I0634683

The
BRUJO'S WAY

The
BRUJO'S WAY

First in the Buenaventura Series

Gerald W. McFarland

SUNSTONE
PRESS

SANTA FE

Sunstone books may be purchased for educational, business, or sales promotional use.
For information please write: Special Markets Department, Sunstone Press,
P.O. Box 2321, Santa Fe, New Mexico 87504-2321.

Book and Cover design › Vicki Ahl
Body typeface › Book Antiqua
Printed on acid-free paper
∞

———————————————————————————

Library of Congress Cataloging-in-Publication Data

McFarland, Gerald W., 1938-
  The brujo's way / by Gerald W. McFarland.
     pages cm -- (First in the Buenaventura series)
  ISBN 978-0-86534-944-5 (softcover : alk. paper)
  1. Warlocks--Fiction. 2. New Mexico--History--To 1848--Fiction. I. Title.
  PS3613.C4393B78 2013
  813'.6--dc23
                            2013007145

———————————————————————————

WWW.SUNSTONEPRESS.COM
SUNSTONE PRESS / POST OFFICE BOX 2321 / SANTA FE, NM 87504-2321 /USA
(505) 988-4418 / ORDERS ONLY (800) 243-5644 / FAX (505) 988-1025

Preface

Almost all the action in *The Brujo's Way*, the first volume of the Buenaventura Series, takes place in the early 1700s in Santa Fe, New Mexico, in Mexico City, and at points between on the Camino Real. The choice of this time and these places comes out of my experience of teaching a college class on the American West, one segment of which dealt with the Pueblo Revolt of 1680 and its roots in intercultural conflict on New Spain's northern frontier. On this foundation of historical realities, I have built a narrative of entirely fictional events, most of which occur nearly a generation after the Revolt.

The story of Don Carlos Buenaventura, a brujo who practices a benign form of sorcery based on his motto "Do no harm," can be read simply as a tale of adventure, romance, and magic, but it is more than that. For all that Carlos is beginning his sixth life as a brujo and eventually remembers a great deal about his previous lives, he has not acquired much wisdom. When in the guise of an ordinary man, he spends his days fencing, racing horses, and pursuing women, and as a brujo he uses his sorcerer's skills to entertain himself, talking with magical animals and transforming himself into hawks by day and owls by night. He lives a largely carefree and unexamined life, and why should he do otherwise? Even if he dies, he knows his consciousness of his brujo self will continue into his next life.

Carlos's devil-may-care attitude is challenged by events throughout *The Brujo's Way*, events that lead him to realize that there are depths of thought and action he has never plumbed. Even though he has no teacher to guide him, he begins an odyssey of self-discovery on what he calls, having no other name for it, the unknown way.

The Brujo's Way had its origins as a short story I wrote for a Spanish conversation group, and I am immensely grateful to two members of that group—Dorothy McFarland, my wife and beloved copyeditor, and Dennis Shapson, whose support was unwavering—for their help and encouragement.

1

Birth

*H*is mother was late in the fifth month of her pregnancy with him when Don Carlos, a brujo of extraordinary powers, realized that something was not right. He was a healthy fetus; that wasn't the problem. Indeed, as in each of the previous times that he had been reborn, he had been enjoying his sojourn in the womb—warmth, ample sustenance, and plenty of time to restfully enjoy his natural animal vitality. Thus he had spent nearly five months happily calling to mind exploits of which he was proud from his former lives. (It was his usual practice not to dwell on any negative thoughts or memories while in the womb.) He also entertained himself by humming his favorite songs.

His recognition that all was not well came only gradually. The first clue was when he heard his mother-to-be use the word "doctor." "Thank you for coming by, Doctor," she had said. Don Carlos found this perplexing. Never, in any of his other births as a brujo, had his mothers called upon the services of a doctor. It was, as far as Carlos could recall, the late seventeenth century, and based on his experiences in previous lives, Carlos had formed the opinion that all doctors were quacks. The delivery of a baby, he believed, should be entrusted to an experienced midwife, and he found the possibility that a male doctor might bungle his birth highly annoying.

Once Don Carlos sensed that something was not quite right, he began to listen to the conversations that took place between his mother-to-be and her visitors. The first such conversation was with a priest, Father Dominic. Carlos noticed a pleading tone in his mother-to-be's voice when she told Father Dominic that she desperately needed the child she was carrying to be a boy. "Two girls so far," she said anxiously, "and if I don't produce a male heir this time, my husband, who has grown most impatient, will find a way of disposing of me."

To this Father Dominic made some soothing noises—Don Carlos could not quite make out the exact words—and urged "my dear Doña Carlotta" (so that was his mother-to-be's name) to pray with him. For Carlos, a skeptic when it came to Catholic priests and Christian prayer, a priest's presence was definitely a bad sign.

Doña Carlotta apparently did not find Father Dominic's pious words particularly comforting, because no sooner had he left than she began weeping and spoke sorrowfully to someone who turned out to be her maid. "Rosita, what will become of me if I do not produce a boy child from my third pregnancy?"

"Mistress, with all due respect, you should try the potion that I brought you from the old midwife in my village," Rosita replied. "It always gives women who want a boy child success in that endeavor."

Don Carlos, well aware that he was already fully formed as a male fetus, observed to himself that folk remedies were useless at this point.

"Oh! I dare not!" Doña Carlotta cried. "If my husband, Alfonso Vicente Cabeza de Vaca, found out that I used magic, he would have me condemned as a pagan and possibly burned as a witch." A tiny dart of apprehension, a largely unfamiliar and very unwelcome sensation, shot through Don Carlos upon learning about his prospective father's beliefs. Instantly, he repressed it. He needed to learn more before drawing any conclusions.

Later the same day, Doña Carlotta discussed her situation with a woman who Don Carlos eventually realized was her sister Mercedes. This sister was even less help than Father Dominic. No words of comfort from her. "Our father," Mercedes remonstrated, "expects you to produce a male grandchild to justify the huge dowry he paid to your husband. Only a male heir will be eligible to carry your husband's title of marquis into the next century."

By now Don Carlos knew precisely what was wrong. He had chosen the wrong parents, a mistake he had never made before, even when he was a young and not thoroughly matured brujo. Always before he had chosen simple working-class people or peasants as his parents, since they could be depended on to understand and even admire his skills as a brujo. However, this time around he had blundered and found his way into an aristocratic family of orthodox Catholics, with a father (at least) who regarded sorcery as heresy and who, Don Carlos knew from past lives, was the type of religious zealot who would not hesitate to kill a brujo that turned up in his family.

Immediately he began to wonder what, if anything, he could do. Confined as he was to Doña Carlotta's womb, he was in no position to search for a peasant woman with a male fetus and change places with that boy-to-be. He could always transform himself within his mother's womb;

transformations were, after all, an art at which he was a virtuoso practitioner. But transform into what? If he changed into a crow and was born as such, his chances of surviving more than a few minutes were nil. To be sure, once dead he could immediately find more suitable parents and start anew the requisite nine-month gestation period. That struck him as a huge waste of time. Besides, he felt some sympathy for Doña Carlotta's plight, her need to have a boy child so that Marquis Alfonso would not, as she had said, "dispose" of her.

His sympathetic response to Doña Carlotta's predicament instantly led him to a memory that explained how he'd gotten in this bad situation in the first place. His greatest weakness as a brujo was his love of women. To be completely successful, a brujo could not permit such human weaknesses. However, in his most recent life he had fallen madly in love with an entrancing beauty named Violeta. Even now he could remember in every detail the first time he had laid eyes on her. It was at a beggars' ball, and she had worn a low-cut gown that exposed her gorgeous breasts. Then, during a passionate dance, she had raised her long skirts and shown her bare, beautiful ankles, with their promise of magnificent limbs above. He was lost. Before the night was out, they were lovers, and it became their custom, after an intense bout of love-making, to lie in each other's arms, naked and exhausted, and drink wine.

On the last such occasion, she handed him a glass of dark red wine and said, "This wine is best drunk quickly," after which she tossed her wine down in one gulp. So besotted was he by her charms that Don Carlos unthinkingly — that is, with none of the caution that is an essential part of the Brujo's Way in which he'd been trained — followed her example. He had just the barest fraction of an instant to notice that the wine had a bitter aftertaste before he fell back in bed, completely paralyzed and not even able to think straight. But he was aware of Violeta laughing with delight, her violet eyes gleaming with joy at his condition.

At that very moment Don Carlos was shocked to see his bitter and relentless rival, the sorcerer Don Malvolio, enter the room. Don Malvolio embraced Violeta passionately and whispered in her ear, "Dear Violeta, you have succeeded where I have so often failed. Now my archenemy is in my control, and I can follow the ancient formulas for disposing of his brujo's soul once and for all."

With this Don Malvolio drew a knife from his belt and, reaching under the bed, brought out a sturdy rope which he secured to the chandelier in the center of the room. Horrified, Don Carlos knew precisely what Don Malvolio intended to do; he would tie Carlos's feet together and hang him upside down from the chandelier. Next, he would knock Carlos unconscious. Finally, he would slit Carlos's throat, causing his life blood to drain out of him, and along with it his immortal soul.

Don Malvolio proceeded to put his plan into action. Paralyzed as Don Carlos was, and with a mind fogged by the drug he had been given, he seemed totally at Malvolio's mercy. But as Malvolio was about to strike him a blow to the head, Carlos, calling from deep within every bit of his remaining power as a brujo, threw his soul out of his body and into the Great Soul Vat from which he would be reborn.

Don Malvolio saw Carlos's soul fly out of the room and cursed angrily. "Enjoy your escape, Carlos, but know that I will once again hunt you down, and next time I will destroy you."

These unhappy and confusing circumstances doubtless accounted, or so Don Carlos now thought to himself, for his poor choice of his soon-to-be parents. It's little wonder, he mused. I fled in such unthinking haste that I was in no position to choose wisely.

Nevertheless, he had escaped, albeit by the barest of margins. Had he died and gone to the Great Soul Vat in an unconscious state, he would have been reborn as an ordinary man, unaware of his true nature. As it was, despite the confused and panicky state in which his soul left his dying body, Don Carlos entered the Great Soul Vat sufficiently conscious of himself to be reborn with memories of his past lives as a brujo—lives in which he had been committed to a Brujo's Way that was altogether different from the kind of sorcery practiced by Don Malvolio. Don Malvolio belonged to the Moon Moiety of sorcerers, the most widely known type of sorcerer and the one that gave all sorcerers a bad name because they used their powers to do evil deeds, taking great satisfaction in the misery they brought into the world. As for Don Carlos, he was aligned with a tiny subgroup of sorcerers who called themselves the Sun Moiety, members of which sought to promote peace and harmony in the world and whose motto, expressing their most fundamental values, was "Do no harm."

Don Carlos had never been one to dwell on misfortune or betrayal. He knew that he could not succeed as a brujo if he expected the world to be other than it was, and the plain fact was that there were many evil and treacherous people like Violeta and Don Malvolio in the world. Turning aside from negative thoughts, therefore, Carlos concluded that Doña Carlotta and Marquis Alfonso perhaps had not been such bad choices as parents. After all, Don Malvolio would be hunting for the reborn Don Carlos and, knowing that Carlos had always chosen to be born into families of simple people of modest means, Malvolio would never think to look for him in an aristocratic, orthodox Catholic family.

This thought so pleased Don Carlos that he did a somersault in his mother's womb, unintentionally giving her such a hard kick that she cried out. "Ouch!" she exclaimed. "What a strong and precocious kick that was!" But far from being dismayed, she laughed happily and said, "It was a kick that only a boy could give."

So it was that Don Carlos decided to go ahead and be born into a titled family as a human infant rather than transforming himself into a crow, a cockroach, a mouse, a rabbit, a kangaroo, a dog or a cat—though he amused himself by thinking of all the many possibilities. In this playful mood, so typical of the cheerful disposition he'd always displayed in previous lives, he for the moment ignored the disquieting thought that being born into a family of enemies of the Brujo's Way would pose one of the greatest challenges he had ever faced. Simply put, in order to avoid detection, he would have to disguise his true nature; and in suppressing any outward sign of his true nature, he was in danger of forgetting who he was.

2

Normalcy

Don Carlos's childhood as heir to the Marquis Alfonso Vicente Cabeza de Vaca's title and fortune did not always go smoothly. Indeed, about the only completely positive feature of his first year in the Cabeza de Vaca household was his mother's choice of a wet nurse for him. Obviously, one could not expect an aristocratic mother to nurse her own baby, so a young Native woman, Juana, who only a few weeks earlier had lost an infant in an accident, was brought into the household to nurse Carlos. He took great pleasure in attaching himself to Juana's ample brown breasts and suckling to his heart's content.

"My!" his mother exclaimed, slightly alarmed. "He scarcely seems willing to stop, even when he surely has eaten enough." But Juana was an easy-going peasant girl, happy to have a baby to cuddle, and she assured Doña Carlotta that she didn't mind the baby's enthusiasm at all.

Even as a nursing infant, Don Carlos was aware that at some time in the future he was likely to clash with Don Malvolio or another sorcerer of the Moon Moiety, sworn enemies, and aggressively so, of brujos of Don Carlos's type. In their war on members of the Sun Moiety, Malvolio and his ilk had a great advantage in numbers, their presence in the world being ubiquitous. By contrast, Carlos's allies in the Sun Moiety were so few in number that in five previous lives from the time that he had completed his apprenticeship, Carlos had met only one other brujo trained to believe and act as he did. The very scarcity of Sun Moiety brujos only intensified Carlos's determination — indeed, as he saw it, his obligation — to preserve the benign version of sorcery to which he was committed, a task he knew required him to dedicate himself to practice and, if possible, to enhance his skills.

This task proved incredibly more difficult than he had expected when he had chosen to enter the world as Doña Carlotta's baby. Although at first he remembered in great detail how a brujo went about his work, a brujo's skills needed to be applied in practice or his control of them would weaken. The trouble was that as an infant and little boy in the Cabeza de Vaca household, he was rarely left alone, a circumstance that prevented him from practicing his brujo techniques.

He was delighted, therefore, one night when he was not yet two, to find that Juana had stepped out of the room and he was alone in his crib. Taking advantage of this moment, he transformed himself into a bat in order to practice flying. But he was so out of practice that he soon collided with a vase of flowers, knocking them to the floor and shattering the vase. Slightly stunned, he flew a wobbly flight back to his crib and managed to transform himself into a sleeping baby just a split second after his father, followed by Juana, burst into the room.

"What could have happened?" his father bellowed, his eyes darting around the room. Turning to Juana, he demanded to know, "Did you see a bat fly over to Alfonsito's bed?"

"No! No!" she replied, clearly frightened out of her wits.

The marquis examined Carlos's body carefully, and finding no marks such as a vampire or bat might have left, concluded that he might not have seen what he believed he had seen. "Juana, I ordered you," he thundered, "to sleep all night on the cot next to Alfonsito's crib, and now I find that you have left him alone. Woe be to you if anything untoward happens to my only son and future heir!"

Such a stuffed shirt! Carlos thought to himself, and what a nuisance that he named me after himself: Alfonsito, indeed.

Fortunately, no one thought too deeply about how the vase came to fall to the floor. "Perhaps an earthquake did it," Juana suggested, as she gathered up the broken pieces. "We have lots of earthquakes in Mexico City."

"I didn't feel an earthquake," the marquis growled, but he was too flustered by events to pursue the topic further.

The next morning Carlos's mother and her maid Rosita came to the nursery. His mother scooped him up and rocked him in her arms. "Poor baby," she exclaimed. "Did something bad happen to you last night? Mama feels so badly about not being here to protect you." Don Carlos gave her the sort of beatific smile babies use to melt the hearts of their mothers and was delighted when his smile had the desired effect. "Oh, Alfonsito," his mother crooned, "you are so dear to me!"

Over the next two years he now and then managed to practice a few secret transformations, but on one occasion he acted impulsively and almost exposed his brujo self. The source of the trouble was his two older sisters, Fortunata and Valentina, who were unhappy at being replaced as the focus of the family's adoration by their brother. They pretended to love him, but, ever jealous of the attention lavished on little Alfonso, they enjoyed tormenting him whenever they were left alone with him. One of their favorite ways of doing so was to make up sing-song taunts using his name:

Alfonsito, Alfonsito.
Patoso como osocito,
Feo, feo cerdocito!

Alfonsito, Alfonsito.
Clumsy as a little bear,
Ugly, ugly little pig!

Most of the time, Carlos responded with laughter, pretending that he didn't mind these ditties, but he lost control one day when Fortunata and Valentina had kept after him for what seemed like hours. When Fortunata left the room for a moment, his anger overwhelmed him and he turned Valentina into a mouse that ran around the room making frantic squeaking sounds.

He was enjoying Valentina's panic when the turning doorknob to his bedroom alerted him to Fortunata's impending return. Luckily, he was able to transform Valentina back into her human form just as Fortunata entered, though Valentina was left sitting in the middle of the room with a dazed look on her face. "What's wrong with you?" Fortunata demanded.

"I don't know," Valentina replied. "I just feel not quite myself."

"Little wonder," Fortunata said. "It's difficult for anyone to keep her wits about her in the presence of our dopey brother." But to Carlos's relief no one except him seemed to notice that anything strange had happened.

What Carlos experienced inwardly, however, was something else, a sense of alarm at the close call his loss of self-control had occasioned. He decided that the only way to keep his capacity for sorcery well disguised would be to stop any effort to practice his brujo techniques and, even more difficult, to repress thinking about his brujo powers. Applying himself more strenuously than ever to the task of appearing to be an ordinary child did indeed have the desired effect of hiding his true self; but his no longer practicing or even thinking about his craft meant that his skills as a brujo gradually grew weaker and weaker.

As a little boy, Don Carlos learned many significant details about his parents from gossip that his mother's personal maid delighted in passing on to him. According to Rosita, his maternal grandfather, Fernando Alvarado, was a banker with no title but an exceedingly large fortune. Carlos's father, on the other hand, had an aristocratic title but little wealth, and prior to his marriage to Doña Carlotta he had suffered the humiliating fate of needing to work for a living—not that his largely honorific duties as vice consul in the Spanish embassy in Mexico City were especially demanding. After marrying Doña Carlotta and coming into possession of her substantial dowry, he resigned from his government post and enjoyed an upper-class life of complete leisure.

In courting his parents' approval, Don Carlos adopted good behavior as a disguise. A bit to his surprise—that is, while he was aware of what he was doing and not yet pursuing normalcy purely out of habit—conforming to the image of a good boy proved not particularly difficult. His mother was a tender-hearted woman, and he delighted in pleasing her by being a dutiful son. He displayed great creativity in finding methods to charm her. One of the most successful was a game that Carlos invented and named Kissy Bird.

The Kissy Bird was an imaginary creature who visited Carlos's mother on mornings when Carlos was up and she was still in bed, which was often because her health was not particularly good from his early childhood onward. The game required that his mother be alone, which was most of the time, since his father usually slept in a separate bedroom. To set the game in motion, Carlos would knock softly and open his mother's bedroom door just enough so he could lean in and announce, "The Kissy Bird is loose in the house again!"

"Oh, my!" his mother would exclaim in mock dismay. "We must catch him!" Whereupon Carlos would burst into the room and run around it several times, flapping his arms and making kissing noises. The game ended, always with gales of laughter, when he would jump onto his mother's bed and she would take him in her arms. "I've caught the Kissy Bird," she would declare, upon which she would kiss him on the cheek, forehead, and ear, and he would do likewise to her.

Don Carlos was slower to warm up to his father, but eventually came to appreciate that Marquis Alfonso, though narrow-minded about religion, was not an ungenerous person, at least not where his son was concerned. The marquis indulged his son's every whim, and Carlos took full advantage.

Don Carlos grew to be a model young aristocrat. His father hired the very best Jesuit tutors to instruct his son in reading, writing, mathematics, and religion, and although Carlos found nothing in his religious instruction to inspire devout Catholic belief, he at least learned to put on a respectful face as he fulfilled his obligations to attend Mass, say his prayers, and go to confession. Due to his generally good behavior there wasn't all that much to confess, except for a few amorous adventures he had enjoyed and didn't feel the least bit guilty about. But since it was obligatory to give the priest some grounds for requiring him to say numerous "Hail Marys," he admitted to sexual misbehavior, the details of which he cynically believed his confessor would enjoy.

Like all his upper-class male friends, Don Carlos felt obliged to assert his manliness by attempting to seduce girls and women. The girls, warned repeatedly by their mothers to beware of boys who plied them with promises of marriage in return for sexual favors, but who would abandon them if those favors were granted, foiled his best efforts to seduce them. Only one girl, ironically named Virginia, did not; she was a wild, willful daughter, a fact so widely known that his success did not seem a huge triumph. The girls' mothers were another story altogether, and several of them, during times when their husbands were out of town, took him into their beds.

By the time he celebrated his eighteenth birthday, Don Carlos had become such a well-regarded young man, unusually mature for his age (he had lived many previous lives, after all), that every upper-class mother in the city dreamed of marrying a daughter to him. He was extraordinarily handsome, and his accomplishments in many areas were superior to those of every marriageable man of his class. His tutor in swordsmanship, the redoubtable Don Ignacio de Tortuga, asserted that in all his seventy years in Spain and Mexico City he had never encountered a swordsman with such swift and creative reactions. Don Carlos also became an outstanding horseman. When only twelve years old, he won the annual race around Plaza Mayor, the main city square, and was showered with praise by men and bouquets by upper-class ladies and their daughters. Moreover, Carlos amazed his tutors by rapidly achieving fluency in Latin, Greek, and French, and even picked up a smattering of Sanskrit from Father Stefano, the most senior of his tutors, who had had a long-standing interest in Eastern wisdom literature. Simply by eavesdropping on the household's maids as they chattered among themselves, he also mastered several Native dialects. No one, not even Carlos, suspected that these successes drew on innate capacities from his previous lives.

In his late teens, Don Carlos found his life entirely satisfactory. The conflicts with his sisters that had once been so annoying had gradually diminished in intensity. His parents seemed to enjoy having him around, with the result that there was no pressure to do anything other than to pass his days in entertaining pursuits that he'd come to enjoy enormously: romancing young women and their mothers, idling away many hours in cafes, fine-tuning his skills as a fencer, and participating in an equestrian drill team that he and a group of other aristocratic young men, drinking friends of his, had established.

Despite the ease with which he learned the lessons his Jesuit tutors assigned him, he had no desire to undertake serious professional or philosophical study at the Jesuit seminary outside of Mexico City. He rather wished that he was inclined to pursue scholarly activities, if for no other reason than because it would please Father Stefano, of whom he was very fond, but he truly wasn't drawn to do so. He had given himself so fully and successfully to the comforts of an ordinary life, the pleasures of play and leisure that were the birthright of highly privileged, upper-class men, that the brujo identity central to all his previous lives had ceased to be even a faint memory.

Shortly after his nineteenth birthday, the relative stability of Don Carlos's life ended following a series of events that had begun two years earlier with the death of his maternal grandfather, the wealthy banker. Sad though this death was to his daughters Carlotta and Mercedes, the immediate effect was to greatly enrich the Cabeza de Vaca family. When, soon after her father's death, Mercedes moved into her brother-in-law's household, everyone's expectation was that the huge dowry she could convey to a future husband would bring swarms of suitors to her door. Suitors came, and came in large numbers, but Mercedes rejected each and every one of them.

"What is the matter with you?" an exasperated Doña Carlotta asked one day.

"I didn't see it clearly until now," Mercedes replied, "but I have no interest in men, marriage, or babies. It's my intention to enter a monastery." Less than two months later, Mercedes became a Carmelite nun.

Inspired by her aunt's example, Valentina, the younger of Doña Carlotta's daughters, declared that she too wished to become a monastic and soon thereafter she followed her aunt into a nunnery. This was not altogether surprising, since Valentina was a shy girl who had never shown much interest in dancing and parties, but Carlos felt some pangs of guilt at the thought that his having once turned her into a mouse might be one source of her timidity.

Carlos's elder sister, Fortunata, was made of different stuff. She welcomed the attention of the many young men who came to court her and, perhaps not coincidentally, to gain a large dowry along with her hand in marriage. After long flirtations with four different suitors, she found one she particularly liked and encouraged him to ask her father, the marquis, to give his consent to their marriage. The wedding was a splendid affair, said by many members of the local aristocracy to have been the most lavish in the history of the city. After the Nuptial Mass, Don Carlos had a wonderful time at the banquet and ball that his parents gave for the newlyweds. The festivities afforded him seemingly innumerable opportunities to flirt with a dazzling array of lovely unmarried upper-class girls—to hold them in his arms and whisper sweet nothings in their ears.

Don Carlos liked Fortunata's choice, Emiliano Alaniz. Emil, as everyone called him, was rich in his own right by inheritance from a grandfather who had made a fortune as a merchant active in trans-Atlantic trade. Although Emil had studied to be a physician, he had added to his inheritance by continuing to involve himself in his grandfather's business. With Emil's wealth joined to Fortunata's dowry, the newlyweds began their life together in great material comfort. Fortunata's attitude toward Carlos having mellowed over the years and having grown even warmer once she'd succeeded so well in her marriage, she and Emil invited him to dinner at their residence once a week during the months after their wedding. However, this practice came to an abrupt halt when Emil decided to move to Lima, Peru, where he was intent on expanding the family's trading interests along the Pacific coast of South America.

Suddenly family life in the Cabeza de Vaca household was much constricted: no Mercedes, no Fortunata, no Valentina—only Marquis Alfonso, Doña Carlotta, and their son.

Two months after Fortunata's departure, the household shrank further. The marquis fell ill with pneumonia and died a week later. Doña Carlotta was deeply distraught at the loss of a man who had protected her against the realities of the world. "This is terrible," she told Carlos. "I have led a sheltered life, protected first by my father and later by my husband, and now I'm on my own." But Carlos sensed that she was not asking for his help, an accurate perception as events proved, for after an almost indecently brief period of mourning she married General Rodrigo Alvarez. Don Carlos's youth was at an end.

3

Impermanence

*H*is father's death and mother's remarriage turned Don Carlos's life upside down. He did not begrudge Doña Carlotta her happiness. He understood that she felt an urgent need to have a strong man at her side and that much as she loved him she did not, as she told him in an apologetic way one day, consider him, still a minor, suitable for that role. General Alvarez, whose first wife had died only a week after Don Carlos's father's death, had all the requisite qualifications: he was ten years older than Doña Carlotta, a domineering man, and well-connected with Spanish noble families. He was also something of a national hero.

In the late 1600s, Spain's control of the northernmost parts of its empire in the Americas had been challenged by rebellious Natives. In New Mexico the 1680 revolt of the Pueblo Indians had led to the deaths of many Spanish colonists and a humiliating forced retreat of the survivors to El Paso del Norte. Not until late December 1693 was a Spanish expedition into the province able to suppress Native resistance and decisively reestablish Spanish control of Santa Fe. General Alvarez, sent from Spain to command the expedition's military contingent, accepted submission where it was offered and brutally crushed any opposition he encountered in Santa Fe and elsewhere in New Mexico.

"Was it necessary to torture and execute so many rebels?" Don Carlos once incautiously asked his stepfather. "Wouldn't a few well-chosen examples have been sufficient?" The general's scornful "No!" was a warning, Carlos realized, not to get on his stepfather's wrong side. Even the suggestion on Carlos's part of the virtues of moderation was taken by the general to be a sign of deplorable, almost feminine, weakness.

General Alvarez plainly had a variety of motives for marrying Doña Carlotta. For one thing, she was still relatively young and definitely attractive. Even more important, Don Carlos soon decided, she was, by inheritance from her father and first husband, very rich. General Alvarez had three sons, all of them unmarried men in their twenties. The combination of the general's reputation as the military hero who had restored Spain's honor in the North and the wealth of his wife's family increased the likelihood that he could bring about exceptionally prestigious marriages for his three sons by his first marriage.

Unfortunately for Carlos, his interests did not rank high among the general's priorities as he sought to promote the social advance of his sons. Indeed, Carlos was something of an impediment to the general's plans because the general's sons compared poorly with Carlos. He was more handsome, more socially accomplished, and better educated than his stepbrothers. Not that it mattered, strictly speaking, since parents rather than their children decided who married whom, but if eligible young women protested too loudly to their parents that they would prefer to marry Carlos rather than one of the general's sons, it could be a problem, and an embarrassing one at that.

Accustomed to command, the general moved swiftly to take control. Less than two months after marrying Doña Carlotta, he persuaded a probate judge to name him as Don Carlos's legal guardian. The first Carlos heard of this was when the general said to him, "While you are a minor, I will manage your estate and give you a monthly allowance." Carlos's heart sank.

Carlos took his stepfather's message to be clear, though unstated. In the nearly two years remaining until Carlos became twenty-one, the general intended to enhance his three sons' well-being at his stepson's expense. At best, Carlos could expect that he would inherit only a small portion of the Cabeza de Vaca family's wealth; he would be, much as his father had been before marrying Doña Carlotta, a man with a title but a small estate. He could not appeal to his mother because she was afraid of angering her new husband.

Don Carlos had been completely unprepared for these shocking changes in his status, and they made him realize that he could no longer drift through life; it was time to do what he could to assert mastery over his destiny. But where to begin? He had no relatives to whom he could turn, and his friends were from stable aristocratic families. None of them had his problems.

One man he could trust, he decided, was his fencing master, Don Ignacio de Tortuga. He went to Don Ignacio's residence and described his situation.

Don Ignacio was characteristically blunt in his response. "Alfonso, you have been complacent, and because of your complacency, you have failed to prepare yourself for the blows life inevitably delivers—a lack of preparation you would never exhibit when fencing. You must realize that the law of life is impermanence; nothing, nothing at all, is permanent."

This, Carlos realized, was all too true. "What is to be done?" he asked, and together they began to plan how Don Carlos could take control of his life.

"Begin by finding ways to become financially independent," Don Ignacio advised. "As long as you depend on your stepfather to give you an allowance and to pay your bills, you are at his mercy—a slave in fact, though not in name."

Don Carlos, who had never earned even a centavo, asked whether any of his skills, particularly swordsmanship and horseracing, might be applied to earn money. Don Ignacio replied that good fortune smiled on him. Earlier that week a highly regarded fencer, a Neapolitan, Giovanni Gemelli, had arrived in the city boasting that no Mexican, "clumsy provincials," as he called them, could defeat him, a boast he fulfilled by besting several of Don Ignacio's students in fencing bouts. "You must challenge this Gemelli fellow," Don Ignacio said.

Arrangements were quickly made. The challenge was delivered by a friend of Carlos's, and a date was set for three days later. Meanwhile, Don Ignacio advised Don Carlos on how to make the bout a paying proposition. Although gentlemen could not properly bet on themselves, their friends could, and Carlos set about to finance these bets. He had some cash on hand, and in order to raise more he pawned two expensive rings his grandfather had given him. He distributed the proceeds to friends with instructions to lay bets with members of Giovanni Gemelli's entourage. Carlos promised to share twenty percent of his winnings with his friends.

The day of the bout began auspiciously. Looking around the ballroom where a large crowd had gathered, Don Carlos realized that he had been cast in the role of the local champion and that, because of Gemelli's arrogant remarks about Mexican "provincials," the honor of his friends and neighbors depended on his success. No matter; he didn't let this impression go to his head. All his energies were concentrated in a splendidly self-disciplined way on the bout to come. Win the bout first, he told himself; now is not the time to celebrate.

At this moment Gemelli entered, a peacock in gold, red, and purple. Don Carlos wore an austere black outfit.

The bout—a best six of eleven touches—began with no preliminaries. Don Carlos had prepared carefully, practicing intensely for two days and discussing Gemelli's style with Don Ignacio. Initially, the bout was closely contested. Gemelli was an excellent fencer who immediately went on the offensive. For his part Carlos was content to pursue a largely defensive strategy that enabled him to study Gemelli's technique, even though he knew he would lose some exchanges that he could have won. To all appearances Gemelli seemed to dominate the bout, winning four of the first six exchanges, and Carlos's supporters were becoming worried.

However, by the time the seventh exchange began, Carlos was seeing the action as though every exchange was happening in slow motion. The experience was not a new one. Indeed, Don Ignacio had once remarked, "At times I believe you see your opponent's moves as though they were being made slowly," an insight so keen that it astonished Carlos. His estrangement from his inner brujo self was so great that it was only later that he realized his capacity to slow down fast-moving action drew on training he'd had in sorcery in past lives.

Now able to anticipate Gemelli's every move, Don Carlos took the offense, easily winning the seventh and eighth exchanges and evening the score at four hits each. He could just as easily have won the next two exchanges also and been victorious in the bout, but he decided not to do so. The closer the bout seemed, he reasoned, the greater the likelihood that the onlookers would bet heavily on a second bout if one was proposed, as he assumed it would be.

Don Carlos let Gemelli win the ninth exchange with a simple move that a fencer of modest accomplishments should have parried easily. Misinterpreting this as a sign of a flaw in Carlos's technique, Gemelli reacted with fatal overconfidence, just as Carlos had hoped he would.

Don Carlos won the next exchange quickly after Gemelli repeated his previously successful tactic (the fool! Carlos thought to himself) and was easily outmaneuvered by Carlos. The bout was now tied, each fencer having achieved five hits.

Don Carlos, completely confident in his mastery of Gemelli, let the eleventh and decisive exchange go on longer than necessary by returning to the defense rather than his usual vigorous offense. His motive was to put on a good show for the audience—a long, seemingly hotly contested bout being more dramatic than an extremely brief one. Finally, shifting again to the offense, he drove Gemelli backward by the ferocity of his assault, then purposely seemed to slip, creating an opening that gave his opponent—who was by this point sweating heavily in the city's midday heat—an apparent path to victory. When Gemelli lunged forward to exploit it, Carlos parried the Neapolitan's assault, struck home, and declared "Touché!"

Gemelli was outraged. "You won unfairly, by a clumsy accident rather than skill."

"Very well," Carlos replied. "I would not wish a guest in our fine city to leave feeling he had been dealt with unfairly. Let's have a best two-of-three bout after a short break"—a short break, he thought, during which his friends could collect their winnings and make new bets with Gemelli's entourage. As for new bets, when Don Ignacio asked whether his friends should bet only the money they had won or that money plus the capital they had originally put at risk, Carlos replied, "Bet it all," and was rewarded with a knowing smile from his master.

Don Carlos had no intention of dragging things out any further. When the bout resumed, he attacked with ardor, giving the Neapolitan no openings and winning the first two exchanges, and the bout, in short order.

Poor Gemelli and the members of his entourage were shocked by this result. Before they had time to gather their wits, Don Carlos said, "Generosity requires that I offer you another chance to defeat me. I see that you have ridden into the city on a fine Arabian stallion named Alcázar. I, too, have an Arabian stallion on which I've won many races. He will be yours if you prevent me from scoring the next five hits, but if I win all five, your Alcázar will be mine."

It was so agreed, and Don Carlos again went on the attack, determined to win five exchanges quickly. He won the first four easily, but during the fifth, Gemelli fenced with a passion that forced Don Carlos to achieve new heights of swordsmanship before he won. After the ensuing cheers ended, Carlos turned to Don Ignacio, bowed deeply, and said, "Out of gratitude for your teaching, I give you Alcázar."

4

Northward

The evening following Don Carlos's triumph in his match with Giovanni Gemelli, General Alvarez leaned across the dinner table and, making little effort to disguise the sarcasm in his voice, said to Carlos, "A noble gesture, giving Alcázar to your fencing master; however, since Alcázar is surely worth a great deal in silver bullion, the gift shows that you have much to learn about the practical side of life."

Carlos said nothing, but nodded his head in an ambiguous way that might be taken to mean agreement. But what he agreed with was that titled men could afford to honor impracticality — not the general's point, of course. Carlos waited for the other shoe to drop.

"It's time for you to approach life more realistically," the general continued, "and I have found a perfect starting point for you. Joaquin (the general's eldest son), through his engagement to Señorita Francesca Saurez (who was seated to Joaquin's right), has brought us great happiness. (And a huge dowry, Carlos observed to himself, since "Francie," as friends called her, was the daughter of one of Mexico City's richest men.) After they're married, Joaquin, as a captain in the army (all the general's sons had followed their father into military careers), will be posted to Santa Fe in command of the royal forces there. The province's military governor is my friend and has agreed to employ you as his secretary."

"Most generous," Carlos replied, knowing it wasn't. "Let's discuss it tomorrow."

Carlos's respect for his stepfather diminished as a result of this dinner-table exchange. How could the general believe that Carlos would not see through the transparent self-interest of his plan? By sending him to the remote northern border of Spain's North American colonies, he would remove Carlos from competition with the general's two younger sons for marriage to the city's upper-class heiresses. The position of secretary would also put Carlos a step below Joaquin in the social hierarchy of Santa Fe.

However, Carlos, unbeknownst to his stepfather, had been preparing for something like this. He had won a substantial sum from bets his friends placed on him during his bouts with Gemelli. Also, he and Don Ignacio had agreed that if Carlos won the Neapolitan's fine horse, Don Ignacio, who coveted Alcázar for a favorite nephew of his, would pay Carlos handsomely for the horse, although in public they would treat the horse as a gift so that Carlos's stepfather could not lay claim to the proceeds of the sale.

At breakfast the next day, with his mother present, Carlos told his stepfather he would go to Santa Fe, if, as heir to the title of Marquis Cabeza de Vaca, he had suitable financial support from his family. To his surprise, his mother chimed in: "Yes, Rodrigo, that must be done." Clearly, she'd sensed that her son was not being treated generously.

Carlos then asked for enough money to buy two horses and to employ a servant. One horse would be for his manservant, the other a packhorse. He intended to trade his Arabian for a third horse that was more suitable for the rigors of cross-country travel.

Possibly a bit taken aback by Doña Carlotta's intervention on her son's behalf and in any case eager to get Carlos out of Mexico City, General

Alvarez agreed to Carlos's conditions and even, to his credit, exceeded them by offering to pay for appropriate firearms for Carlos and his servant and two suits of clothes for riding in backcountry regions, suits he would direct his tailor to make for Carlos.

The first order of business, as Carlos saw it, was to find a suitable manservant. At Don Ignacio's suggestion, he contracted with a mestizo named Pedro Gallegos. "He is everything you could wish for," Don Ignacio had said. "Strong, loyal, intelligent, and a veteran soldier. He is thirty-three, the son of a Spanish foot soldier and an Indian woman with ties to several northern borderland tribes. He walks with an awkward limp, the consequence of a wound he suffered in battle, but on horseback there is no sign of this infirmity."

Pedro proved to be everything Don Ignacio had promised, and Don Carlos and he immediately liked each other. To prepare for a potentially dangerous trek through areas where Native raiders were active, the companions spent hours practicing with the muskets that they intended to carry on the trip north. Knowing that they needed to be saddle-hardened to make the trip, they took long rides outside the city—Carlos on his recent acquisition, Eagle, a sturdy black Andalusian, and Pedro on Pepper, a gray gelding of the same breed.

On the longest of these rides the two men traveled northwest from the city to the Jesuit Seminary at Tepotzotlán, a location known for the learned priests and monks who lived there and also for the magnificent architecture of some of its buildings. Don Carlos had a double purpose in choosing that particular destination. He wanted to show the place to his new friend, and he wanted to bid adieu to an old mentor, Father Stefano, his favorite among his Jesuit tutors. Only a few inquiries were needed to track his Jesuit mentor down. Father Stefano greeted Carlos warmly. "What brings you here?" he asked. "I could hope that you've at last decided to take my advice and spend a few years here studying, but I know you too well to be confident that such is the case."

"With all due respect," Carlos replied, "your assumption is all too true. Rather than coming here to study, I am about to leave for Santa Fe in New Mexico, where I have an appointment as personal secretary to the province's military governor."

"Given your many skills," Father Stefano declared, "I know you will do well. If anything, your skills and your education make you overqualified for that position. Why have you chosen to move to such a remote location?

I trust it's not some romantic hope that you'll have many adventures on the northern borderlands of New Spain."

"The possibility of having adventures didn't enter into it," Carlos said. "I've been essentially forced by my stepfather to accept this post. Frankly, I'm afraid life in Santa Fe will be boring, after the abundant social pleasures that Mexico City offers."

"From what I've heard," Father Stefano remarked, "Santa Fe was completely abandoned by its Spanish residents during the Pueblo Revolt and its population still hasn't recovered its former numbers, which were not large to begin with. My assumption has to be that you, as a young man with many talents and such great promise, won't become a permanent resident of such an unprepossessing place."

"You're too kind in your description of me," Carlos replied. "As for my plans regarding Santa Fe, let's just say that I hope to do well in my post and then return here two years from now, when I reach twenty-one and inherit my father's title and estate. But should events take me in another direction, I didn't want to leave Mexico City without saying good-bye to you and expressing my appreciation for the education you gave me and for your patience with my wayward life."

"Wayward is too strong a word," Father Stefano assured him.

"If I may," Carlos inquired a bit hesitantly, "permit me to ask you for some words of advice with regard to my forthcoming life in Santa Fe."

"That's a tall order," Father Stefano observed. "You'll recall my counsel that simplicity is preferable to complexity. Now that I think of it, life in Santa Fe may prove valuable in that regard, since there surely won't be as many distractions as there are here: fast horses, aristocratic companions who live a life of total leisure, and, dare I mention it, so many beautiful women to be courted."

"There's wisdom in your words," Carlos replied, "though I'd be less than honest if I didn't admit to hoping that there will be at least one or two pretty unmarried women to court. Could I paraphrase your advice as meaning that in Santa Fe I may benefit from being closer to life's essentials?"

"Good boy!" Father Stefano exclaimed quietly, clapping Carlos on the shoulder. "Let simplicity be your watchword. Now if you'll excuse me, the bell for afternoon prayers is sounding and I must attend. Go in peace, my young friend."

Don Carlos found that his conversation with Father Stefano left him in good spirits, having given him a way of looking at his future situation as something other than a period of exile to which his stepfather had consigned him.

A ride of quite a different sort followed two days later, when Pedro and Carlos were joined by a boyhood chum of Carlos's, Jorge Oñate. Jorge was the eldest son of one of most prestigious families in the city, the future heir to a great fortune. Although he had not yet inherited the vast properties that his father controlled, his parents were exceedingly indulgent of Jorge's every whim. Not for him to have to work, or study, or even to settle down. His parents believed that such activities were inappropriate for an upper-class male in his late teens. So Jorge spent his days socializing, gambling, calling on pretty unmarried girls, and generally enjoying himself.

Don Carlos knew all too well that had his own father been richer and had he lived, the life he, Carlos, would have continued to live would have been much like Jorge's. No matter. They were close enough in social standing to spend a lot of time together, and Carlos was sure that Jorge would enjoy a horseback excursion into the country with him and Pedro.

The three men rode a long way outside the densely populated part of the city, stopped for lunch and wine at a small country inn, and discovered to their delight that several young upper-class women from their circle were at the inn to attend an anniversary party for an older couple. Carlos was particularly pleased by the presence of Isabel García, a pretty brunette with smiling eyes. Well trained by her mother, Isabel had more than once fended off Carlos's best efforts to bed her, always responding with a laugh and the comment that there would be plenty of time for intimacies once they were married. Of course, as she well knew, he had no intention of proposing marriage, but the back and forth of flirtation was a harmless game that both of them enjoyed greatly.

After a pleasant lunch, marked by serenades for the couple and many laughs with the girls in the party, Carlos, Pedro, and Jorge continued to an even more remote spot where they practiced marksmanship with their muskets.

On the way home Jorge, who was an inveterate gambler and careless with money, challenged Carlos to a race back to a plaza on the outskirts of Mexico City. "The wager will be all the pesos you can hold in your right hand," Jorge called, as he spurred his horse to a gallop.

Don Carlos had little doubt that Jorge, despite being a risk-taker, had decided that his elegant mount was faster than Carlos's Eagle, sturdy and well-conditioned though Eagle obviously was. What Jorge did not take into account was that Eagle, even if he was not the complete equal in bloodlines to Jorge's stallion, was more than his match in heart.

Seeing the other horse in the lead, Eagle took off after Jorge and soon caught up, as Don Carlos was sure he would. Eagle simply would not allow another horse to outrun him, and he and Carlos reached the finish line a good five yards ahead of Jorge.

Jorge was surprised. "I certainly underestimated the heart and stamina of your Eagle," he said graciously. "If I must lose a bet to anyone, you'd be my choice. As you know, I have plenty of money, and a handful of pesos — perhaps even two handfuls — is the least I can give you as a farewell gift."

So the days passed in useful and pleasant ways until his stepbrother's wedding. Then, while dancing after the ceremony with all the pretty upper-class girls, he was keenly aware of their eyes, arms, and bosoms. "I'm leaving this," he thought sadly. "All is impermanent."

Three days after the wedding, the party that Joaquin was to lead northward assembled on Plaza Mayor. They were thirty-two in all: the newlyweds, Joaquin and Francesca, and their three servants (two women and one man), a squad of nine soldiers under Joaquin's command, Don Carlos and Pedro, and sixteen colonists, twelve men and four women. The colonists were craftsmen, farmers, or servants, and representatives of various races — mostly mestizo, but one pure-blooded Spaniard and two mulattos — all of them hoping to find a better livelihood in Santa Fe.

The farewells were tender. Doña Carlotta slipped some heirloom gold rings of hers into Don Carlos's pocket and, with tears in her eyes, hugged him tightly: "Go with God, dearest son," she said. "I can barely stand to let you go." Her husband clapped his stepson on the back and, with surprising and seemingly genuine warmth, said, "Good luck."

The first three days of the trek were through well-settled and reportedly safe districts; nevertheless, Don Carlos got Joaquin to agree that he and Pedro should ride ahead of the main party to be sure that the gangs that had been robbing travelers were nowhere in evidence.

Observing all the members of the party, Don Carlos was most drawn to one of Francesca's maids, a young woman about his age who had blonde hair, luminescent golden skin, and — most startling of all — blue eyes. Joaquin, noting the direction of Carlos's gaze, pulled him aside and said, "Her name's Camila Lobo, an orphanage-raised foundling. If you dishonor my wife by seducing her maid, you will incur my undying enmity. Understood?"

Don Carlos had no intention of offending Joaquin and Francie, and in any case his attention was increasingly focused on a strange mental sensation he'd begun to experience four days into the trip as the party entered a high mountain desert region with few villages and ranches. This odd sensation grew stronger as the party moved on, but its precise nature eluded him, hovering just beyond his conscious reach—quite like the experience of trying to recall an old friend's name but not being able to remember what it was.

On the fourth day he was perplexed by several moments in which he had vividly detailed flashes of images of the countryside from overhead, as though he was seeing it from the perspective of a bird coasting along above the caravan. It was a particularly hot day, and he was half convinced that he was suffering from hallucinations as a result of the heat. Concerned, he made certain that he was drinking plenty of water. The images nevertheless persisted and came to seem more like memories than hallucinations. Single images linked themselves into sequences of events, as if he was remembering things he couldn't place in time. Suddenly, with a clarity that astonished him, he knew he was recalling fragments of past lives.

That evening, after the rest of the party had bedded down for the night, Don Carlos walked up a dry arroyo near the camp and sat underneath a tall pine tree. He hadn't been there long before a large owl flew over his head. Along with the sudden, close presence of the owl came a kind of knowledge—that he knew how it would feel to be an owl flying above a moonlit landscape. Simultaneously, he experienced strange sensations in his arms, and, raising his hands in front of his face, he saw that the tips of his fingers had feathers, owl feathers. He shook his hands vigorously, but the feathers did not immediately vanish. In the depths of his being he was both thrilled and disturbed. Recollections flooded over him. He realized that he had once been adept at transformations. The word "brujo" popped into his head.

Upon Carlos's return to camp, Pedro turned under his blanket and said, "You were gone a long time." Laughing, Pedro added, "I hope you're not suffering from constipation."

"Not at all," Carlos replied. "I just needed to be alone in order to think things over."

Pedro grunted and rolled over. "Some men think best while using the latrine."

The next day Don Carlos was restless. The mountain desert seemed very familiar, despite the fact that he'd never been in this region before. Perhaps in a past life, he said to himself, although with less certainty than he had felt last night. He wondered whether the barren landscape was causing his imagination to run wild.

That night he again left the camp after dark and hiked for some distance. He sat down on a rock and focused his mind on the owl he had seen. He was not conscious of the moment of transformation; he was an owl. Loosely encircling him in a soft pile were his shirt and pants. Extricating his wings and stepping high, he lifted himself out of his clothes and boots and launched into flight. By the light of a full moon, he followed the contours of the road ahead, astonished at the minute details his owl eyes could detect. After two exhilarating hours, he returned, somewhat reluctantly, to his starting point, changed back into his human form, dressed, and walked into camp.

Pedro greeted him again. "Thinking or shitting or both?"

"We'll talk in the morning," Don Carlos said somewhat curtly.

Riding ahead of the rest of the party the following day, Don Carlos decided he needed to tell Pedro about his owl experience and hope his manservant wouldn't think he was crazy.

Upon hearing Carlos's story, Pedro simply said, "You're a brujo and a powerful one. My mother's father was a brujo, but he couldn't do what you just did."

Freed by Pedro's acceptance to pursue his practice of sorcery, Don Carlos went flying again the next night. The party had stopped just short of a canyon where bandits had been active. As he skimmed along the ridge above the canyon, Carlos saw a bandits' camp.

Returning to his own camp in human form, Don Carlos woke Pedro and told him about the bandits. "Let's surprise them with a night attack," he said. "There are only eight of them."

Pedro took this calmly. "Two against eight? Very well; let's check out the situation."

It took nearly an hour of scrambling through rough terrain to reach a position above the bandits' camp. Seven of the bandits were sleeping around the embers of a dying fire, while the eighth was positioned some distance off watching the gang's horses.

"Pedro," Carlos asked, "can you deal with the man guarding the horses and lead the herd down the canyon to our camp?"

Pedro grinned and crept stealthily across to a spot near but behind the guard. Don Carlos saw his companion draw a long, thin object, a tube of some sort, from his pack. He inserted a dart in one end of the tube, blew strongly into the tube, and watched as the guard slapped at his neck, exclaiming, "Damn bugs!" before collapsing due to the paralytic properties of the drug solution in which Pedro had soaked the dart. "It's something I learned while campaigning in southern jungles," Pedro told Carlos later, clearly pleased with himself.

While Pedro led the horses away, Don Carlos, carrying two large bags, crept up on the sleeping bandits. As silently as a shadow, he moved through the camp, carefully placing the men's boots into one bag and their muskets into another. With both bags fully loaded, he walked down the slope, rendezvoused with Pedro, and together they returned to their own camp.

Keeping the bandits' horses near the travelers' camp proved quite easy, since Don Carlos's Eagle was a born herd leader, and the bandits' horses settled down to graze near him.

At first light, before anyone in their own camp was awake, Don Carlos and Pedro walked up the road toward the bandits' hiding spot. As they rounded a corner, they saw a dejected-looking barefoot bandit, a mestizo, approaching. "My name is Manuel Tapia," the robber said. "My horse and the horses of my friends have wandered off during the night."

"Apparently, your boots also wandered off," Pedro said with a grin.

"Let's not waste time with lies," Don Carlos said sternly. "We know you are part of a bandit gang. We've found your horses, boots, and weapons and saw silver ingots from the Chulamate Mine in a bag hidden in your musket's scabbard. We can help you recover these items, but if you want to live out the day you must do exactly as I say, because if our captain learns that you are bandits, he will take great pleasure in hanging you by the neck before the sun has reached its zenith.

"Here's what you must do. Tell our captain that your men are on the road to the northern mines—I'm assuming some of you have been miners (a question that brought a nod)—and are hoping to find work there. You haven't entered the canyon for fear of robbers, but if you can join our party, our combined numbers will discourage bandits from attacking."

Joaquin, when he arose, initially reacted with suspicion because the newcomers' horses were of fairly good quality, but since the bandits appeared to be poor men who lacked boots and weapons, he eventually approved Carlos's plan. The two parties then entered the canyon with the bandits at the head of the column, followed in order by Carlos and Pedro, Joaquin and his nine soldiers, the carriage with Francesca and her maids, three mule-drawn supply wagons, and the rest of Joaquin's group last in line.

About midway through the canyon Manuel dropped back to speak with Don Carlos. "I admit," he began, "that despite your numbers, we were tempted to try a surprise attack on your column in hopes of kidnapping the captain's wife for ransom. However, the omens were all bad. Early last night I saw a large owl of a type not seen here this time of year circling over our camp as though it thought of us as potential prey. Then this morning we awoke to find our boots, muskets, and horses gone and some items missing from our saddlebags. We were terrified! Perhaps we had encountered one of the witches said to inhabit this region."

"Perhaps so," Don Carlos replied with an inner smile.

Pedro couldn't let the point pass. "My mother was a pure-blooded Indian," he said, "who taught my brothers and me that witches often take the form of owls. It seems altogether likely that what you saw was a witch who was sizing you up for an attack."

"At least this witch wasn't one of the soul-grabbing type," Don Carlos added, thinking it might be useful to show Manuel that things could have been worse.

"And how would we know that?" Manuel asked. "One of my men, the one who was watching the horses, felt a pinprick in his neck and fell to the ground, unable to move or speak. Could he have been bitten by a soul-grabber?'

"I doubt it," Pedro replied. "Had he been attacked by a soul-grabber, he would look like a ghost this morning and would have wanted nothing to do with the rest of you. More likely, a witch cast a temporary spell over your guard and the rest of you and then stole into your camp to take your goods."

"I've been wondering how you came to know where those items are hidden," Manual inquired.

"Pure chance," Don Carlos said. "As you saw, Pedro and I were walking up the road to see its condition, when we spotted your items off to one side. Your horses, by the way, apparently ran off once they weren't being watched. Fortunately, my horse has a commanding personality. He's a lead horse, and once your mounts met up with him, he displayed his dominance by adding them to the rest of our herd."

By now the travelers had reached the far end of the canyon where the road forked, and the bandits and colonists went their separate ways. As they parted, Don Carlos told Manuel where his gang could find their boots and weapons. Lastly, he handed Manuel a silver ingot he had taken from the bandits' stash and said, "I have done you a very great favor; indeed, I have saved your life, and should I ask for your help at some future time, I expect you to return the favor."

5

Santa Fe

*F*or several weeks after their encounter with the bandits, Joaquin's party moved ahead at a steady pace. However, one afternoon after torrential downpours had fallen in the mountains to the west, Don Carlos and Pedro came to the next ford only to find the river dangerously swollen by runoff from the mountains. Carlos rode back to the main party to speak with Joaquin, who was riding next to the carriage carrying his wife and her two women servants.

"Joaquin, the river is running high and the current is so strong that we might do well to wait until morning to ford the stream. Would you like to see for yourself?"

Joaquin spurred his horse forward, and Carlos was about to turn Eagle to follow when the blue-eyed beauty, Camila, leaned out of the carriage and said, "You're an odd one. In fact, you're doubly odd—because you're in a party with your brother and sister-in-law and never dine with them, and because—though Doña Francesca says you were quite the ladies' man in Mexico City—you never socialize with anyone except Pedro."

"Joaquin and Francesca are on their honeymoon, and I didn't want to intrude. And Pedro is very good company."

"Oh?" Camila replied in a speculative way. "I've heard that soldiers are like that."

"Not that kind of company," Don Carlos said to everyone's amusement. He wheeled Eagle about and galloped off.

The next morning, to Don Carlos's surprise, Joaquin stopped by to apologize for what he called Camila's "impertinence." "Having spent nearly twelve years in an orphanage," Joaquin added, "she did not have an upbringing conducive to good manners. Nevertheless, I appreciate your efforts to keep your distance from Francie's maids."

"Think nothing of it," Carlos replied. "I don't take things servants say seriously."

In fact, by morning—after a night of flying about in the form of an owl—Don Carlos's mind was on other things. He was remembering more and more of his past lives as a brujo and had regained his skill at transforming himself. The key to success was to concentrate on every detail of the animal he wished to become until he became it. Changing the form of other things proved more difficult. He experienced some success transforming one type of plant into another, and he felt a sense of great accomplishment when he managed to make a yucca bloom despite it not being the season for yucca blossoms. However, he had no luck at all working with inanimate objects— stones, crystals, and sand. He concluded that as a being whose life depended on breath, he could successfully draw on the energy of his breath and the circulation of his blood to identify with and utilize the life force within all living things: plants, trees, and animals. An inanimate object, he concluded, must require a different brujo technique, which he'd either forgotten or never known. Nevertheless, he congratulated himself, observing that he was making some progress at regaining his old skills, and having turned to that happy thought he was immediately distracted from pondering how to work with inanimate things to wondering whether he could change another person into one of the owls that he became with such ease. Possibly so, but he wasn't about to attempt it for fear of doing someone great harm, which would certainly be the case if he couldn't reverse the process. (He had forgotten, for the moment, that as a little boy he'd once transformed his sister into a mouse and had successfully returned her to human form.)

At noon, the party came to Nombre de Dios (present-day Chihuahua), a settlement in a rough silver-mining and cattle-raising region where Franciscans had recently established a mission church beside the Chuviscar River; everyone paused there to water their animals. Don Carlos was amused to see Eagle, always the dominant one, push Pepper away to take the best spot at the watering trough.

A melodious voice broke his reverie. "Nothing shy about your Eagle,"

Camila said. "Joaquin scolded me for not being respectful yesterday. I guess I owe you an apology."

"I agree that you were too forward. You must be more careful in the presence of others, especially your mistress. However, I wasn't offended, because I like high-spirited people."

"Even high-spirited women?"

"Especially high-spirited women, though just now I'm preoccupied with other things."

As he turned and led Eagle away from the watering trough, he thought to himself, I'd better be careful. I find this blue-eyed woman very attractive, but I've promised Joaquin that I'll keep my distance.

Three weeks later the travelers reached the Rio Grande and the small settlement of El Paso del Norte. Their trip had been arduous, and they were fatigued. Joaquin, whose solid leadership skills Carlos had come to respect, declared that everyone needed to rest for several days. Besides, they'd arrived on the eve of a local religious feast day dedicated to Our Lady of Guadalupe, in whose honor a mission had been established in the town in the mid-seventeenth century.

Joaquin had apparently gone out of his way to learn something about the history of New Mexico province, which he and the rest of his party were about to enter. "You know about Our Lady of Guadalupe, I suppose?" he asked Carlos.

"I'm familiar," Don Carlos replied, "with the story of Our Lady's appearance to an Indian peasant near Mexico City in December sometime early in the 1500s. I assume that the residents of El Paso del Norte hold this particular feast in mid-December in commemoration of that miraculous event."

"Yes," Joaquin commented. "I'm sure you're right. We're fortunate to arrive here at this moment. It will make our stay more enjoyable."

"Agreed," Carlos said, with a nod.

"I didn't know you were so well informed about religious history," Joaquin remarked. "From what I heard you always seemed more interested in the pleasures of secular life."

"Some credit has to go to my Jesuit tutors," Carlos replied with a laugh. He clapped Joaquin on the shoulder and said, "Now if you'll excuse me, I want to find a stable where Eagle can eat and rest while we're here. I'll see you at Colonel Encarnación's tonight."

Colonel Gabriel Encarnación, the commander of the local army garrison, happened to be an old friend of Joaquin's, and he invited Joaquin and Francie to stay with him. Don Carlos was also invited, but he could see that even one more guest would make the colonel's residence overcrowded, so he had politely declined, though he had been pleased to accept an invitation to join the Encarnación household nightly for dinner.

Pedro and Don Carlos found a room for themselves in a small boardinghouse that catered to Native and mestizo visitors to town. Carlos kept the location of their lodging a secret because he knew his upper-class friends and relatives would be puzzled if they learned that he, heir to the title of marquis, had chosen to rub shoulders with Indians, who were at the very bottom of the social hierarchy; yet Carlos, for reasons he didn't understand at this time, felt a special affinity for New Spain's humbler folk.

El Paso del Norte's Feast of Our Lady of Guadalupe was a modest affair when compared with feast days in Mexico City. Nevertheless, everyone in Joaquin's party had a good time. The procession to the church and the High Mass that followed were done solemnly and with some flair. After Mass there were all sorts of activities, including dances and horse races, the longest of which Eagle won for Carlos. Don Carlos introduced himself to several of the local Spanish residents, families of merchants and traders, and enjoyed dancing with their daughters. He concluded that pretty girls could be found nearly anywhere.

Evenings at Colonel Encarnación's also proved diverting. The colonel was a genial host who served the best available food to his family and guests. On the second night at his hacienda, the colonel suggested that everyone draw straws. The three persons who drew the longest straws were obligated to entertain the rest.

The colonel's son, a bright, playful nine-year-old named Benito, drew the first long straw and treated everyone to an adept rendition of a popular violin piece.

Camila drew the second long straw. Accompanying herself on a guitar, she sang with deep emotion a ballad that included the words, "I never will marry; I'll be no man's wife; I intend to stay single all the days of my life." Such feeling; such beauty. Tears flowed freely.

Don Carlos drew the third straw. He wondered aloud what to do.

"How about a magic trick?" Camila suggested. "Yes! Yes!" Benito chimed in.

"Good idea," Carlos replied, "though my tricks depend on sleight of hand, not magic." This was not entirely true, but it was a necessary claim to make when among Catholics. "I will do three tricks," he announced. "Watch closely to see if you can detect how each is done."

For his first trick he invited Benito to sit next to him. He cupped his hands over the boy's left ear and pretended to be tugging very hard at something. Out came a two-reales coin that he gave him to keep.

For his second trick he placed an empty vase on the table and covered it with a napkin. To make his performance more dramatic, he waved his hands above the napkin and muttered an incantation of sorts, which was a Sanskrit phrase he remembered from his studies with Father Stefano. He lifted the napkin only to see the tiny vase sitting there, completely unchanged. Shaking his head in mock frustration, he covered the vase and announced, "Clearly, this is going to take stronger measures." He took a spoon, scooped some salt out of a condiments dish, and sprinkled the salt on the napkin, repeating his Sanskrit incantation more loudly and enunciating the words with great clarity. (He was confident that no one else in the room would recognize that the Sanskrit words meant "You will see many things, though without understanding any of them," a phrase that had stuck with him because it seemed to embody a profound truth.) When he drew the napkin aside this time, doing so with a wild flourish, the tiny vase now contained a small flower that he'd been hiding up his sleeve.

He next went to the patio and returned with a rock about twice the size of his fist. He covered it with a large napkin. When he withdrew the napkin, the rock sat there unchanged. With a shake of his head he declared, "My casual approach, born of overconfidence, has proven inadequate." He hadn't intended to repeat the bit of showmanship he'd displayed in the second trick, but it seemed timely to do so. "Let's try again," he said. Everyone laughed, amused at what they assumed was simply another dramatic device on his part.

He made a show of concentrating intently on the task. This time when he pulled the covering away, a small, multi-colored bird was sitting there. The little creature took off and circled the room several times, singing excitedly, before flying out an open window.

Everyone applauded enthusiastically, though Don Carlos noticed that Camila was giving him a speculative look. "All this proves," he said, "is that the hand is quicker than the eye." (The truth of the matter was a bit different. He had purchased the little bird as a present for Benito Encarnación and had hidden it in a cage with other birds in the patio. To transport the bird unseen to the dining room he had used a brujo's technique he'd remembered only the previous day: changing an animal or plant into a tiny compact form to move it from place to place and then restoring it to its original size at an appropriate time.)

At the end of the evening, Colonel Encarnación drew Joaquin and Carlos aside with a solemn look on his face. "Please be very careful on your northward journey," he said. "There are many reports of hostile Natives along the route to Santa Fe. Four merchants who were crossing through the Jornada del Muerto section of the Camino Real last week were attacked and barely escaped with their lives. To make a successful run for it, they had to abandon their pack animals and all their goods except the clothes on their backs. Successful raids of this sort simply serve to embolden Native war parties all the more."

With this warning in mind, the travelers proceeded northward in a cautious mood. Each night Don Carlos, as an owl, ranged widely scouting for hostile Natives. In the first five nights he located only one campfire, which, on close examination, he saw was surrounded by a small family group that did not appear to be a war party. But on the sixth night of the trek, just after the caravan had reached the barren Jornada del Muerto part of the trail, he saw a party of twenty men, all mounted and armed.

Don Carlos flew back to camp, changed into his human form, and reported that he'd walked outside the camp's perimeter and had spotted a good-sized war party nearby. Joaquin didn't seem as worried as Carlos had expected him to be. "What can a few Natives with spears and bows do against well-armed Spaniards?" Joaquin asked.

"Quite a lot," Don Carlos replied, "if they catch us unawares in the type of pre-dawn attack they favor."

"You're right, of course," Joaquin said, and he doubled the normal watch and instructed his soldiers to sleep with their swords, daggers, and muskets, the latter fully loaded, by their sides. Carlos and Pedro and several other civilian members of the party who were armed did likewise.

Just before dawn all hell broke loose, the raiders having escaped detection until the very last minute. Don Carlos and Pedro were on one side of the camp, Joaquin and the ladies on the other. A group of fifteen warriors emerged on Carlos's side and bore down on the camp with blood-curdling screams. Carlos, Pablo, and the armed men, three soldiers and two male colonists who'd been sleeping near them, leaped up and prepared to fight. The army unit's bugler sounded the alarm. Pedro, a veteran of many skirmishes, told his less experienced companions, "Hold your fire until they're almost on us. They're hoping we'll waste our ammunition by firing a volley while they're too far away to guarantee success."

Arrows and spears rained down on the Spaniards, but by using their shields to protect themselves and showing patience in waiting to fire back, they held their own and managed to kill two attackers. The survivors retreated hurriedly, several of them badly injured and needing help to escape. It was then that Carlos realized that other Natives had attacked Joaquin's part of the encampment, and with greater success. Indeed, Joaquin was grappling with a knife-wielding warrior and was getting the worst of it. Another warrior had one of Francie's maids by the hair and was dragging her away.

Certain that he couldn't safely take the time needed to reload his musket, Don Carlos picked up a spear that had fallen nearby and, drawing on his brujo powers, hurled it with incredible force at the warrior who was about to deal a death blow to Joaquin. The spear pierced the warrior's neck, killing him instantly.

Carlos and Pedro ran toward the skirmish across the way, their daggers drawn. There were only three warriors left, all three now in full retreat, including one that was trying to throw the struggling maid he'd captured onto his horse. Carlos raised his hand with the dagger in it and, aiming carefully, threw the dagger at the warrior, who jerked backward and collapsed. Only then did Carlos see that Camila, dagger in hand, had also pursued the Native with the intent of attacking him. "What took you so long?" she asked with a wry smile, when he, a little out of breath, reached her side.

"You certainly were doing your part with cool determination," he replied.

"There was nothing calm about my feelings," she confessed. "I was frightened out of my wits, but I couldn't stand by and do nothing. I thought the very least I could do would be to distract him long enough for you or someone else to get here and help."

Despite her disclaimer, Carlos was impressed and told her so. "What you did, Camila, was incredibly brave. You were intervening to help your friend at great risk to yourself."

"I don't even want to think about it," she replied. "Fortunately, at the time I wasn't thinking things through. I acted on impulse."

Carlos, in an effort to lighten the mood of the moment, injected a teasing tone into their exchange. "I guess I got things wrong," he said. "I thought you were simply applying the lessons you learned at the orphanage."

She looked perplexed and asked, "What was that?"

"All the instruction you received during the drills they called 'How to Ward off Attacks from Native Warriors.'"

Camila rewarded him with a wan smile and rallied to adopt the lighter tone he'd introduced, saying, "Yes, Reverend Mother insisted that we work on that lesson at least once a week."

They didn't pursue the joke further because serious business demanded their attention. María, the maid who'd nearly been carried off into captivity, embraced Camila tightly, sobbing, "Camila, I was terrified."

"I was too," Camila told her.

Turning their attention to the rest of their party, they found that although the attackers had been driven off, they had done much harm. Two colonists and one soldier had been killed, and Joaquin was severely injured. As his friends did their best to bind his wounds, he slipped in and out of consciousness. He was loaded into the party's only carriage, his life hanging in the balance. Camila and María immediately agreed to yield their seats to him and to ride in one of the supply wagons for the rest of the trip to Santa Fe.

Progress toward Santa Fe seemed to go slowly due to the somber mood that prevailed in the party in the aftermath of an attack that had left three of their companions dead. Joaquin's condition was a constant worry, especially for his bride of less than four months. Fortunately, his condition soon improved sufficiently to indicate that he would, given a long period of convalescence, recover completely.

During the days after the battle, Carlos often rode next to the carriage bearing Joaquin and Francie and did his best to keep them in good spirits. He could tell that Francie appreciated his efforts. At one point when Joaquin was sound asleep, she ventured a comment about Joaquin's father, Carlos's stepfather. "I didn't like," she asserted, "the way the general practically ordered you to leave Mexico City. It seemed to me that the least he could have done was to give you more of a chance to refuse."

Carlos, not seeing any point in stirring up the coals of that fire, replied, "He's used to command, and once I'd decided not to defy his wishes, I resolved to make the best of it without any protest."

Later the same day Camila approached Carlos at a rest stop and commented, "I couldn't believe how powerfully you threw that spear practically the whole distance across our camp."

"I suppose a bit of luck was involved," he replied.

"I wasn't referring to the precision of your aim," she told him, "though that was remarkable in its own way. It was the force behind your throw that seemed almost incredibly strong."

"When I was about twelve or thirteen," he said, making up a story to explain the power he'd shown, which, in fact, had called on his brujo training, "some of my friends and I used to play a game we called Spaniards and Indians. The Spaniards got to use muskets, and the Indians spears. We didn't attack each other; we simply did target practice to see which side could hit a barrel set some distance away. I almost always drew the straw that meant I would be one of the Indians. My competitive spirit was so strong that I used to sneak off and practice for hours on end until I could hit the barrel much oftener with spears than the Spaniards did with their muskets."

"You rich boys definitely had more leisure for time-passing activities," Camila observed with a bit of a grimace, "than we orphanage girls did. Our days were a constant round of lessons in sewing, cooking, proper deportment, and a small dose of reading and writing."

"I spent a lot of time with Jesuit tutors," Carlos replied. "That wasn't much fun."

Camila's rejoinder indicated that his defense didn't impress her. "I'm sure," she said, "your Jesuit tutors didn't require you to learn sewing and cooking, the assumption being that you had cooks and maids to perform those mundane services."

"I can't deny it," he conceded, observing to himself that Camila used verbal jousting in somewhat the same way aggressive fencers attacked vigorously to keep him on the defensive.

Two weeks later their sad and bedraggled party at last glimpsed Santa Fe ahead. The sight left Don Carlos feeling disheartened. What he saw was a tiny town consisting of mostly one-story adobe dwellings scattered about amidst cornfields. His first reaction was a bitter one. To think, he observed, that I left a vibrant city of 100,000 to try my luck in this backwater, a town without any grand boulevards, splendid plazas, handsome cathedrals, or fine homes. He knew it was possible that in time he would come to appreciate whatever pleasures and possibilities this rustic place had to offer, but for the moment he simply felt that he had reached the farthest edge of the civilized world as he, a Spaniard, defined civilization.

6

Murder

*D*on Carlos, Pedro, and the rest of Joaquin's party arrived in Santa Fe as night fell. Carlos and Pedro were offered a small room in the Presidio barracks. After a quick meal, they went to bed.

Don Carlos, more tired than he had realized, slept later than was his custom, and at eight o'clock in the morning he was still in bed, dozing, when Pedro came in and shook him. "Time to get up," Pedro said. "There's a lot to do, beginning with breakfast, after which you must dress in your best suit and call on the military governor, General Juan Villela. A servant of his just came by to say the governor wants to see you as soon as possible."

Don Carlos bounded out of bed, his energy restored by a night's rest, and dressed quickly. After gulping down the hearty breakfast Pedro had prepared — an omelet made with fresh eggs, cornbread still warm from the oven, and strong coffee — he was ready to set off to see the governor. "Any advice?" he asked, not really expecting an answer.

"Yes," Pedro replied, with a solemn look at his master. "I urge you to be very careful. It was one thing to pursue your brujo path while we were crossing through desert country, where the chance of being exposed was small. However, in Santa Fe many eyes will be watching us. Don't forget that your new boss is one of the Spanish leaders who curbed Pueblo shamanism after the Revolt. It would be very bad for you if he learned that you are a brujo."

Don Carlos recognized the wisdom of Pedro's counsel and thanked him for speaking so frankly. It was, therefore, in a wary mood, wondering how he would be received, that he walked the short distance to the Palace of the Governors and was admitted to His Excellency's office. He need not have worried. Governor Villela welcomed him warmly. "We are delighted to have you here at last," he said. "My old friend, your stepfather, General Rodrigo Alvarez, had nothing but praise for your talents as a swordsman and as a highly educated young man. And," he added, gesturing to a desk with piles of papers on it, "as you can see, your secretarial skills are much needed."

"I will do my best to serve you well," Don Carlos replied.

The governor next expressed an interest in the details of the attack their caravan had suffered and stated in no uncertain terms that marauding Native raiders needed to be dealt with harshly. He added that although the casualties the Spanish party had suffered were extremely regrettable, in his judgment the losses they had inflicted on the Natives were probably severe enough to discourage further attacks on Spanish travelers in the near future. After a brief exchange about other aspects of the trip Carlos had just completed, including news regarding the status of the army's garrison at El Paso del Norte, the governor left Carlos to the paperwork.

There was a lot of it; and it wasn't only the governor's papers and documents that needed to be drafted or copied. The province's vice governor and the town's mayor also had left many documents for Carlos to prepare. Apparently, none of Santa Fe's top officials had completed official reports for the better part of a year.

Working through most of the day without a break and, after a quick bite to eat, late into the night, Don Carlos readied everything in the pile of "urgent" items for the governor's signature and immediate dispatch to Mexico City. The governor was very pleased when he stopped by to check on Carlos's progress. Carlos congratulated himself: I've taken the first step, a necessary one mentally, in transforming myself from a brujo into a bureaucrat.

After breakfast on his second day in Santa Fe, Don Carlos paid a visit to the house on the Presidio grounds where Joaquin and Francie were quartered. Too weak from his injuries to consider taking command of his soldiers at any time in the immediate future, Joaquin clearly had been looking forward to Carlos's visit. "Alfonso," he said, addressing Carlos by his proper name, "until I'm on my feet, I need you to act as our family's emissary to the first families of Santa Fe. Please arrange to accompany Francie on formal visits."

Don Carlos, flattered to be entrusted with such an important social role, agreed readily, but excused himself soon thereafter because he could see that his stepbrother badly needed rest.

He and his sister-in-law chatted briefly about when to make the proposed introductory visits; then, as Carlos turned to go, Francie fixed him with a questioning look and asked, "Camila seems to believe that your magic is less sleight of hand than sorcery. Is there anything to that?" Camila was across the room, watching alertly.

Don Carlos knew that this line of speculation needed to be squelched. With seeming unconcern, he laughed, "Didn't I tell you the hand is quicker than the eye? I gather that you didn't see that the flower was up my sleeve or that I concealed the little bird the same way. I shouldn't admit to how the tricks were done, but the key is to distract the onlookers' attention by dramatic flourishes that cause them to look elsewhere while the flower or bird or whatever is brought out from a hiding place."

"Is that so?" Francie replied skeptically.

"Yes, I bought the bird from a peddler as a gift for Benito and hid it in the patio. When I went to the patio to bring back a rock, I disguised my real goal, which was to retrieve the bird."

Don Carlos was relieved that his explanation seemed to satisfy Francie.

Don Carlos and Pedro needed a better place to live than the tiny room in the Presidio barracks where they'd spent their first few nights. Carlos, preoccupied with the mountain of paperwork at the Palace of the Governors, left it to Pedro to locate lodgings. Pedro soon found an abandoned wreck of a house with a small garden plot and a corral attached to it. The place was barely a block from the plaza, one side of which was plainly visible from the house's front porch. The house's previous occupants had been killed during the Pueblo Revolt and the house itself nearly leveled. Eleven years after military forces led by Carlos's stepfather had begun to reestablish permanent Spanish control of Santa Fe, the house still stood empty and the garden plot lay fallow. Since no heirs had been found, the governor offered to grant the property to Don Carlos. He gratefully accepted, and the transfer of title was quickly consummated. Pedro, a capable carpenter, set about rebuilding the house.

After five weeks of intense labor, Pedro, aided by several Pueblo Indian workers, one of whom was an orphan boy named Diego, had rooms ready for himself and Carlos. A week later, the men were able to move their horses into the stable in back of the house, and Diego, whose parents had been killed in the Pueblo Revolt and who had been living with a distant cousin, asked to be allowed to sleep in the stable's hayloft in return for doing odd jobs. "He'll be handy to have around," Pedro argued, "and we'll learn Pueblo languages from him." Carlos, who felt sympathy for the young orphan, agreed.

Over the months following his arrival in Santa Fe, Don Carlos settled into a comfortable routine of work and play. During the trip north, a wild spirit within him that drew on energy from the desert landscape had led him to pursue acts of sorcery. Once he became a town-dweller, he lost contact with that wild inner spirit and became absorbed in, one could say domesticated by, life that moved along tame, conventional lines.

In addition to his work as a civil servant, he was drawn into ordinary social life. He escorted his sister-in-law on obligatory visits to the homes of the town's social elite. There were only a few such families. Although Governor Villela and his wife had no unmarried daughters, they did have a twenty-three-year-old son, Rafael, a member of the army garrison at Santa Fe whom Carlos liked and undertook to tutor in fencing.

Two of the remaining elite families included unmarried daughters of eligible age. Vice Governor Ignacio Peralta and his wife had twin girls, Juliana and Victoria, who, though pretty, failed to interest Carlos because they were not terribly bright. Elena, the daughter of the town's leading merchant, Javier Beltran, was intelligent enough, but she was plump to the point of being portly. Don Carlos had always found slender young women more to his taste.

After the first round of visits to these families, Carlos's sister-in-law turned to him and, with a slight edge in her voice, said, "All these years, and you haven't changed; you never took a serious interest in me because I was neither slender enough nor clever enough for your taste."

Carlos's reply—that he'd been too young to appreciate her charms— at least led her to smile.

Of all his social relationships, Carlos most enjoyed his time with Pedro and Diego. Diego earnestly tried to please the two older men, and they applauded his every effort. The one initiative that didn't work out too well was Diego's first attempt to cook a meal. He planned to serve enchiladas, but misjudged the amount of time the tortillas would take and scorched them badly; consequently, smoke from burned tortillas filled the house. The three men raced around throwing windows and doors open. Diego was afraid he would be punished, but Carlos told him he was sure that Diego would not make the same mistake twice, and Pedro poured wine for them to drink while sitting on the house's front veranda waiting for the smoke to clear.

Pedro had begun to entertain his friends with amusing stories of his own youthful errors when a male dog, all white except for one black eye and with a severe limp in his left hind leg, approached. (There were many stray dogs in Santa Fe.) "See!" Pedro declared. "A guest has come to dinner."

"Can he stay?" Diego asked, his heart moved by the dog's limp and his skinny body.

Amused, Carlos replied, "He can stay, if he'll eat your tortillas." No problem. The hungry dog wolfed down the burned tortillas and begged for more.

"He has a lot of fleas that I don't want in the house," Pedro announced.

"I can fix that!" Diego declared. "I'll give him a bath with cedar oil and he'll be fine."

After his bath, the skinny dog, facetiously named Gordo, joined the household as a loyal companion and guard dog.

As the months passed and spring gave way to summer, Carlos found that he was enjoying his quiet life in Santa Fe more than he had expected — conversations with friends, a job that introduced him to new political and financial topics, and socializing at dinners and parties. All these activities were proving to be quite pleasant. But one hot day in mid-August his daily routines were disrupted by an act of violence.

Shortly after breakfast on a Saturday, Carlos and Pedro were sitting on their house's veranda when Diego, out of breath and highly agitated, ran up to them and announced, "A soldier has been murdered, and my friend José Lugo has been arrested for the crime!"

Carlos and Pedro followed Diego to the Barrio de Analco, a neighborhood where many Natives lived. On the way they passed two constables, each of whom had a firm grip on the upper arm of a slender, frightened-looking Pueblo youth whose hands were tied and who was being force-marched between them. The distraught captive kept his head downward. "That's José," Diego whispered. "I can't believe he'd murder anyone; he's never even been one to get in fights."

When they reached the Barrio de Analco they found a small crowd gathered outside a shabby, abandoned adobe building. As an important government official, Don Carlos was able to push his way through the gawkers, followed closely by Pedro. They saw, sprawled face-up on the dirt floor, the body of a dark-haired, well-built soldier. There was an ugly gash on his neck, and a blood-covered flint knife lay on the floor nearby. The town's police chief, Mauricio Castillo, a fat, middle-aged man, was surveying the scene. Don Carlos addressed him firmly. "Tell me what happened here."

"Yes, Sir. The victim is Corporal Estavan Morales, stationed at the

Presidio. He was known to be courting an Indian girl, Ana Lugo. Her brother objected, and obviously the brother, José, attacked and killed Corporal Morales."

"Obviously? You mean there were witnesses?"

"No, Excellency, but all the evidence points to that conclusion. It looks as though Corporal Morales had visited the Lugo girl, and on his way back to the barracks, while still in the Indian section of town, he was attacked by the girl's brother, who had argued with Morales and threatened him."

"I'm left wondering," Carlos stated, "whether you've yet had a chance to check at the Lugo house whether Corporal Morales indeed visited them last night."

Chief Castillo was sufficiently intimidated by Don Carlos's high standing in the provincial government to try not to let his irritation show; nevertheless, he couldn't altogether disguise his annoyance when he replied, "No, we haven't talked with Lugo's family. What would be the point? They'll just lie to protect him."

"I suppose that remains to be seen," Carlos said, making it plain that the matter wasn't settled as far as he was concerned.

After examining the scene carefully, Don Carlos left with Pedro and Diego in tow. As they walked back to their house, Carlos asked, "Did either of you see anything that didn't fit well with Chief Castillo's explanation?"

"Quite a bit," Pedro replied. "For one thing there was no sign of a struggle, and it's not possible that a slender boy like Lugo could have overpowered a tough soldier twice his size."

"Agreed," Carlos said, "unless he had help from accomplices."

"Possibly, but even so, it would have taken a major scuffle to subdue such a large man. Also, that knife is definitely not the murder weapon. Over the years I've seen many knife wounds, and this one was made by a very sharp steel blade, not a flint knife."

To this Carlos added, "I thought it odd that there was no blood on the floor. A wound that deep surely would have left at least a small pool of blood. What do you make of this?"

Pedro was decisive. "Corporal Morales was killed somewhere else and brought to the edge of the Indian district, with the flint knife and location meant to incriminate José Lugo."

"I share your view," Carlos replied. "José is being framed. But can we prove it?"

7

Pursuit

*I*t being Saturday morning, Governor Villela was not at his office, so Don Carlos went directly to his residence. A maid answered the door and announced his arrival. The governor appeared immediately and welcomed Carlos warmly. "Dear boy, I suppose you've heard the news regarding this dreadful business about Corporal Morales. Chief Castillo just came by to say that they've already made an arrest, an Indian boy whose uncle was one of the most defiant rebels in our time of troubles."

"Yes, Excellency, and that incident is what I'd like to discuss. I reached the place where Morales was found less than a half hour after the news of his death became public. I saw certain details in the crime scene that don't seem to fit Chief Castillo's theory about who did this ghastly deed. Among other curious facts, it doesn't seem reasonable to assume that a slender boy could overpower and kill a soldier who was twice his size. Perhaps he had accomplices, and, if so, they need to be caught. I'd like your permission to conduct an investigation of my own to determine whether or not my doubts about José Lugo's guilt are justified. Please give me a few days. I'll make every effort not to step on Chief Castillo's toes."

Governor Villela stood looking thoughtfully out the window for some time, then turned to Don Carlos and spoke. "Alfonso, a successful investigation of the sort you propose must be led by a man with a certain gravitas, who can command respect, even fear. You're obviously very young; yet you've always seemed to me older than your years, so much so that I've often had to remind myself that you're not yet twenty-one. The seriousness you've displayed in pursuing your work for me has led me to admire your diligence and intellect. Considering those qualities of yours, I'm inclined to agree to your proposal; however, a few days' time is all I can allow unless you turn up something substantial right away."

Pleased to have the governor's authorization, but feeling under pressure to work very fast, Carlos returned to his house and called Pedro and Diego together. "To achieve quick results," he told them, "we'll need to divide the investigation among ourselves. Diego, you know the Lugo boy; do you also know his mother and sister?"

"Only a little," Diego replied. "I once took them a message from Father Benedicto."

"That's good enough. Here's what I want you to do. Visit them, and tell them, as you told us, that you can't believe that José killed Morales. Find out as much as you can: Was Morales bothering José's sister? Did José and Morales argue? Most important of all, did Morales come by the Lugo house last night before he was killed?"

Turning to Pedro, Carlos said, "See if you can find out where Morales was murdered. Take Gordo along. I have a feeling that he's got a good nose for scents. Let him sniff around the place where Morales was lying. Then take him outside and go street by street until, as I hope he will, he picks up Morales's scent. If I'm right, there won't be any trail until you get some distance from where Morales was found because he didn't get there on his own two feet."

With his two friends headed off on their assignments, Don Carlos walked quickly to his stepbrother's residence at the Presidio. Camila answered the door. "You're up early for a Saturday," she said. "Shouldn't you be sleeping off a party or a drinking bout?"

"Don't be insolent," he replied. "I'm here to see Joaquin. Please let him know. I wish to speak with him about a matter of some urgency."

Joaquin, now fully recovered from his wounds, came to the hallway and invited Don Carlos to join him in a parlor. Before Joaquin could say anything more, Carlos said, "I need a favor and hope you will be willing to help me."

Joaquin's answer was affirmative. "I owe you a great deal, Alfonso, not just because you escorted Francie on her formal visits, but even more so because you saved my life in the desert. If your request is in my power to fulfill, rest assured that it will be granted."

"I'm sure that the murder of a soldier under your command," Carlos began, "is gravely troubling for you. I'm equally sure you want the doer of the deed caught."

"You don't believe it's this Indian fellow, the nephew of one of the most notorious of the Pueblo rebels and a brother who was angered because his sister was courted by Morales?"

"That's certainly the most obvious possibility," Carlos acknowledged, "and Chief Castillo has leaped to that conclusion." Carlos then told his stepbrother about his doubts. "What I'd like to do, with you present, is to ask Corporal Morales's comrades some questions. We'll call them into your office one at a time. If you preface every interview with a stern warning that they had better answer my questions fully, it would have a beneficial influence. You'll soon see where I'm headed with my inquiries."

The interviews were quickly arranged. Most produced nothing of note; however, Don Carlos's questions turned up potentially useful information from two individuals.

Each soldier was asked what he knew about Corporal Morales's alleged courtship of José Lugo's sister. Every soldier but one told the same story — that Morales had found her very attractive and had been annoyed by her brother's hostility. The exception came from the garrison's youngest private, Pablo López. "Corporal Morales and I were friends," he said, "because we grew up in the same town outside of Mexico City, and we enlisted together. I knew he was interested in the Lugo girl, but — well, two weeks ago at the market we practically bumped into the Lugo girl and her mother. The girl shrank away from him and turned her back, and her mother lit into him. She told Estavan in no uncertain terms never to come near her daughter again, grabbed the girl by the arm, and marched away with her. Estavan said to me, 'That mother is a harpy! She's welcome to the girl. I don't want her!'"

"Did Morales try to see the girl again in the past two weeks?" Don Carlos asked.

"I'd have no way of knowing for certain, but he certainly seemed to have lost interest."

The last soldier Carlos and Joaquin interviewed was the unit's first sergeant, Hector Sinoba. The other soldiers, when Don Carlos had asked them what Corporal Morales had done on the previous Friday night, replied that they assumed he'd gone out drinking, although no one knew with whom. But Sergeant Sinoba had a different opinion. "I don't think he ever went drinking, which is why no one can say they drank with him. No, Friday was his night to gamble. I know because when he lost, which was often, he came back to the barracks grumbling about his bad luck."

"Did he say where he gambled, or with whom?" Joaquin asked.

"No. Sorry I can't help you on that count. When I asked, he refused to say."

After Sergeant Sinoba left, Joaquin turned to Carlos. "Alfonso, I think you're on to something. Morales must have started the stories about José's hostility to him to explain why he stopped pursuing the girl. It wouldn't have seemed manly to admit that it was the girl's mother who chased him off. Gambling, and the conflicts that often arise from it, might provide a motive for murder. That's worth checking."

Don Carlos walked to his house and found Pedro and Diego waiting to report.

Diego had talked with Father Benedicto as well as José Lugo's mother and sister. "Father Benedicto was surprised," Diego said, "upon hearing that José was arrested for murder. 'That doesn't seem at all like him' — those were his exact words. And both Señora Lugo and Ana swear up and down that Morales did not come by their place last night."

"Good work, Diego," Carlos replied. "Having Father Benedicto as a character witness may help at some future point."

Pedro told what he had found. "The credit goes to Gordo. We first went to the place where Morales's body was discovered. Gordo sniffed at the spot for a long time. Then we went along all the nearby streets. At the entrance to a stable in the Spanish part of town only three house lots from here, Gordo got very excited. Inside, underneath straw, we found blood and marks of a struggle."

"Excellent!" Carlos exclaimed. He turned and scribbled a note which he gave to Diego. "Take this news to my stepbrother; then escort him to the stable Gordo found."

Turning next to Pedro, Carlos said with some urgency in his voice, "Go back to the stable and be sure that no one tampers with the scene of the crime. I'll go to see our police chief and bring him along too. By the way, I've never known who runs the stable. Do you know the name of its owner?"

"Yes. That would be Arturo Barbon. His brother Roberto owns the inn just off the plaza."

Each of the three friends went his separate way. Don Carlos found Chief Castillo just sitting down to lunch and in no mood to "chase fantasies," as he put it. But he couldn't risk offending someone so highly placed in the Crown's service, so he came along.

When Don Carlos and Chief Castillo arrived at the stable, Joaquin was already there with Diego. Pedro had carefully removed the straw that covered the bloodstain. There were also signs of a struggle. Arturo Barbon stood off to one side.

To his credit Chief Castillo immediately understood the significance of the large bloodstain on the floor. Carlos was glad that this recognition led the chief to take the lead in questioning Barbon. "What happened here?" he demanded.

"I have no idea, Sir," he said.

"Bah!" the chief exclaimed. "A soldier from the Presidio gets murdered in your stable, and you know nothing. Well, we know you let your tack room be used by gamblers. So cooperate or you'll be in trouble."

Grudgingly, but in some detail, Barbon admitted that he knew quite a lot. Yes, he let gamblers use his tack room. Yes, Corporal Morales had been one of the regulars. Yes, Morales had been gambling until late Friday night. Yes, he'd been winning in a big way. The three men with whom he'd been gambling were angry and finally said they wouldn't play any longer. At that point Barbon, believing the evening's games were over, had gathered up the cards and chips and left the room. He had no idea what, if anything, happened after that, or so he said.

"Who were the three other men?" Castillo asked. "And where are they now?"

"The three other gamblers are mestizos. They told me that they were from a ranch north of Jemez Pueblo, and that they intended to head back there early today."

"Assuming that's true," Pedro observed, "we ought to be able to catch up with them on the road to Jemez Pueblo, which is the better part of a two-day ride from here."

Carlos asked Barbon, "What sort of horses did they have?"

"Two were pinto geldings; the other was a black stallion, though not of high quality."

Don Carlos consulted with Joaquin and Chief Castillo. They agreed to organize a posse to set out after the three. Chief Castillo ordered one of his deputies, Faustino Ruiz, to go, and Joaquin chose Sergeant Sinoba, whom he described as "a highly reliable soldier," to join Carlos and Pedro.

"Good," Carlos declared. "Let's saddle up and leave immediately."

The foursome set out at a brisk pace, sometimes even breaking into a canter. They had not yet overtaken the three gamblers when they reached a place where the road forked. "What now?" Pedro asked. "Dividing is not safe."

Don Carlos motioned to his companions to stop well short of the place where the road split. He and Pedro were sure that the freshest hoofprints on the road they'd been following were those of the three gamblers. Unfortunately, where the roads came together, there was a confused mixture of hoofprints and bootprints.

Carlos dismounted and studied the fork and the area around it. At the center of the fork he found a small pile of ashes. He bent down, sniffed at it, and then gazed at it using his peripheral vision only. Without knowing how he knew it, he said, "They made an offering here. This is the place where three roads cross, sacred to an ancient goddess of death, which is a pagan superstition from Europe, not a Native belief. These gamblers are half-Spanish. I think this means that they are our killers."

He stood up and began to look at the hoofprints in each of the two forks of the road. After a few minutes he began to see luminescence coming from one set of tracks, and these had taken the right-hand fork. Carlos realized that these tracks were the black stallion's. Mounting, he simply said, "This is the road they took. Follow me."

A clear night and a gibbous moon enabled the posse to keep going after dark. The dusty road shone almost white in the moonlight, and off to their right they could see the pewter gleam of the river. Far ahead, between the road and the river, Carlos's gradually reawaking sorcerer's vision enabled him to see a pinpoint of light—a campfire. Whispering to his comrades to stop, he told them to dismount quietly and lead their horses into the sparse roadside brush. "They are up ahead," he said, still whispering. "They will hear our horses on the road, so we must approach on foot."

Leaving their horses ground-tied, they stealthily crept toward the distant campfire. They silently passed the gamblers' horses, tethered nearby, and stopped at the edge of a small clearing. The three suspects were sitting with their backs to them, close to the fire, talking in an animated way and laughing loudly as they passed around a half-empty bottle that Carlos assumed contained an alcoholic beverage, probably quite potent, since they seemed very drunk.

In complete silence Don Carlos and his companions exchanged looks and checked their muskets to be sure they were loaded and ready to fire. At Carlos's signal, the four members of the posse leaped out of the brush and Carlos shouted, "Put your hands up; any resistance and we'll shoot to kill." Looks of surprise and total dismay came onto the three mens' faces and they complied instantly with Carlos's demands. Members of the posse quickly bound the suspects' hands and feet to prevent future resistance or attempts at escape.

A search of their saddlebags led to the discovery of a silver crucifix that had belonged to Corporal Morales and a small bag filled with reales. Most or all of these, Carlos assumed, were the corporal's winnings, taken from him after he'd been killed.

"Any idea how we can find out which one murdered Morales?" Don Carlos whispered to Pedro and Sergeant Sinoba while Deputy Ruiz kept a close watch on the three men.

"Yes," Pedro volunteered. "Untie the feet of one of them, put a rope with a slip-knot around his neck, and lead him off into the brush for questioning. Bring him back and do the same with each of the next two. Then take the first one off again and tell him that one of the others has said he's the killer. Do the same with the other two and see what you get."

In the course of applying Pedro's method, the posse members found that everything progressed pretty much as Pedro had predicted. The three men, whose names turned out to be Rico, Cesar, and Antonio, each initially denied that they knew anything about Corporal Morales's death. Cesar, the tallest of the three, went so far as to say, "He was in good health when we went off to the inn to get some sleep." Antonio, a thin, swarthy man, and Cesar, a burly tough-looking fellow, both shrugged casually and feigned ignorance when asked what had happened to the corporal.

The second round of interrogations quickly got results. Antonio was the first to break. Having taken him back into the brush, Pedro told him that Cesar had singled him out as the killer. Antonio grew angry and said, "No, it was Cesar who slit the corporal's throat. He's just trying to get off the hook by blaming me." Pedro later pointed out that Antonio, at least, knew the method by which Morales had been killed, knowledge he wouldn't have had if he was completely innocent.

Precisely which of the accused had wielded the knife became murkier when members of the posse repeated the same trick on Cesar and Rico. Upon hearing that Antonio had said Cesar had murdered the corporal, Cesar immediately stated that he was innocent; Rico had done the deed. But Rico denied having had any part in the actual killing and asserted that Antonio had slashed the corporal's throat using a fine knife that his inquisitors would find in Antonio's saddlebags. The knife, apparently the murder weapon, showed up in Antonio's saddlebags, but it remained unclear whether he'd been the one to use it on Morales. Nevertheless, the interrogators had discovered another of the suspects who knew that Morales had died of a slit throat.

Leaving the three men, once more bound hand and foot, by the campfire, the posse members withdrew a short distance to compare notes, keeping a close eye on the three gamblers. Deputy Ruiz burst out, "I'm completely confused about who murdered Corporal Morales. Antonio accuses Cesar; Cesar says Rico did it, and Rico lays the blame on Antonio. The murder weapon was in Antonio's saddlebags, but a search of the other two's saddlebags turned up the corporal's silver crucifix in Rico's possession and most of the money in Cesar's stuff."

"There's no telling which story is true," Don Carlos observed, "but we've tricked them into confessing that there was a murder and that they were in on it."

"From what we found in their saddlebags, we also know," Sergeant Sinoba added, "that robbery played a big role in motivating the murderers."

Deputy Ruiz mulled this over in silence for a few moments. "I admit," he said at last, "that when we started after these men, I thought Chief Castillo was right in arresting José Lugo. But I'm now convinced that Lugo should go free and that these three should be put on trial for robbery and murder."

Concurring with Ruiz's conclusions, Don Carlos sent Pedro to retrieve their horses and bring them to camp, where the posse members would rest until dawn and then take the three gamblers back to Santa Fe. Early the next day they set out for Santa Fe and reached the town just before dusk. Buoyed by their successful pursuit of the murderers, the four members of the posse agreed to get together again soon for a round of drinks and good fellowship.

The wheels of justice moved swiftly on New Spain's northern frontier. The trial of the three gamblers took place before a magistrate less than a month after their arrest. All three of the accused maintained their innocence, but each also admitted that he thought it was possible that one of his comrades might have returned to the stable from their rooms at the inn and robbed and killed Corporal Morales. The timing this story implied—that Morales had tarried at the stable rather than leaving it immediately to go to his barracks—struck everyone as improbable in the extreme. Unable to sort out precisely who had done what, the magistrate declared that in the light of the men's mutual accusations, none of their alibis was in the least persuasive. The most likely scenario, he concluded, was that one gambler had struck the fatal blow while the other two held Morales down. As thieves and accessories to murder, all three were declared guilty of a capital crime. The three men were hanged two weeks later.

Shortly after the execution, Pedro told Carlos, "Alfonso, by saving José Lugo, you've become a hero among the local Indians. I'm confident you will benefit from their gratitude someday soon."

8

Camila

For a man who, through many lifetimes, had always loved women, the one thing lacking in Don Carlos's life in Santa Fe was a romantic interest. This became all too evident on the occasion of the town's late-autumn masked ball. The small settlement's residents of all classes looked forward to the All Saints' Eve Ball with great anticipation. The town's womenfolk spent months preparing their gowns, and the men planned their costumes with great care.

Don Carlos dressed as Don Quixote, a would-be knight errant besotted with chivalric romances. Pedro went as Sancho Panza, his rustic squire. Don Carlos danced with all the upper-class ladies: Governor Villela's wife, Isabel, Señora Peralta and her twin daughters, and the Beltran girl and her mother, and tried to imagine them as far more entrancing than they were. None of them truly touched his heart.

After one particularly vigorous dance, this time with his sister-in-law Francie, he was inspired to give her a genuine compliment. "You look especially fetching tonight."

"I suppose it's because Joaquin is well again and has fulfilled my wish for a child." Blushing at her admission, she continued, "Happily, I have only seven more months to wait."

"That's wonderful!" Carlos exclaimed. "I'm sure Joaquin is happy too."

"Of course, but as long as we're speaking frankly, I've been wondering why you haven't asked Camila to dance. She worked many hours on her gown, and you must admit that the result is dazzling. She's a great beauty."

"Francie," he protested, "I promised Joaquin that I wouldn't romance your maids."

"A euphemism for seduce. Call it what you will, one dance won't break your pledge. Do I have to walk you over to her like I would a bashful boy?"

"Encouraged by that threat, I'm on my way right now."

So it was that Carlos and Camila had their first dance. She had a shapely figure and, in the candlelight of the ballroom, soft and vulnerable eyes. Enchanting was the word that came to his mind, a perception that led his imagination to enrich her appearance even more. Finding himself curiously tongue-tied, he said, "You're an excellent dancer."

"Are you surprised?" she asked. "Doña Francesca has generously seen to my education in social matters, apparently hoping that I will gain the attention of some respectable man, perhaps a corporal in the army or a skilled craftsman—not that either appeals to me."

"Given your very great beauty, you certainly can aim higher than that, though I remember you singing a haunting verse to the effect that you never intend to marry."

"I'm a practical person. Foundlings have to be. I believe it's my fate not to marry, so I've made it my preference too. But tell me, Don Alfonso, why are you always so cold to me?"

"I thought that started with you and your penchant for verbal combat with me."

"That's no answer at all," she declared, "and unworthy of such a skillful fencer."

A bit angry, Carlos said, "Would an honorable man romance his sister's maid?"

"So that's it," she said, turning away from him, her eyes glistening with tears.

She hurried out of the room and when she hadn't returned a half hour later, Carlos excused himself and went home.

The morning after the All Saints' Ball Don Carlos got up in a bad mood—grumpy and out of sorts—rather than his normal high spirits.

"Love troubles?" Pedro asked from across the room.

"I don't want to talk about it."

"Yes, you do," Pedro replied firmly.

"All right. Last night, just as the music stopped, I said something that, completely without my intending to do so, hurt Camila's feelings. She pulled away from me and started across the room. I was going to follow and try to make amends, but Governor Villela took my arm and insisted on introducing me to a visitor. By the time our conversation ended, Camila was nowhere to be found."

"Precisely what was this inept remark?" Pedro inquired.

"She accused me of being cold to her, and my answer was the truth — that I had promised Joaquin that I wouldn't romance his wife's maids."

"That was the word you used, 'romance,' which is a polite substitute for seduce? No wonder she became so upset."

"I don't quite see how," Carlos protested. "I thought my statement would lead her to conclude that I was respectful of her honor. Instead, she's twisted my words into some sort of insult."

"You are not that dumb," Pedro chided him, "or at least I'm surprised if you are. By admitting that you had promised your stepbrother not to 'romance his wife's maids,' you reminded her of the inferiority of her social position."

"That's not what I meant," Carlos said sharply.

"No," Pedro said. "But what now?"

"I have no idea," Carlos replied.

"Don't be an idiot. Having failed to find her last night, you need to find her today."

Pedro was right, of course, and Don Carlos dressed carefully and walked to Joaquin's residence at the Presidio. Francie's second maid, María, answered the door. Carlos said, "I've come to see Camila."

"She told us she doesn't want to see anyone today. But here's Doña Francesca."

Francie reproached him. "You certainly managed to spoil Camila's evening."

"Surely you don't believe that was my intention. I'm here to apologize for any injury that I've unintentionally caused her."

"She made it clear that you were the last person she wanted to see," Francie told him.

"That won't solve anything," Carlos replied. "Help me clear the air. I'll wait here in hopes that you'll be able to persuade her to speak with me."

After a long interval Camila came to the drawing room where Carlos was waiting. "I've agreed to see you only because of Doña Francesca's urgent pleas on your behalf."

"Thank you for doing so. I came to apologize for hurting your feelings. Nothing was farther from my mind. I enjoyed dancing with you and have always admired your high spirits."

"Yet you said you couldn't, as you put it, 'romance' me, which could have had a number of different meanings, all of them insulting. It could mean that you viewed me as a loose woman whose virtue you could compromise by seducing me, but had chosen not to. Or it could mean that you couldn't consider a friendship with me because I was only a maid, the clear implication being that a foundling servant girl is an insignificant person to a man of your high status."

Choosing his words carefully, Don Carlos tried to prove his respect and affection for Camila by manifesting them in a practical way. With great earnestness, he said, "I would like you to regard me as your friend because of deeds rather than words. As a first proof, I hope you will allow me to accompany you, Joaquin, and Francie to Mass tomorrow." Noting her questioning look, he added, "Being with Joaquin and Francie will maintain, as I'm sure both of us wish to do, outward proprieties and prevent local gossips' tongues from wagging."

Camila stood silently, gazing past Don Carlos into the next room. Finally, she looked directly into his eyes and said, "If you wish, I will offer you the chance to be my friend—a friend, and not, in any sense, a romantic partner. If you respect the line I've drawn, then we can begin."

When Don Carlos called for Camila the next morning, she was no longer in a somber mood. She greeted him at the door wearing a white dress and a white lace mantilla over her shoulders. "What do you think?" she asked, twirling to show him all sides of her dress. "Will Father Benedicto believe that my inner soul is as pure as my outer garments?"

"I can't be sure what he'll think, but he'll definitely be distracted from the liturgy by your presence in the front pew." Camila responded to his words with a light laugh he'd never heard before.

Joaquin in full-dress uniform and Francie in an attractive apricot-colored dress joined them and walked next door to attend Mass in the small chapel located in the *terreón* (defense tower) at the southeast corner of the Palace of the Governors. (The town's other two churches—the Chapel of San Miguel and the parish church—had been destroyed in the Pueblo Revolt of 1680 and had not yet been rebuilt.)

After Mass, Carlos and his friends returned to Joaquin and Francie's residence for a leisurely lunch served by Camila and María. Once the dishes had been cleared, Francie teasingly addressed Carlos and Camila. "Joaquin and I are going upstairs. You are welcome to visit together in the parlor, assuming you can be trusted to behave yourselves without a chaperone."

When they were at last alone, Don Carlos turned to Camila and asked, "Friendship with a woman without romance is a new concept to me. Can you tell me how you think of it?"

"I don't see that it's so strange," Camila replied. "Think of me as a sister with whom you can be comfortable speaking freely and frankly on all topics, particularly those of the heart. Is that inconceivable to you?"

"No, and in fact, it sounds appealing, though I've never experienced it. I have two sisters, both older than me, and for a long time we were rivals for our mother's affection rather than friends of the sort you describe. How do we start down the path you propose to follow?"

"I suppose we can take turns. Since you've said you want to prove your friendship through deeds, I think you're obligated to go first, preferably by answering my questions."

"That sounds like a game my sisters used to play: 'Tell or Do.' Had they asked me to play, I would have chosen to 'do' a difficult task; now you're asking me to choose 'tell.'"

"The two may not be so different, Alfonso. For example, my first question would be why is it that you're so different here in Santa Fe from the way you were when in the desert?"

That, he thought, is a dangerous question to answer truthfully. Nevertheless, he plunged in. "In the desert I seemed to imbibe a certain wildness of spirit from the landscape. Seeing owls fly over us at night and coyotes move through the underbrush, I felt drawn to join them in their freedom from society. Here in Santa Fe I feel tamed by close society with other people, and that leads me to behave conventionally."

"I'm sure there's much more to it than that," Camila said, "but that's a start. Your turn."

"Allow me," he said, "to ask you about your first question. If you sense a great difference between me as you perceived me in the desert and as I seem to be here in Santa Fe, which Don Alfonso, the desert Alfonso or the Santa Fe one, do you believe would make a better friend of the sort you've proposed I might be to you?"

"A difficult question," she replied with a frown. After a long pause she said, "There are qualities to like in both the desert Don Alfonso and the Santa Fe Don Alfonso. However, there are risks in both too, risks involving trust. The desert Don Alfonso seems to have an ungovernable spirit that won't ever be predictable. The Santa Fe Don Alfonso seems to be a man in a disguise, acting conventionally, while having an inner self that imbibes, as you put it, 'a certain wildness of spirit from the landscape.'"

"Your answer didn't really clarify," Carlos pointed out, "which Don Alfonso would make a better friend for you."

"I think if you review my words carefully," she asserted, "you'll find that all the clues are there. Now it's my turn, and I would like to know which Don Alfonso is the true Don Alfonso."

This was a little too close for comfort. Thinking quickly he answered by saying, "Each is true, and the main difference arises from the context in which I find myself—freedom from convention surfacing strongly in the desert setting in which there are no fences or walls, and comfort with conventional society when I am moving in those circles."

"Interesting," she mused, "but your answer wasn't really an answer either, leaving me with the feeling that I have to accept both versions of Don Alfonso or neither."

"I would hope that you'd accept both," he replied. "Now, if I may have a turn again, let me say that I'm curious about your conviction that you'll never marry. You're beautiful, unusually so. You're also intelligent and witty. I sincerely mean it when I say that I can't see any limit to the type of suitor, no matter how high in status, you can attract."

"True enough in theory, though I experience my beauty as a burden because men are drawn to me by my outer appearance rather than my soul. A bigger issue for me is that I don't know who I am or, more accurately, where I came from. Who were my parents? The question torments me."

"You have no idea?"

"None at all; that's a foundling's fate. I arrived in a basket one morning on the steps of the orphanage with a note: 'This is my dearest Camila, born December 6th.' I don't blame my father. Men are like that; they take their pleasure and leave. What I can't bear is the thought that my mother gave me up." Beginning to weep, she asked, "How could any mother do that?"

From Camila's words, Carlos saw again, as he had on the night of the All Saints' Ball, that underlying her apparent unconventionality, her directness and witty repartee, was a deep vulnerability. His tender feelings were aroused, and he tried to reassure her that her mother loved her.

After this first conversation, Carlos and Camila got together to talk as often as possible. They disguised their relationship—a marquis and a ladies' maid being so intimate would definitely have scandalized most members of Santa Fe's elite—by meeting at Joaquin and Francie's residence after Mass on Sundays. They also managed a few supposedly "chance" encounters at the market, after which Pedro and Carlos would walk Francie's maids home and Carlos would talk with Camila in the parlor, while Pedro, who liked María, would visit with her in the kitchen.

Doubtless these maneuvers did not fool many; however, only Carlos's boss, the governor, ventured to comment. "You're spending a lot of time at your stepbrother's."

"We are family, after all," Carlos replied. With a start, he saw a truth. After many lives in which family was mostly a convenience necessary to get started in life, he for the first time felt he was part of a family, albeit an odd one in which his spiritual sister was the family's maid.

9

Marriage

Don Carlos and Camila were lounging in the parlor, sipping wine. He was musing on how comfortable their relationship had become. "Pay attention," Camila said, breaking his reverie. "I have a topic to discuss: marriage."

Don Carlos had expected the subject of marriage to come up sometime, and he'd thought carefully about what to say. Although his memories of his many lives as a brujo had become quite faint over the past year—fading to the point that he scarcely remembered specific past lives—he was quite certain that he had never married and that brujos did not marry. But what did that mean for him now? If he was no longer a practicing brujo, did whether or not he'd married in past lives have any relevance to the present, in which he was living the life of a conventional man?

Camila nudged him, "Alfonso! I asked you to pay attention. I've told you my attitude toward marriage, and it's unfair that you haven't shared yours. After all, less than a year from now you'll come of age and take your rightful place as a marquis—a titled, wealthy man. You already have all the unmarried girls of Santa Fe and doubtless a much larger number in Mexico City eager to marry you. Your indifference is driving their mothers crazy."

"Wait a minute," he protested. "It's not really true that you've said all there is to say on the subject of Camila and marriage. Your only reservation seemed to be that you didn't know who your parents are. Suppose you found out? What then?"

"That's so unlikely that I never waste time speculating. Quit stalling and answer my question. What about you?"

Now he was unavoidably on the spot, and an extremely awkward spot at that. Are we talking about marriage in theory only, he wondered, or is Camila indirectly asking whether I can imagine marriage to her, something, as best I could tell, she ruled out? Moreover, if I'm no longer a brujo, does that mean that my fondness for Camila might evolve into a romantic relationship? What a muddle!

Picking up on the word *muddle* that had just crossed his mind, he struggled to give Camila an answer regarding marriage without revealing, as he sensed he never could, the obstacle that his brujo self, the desert Don Alfonso, presented. "To be completely candid," he began, "my thoughts on marriage, marriage and me, that is, are a muddle. I've always enjoyed the company of women without any intention of marrying. Marriage always struck me as a prison of obligations and prescribed behaviors, an unappealing prospect."

"Surely, affection ought to come into play," Camila interrupted. "Haven't you noticed that when they're out of the public eye, Joaquin and Francesca often look at each other with great tenderness? They have a very loving relationship."

"Yes, that's the best example I could offer of displays of affection between a married couple, and it's thoroughly charming. I've never before come across a marriage quite like theirs. While growing up, I never witnessed open displays of physical affection between my father and mother or my mother and stepfather. And the same was true of the parents of my best friends. None of them ever showed anything remotely resembling ardor for each other in their public conduct. Even if they subscribed to a code that required extreme discretion, I can't believe that true lovers could have avoided revealing at least some flashes of passion when I was around. I'm too much of a romantic to settle for that kind of marriage, as my choice to portray Don Quixote at the All Saints' Ball should suggest."

Camila fixed him with a look, the meaning of which he wasn't certain until she put her reaction into words. "I guess I'm a little surprised that you're such an idealist," she said. "You approach your public life in such a practical, rational way that what you said a moment ago is quite different from what I expected. Is this idealistic Alfonso a private self that I've never even glimpsed previously? Please tell me more."

Carlos fell silent, unsure of what to say. To his relief, before he could respond to Camila's latest question, a soft knock at the parlor door announced Francie's presence. "My!" she remarked. "Serious talk, I gather. Excuse me for interrupting, but the party of new colonists we've been expecting has reached the town's outskirts. Joaquin, who will welcome the soldiers in the party, is putting on his uniform. Let's see who else is along."

The arrival of new colonists was always an exciting occasion. Given the small size of Santa Fe's population, the appearance on the scene of even a few new colonists promised to add savor to a social stew that had gone flat. The day's arrivals did not disappoint. In addition to a half dozen soldiers, replacements for six members of the Presidio garrison whose terms of service had expired, there were ten servants and craftsmen. But the prize that delighted the town's elite was the presence of two upper-class families. The first of these was the Nicolas Arculeta family, consisting of an eighteen-year-old son, a mother, and a father who was to become the king's attorney for the province. The other members of the elite in the party were a physician, Dr. Loreto Tiburcio, and his daughter, Inéz de Recalde.

When he was introduced to Nicolas Arculeta and his wife, Don Carlos was impressed by what a friendly people they seemed to be. Next, Dr. Tiburcio stepped forward. Apparently feeling the need to explain why his daughter's family name was different from his, he announced that she was, unfortunately, recently widowed.

The young widow was a striking beauty, with gray eyes and jet black hair. With a brilliant smile she turned to Carlos. "So you are Alfonso Cabeza de Vaca." Reaching into her purse, she pulled out an envelope. "Your mother," she said, "asked me to give this to you. She also asked me to give you this," leaning forward to kiss his cheek. The kiss lasted longer than was usual for formal greetings. Over Inéz's shoulder he saw Camila watching. Involuntarily, he blushed.

Inéz laughed in delight, revealing a perfect set of very white teeth. "As handsome as they come and shy too—a combination that's rarely encountered," she declared.

Don Carlos was relieved when the governor tugged at his sleeve, pulling him away and saving him from further embarrassment. "I urgently need you to work tonight, even though it's Sunday, and all day Monday and Tuesday too, if necessary, as is likely. There are many reports I need to finish to send back with the party of soldiers that will leave Wednesday."

Despite the governor's request, Don Carlos did not immediately head for his office. He walked several blocks with his family and friends in hopes of learning what Camila was thinking about the kiss Señora de Recalde had bestowed on him. The topic came up only indirectly in an exchange that followed a remark of Francie's. "Didn't you think it curious," she ventured, "that Dr. Tiburcio is so dark, almost a mulatto, while his daughter has such a fair complexion?"

"We know nothing of her mother," Joaquin commented, "which might explain quite a lot." He added that he'd heard that Dr. Tiburcio and his daughter were Basques, but immediately admitted that that didn't in itself offer anything by way of an explanation of the differences in their appearance.

Camila chimed in. "I'll bet Señora de Recalde's husband didn't die of natural causes."

"Camila!" Francie exclaimed. "What a strange thing to say, especially without any grounds for venturing such an opinion."

"My response," Camila replied, "was intuitive, not based on any known facts, though I notice even you observed that there's something odd about the father and daughter. No matter; time will tell," she declared, giving Carlos a look he wasn't sure how to interpret.

Like Francie, Carlos was puzzled by Camila's response to Dr. Tiburcio and his daughter. He was thinking that he ought to have scanned the auras of the two newcomers while they were standing beside each other to see what he could learn about them, but he had missed the moment. Then Governor Villela, who was walking by, spoke to him peremptorily, "Please start immediately on the paperwork I mentioned a moment ago. You can talk with your friends later."

Governor Villela hadn't misled him about the paperwork, which took until late Tuesday to complete. He didn't mind the work itself, but he was frustrated because it kept him from visiting Camila.

Wednesday morning Don Carlos arose in a good mood and ate a hearty breakfast. The party of six soldiers who had completed their terms would be sent off this morning with a proper ceremony at the plaza. He planned to attend it and then walk to his stepbrother's residence to seek a private interview with Camila, at which he would make amends, if needed, for perhaps seeming too pleased by the kiss he'd received from Señora de Recalde, about whom Camila seemed to harbor suspicions.

A large crowd had assembled around the plaza. When Carlos, Pedro, Diego, and Gordo arrived, the departure ceremony was about to begin. Don Carlos saw Camila at the corner of the square with Francie and María. He tried without success to get her attention.

He had intended to head over to talk with Camila as soon as the departing soldiers marched off at the end of the brief farewell ceremony, and as he was about to start in her direction he became aware of the sound of hoofbeats coming up the street behind him. A tap on his shoulder caused him to stop and turn around. Inéz de Recalde was standing there holding a handsome black Arabian stallion by the reins. She was wearing a long skirt split down the middle to permit her to ride astride her mount, and because the sun was directly behind her, her head was surrounded by a halo of light. The effect was breathtaking. "Good morning, Don Alfonso," she said amiably, reaching down to rub Gordo's tummy, which he had rolled over to expose to her.

Surprised, Don Carlos remarked, "I've never seen him do that before."

Inéz laughed. "Males, both two-legged and four-legged, like me. Please give me a leg up onto Diablo." Once mounted, she tapped his shoulder with her whip and said, "Thank you."

As Inéz rode off, Don Carlos looked for Camila, Francie, and María and finally spotted them leaving the plaza. He ran after them, catching up just as they reached the gates to the Presidio. Camila dropped back behind her companions and remarked, "My, aren't we chummy with the pretty widow. Have you found your soul mate? Gordo certainly is smitten with her charms."

"I was simply trying to be polite to her," he protested.

"So you say," Camila replied, "but it's obvious that she knows how to get dogs and men to do her bidding.'" She continued with what struck him as an irrelevant addendum: "I can't stand women with naturally curly hair."

Francie came to his rescue. "Alfonso, this week is Camila's eighteenth birthday, and we're having a ball in her honor on Saturday. It will offer a good occasion for introducing the new arrivals to all the residents who've lived here a while. Consider this your invitation."

Carlos indicated to Francie that he wanted a chance to speak with Camila alone, only to be rebuffed. She and her two maids, she told him, were going directly home to sew their gowns. Visits to the Alvarez residence on Thursday and Friday were no more successful. The three women were always together, intent on their sewing. He never found Camila by herself.

Saturday evening came and, dressed in their best suits, Don Carlos and Pedro—the elite's servants were invited too—joined in the festivities. Although the custom at such balls was for everyone to dance with everyone else, Carlos hoped for several dances with Camila.

As it turned out Don Carlos ended up dancing three dances with Inéz and only one with Camila, who looked lovely in her new gown and who had numerous men vying to dance with her. It's almost like a coming-out party for Camila, Carlos thought. He noticed, and then was surprised that the observation troubled him, that the governor's son, Rafael, was Camila's most frequent partner and that she constantly rewarded him with brilliant smiles.

Inéz had insisted on a second and third dance with him, and she was, by all odds, a very beautiful woman and a skillful dancer. Carlos took great pleasure in holding her in his arms. Besides her beauty and her clever conversational gambits, the most memorable thing was her perfume. He couldn't place the scent but its effect was mesmerizing. He felt almost faint, or at least dizzy. Inéz, noticing his state of mind, laughed at what seemed to be a private triumph, and at that very instant the memory of Violeta, a woman from a previous life, came to mind. Violeta and Inéz didn't look a great deal alike, but he found Inéz's seductive way of relating to him, so reminiscent of Violeta's, most discomforting.

Finally extracting himself from Inéz's attention by introducing her to Vice Governor Peralta, he brusquely chased off other partners and secured a second dance with Camila.

"I could tell," she said, "that you were very taken with Señora de Recalde while dancing with her. It looks more and more as though she's won your heart."

"Not at all! Only tonight I realized that she reminds me of a woman who once did me grave harm."

"I'd love to hear more, if I weren't preoccupied with a problem of my own. Rafael Villela has proposed marriage to me, and I have to carefully consider my answer."

Don Carlos felt as though the floor had dropped out from under him. He didn't have any claim on Camila or any right to interfere with her decision. From society's viewpoint, she, a foundling, would achieve a huge leap upward in status if she accepted Rafael's offer, and certainly he, Carlos, had not offered her an alternative. But he had opened himself to her in friendship in a way he had never done before, and he had never considered, given her often expressed reservations about marriage, that she might turn away from him for another man. Though stunned by her words, he murmured something to the effect that he wished her well no matter what she decided.

He soon left the ball, giving the lame excuse that he didn't feel well. Once home, he was overtaken by a sense of loss and had no idea what to do. He tried to drown his sorrows in glass after glass of wine, which didn't help at all; it only made things worse by giving him a terrible headache.

After breakfast Sunday morning, he determined to go to his stepbrother's residence and say something to Camila, though he wasn't yet sure what that would be. At the very least, he had to tell her how dear she had become to him.

When he arrived at Joaquin's place, he was surprised to have Francie answer the door. She was beaming from ear to ear. "Come in, Alfonso. We have great news that has made us very, very happy. We're in the drawing room."

Joaquin, Camila, and María were there all smiles. "The news we have," Francie announced, "is that there's going to be a marriage in the household."

Carlos's heart sank. Had Camila accepted Rafael's proposal?

But Francie continued by saying, "I'm delighted to announce that Pedro has asked María to marry him, and she has accepted his proposal."

10
Troubles

"*I* can see by the look on Don Alfonso's face," María began, "that Pedro hasn't told him about our engagement. That big coward! I will chide him in no uncertain terms the next time I see him." She didn't stop there, displaying a volubility he'd never noticed in her before. "Pedro and I have worked everything out in a way that I hope will win your approval. Our marriage banns will be announced at Mass next Sunday. We'll marry three weeks later on the first Sunday in January. That will allow time to spruce up the two rooms on the back side of your house, the one Pedro's used as a bedroom and the unused room that's currently storage space. That's more than enough space for Pedro and me, assuming we can share the kitchen with you. I'll continue to work part-time for Doña Francesca, and Camila and I will train Ana Lugo to be a second maid. Doña Francesca is agreeable to this arrangement and we hope you'll go along with it."

This sounded fine to Don Carlos, and he told everyone so. However, he still had urgent business with Camila. When there was a pause in the conversation, he asked Francie, "Will you permit me to speak with Camila?"

"Of course," Francie replied. Camila rose and together they stepped out into the hallway.

"You might have asked whether I was willing to talk with you," she said, but without ill feeling. "What now?"

Don Carlos had decided what he needed to do, and he attacked the issue boldly. "After last night, I realized that I love you a great deal. I'd had some questions about marriage for myself that were unresolved, and you yourself seemed to close off the possibility. Now that's changed for me and evidently for you as well. If you are willing to consider marriage, I implore you to say you'll marry me."

Camila responded to Carlos's declaration in a playful way. "My word!" she exclaimed with a wry smile. "A girl turns eighteen and all at once proposals of marriage come her way from every direction. I must start a list to keep track of my suitors."

"Camila, please be serious; I am. You know that I love you."

"I know," she replied, relenting a little. "You'll just have to give me some time. Bear in mind that I'm the one who's always rejected the idea of marrying until I find out who my mother is. That piece of business is still unfinished. Besides, you're not much older than I am and have more than half a year to go until you receive your full inheritance." Putting her hand gently on his arm, she said, "I'm touched by your proposal, especially since I feel it might come at some cost to your ideals. I need time to think, and in any case Rafael will be arriving any moment to describe his intentions in greater detail than was possible on the dance floor last night."

Rafael was indeed on his way. Don Carlos and he met only fifty feet from the door to Joaquin's residence. Carlos greeted Rafael and asked to speak with him for a moment. "I know you're eager to see Camila, but there's something I want to tell you first. We've always been good friends, and I greatly respect you and your father. I hope the fact that I've just now asked Camila to marry me, which makes us some sort of rivals, will not in any way harm our friendly relations."

Rafael took this better than Carlos felt he had any right to expect. "You've always bested me at swordsmanship, but I will compete ardently for Camila's hand and hope to prevail in the end. May the best man win!"

"Perhaps it's less a case of which of us is the best man than which of us Camila believes will bring her the most happiness — a prospect that both of us, I'm sure, wish for."

With that, the two men parted. Upon his return home, Don Carlos found that Pedro had a message for him. "One of Doña Arculeta's maids stopped by a few minutes ago to ask you to visit her today at your earliest convenience. As you may know, the Arculetas have taken up residence in the rose-colored house to the west of the governor's offices. The invitation was delivered with some urgency. If you hurry, you'll get there before lunch."

Carlos found Doña Arculeta in a highly agitated state. She rushed through perfunctory greetings and spoke in a voice charged with emotion. "Before I say anything I must ask that you, as an honorable gentleman, not tell anyone under any circumstances what I'm about to say."

After receiving Don Carlos's pledge to keep their conversation a secret, she continued. "At Camila's birthday ball last night I suddenly realized that Camila was born on the exactly the same date, December 6, 1686, as the illegitimate daughter of one of my dearest friends. So I must ask you some questions about this young woman Camila Lobo, with whom you are said to be good friends. Has she ever told you how she came by her name?"

"Yes, she is a foundling who was left as a newborn on the steps of an orphanage. A note in the basket gave her date of birth and referred to her as 'My darling Camila.'"

"And what was the origin of her last name?"

"The nuns came up with that because from the first she was very self-possessed, like a lone wolf, one of the sisters said."

This information did not calm Doña Arculeta in the least. "Remember that you are sworn to secrecy. I believe, indeed I'm nearly certain, that Señorita Lobo is the illegitimate child of my friend, whose name shall remain unmentioned. This friend and I grew up in Puebla and loved each other like sisters. The two young men who were courting us nearly twenty years ago happened to be cousins. Such were the close bonds between the four of us that the men proposed to my friend and me on the same day, and we planned a double wedding for a year later. My friend's mother and my mother were delighted and took my friend and me to Mexico City to shop for our wedding trousseaus. The second night we were in the city, the four of us went to the theater, and after the play we were invited backstage to meet the actors. The male lead in the play, an extremely handsome blue-eyed Basque, took one look at my friend and whispered in her ear an invitation to meet him late that night at his hotel, which happened to be the one at which we were also staying. My friend experienced, for the first and only time in her life, an overpowering infatuation. I conspired to help her slip out of our rooms and go to the actor's room. It was a betrayal of my mother's trust and of her fiancé also, but we were young and impulsive, intoxicated with excitement at being in Mexico City. The next morning the actor and the rest of his troupe left for Spain before we got up. All seemed well until three months later when my friend became certain that she was pregnant. There was nothing to do but to go to my mother — we didn't dare go to my friend's — to confess. She was furious, but also unwilling to ruin my friend's marriage and probably mine as well.

"It's a miracle that the subterfuge we concocted actually worked. My friend was a plump girl, and by wearing loose garments — it helped that cloaks and loose-fitting dresses were in style that year — her pregnancy was not in danger of becoming obvious until she was six months along. At that point my mother dispatched my friend to Mexico City with the excuse that a favorite aunt was ill and in need of my friend's companionship. Although this was a ruse, it worked; the aunt agreed to help; the baby was born and given up. The birth date was precisely the same as Señorita Lobo's and her given name, Camila, was the name my friend intended to give her first-born girl child. My friend and I and our fiancés had our double wedding and have had happy marriages ever since.

"But you must see my dilemma. I don't want to speak a word of this to anyone, certainly not to Señorita Lobo, until I've written my friend and asked her whether she wants to acknowledge that this blue-eyed eighteen-year-old was fathered by a fair-haired, blue-eyed Basque lover. I am very fearful, as I think she will be also, that if this story comes to light, it will have disastrous consequences for my friend's marriage. I don't worry much about mine, since my husband is an easy-going man who's likely to say, 'At least you weren't the one to become pregnant by a Basque actor.'"

"What do you want of me?" Don Carlos asked. "I don't see how I can help you."

"Could you perhaps find some reason to travel to Mexico City, where my friend, her husband, and their five children recently moved, and deliver a letter from me? I believe that you, as someone who knows the young woman well, can put the situation in the best light to my friend."

Aware as he was how deeply Camila desired to know her mother's identity, Don Carlos could not refuse. He told Doña Lucila (it was time to be on a first-name basis) that he had recently received a letter from his mother reporting that she was not in good health. That news was very worrisome. She hadn't been completely well for some years. If she was worse now, his genuine concern about her would provide a logical justification for saying he needed to go to Mexico City to visit her. However, he added, the trip would have to wait until after Pedro and María were married a month from now. By that point he hoped to have his own affairs in better order than they were at the moment.

On Monday Don Carlos attempted, without success, to do some work at the governor's office. He kept finding himself staring out the window, his thoughts on Camila. Brujos don't marry, he told himself, but I am no longer a practicing brujo. My life is entirely that of an upper-class civil servant. What's more, I like my life and love Camila.

At the end of an unproductive day, he was putting away papers when Rafael came in the door. "I've had a message from Camila," Rafael said, "inviting the two of us to come to the Presidio. A friend of Doña Francesca's has sent the family a recipe and the makings for a hot chocolate drink, and Camila wants to try it on us."

Camila greeted her suitors at the door. She was wearing a somber, dark brown dress. Not a good sign, Carlos thought. Rafael and he sat in the parlor watching in silence as she prepared the drink. Her hands were elegant, and she served the drinks as gracefully as any upper-class woman. Clearly she had taken her social training to heart.

When she finally settled back in her chair, Camila said, "I have a little speech to give. I hope you won't be displeased by what I say. I deeply appreciate your affection and friendship. I'm greatly honored to be the recipient of your marriage proposals. Still, as you know, there are circumstances that make me hold back, even though Doña Francesca is most annoyed with me on that account."

She looked down and fell silent before continuing. "You're aware that I'm loath to marry without knowing my mother's identity. Although that may prove to be an impossible dream, I am making one last attempt to solve that mystery. I've sent a letter with Private Pablo López, who is on his way to Mexico City, and have asked him to deliver it to the mother superior of the orphanage where I grew up. The letter pleads with Mother Veronica to ask the older nuns whether any of them can provide information regarding my mother's name."

Addressing each of her suitors separately, she said. "Rafael, Don Joaquin has told me that your military commission as a lieutenant in the army has arrived at last. You have my congratulations and admiration. Perhaps you can find it in your heart to wait for an answer from me while you assume your new duties."

"Alfonso, you aren't yet twenty-one and won't receive your full inheritance until you are. Surely you won't want to marry before that's settled, and I hope that fact will allow you to give me more time to make my decision."

With these words Camila's eyes filled with tears that ran, unhindered, down her face. She looked so irresistibly, incomparably beautiful that Don Carlos felt close to crying himself. He didn't know for certain, but Rafael would have to be hard-hearted not to feel likewise.

Gathering herself, Camila spoke in a barely audible voice, "What I'm asking of you is that you do me the favor of patience. Give me time, a year even, before I must make a decision regarding your proposals. I promise I will honor whatever deadline you set."

Rafael spoke first. "Before too long I may be assigned to serve elsewhere. Could you perhaps give us your answer no more than six months from now?"

"Why not split the difference?" Don Carlos suggested. "That would make our self-imposed deadline nine months, that is, early September 1705. That will allow me to travel to Mexico City to check on my mother's health and return before the deadline is reached with whatever I can learn while there about the name of Camila's mother." This compromise seemed satisfactory to all involved.

Once the deadline was set, Don Carlos resumed his amiable routines of work, play, and domesticity. A task that required immediate attention was completing the conversion of two rooms in Carlos's house into an apartment for Pedro and María. Pedro set to work right away, and soon thereafter two Pueblo Indians with carpentry skills showed up and volunteered to help. They refused Carlos's offer to pay them the going wage. It turned out that they were relatives of José Lugo, the boy he had saved from being executed for murder, and they said their assistance was in gratitude for his intervention. "Your good deeds are coming back to haunt you," Pedro said with a chuckle.

José Lugo's sister Ana began training for service in Joaquin and Francie's household, and she learned her duties so swiftly that María was soon able to spend more time at Don Carlos's residence, sewing curtains, blankets, towels, and the like for the rooms she and Pedro would occupy. Camila often joined her on afternoons when the sun was warm enough to permit the two women to do their work on the veranda, a practice they followed at Francie's suggestion that being in plain view of neighbors was the best way to keep tongues from wagging about two unmarried women who visited a residence occupied by three unmarried men.

Carlos, Pedro, and Diego joined María and Camila on the veranda when they could, and to assure Rafael that this was not a way for him to monopolize Camila's attention, Carlos invited Rafael to come by regularly. It turned out that this odd group of six — Carlos, Rafael, Pedro, Diego, María, and Camila — had a good time together. Sometimes they simply listened to María rattle on happily about this and that. She had become, Carlos observed, quite a chatterbox — a good balance to Pedro's more laconic manner. At other times Carlos and Rafael took turns reading passages from Lope de Vega's *La Dorotea*, a prose romance whose many twists and turns of plot endlessly amused them.

Into this quiet domestic scene rode none other than Inéz de Recalde.

She was, as always, dressed to draw maximum attention, this time in a red riding outfit with gold trim that served to highlight her black hair. "Good afternoon, everyone," she said, flashing a dazzling smile directed mainly at Carlos. "May I borrow Gordo?" (Gordo had already indicated his assent by waging his tail so furiously that he almost fell down.)

Carlos, displaying his excellent manners, had stood up and stepped off the veranda to greet her. "That's fine by me," he said.

"Thank you," she replied, tapping him on the shoulder with her whip. Calling to Gordo, she said, "Come along, sweetie," and off she went, Diablo prancing prettily, and Gordo running fast to keep up.

"Sweetie?" Pedro said grumpily. "That's the end of Gordo's career as a watch dog."

"How so?" Don Carlos asked. "He's always raised a huge ruckus at the approach of anyone except you, me, and Diego."

"When you leave for work these days," Pedro replied, "Gordo runs off to spend the day at Señora de Recalde's house. He wouldn't let out a peep if she were to steal into the house in the middle of the night."

"And head directly for Alfonso's bedroom," Camila added, perhaps with some malice.

"Whoa!" Carlos exclaimed, rising to his own defense. "I don't have any intention of inviting her into my bedroom, or my house, for that matter."

"Who said she needs an invitation?" Camila replied. "The proprietary way she taps your shoulder with her whip is a declaration of ownership. Wake up. She's out to get you."

Don Carlos scoffed at Camila's assertions, only to have her point proven that very afternoon. Carlos was sitting by himself on the veranda when Inéz returned from her ride. "Thank you for the loan of Gordo," she said. "By the way, even before we left Mexico City, I heard that you are an incomparable swordsman. I have studied with several fencing masters in Northern Spain, and I would enjoy testing my skills against yours."

"I've never fenced with a woman," he replied.

"Is that a problem? I assumed you would enjoy a challenging opponent, whether a man or a woman."

"It's no problem. I was simply making a statement of fact."

"Then it's settled? I've had workmen prepare a fine fencing strip in the patio of our house. Shall we say tomorrow at noon, when everyone else is beginning their siestas?"

The next day he knocked on Inéz's door at the appointed hour. She let him in and walked ahead of him to the patio. She was wearing a leather fencing shirt and skin-tight fencing pants that revealed the shape of her hips and legs. Practical but provocative, he thought.

In the patio, next to a statue of the Virgin Mary, was a well-designed piste (fencing strip). A table off to one side had a wine bottle and two glasses on it, to which she gestured: "Available should we wish to pause for refreshment. Let's begin." Inéz was a left-handed fencer, unusual in itself, and her style of attack was unfamiliar to him. She was very good. He parried her early thrusts, but she finally managed to penetrate his defenses. "Touché!" she cried, clearly delighted. "I'm pleased to present new challenges."

As they continued to fence, Inéz won several more exchanges, and Carlos observed that he had not kept himself in top condition. Nevertheless, he gradually sorted out her approach and won more and more exchanges until he succeeded in scoring five hits in a row. "Ah!" she said. "You are every bit as good as described now that you've warmed up. And speaking of warming up, I'm positively hot in the sun. Let me take off this top, while you pour us wine."

She unbuttoned her leather shirt, and by the time he turned back to her to offer her a glass of wine, she had stripped to a black undergarment that left her shoulders and arms bare. Amused at his appraising look, she laughed, "I hope you don't mind, but I'm much more comfortable now."

"I worry that your arms and shoulders will be bruised by a successful hit to them," he replied.

"If that concerns you," Inéz said, "you can simply target only the torso covered by this corset, which is sufficiently padded to protect me."

"Very clever of you," he observed. "You gain freedom of movement while limiting the areas of your torso I may target."

"A fencer with your great skill shouldn't find that limitation an insurmountable obstacle," she replied with a smile. After they'd each sipped a small amount of wine, they resumed their practice. Several times in the next series of exchanges, they found themselves locked together in close quarters, body to body — was this her intention, he wondered? — and he became keenly aware that her shoulders were gleaming with sweat, her skin flushed from her exertions. She was wearing the same perfume that she had worn at the birthday ball, and the scent grew more powerful as their exchanges went on. He began to feel a bit faint, and when his concentration flagged, she won an exchange.

Very pleased with herself, she declared, "That was most satisfying for me. Let's have one more exchange, winner take all."

"And the prize?" he asked.

"To be negotiated to our mutual satisfaction."

Something in her manner reminded him again of the treacherous Violeta, the memory of whom was accompanied by an upwelling of anger, and his foggy mind cleared. He became totally concentrated on the task at hand and fenced aggressively. Inéz was driven backward but defended herself with great inventiveness, parrying his best innovations with innovations of her own. There was, he was aware, an erotic element to the whole affair. Finally, he broke through her defenses and scored a hard touch on her left shoulder. "Sorry," he said. "That was in your unprotected area and may leave a bruise."

"I don't mind at all!" she exclaimed. "That was marvelous! I don't mind a bruise when I'm doing something I love. Let's stop for now and agree to resume our practice someday soon."

They sat at the table and drank wine without speaking. She took a chair close to him and did not put her shirt on again. Finally, she spoke. "It's said that you've proposed marriage to that pretty maid of Doña Francesca's. I can see the attraction, but I admit I was surprised—a marquis and a maid, especially when you can have all of this," she said, presenting her body in a way that made it plain what "this" was. "You won the winner-take-all exchange. What prize do you propose to claim?"

Don Carlos, doing his best to resist his desire for this provocative woman, stammered, "I'm very loyal to Camila"—a rather lame reply, he thought.

Inéz laughed. "Dear naive boy! All virile men take their pleasure both with their wives and at least one mistress."

"I think," he said, "if we're to continue these fencing sessions, which I would enjoy, we'd better stick to fencing until I know whether Camila accepts my proposal."

"Perhaps that's the prudent course for now," she agreed, "although I'm not usually inclined to be prudent. Since I don't want these sessions to end, we can discuss your prize another time."

With this somewhat ambiguous reference to his "prize," they parted, having agreed to meet again in a week. As he walked the short distance to his house, Don Carlos examined his motives in agreeing to another session. To be sure, he had enjoyed the challenge Inéz presented as a fencer, and he'd hoped that offering to meet again was a concession that would satisfy her for the moment and thus lead her to avoid pressuring him for anything more intimate than flirtatious talk. But he couldn't deny that he found her sexually alluring. I'll have to be careful, he told himself, and not forget that Inéz resembles Violeta, that black widow spider who lured me into her web with fatal consequences.

11

Love

*T*he day after Pedro and María were married in a simple but totally satisfying Nuptial Mass, the weather changed. The temperature soared well above normal for early January and there were dark clouds in the west, with veils of rain falling in the distance, though overhead it was clear. Carlos arrived at the entryway to Inéz's residence at noon to keep their weekly fencing appointment. Their recent sessions had passed without Inéz making any personal overtures beyond an occasional reference, which she delivered in a light tone, to the winner-take-all "prize" he hadn't yet claimed. He knocked on the house door and a maid, who was carrying a shopping bag, let him in. (He had never seen this maid before and hadn't even known whether the household had servants, though he'd assumed there must be some.) "I'm going out shopping," the maid said. "Madame is waiting for you in the patio."

Don Carlos found Inéz standing next to the statue of the Virgin Mary. Her outfit was not the usual one, except for toreador-style pants, although even these were a deep red rather than the usual black. She was barefoot and wore a simple white long-sleeved linen shirt and had let her naturally curly black hair fall loose down to her shoulders. Something about her posture and expression led him to ask, "Are you all right? You seem sad."

"True enough," she replied, brightening a bit, "but let's not waste time on that topic. Do you mind if we fence barefoot?"

"Barefoot is fine," he replied. "However, I feel it's unsafe for you to fence without a padded top for protection." (The fabric of her shirt was thin enough that he could see she had something red around her waist and midriff and a black band around her bosom, but the latter was not the corset-like undergarment she'd worn in previous bouts.)

Inéz gave him a wry smile. "You're so superior to me as a fencer that I've planned to give you greater challenges today." She lifted the bottom of her shirt to show him a broad red waist sash. "This piece of clothing," she said, "is called a cummerbund, an item Loreto had imported for me from the East Indies. It will absorb any hits you make on it; as for the rest of my torso, I've bound my bosom in a wrap."

"Surely, that wrap won't prevent you from being bruised by hits in that area."

"Probably not," she agreed. "Nevertheless, I give you leave to hit there too, although I'm confident that you're too much of a gentleman to avail yourself of that offer."

He settled for declaring, "I will try to limit my touches to the area covered by the cummerbund, which will be, as you suggest, a challenge, but a worthy one."

He kicked off his shoes without further comment, and they immediately began fencing. She was, he noted, fencing with great intensity today. Usually, she let him go on the offense—which was, in any case, his preference—but today she went on the attack with such ferocity that he was forced to retreat as often as he was able to be an aggressor. This novel situation brought out the best in both of them, forcing them to new heights of creativity. He was thrown into a state he'd always relished, a clarity of mind that saw every thrust and parry in slow motion. Inéz seemed to be experiencing something comparable. The effect was exhilarating.

At that moment the clouds, which had been billowing toward them, let loose a torrential rain, drenching both combatants to the skin. Carlos stopped and gestured toward the house to suggest they get out of the rain. "No," Inéz said, without hesitation. "We must continue. This is too glorious to abandon."

The rain stopped as suddenly as it had begun, and they returned to their exchanges which, if anything, were even more intense in the aftermath of the heavenly outpouring. Carlos's leather fencing shirt had become so soaked that it was restricting his movements; consequently, Inéz scored two hits in rapid succession. Annoyed, he took off the shirt. The only top he had on now was a sleeveless undershirt that exposed his well-muscled arms.

Inéz looked at him appraisingly and observed, "Aren't you the one now in danger of getting bruised by my hits?"

"Not if I defend myself with greater freedom," he replied, and in fact he once again began to win exchanges despite her best efforts to break through his defenses.

Inéz's shirt, which had become soaked through, clung to her body like a second skin, and she was having trouble with the wrap around her breasts. Whatever she'd used to secure it tightly around her had come loose and one end had slipped down to her waist. "Damn thing!" she exclaimed, grasping the loose end and tugging on it until the whole wrap came off. She was not wearing anything underneath. He found the sight thoroughly distracting and his relative inattention gave her an opening to score a hit on their next exchange.

Annoyed with himself for letting his attention drift, Don Carlos also realized that both of them were almost too exhausted to continue. Collecting his wits, he suggested, "How about three more hits and then stop?" She nodded in agreement and they resumed fencing.

Each of the final three exchanges was prolonged as both Carlos and Inéz fenced with passion and great skill. Inspired by the intensity of the effort required, Carlos achieved what seemed to him something akin to bliss. He also won all three exchanges. Inéz didn't seem to mind. With a smile of delight, she moved close to him and said softly, "That was unforgettably wonderful!"

"But you're still sad," he observed, without being aware of how he knew.

"Underlying sadness," she replied, "one always finds anger." After a brief pause, she seemed to change the topic: "I have a favor to ask, something you can help me with, if you're willing."

He stood waiting for her to continue. "My lover seems to have become bored with me." (This struck Carlos as inconceivable, but then, he hadn't known she had a lover. Town gossip had not even whispered to that effect.) "What I need to do is to make him jealous, and the quickest means to that end is for him to find a love mark on me. Will you" —and this was said shyly —"bite my neck?" She pulled her shirt's collar aside to expose the nape of her neck. When he seemed to hesitate, she insisted: "Please don't hold back; just do it."

Carlos leaned forward and placed his lips on the spot she'd indicated. The skin of her neck was damp and soft as a baby's. Touching her was a delicious sensation. She told him what to do. "You must bite with your teeth as well as your lips." He began to do so. She pressed against him and placed a hand on his lower back to draw him even more firmly to her.

Wondering whether their encounter was approaching a boundary he wasn't sure loyalty to Camila should permit him to cross, he made a move to separate their pelvises. "Don't!" she pleaded so compellingly that he gave in. Throwing caution to the wind, he put an arm around her and stroked her back. She responded by taking his other hand and sliding it under her shirt to her breast. A moment later she gave a small cry and relaxed all over.

Pulling back ever so slightly, Inéz kissed him gently on the lips and stroked his bare arm. She sighed. "That was very nice. Can you see the beginning of the bruise on my neck?" Before he could reply, she added, "When my lover sees that, he will go crazy with desire. Thank you, but go now. Hurry! My lover will be here any minute and it will spoil the effect if he learns who you are. Use the back door to avoid a chance encounter."

After struggling into his wet shirt and putting on his shoes, Don Carlos followed Inéz to the back door, where she said, in her usual provocative way, "I hear you're leaving for Mexico City day after tomorrow. If I don't see you before you leave, count on me to visit you in your dreams and to haunt your daytime thoughts with memories of today."

They parted without saying another word. Don Carlos felt ambivalent about what he'd done in the heat of the moment. He tried to convince himself that this one episode didn't set a precedent for the future. If she asked for similar favors, he would show more restraint. On the whole, it was a good thing he was leaving Santa Fe for a while.

As he turned the corner onto his street, he could see Pedro, María, and Camila sitting on the veranda of his house. "You look bedraggled," Pedro commented with a laugh.

"Possibly guilty," Camila suggested.

"I got caught in the rain," Carlos told them with as much aplomb as he could muster. Still, he had to admit that he was feeling guilty, and though he joined his friends on the veranda, his mind drifted off as he mulled over his situation. He felt uneasy about the recent episode with Inéz, which seemed a betrayal of his love for Camila. He had indulged in erotic pleasures with a seductive, sexually experienced woman, while thoughts of the virginal, innocent friend to whom he had proposed marriage had barely entered his mind. Hadn't Pedro said that according to María, Camila had told her that she didn't expect to be kissed by a man in anything other than a perfunctory formal way until she was married? That meant, she had added, that if she never married, she might never receive such a kiss.

The more serious source of guilt concerned his conduct with women in general. He seemed to have a habit of acting in an impulsive way where women were involved, as when he'd unthinkingly tossed down the wine Violeta gave him, an act that led to his death and nearly caused him to lose his soul. Today he had again acted on impulse, granting Inéz her every wish without a second thought or even a first one. No untoward consequences had arisen from his actions, at least not yet, and he had enjoyed enormously giving in to guilty pleasures. Still, this was not wise behavior.

Even his proposal of marriage to Camila had been an impulsive act. He had not thought through what he was doing, acting out of fear that he would lose her if she married Rafael. But if he, Carlos, married her, wouldn't he have to sever all connections with his deep inner self, his brujo soul? Marrying went against everything he knew about brujos. They didn't marry because their way of life required absolute freedom from conventional social attachments. And if he did sacrifice sorcery for love's sake, didn't that mean that he would no longer retain the consciousness of his brujo self that was necessary to be reborn with memories of his previous lives as a brujo?

He fell into a deeper state of reverie than he was accustomed to and began to recall a lesson he had received many lifetimes ago from one of the greatest brujos of any age, Don Serafino Romero. "There are," Don Serafino had told him, "two ways to live, though the first of these, the way of the ordinary man, can scarcely be called living. The ordinary man is immersed from dawn to dusk in reacting to everything he encounters out of either desire or fear. He believes his happiness depends, in the first case, on gaining what he desires: wealth, fame, success, a certain woman, and the like; or in the second place, he reacts to things he dislikes by pushing them away, thinking that this will save him from depression, pain, sickness, and even death. The trouble is that when he achieves what he thought he wanted, it doesn't bring him happiness, and he immediately pursues another object of desire or seeks to avoid whatever new sources of aversion arise. Happiness is always temporary; thus it eludes him. And, of course, there is no way he can totally eliminate from his existence pain, sickness, and the knowledge that he will die. He is trapped in a state of continual suffering."

So deeply was Carlos immersed in these memories that he was no longer simply remembering Don Serafino's words but actively listening to them. Don Serafino went on. "The second way to live is the brujo's path.

Brujos of our Sun Moiety train themselves never to depend on transitory things. Although they can appreciate the beauty of the physical world, including the beauty of women, they see everything through the eyes of a realist. They know that everything is impermanent and therefore incapable of bringing lasting happiness. You might suppose that the life of a brujo of this sort is a lonely, cold-hearted path because he cannot, except at his peril, form attachments to people, places, or physical objects. However, his path is the only way to truly live. Where the ordinary man acts on impulse and is dominated by desire and fear, the brujo sees that every aspect of the world, in its coming into being and falling away, is just as it should be. This perception, which allows the brujo to move through life in peace and equanimity, is the ultimate treasure of the Brujo's Way."

In the inner silence that followed these words, Don Carlos felt himself standing apart from his recent actions and regarding them from a deeper perspective. He saw that where Inéz and Camila were concerned, his impulsive behavior showed him to be an ordinary man. But as he returned to surface consciousness, the power of Don Serafino's words faded, and Carlos's awareness shifted to his feeling that he found much to enjoy about the conventional life.

Pedro's voice interrupted his thoughts. "Alfonso! I asked you a question! Are your travel plans all set? You're leaving at dawn the day after tomorrow."

Carlos's attention sprang back to the present moment. "Sorry," he said. "I was distracted. I've got a lot on my mind."

"I apologize for snapping at you," Pedro said. "For the past month I've been preoccupied with our wedding plans and haven't kept up with your situation. How long do you expect this trip to take?"

"My hope is that we can get to Mexico City in seven or eight weeks."

"That's really pushing it," Pedro replied. "That doesn't allow much time for taking breaks. Won't you and anyone who's accompanying you need to rest your horses or somehow acquire fresh mounts along the way?"

Carlos tried to spell things out. "My thinking goes like this, old friend. I'll push hard to get through hostile Indian territory to reach El Paso del Norte as quickly as possible. I'll rest a day or two there. Then I'll try to get to Nombre de Dios in seven or eight days. If necessary, I'll acquire a fresh mount in Nombre de Dios, the wisest choice, though you can imagine how reluctant I am to put Eagle out to pasture until I can reclaim him on the return trip."

"The round trip could take five months or more," Pedro said, "assuming you can complete your business in Mexico City in two weeks or less."

"I agree," Carlos replied, shaking his head. "I hope I can do it faster."

Camila interrupted the two men's conversation. "This whole topic depresses me," she announced. She stood up abruptly and spoke to Carlos: "Please come by the house early this evening, before dinner." Without waiting for an answer, she left.

That afternoon, after putting on fresh clothes, Don Carlos walked to the Presidio. Camila met him at the door. She had changed her dress and was wearing a beautifully embroidered blouse. "That's new, isn't it?" Carlos asked. "Or at least I've never seen it before."

"Yes, I've been working on it for months now. Come in and have some hot chocolate."

They settled down with their chocolate and sipped it in a silence that was not altogether comfortable. Why, Carlos wondered, had Camila summoned him so peremptorily? Why had she left the group on the veranda so abruptly and, he thought, angrily?

"I'm afraid for you," she said at last, breaking the silence.

"Whatever for?"

She shook her head, as if annoyed. "You were so…," she began. She took a deep breath and went on. "So distracted. It was as if you weren't there at all, until Pedro called you out of your trance. And then you talked about your trip, but that wasn't what you had been thinking about, I know it wasn't. You'd been with Inéz, hadn't you? I suppose it's none of my business—we're not engaged—but I don't like that woman. I especially don't like her proprietary manner with you. She makes me afraid for you." Camila looked up at Carlos earnestly, her eyes filling with tears.

Carlos was astonished at how much she had perceived, as well as her speaking so frankly about it. "Yes," he admitted. "I had come from fencing with Inéz, and I was tired from the exertion. I'm sorry I paid you no attention."

"Oh!" she exclaimed. "It's not that I'm jealous. I know you love me. I don't think you love her. But she's *dangerous* for you." Camila said this in a tone of great intensity.

Trying to shift the mood, Carlos said lightly, "I'm much more likely to be in danger from hostile Natives I might meet on the trip." This, however, did not help.

"And that, too!" Camila replied. "I'm frightened for you! Must you make this trip to Mexico City? For months now Native raiders between here and El Paso del Norte have been attacking travelers through the Jornada del Muerto section of the Camino Real."

"As for the 'must' part of your question," Carlos replied, "my concern about my mother's health means I must go. Her situation is extremely worrisome. Regarding the threat of being attacked, don't worry. Joaquin is sending three soldiers with me. We won't be encumbered by carriages and baggage as we were in the party that brought us here. The moon is almost full. We'll be able to move swiftly through the most dangerous regions using moonlight to find our way."

Camila rose suddenly and put a hand on his arm as he too stood up. Looking solemnly into his eyes, she said, "It's just that I can't bear the thought of any harm coming to you."

Don Carlos was deeply moved. "Rest assured that nothing will prevent me from returning to you," he said.

Tears began to slide down Camila's cheeks, and she lowered her head. Carlos lifted her chin so that he could see her face. The tears only made her more beautiful. Without thinking, he bent to kiss her. Their lips met in a kiss that was tender and long-lasting. The kiss ended, but they still held each other in a close embrace.

After a few moments she freed herself from his arms. "I'm not sure that was a good thing," she declared. "Oh well, it was certainly a good thing, but what if someone had seen us? My reputation would be ruined, and foundlings don't have much social standing in the first place." She gave him a radiant smile. "I don't care; I got away with it, and I'm glad it happened whether it was proper or not. Perhaps its memory will serve to keep you from forgetting me."

"Forget you? Impossible!" he protested. "I'll be back as soon as I can."

Two days later, at the very crack of dawn, Don Carlos and the three soldiers Joaquin had assigned to accompany him stood with their mounts and two packhorses in front of the Palace of the Governors. The weather had shifted again, and snow had fallen overnight, and all of Santa Fe was covered with a thin blanket of whiteness. With each exhalation, the horses and the humans alike made clouds in the chill January air. Carlos's Eagle sensed that something big was happening and was restless to get started.

Despite the early hour, nearly everyone Carlos knew in Santa Fe was there to see him off. But when he surveyed the sea of faces around him, he couldn't spot Inéz. Camila stepped forward with a turquoise crucifix of Indian make on a silver chain. Brushing his cheek with hers in a formal kiss, she said, startling him with how well she read his thoughts, "She's not here so it's no use to look for her. This small gift is to protect you and to insure your safe return to me."

Don Carlos's heart leapt with happiness because Camila had said "return to me" — not, as she might have, "to Santa Fe."

As his party set off at a brisk pace, Carlos reflected on the very great differences between the two women in his life. Inéz, passionate and provocative, had warned him that she would invade his dreams and haunt his daytime thoughts. By contrast, Camila had asked for nothing except his safe return, and it was the tender first kiss he'd shared with Camila that was foremost in his mind as he and his companions headed south toward Mexico City.

12

Bewitched

Don Carlos and his three companions made good time the first day. They moved ahead at a steady pace until they reached the ranching area known as El Bosque de Doña Luisa and camped there for the night. He thought of the three young soldiers as boys, although they were only a few years younger than he was. One, Alejandro, was seventeen; Luis and Gonzalo were sixteen. They were mestizos from a small town in the mountains west of Santa Fe. They had come to Santa Fe and joined the army for — what? Perhaps they sought a better life — regular meals, free housing, and a small salary. Or perhaps they were hopeful of escaping the dull routines of their village for the supposedly more lively society of Santa Fe, small settlement though it was, or the possibility of adventure in military combat.

Who knows? But the fact was that they were good fellows. They were sturdy, ready to ride hard for long hours without complaint, and respectful of Don Carlos, whom they called 'Excellency,' until he told them he preferred to be called Don Alfonso.

By nightfall the party had traveled a long way for a one-day ride. They camped by a small stream and didn't worry much about Indian attacks since those usually occurred, when they did, at a point considerably farther south. Nevertheless, they divided the night into four parts of two and a half hours each and kept watch on that schedule, each man taking his turn until first light the next morning.

Don Carlos took the second watch, which began at eleven thirty. His choice was determined by a hunch that his young companions, weary from the day's ride, would sleep soundly through the period from eleven thirty to two in the morning. That being the case, they weren't likely to notice when he slipped out into the brush and practiced his favorite form of sorcery, transforming himself into a bird or animal. Much to his disappointment, none of his initial efforts to become an owl succeeded. Apparently, he had been so domesticated by his life as a bureaucrat and conventional man that his skills as a brujo had atrophied. He didn't let this bother him much, remembering that it had taken a few days in the high desert country on his trip from Mexico City to Santa Fe to get in touch with his powers as a brujo. At the end of his watch, he returned to camp, woke Gonzalo, who was supposed to take the next watch, and rolled up on the ground in a blanket, resolving to attempt transformations on future nights.

Inéz had told Carlos that she would come to him in his dreams. He hadn't taken her assertion seriously, but if he thought he was going to be rid of her, albeit temporarily, by leaving Santa Fe, he soon learned otherwise. He had no sooner fallen asleep than she appeared to him in a dream. She was dressed in the wet linen shirt she'd worn the last time they'd fenced. With a seductive smile, she spoke. He couldn't hear what she said, but her lips shaped the words so clearly that her message was obvious: "When are you going to claim your prize?" The temptation to respond in some way — but how could one respond to a figure in a dream? — stayed with him for a few moments, and Inéz repeated her question twice before he realized he should exercise the restraint he'd decided he should use toward her. In hopes of driving her off, he somehow managed, despite being asleep, to instruct himself to flip over to his other side. The movement jarred him awake and she was gone, only to return twice more in identical dreams.

The next morning as the men grabbed a hurried meal Alejandro Guzman, the eldest and most talkative of Carlos's companions, observed quietly, "You were very restless last night. I hope you got enough sleep, Don Alfonso."

"I woke a lot," Carlos admitted. "It's a good thing I've never needed much sleep."

The party pushed on at a faster pace than long-distance riders would usually have done. Late in the day they spotted a ranch to the east of the road owned by a man named Peralta. The genial proprietor agreed to let them stay overnight in the hacienda's bunkhouse. "You're lucky," their host told them. "Five of my hired hands are away for the night, rounding up some of my cattle that strayed away during a storm."

Perhaps it was simply that he once again had a roof over his head, but Carlos didn't dream of Inéz that night. However, in his sleep his mind drifted to images of Violeta. For the most part the dream, actually pieces from several dreams, consisted of fragmentary glimpses of this woman with whom he'd been so besotted that he had failed to be wary of her motives. The images themselves were certainly riveting: Violeta's pleasure in displaying her breasts; her practice of getting out of bed shortly after they'd made love and doing a provocative dance for him, and her use of an intoxicating perfume, the scent of which nearly made him faint, all too reminiscent of his recent experiences with Inéz's perfume. When Carlos woke up, he told himself that these dreams were useful reminders that erotic enchantment could be used to bring pleasure, but also to do harm.

Around noon two days later, Carlos and his companions reached the vicinity of a once-thriving town, Socorro, which had been abandoned during the Pueblo Revolt of 1680. By the present year, 1705, only one Spanish family was to be found in the area. This family, the Chavezes, had built a good-sized ranch house on the east side of the Rio Grande that doubled as a family residence and an inn that afforded travelers a place to eat and stay overnight, if they were so inclined. Carlos's party stopped for several hours to water their horses and let them eat grain that Carlos purchased. After that they continued their journey, making camp at the Fray Cristóbal rest stop at the northern end of the Jornada del Muerto as the sun was setting. Carlos was pleased; they'd covered precisely the distance that he'd planned. The toughest part of the ride to El Paso del Norte would come next.

Don Carlos again took the second watch. While his companions slept, he tested whether his skills in sorcery were emerging in response to the desert environment. Once again, nothing came of the test, even though he attempted a transformation that had previously come easily: changing himself into a screech owl. I'm out of practice, he said to himself, although the non-result seemed more due to lack of any available powers than to simple lack of practice.

When his watch was over, he lay down and, as was nearly always the case, fell asleep immediately. He soon drifted into a dream state, and Inéz made her appearance. She was again wearing her soaked-to-the-skin shirt. She ran her tongue over her lips to wet them. It seemed to Carlos that a jolt of erotic energy passed between them. Aware of the effect she was having, Inéz walked slowly toward him and spoke. As with the previous night, he couldn't hear her, but her words were clear: "This is your prize; don't you want to claim it?"

Despite his resolve to be careful where Inéz was concerned, he was stirred by her initial approach and only when she was close enough that it seemed their fingers were almost touching did he wrench himself into an action he'd planned for just such an occasion. Having foreseen the possibility of a repeat appearance by Inéz, Carlos had instructed himself to again turn over abruptly in his sleep and to add an innovation that had occurred to him earlier in the day. He reached to his chest and held the turquoise crucifix Camila had given him in the palm of his hand. Inéz pursed her lips in a pout, which served to make her look sexier than ever. "Bad boy," she said, but she disappeared immediately.

On the fifth day of their trek, Carlos and his friends made their now-customary early start, but he told them they would stop well before sundown as soon as they found a suitable place to rest. While the sun was still high, they located a spot next to a low mesa cliff that gave them a shady site to camp. The boys, used to the all-day pattern of their rides, gave him questioning looks. "I'll explain as soon as we settle in," Carlos told them.

When they finally gathered around a fire and were cooking some beans and corn tortillas, Don Carlos described his plan for the next two days. "The area we've begun to cross today, known as the Jornada del Muerto (Journey of the Dead), is a ninety-mile stretch of inhospitable desert. It's also the most dangerous stretch we'll pass through. Native raiders, probably Apaches, have struck travelers in this section of the trail many times in the past three months. I have little doubt but that they're following our movements closely and, because we're a small party, preparing to attack. I hope to fool them and thus escape attack by riding through the night. Once night has fallen, we'll break camp as silently as possible, leaving our campfire burning, and ride on at the fastest pace we can sustain. The moon is nearly full, which will make the trail easy to follow. These Natives favor pre-dawn attacks, but when they descend on this site, they'll find us long gone. Take naps now and be ready to go as planned."

The three boys had neither comments nor questions, and they followed Don Carlos's plan perfectly when night fell. Riding on a moonlit night had a magical quality that delighted Carlos, although he didn't feel his brujo powers stirring in the least. Shortly after dawn the party, though exhausted by a ride of sixty miles, had reached a camp known as Ojo del Perrillo, which was close to the southern end of the Jornada del Muerto and beyond the area where most Native attacks had recently occurred. Carlos told his companions that today they'd take turns sleeping until early afternoon, resume their ride until midnight, sleep in turns again until dawn the next day, and then make a final push for El Paso del Norte, hoping to reach the town by dusk or shortly thereafter.

Although the four companions had the Ojo del Perrillo rest stop to themselves, when Don Carlos walked around the area he spotted many signs that Natives had occupied the camp and watered their mounts at a small spring to the west of it. He began to wonder whether he'd been right in assuming that the danger of being attacked by a war party of Natives was largely over. He climbed to the top of a low ridge on the southeast corner of the camp and scanned the horizon in every direction for signs of hostiles in the area. It was frustrating not to be able to transform himself into a red-tailed hawk, which was the raptor form he ordinarily would have chosen for doing a daytime reconnaissance. But even if he'd been able to do so, he would have avoided doing a transformation during the day for fear of being observed by one of his companions.

He sat absolutely still on the slight promontory and simply watched for what he could see. He had a strange sensation that someone or some animal was standing behind him, but when he turned to look, all he saw was a small cactus plant. He concentrated on the landscape to the northeast of the camp and finally spotted a small dust cloud of the sort a party of mounted raiders would produce—or perhaps it wasn't a dust cloud at all but an aura emanating from the presence of humans that his sorcerer's vision enabled him to see. Encouraged by the thought that his brujo powers were possibly returning, he stood up so quickly that he felt a momentary attack of dizziness. It's been too long since I ate, he told himself, and he took a step down the slope toward the place where his three-man escort was trying to nap.

Before he could take a second step, the feeling that he was being watched returned. It was as though eyes were boring into his back. He spun around to see who it was. Where he'd previously seen the cactus, he was sure he saw a fleeting image of a woman standing there—or more accurately, the figure, half woman, half cactus, was visible for only a brief moment; then the half-woman part of the figure disappeared and only the cactus remained. The woman he'd seen was none other than Inéz, haunting my daytime thoughts, just as she promised, he observed to himself with a mixture of amusement and annoyance.

The immediate issue was what to do about the distant dust cloud he'd spotted. It was possible that the cloud wasn't being raised by a war party, or if it was, that the warriors weren't headed for Ojo del Perrillo. The chance of being attacked was probably less than fifty-fifty. Despite the fact that he had always enjoyed, even sought out, risky situations, he reminded himself that his primary purpose in making this journey wasn't to seek adventure, but to visit his ailing mother and to track down Camila's mother. Prudence demanded that he and his companions get moving again. With some regret at waking them so soon, Don Carlos walked over to where the three soldiers were sleeping and shook them until they were conscious. He explained the situation and suggested that they saddle up and keep going until they'd put some distance between themselves and any Native raiders in the vicinity. "Once we're safely out of harm's way," he said, "we can set up camp again and get some more sleep."

Luck was with Carlos and his friends. Shortly before midnight, they came upon a recently established hacienda and turned up the lane to the main house. Three guard dogs greeted them loudly and in a definitely unfriendly way. But the master of the house, who soon appeared at the front door, was exceedingly gracious and invited the four travelers to water their horses at a nearby spring and spend the night with his vaqueros in their bunkhouse. Carlos was touched by how uncomplainingly the cowboys shifted around in their sleeping quarters to make room for the unexpected guests.

In spite of having the luxury of a bunk with a straw mattress, Don Carlos didn't feel the least bit sleepy. After lying in bed for two hours listening to a couple of the vaqueros who had exceptionally loud snores, he eased out of the room and spent the rest of the night sitting on the bunkhouse's veranda. He didn't attempt any transformations and decided that the virtue of not sleeping was that Inéz wouldn't show up, though he wondered about two of the day's events—the Inéz image imposed on a cactus plant, and the dust cloud that might have been an aura of the sort only brujos could see — and mulled over whether either incident indicated that his brujo's powers were reviving. He decided the evidence was inconclusive.

The rest of the trip to El Paso del Norte went smoothly. Carlos and his escort enjoyed a hearty breakfast with the hacienda's owner before setting out again on their journey. Late that day, the travelers, saddle sore and underslept, were relieved to see El Paso del Norte ahead. Having been a visitor to the town in the past, Don Carlos didn't need to ask directions to the local presidio. He steered his companions to the commandant's residence, where they were greeted warmly by Colonel Encarnación. The plan, as Don Carlos reported it to the colonel, was that his three-soldier escort would join the town's small army garrison and wait there to rejoin him on his northward return journey from El Paso del Norte to Santa Fe. This arrangement was highly satisfactory to the colonel, since the unit under his command was seriously undermanned at the moment. The three boys from Santa Fe were delighted too because they were getting to see new things and new places.

Carlos dined with Colonel Encarnación and his family that night and went to bed very early, pleading weariness from the long ride he'd just made and the need to rest for the still longer ride ahead. Much to his relief, Inéz did not show up in his dreams that night. Perhaps, he mused, I threw her off by making night rides and not giving her a chance to appear in dreams I wasn't having. She may have lost track of me altogether.

Nothing could have been further from the truth. The next day Don Carlos walked around El Paso del Norte with Private Alejandro Guzman, whom he'd come to like a great deal in the short time they'd been together. Carlos found himself afflicted with a strange phenomenon. Time and time again, he would see female residents who had Inéz's face, regardless of their personal traits. If he shook his head, slapped his cheek, or splashed water on his face, Inéz's face immediately disappeared and was replaced by the faces of local women: little girls, young mothers, middle-aged Indians, and mestizo crones. So this, Carlos said to himself, is what Inez meant when she said she would haunt my daytime activities. The image he'd seen of a cactus that looked like Inéz could be explained away as a fantasy or a hallucination, but the phenomenon of seeing Inéz's face on many women was definite proof of her capacity to haunt him.

As Don Carlos continued to behave in this strange way, Private Guzman became concerned. "Are you all right, Don Alfonso?" he asked anxiously. "Should we get out of the sun?"

"I know I'm acting oddly, Alejandro," Carlos replied, "but rest assured this is simply my time-honored way of clearing my head of bad thoughts. And they seem abundant today."

"Ah!" Private Guzman murmured. "You do have an extremely challenging ride ahead."

After a rest break of two days, Carlos and Eagle, accompanied by one packhorse, set off again. Their next destination was the mission and town at Nombre de Dios. Carlos hadn't particularly looked forward to being totally on his own through rough country where bandits might be lurking, and a few miles down the road he was relieved to meet two silver-mine owners who had been visiting relatives in El Paso del Norte and were now headed back to the Nombre de Dios area.

The two mine owners were saddle-hardened riders and agreeable to setting a good pace, though not one as fast as Carlos had taken on the ride to El Paso del Norte. They hoped to reach Nombre de Dios in nine days. Carlos had planned to take seven or eight.

On the first night out of El Paso del Norte, Inéz returned to Carlos's dreams. She was more provocative than ever. She showed up wearing the now-familiar wet shirt and the pouty look she'd had when he'd last dreamed about her. She shook her finger at him and repeated her earlier "bad boy" comment. Then she started toward him and began to unbutton her shirt. He read her lips: "Stop stalling! Your prize is here!" At this point she bent forward to kiss him on the mouth, and he thought he could feel her body against his. He tried to pull back, but he seemed paralyzed by her intense erotic appeal. The odd thing was that there seemed to be a nearly invisible transparent membrane between them. He managed to grasp Camila's crucifix, and Inéz began to fade away. "Very bad boy!" she said, just before disappearing completely.

The next morning at breakfast he was again subject to good-natured jibes about what a noisy, restless sleeper he was. For his part, Carlos was thinking hard about what was happening, particularly the fact that he had, at best, weak powers of sorcery, despite his expectation that the desert environment would empower him again. He concluded that his obsession with Inéz was keeping him from drawing on his inner brujo soul. Under his breath he said, "I've got to head this off tonight." He began to plan.

During the next day's ride he hung back a bit, mulling over the problem of what to do about Inéz. If this kept up, he would gradually be depleted of all his energy, not just his brujo powers, but his ordinary vitality as well. Precisely what triggered the memory he couldn't remember later, but an old sorcerer's exercise called "entering the dream" came to mind. He determined to try it that night, and consequently waited in a positive state of mind for Inéz to appear.

Inéz, when she did appear in his dream state, had apparently decided to take stronger measures to deal with his refusal to take her as his prize. Instead of remaining several yards away from him, she fixed her eyes on his and walked toward him, moving her pelvis in a seductive fashion. She clearly intended to embrace him.

Carlos knew from fencing that there are times when the best defense is a strong offense. Instead of retreating, he tried the sorcerer's technique of "entering the dream" and moved forward to meet her, forcing his way through the thin membrane that had separated them the previous night. He could hear her clearly, and he could also smell her favorite perfume. Although she reproached him with her now-standard "bad boy!" line, she was definitely pleased that he had at last moved toward her. Only at the last moment did she realize that he intended to fend her off rather than take her in his arms.

Always an impetuous, aggressive fighter, Inéz lunged at him, making a grab for the turquoise crucifix that Camila had given him, but he managed to grasp it first. Undeterred, she reached around him and pulled their bodies close together. As she did so, she smiled slyly and asked, "What now? It's your move."

Don Carlos was strongly inclined to give in and make love to Inéz. Instead, he said, "We need to talk."

"Talk?" She almost spat the word out. "Talk is little more than hot air. Deeds are what count."

Testing his willpower by making no effort to escape Inéz's grasp, Don Carlos replied, "Hear me out. You're making this journey very difficult for me. Enticing though you certainly are, your appearances in my dreams leave me little time for sleep. The moment has come for me to collect the prize I won in our winner-take-all contest, and the prize I want is for you to leave me alone, both in my dreams and my daytime thoughts, until I'm back in Santa Fe."

Inéz gave a cry of dismay. She seemed hurt by his choice. "You're a clever one. I'll do as you ask," she said, "if you'll grant me one small favor in return."

"And what's that?" he asked skeptically.

"I'll leave you alone during your trip, no matter how long it takes, if, upon returning to Santa Fe, you come to my house and lie in bed with me for a full day, doing my bidding."

The part of Inéz's proposal about lying around with her for a whole day was enormously appealing. However, the phrase "doing my bidding" warned him off. "No, Inéz, I won't do that," he said.

She fixed a solemn gaze on him, not, he thought, in anger (which wouldn't have surprised him), but as though she'd had a sudden realization about him. "It's just as I suspected; you're not an ordinary man."

"Meaning what?"

"Don't play dumb, Alfonso. An ordinary man couldn't possibly have stepped into your dream and met me body-to-body in this alternative world. That being the case, I'm asking you to grant me a single wish. When you get back to Santa Fe, come visit me for a fencing match, after which we'll sit at my patio table, fully clothed, drink wine, and you will tell me about the romantic adventures you'll have had on this trip. Is that too much to ask? "

"No, it isn't," he replied. "Now will you give me a good night kiss (a foolish and impulsive request, he observed) and go away?"

What followed was a long, deep kiss. When they separated, Inéz said, "Nice," gave him a friendly pat on the cheek, and disappeared.

The next morning he woke up feeling pleased with himself. He'd seized the initiative and decisively told the dream Inéz to go away. Although the strength of the dream faded as the day progressed, he felt content and energized by the solution he'd found.

13

Embattled

After chasing Inéz off, Don Carlos found that his powers of sorcery came back with impressive force. The desert environment was having precisely the effect he'd hoped it would. At times when his two companions could not see him, he tested the strength of his returning powers. Every night he transformed himself into an owl and thrilled to the experience of using rising air currents next to cliffs to soar above the landscape. Even during daylight he was able to go off by himself, ostensibly to attend to a call of nature, to explore his powers. He easily turned a small pine tree into a cactus plant, and then for good measure added some lovely blooms, although mid-winter was not the season for them. To transform the tree he used a technique that he'd learned in a previous life from an old Indian woman who had taught him a few words to say to change the energy of an object he wanted to transform. He had a vague memory that Don Serafino had cautioned him against using this kind of magic, which depended on spells and incantations rather than enhanced natural capacities — concentration, intense awareness, and visualization — and had told him that it was not appropriate to brujos of their type. But in his excitement at the return of his brujo powers, Don Carlos shrugged aside Don Serafino's warning, which in fact he hadn't fully understood in the first place.

In addition to practicing transformations, he attempted and succeeded at physical tasks that would have been well beyond the capacity of an ordinary man. In the first such case he was walking through the brush and found that a huge boulder, nearly as high from top to bottom as he was tall, had rolled down a hill, coming to a stop across his path. He could have slipped around the boulder, but, almost on a whim, he wondered whether he could move it out of the way. From some past life he recalled that the key to such acts was for the brujo to use his breath in a certain way, inhaling fully and then concentrating all his energy at a place inside his body between his navel and his groin. Without any recent experience of performing such a feat, he nevertheless felt confident that by using this method he could roll the big rock off the trail, and he did so with ease.

Almost giddy with the strength that had flowed through his body as he had moved the huge obstacle out of his way, he looked for a second test of his brujo-induced power. He spied another boulder beside the path ten yards ahead, the sight of which tempted him to try something even more audacious. The rock was the size of Don Carlos's upper torso and must have weighed three hundred pounds. Unlike the previous boulder, however, this one was small enough that he could put his arms halfway around it, gripping its sides with his hands. Centering his concentration on his deep abdominal power spot, he picked the boulder up and heaved it twenty feet down the slope. It made a thoroughly satisfying crashing sound as it tumbled to the bottom of the shallow arroyo below the trail.

When Don Carlos returned to camp, both his companions looked up from the snack they'd been having, and one of them asked, "What was that racket a few minutes ago? It sounded as though a huge chunk of the arroyo wall broke off and came thundering down."

"Not quite," Don Carlos replied. "It was only a single boulder that came hurtling down the slope and knocked other rocks around as it made its way to the bottom of the arroyo. Fortunately, I was not in its path."

"Lucky you," his companion commented, "but it sure sounded like an avalanche, not just one boulder."

"You know how it is with sounds in the high desert," Carlos said. "It's like what happens when you hear coyotes yipping. From the opposite side of a hill it sounds as though there must be a dozen beasts howling their heads off. Then you come over the rise and you see that there were only two of them all that time. I'm sure you've hit something like that one time or another."

Both men nodded, obviously familiar with the phenomenon, and everyone had a good laugh about it.

The final night on the trail before reaching the mission town of Nombre de Dios, Carlos walked some distance from camp to a watering hole he'd spotted and sat beside it for six hours without moving. He'd recalled that in previous lives he'd often won bets with ordinary men by wagering that he could sit still longer than they could. (Brujos called this technique Watching.) He had always outlasted his opponents.

Tonight Don Carlos watched in delight as creatures small and large came to drink. Deer, muskrats, rabbits, two foxes, a porcupine, and several mice showed up. They were aware of his presence, but they displayed no fear of him. It was getting close to dawn when a big female mountain lion emerged from the brush. She took a leisurely drink from the watering hole and then came toward him. He wondered, but only for an instant, whether she intended to attack him, though nothing about her manner was hostile. When she spoke, he realized that this was no ordinary mountain lion, and, simultaneously, he saw that her body glowed with a golden radiance. She gave him a friendly lick next to his ear and said, "It's nice you stopped by." And not wasting time with further social niceties, she asked, "Why don't you transform yourself into a male cougar so you can mount me?"

"Your proposal is an attractive one," Don Carlos said, not wanting to offend her, and he was tempted to try it except for reasons that sprang instantly to mind. "The trouble," he told her, "is that it's daylight now and

I've already stayed away from my companions too long. I'm sure you can understand that it would be dangerous for me to have them discover that I'm a brujo."

"You could always kill them, if they did," the lion observed in a reasonable tone of voice.

"I could," Carlos replied, "but I won't. I don't use my powers to harm anyone unless absolutely necessary, and these men have been good companions. It wouldn't be honorable to injure them in the slightest."

"All right, if that's how you feel," the cougar said as she turned away. "Come and visit me, if you pass this way again."

His companions were starting breakfast by the time he returned to their camp. "You were gone a long time," the elder of the two said with a questioning look on his face.

"Something I ate clogged my innards. I needed to squat for a long time to get rid of it. I don't recommend the experience."

This explanation seemed to satisfy the two silver-mine owners, and the three of them were soon on their way. Shortly after noon Nombre de Dios, on the banks of the Chuviscar River, came into view. The settlement had undergone significant changes since Carlos had passed through less than a year earlier. The week after Joaquin's party had moved on, a fire had damaged five houses in town. The townspeople, their resources swelled by riches from the nearby silver mines and cattle ranches, had rallied to refurbish the fire-scarred buildings. In addition, there had been new construction in response to the rapid expansion of the local economy. Nevertheless, Carlos instantly recognized one familiar spot, the well and watering trough in front of the mission church, where, on the trip northward nearly a year ago, he had told Camila that he liked high-spirited women. Seeing it again brought her strongly to mind. From the way she always addressed me, he thought, it was as though sharp repartee was the only way she knew to relate to men, a habit, perhaps, she acquired from the rough-and-tumble life in an orphanage. That memory only made him feel more love for her and to realize that he'd been missing their friendly exchanges.

Much as he didn't want to leave Eagle behind while he went on to Mexico City, Carlos knew his horse was tired from the hard pace and long distance they'd traveled together. It wouldn't be good horsemanship to demand more. Carlos remembered that there had been a large livery stable on the edge of town that provided mounts for the local miners, and he led Eagle down the street toward this stable. It was even larger than he'd remembered, with ample pasture that had several dozen horses grazing in it. Carlos went to the barn and spoke with a stable hand. "Is your boss around? I have some business for him."

Before the worker could say anything, a well-dressed man stepped out of a small office. "I'm the boss," he said, and then gave Don Carlos a piercing look. "Aren't you Don Alfonso? Do you remember me—Manuel Tapia?"

"I remember you very well, Manuel, and I'm glad to see you. What are you doing here?"

"Come in my office so that we can speak in private. I'll tell you how this came about. Give your horse to Ramón here to feed and turn out to pasture, if that's okay with you."

It was fine by Carlos, and once the two men had settled down on chairs in the office, Manuel began to tell his story. "I'm well aware that you saved my life by not exposing me to your captain's wrath, and you also enriched me by letting me keep the silver ingots my gang had stolen. Once my men and I had split the loot, I decided I no longer wanted to risk my neck by following a life of crime. I came here to Nombre de Dios to think things over. When I heard that this stable was for sale, I knew it was the perfect business opportunity for me because the town is growing swiftly. As for the stable itself, I'm proud to say that in the brief time I've owned it, I've improved the operation a great deal. I now have more horses, a better barn, a larger pasture, and excellent connections with stables in other towns. I specialize in providing mounts for riders headed for Durango, where, as it happens, I own another stable. The horses shuttle back and forth. If you need a mount to ride to Durango, I have a fine one that you can have for free. I haven't forgotten the great favors you did for me."

Don Carlos and Manuel chatted briefly about Carlos's life in Santa Fe, but Carlos sensed that Manuel had something else he wanted to discuss. "Is there anything else on your mind, Manuel?" Carlos asked casually.

"Yes, I guess my worries show. Although I'm already in debt to you, I'm wondering whether you can help me with a situation that's weighing on my mind. In the mountains not far to the west of here there's a small village whose residents are all Indians. Until recently, this village prospered. The valley has good soil and plenty of water. The inhabitants specialized in raising sheep for wool. They were self-sufficient and seldom came to town. I've always had friendly relations with several of the families who live in that town.

"The trouble is," Manuel continued, "that a Spanish man named Mateo Pizarro has moved in among them and for all intents and purposes enslaved the canyon's residents. According to reports, he takes whatever he wants: food, sheep, and women. The women, married or not, he rapes, even young girls. Men who initially tried to stop him were beaten up and warned that if they resisted further, he would have his men—he has four henchmen—gang-rape the men's wives."

"Why don't the Natives run away?"

"Although it's a fairly broad valley, it's surrounded by unscalable cliffs and there is only one entrance, a place where the cliffs come so close together that there's barely room for a road. Pizarro's henchmen live in a cabin at that spot and grab anyone who tries to leave and stop anyone who tries to enter. Pizarro pays these thugs with money from wool they sell for him and gives them access to Indian women to abuse sexually.

"I became worried about the situation when one of the Indians escaped and came to me with stories about Pizarro's treatment of the canyon's residents. I rode to the entrance of the canyon and tried to enter it, but Pizarro's henchmen turned me back. They told me that they'd discovered silver ore in the canyon and weren't going to let any competitors in to see their mining operation. They also claimed that the Indians had agreed to stay in the canyon and help mine the ore in return for a share of the profits."

"Did you try to involve the local authorities, asking them to investigate?"

"Pizarro has them in his pocket. He bribes them to ignore the situation and, in any case, the local police chief is a cousin of Pizarro's. When I approached him, the police chief scoffed at my story. 'Those Indians,' he said. 'A couple of them came to me with stories that Mateo Pizarro is a sorcerer. A sorcerer? They're typical Indians, scared of their own shadows and their heads full of superstitions and tall tales. There's no point in investigating fantasies.'"

Manuel continued: "Here's my thought. Given your high social status, if you were to investigate and report to the provincial authorities that you'd found that Pizarro is mistreating the Indians and forcing them to work for him, they'd take you more seriously than they do me. They'd then order the local police to make Pizarro free the Indians from his control. Please," Manuel went on, "don't say no until after I have a chance to offer additional evidence of how desperate the situation is."

Manuel went to the door of his office and stuck his head out. "Ramón," he called. "Bring Felipe here to speak with our guest." (Don Carlos was glad that Manuel didn't mention his name. Intuitively, he was sure he didn't want his name connected with this situation.)

A short, full-blooded Indian man soon appeared at the door and, trembling with fear, entered as Manuel told him to do so. "This is Felipe," Manuel said. "He was the last person to escape from Querobabi, the village I've been telling you about. He made it out the day before Pizarro's gang completed the cabin and fence that block the exit to the canyon. What he saw before leaving has left him traumatized. Pizarro was going about the town, demanding that men surrender their mothers, wives, and daughters to him for his sexual pleasure. If they resisted, he beat them up."

Something had been bothering Don Carlos. "Although Pizarro certainly sounds like a beast, everything you've described to me could be done by an ordinary bully. What has led the Natives to believe that he's a sorcerer?"

"Felipe saw Pizarro go to Felipe's brother's house, grab his wife, and start to take her to his cabin. When Felipe and his brother tried to stop him, Pizarro knocked them down."

"But," Carlos protested, "an ordinary man could do that, if he were strong enough."

Nodding, Manuel agreed. "The difference is that when he knocked them down, they were twenty feet away from him. They were thrown down by an invisible force and paralyzed. Felipe lives in dread that Pizarro will rape his brother's daughter. This niece is only twelve, and don't say it's impossible. Pizarro already raped and impregnated a fourteen-year-old."

Upon hearing Manuel's description, Felipe began weeping and fell to his knees, his hands clasped as if in prayer, and looked imploringly at Don Carlos. Carlos spoke gently to the distraught man. "I will investigate and see what I can learn."

Manuel showed Felipe out the door and spoke solemnly. "I was hoping you would agree to help."

Before he could say anything more, Carlos interrupted and asked, "Are you assuming that I'll somehow get into the canyon? Surely these thugs will turn me away if I try, just as they did you."

"What I had in mind is for you to follow a trail that goes along the rim of the canyon. At the very least you'll be able to see whether the story about the mining operation is true."

"I suppose I can do that," Carlos agreed.

"Excellent!" Manuel exclaimed. "And since I'm already in your debt, please allow me to reward your generosity in practical ways. To start with, I can offer you the use of several of my horses and the companionship of three of my hired hands for the rest of your trip southward. I also want to give you a substantial sum in silver no matter how this turns out."

Don Carlos hesitated for a moment. "Usually, I wouldn't accept money, especially for simply seeing what I can find out, which is all I've promised to do; however, my expenses in Santa Fe are outrunning my resources, and I could certainly use some extra funds. Thank you for offering."

"Think nothing of it," Manuel replied. "It's the least I can do. Is there anything I can do to aid you?"

"Manuel," Carlos said, "bear in mind that all I've agreed to do is to investigate the situation and report back to you. Nevertheless, to protect myself in the process I need a few items that I don't have in my saddlebags. Can you supply the following: a small bag made of tough canvas, two very sharp knives, and six of the galena pieces you have on the shelf behind you?"

"Galena? I can give you pure silver nuggets almost as large and more valuable."

"No, my friend," Carlos replied with a smile. "I'm not trying to buy this fellow off. Pure lead in crystal form, heavy cubes with sharp edges, will be more useful for defending myself." (Don Carlos knew that galena had some quality that most sorcerers found difficult to ward off, though he didn't share this information with Manuel.)

Manuel soon found all the supplies Carlos had asked for. He put the galena and knives in the canvas bag and asked Manuel to ride with him into the countryside to point out the location of the canyon in which Querobabi was located.

The ride was a short one, no more than five or six miles. They stopped at a bend in the road that Manuel said was just out of sight of the cabin at the canyon's entrance. "What do you want me to do with your horse?" he asked.

"Why not take her back to the stable?" Carlos suggested. "If we leave her here, the thugs might spot her and realize that someone's snooping around. Besides, I don't know when I'll return and when I do, Nombre de Dios isn't that far away. I'll walk back."

Directed by Manuel to a trail off the right that headed up to the ridge around the canyon where Querobabi was located, Carlos told Manuel that he'd climb up to the ridgeline to see what he could observe from above the canyon. "There's no route into the canyon," Manuel warned him.

"That's fine by me. Although I have a reputation among my friends as a mountain goat able to climb cliffs no one else can traverse, I have no need to go into the canyon. I'll see what I can see from the ridge, including whether there's a mining operation in progress, and then perhaps I'll return here and have a conversation with Pizarro's henchmen."

Manuel seemed satisfied by Carlos's description of his plan and left, expressing fervent wishes for the success of Carlos's mission. For his part, Carlos was questioning the wisdom of the whole enterprise. What on earth am I doing? he thought. If I'm not careful even an investigation could be dangerous. Camila would be furious with me, if she knew. I promised myself to make this trip as quickly as possible and not go looking for adventures. But was it, he asked himself, the pull of adventure — investigating the actions of a man alleged to be a sorcerer — or Manuel Tapia's plea to help people in desperate need that made me agree to do this? No matter, he told himself, these Indians are in need, and if I can gather information that helps them without becoming directly involved with Pizarro, that's an honorable thing to do.

Don Carlos waited until the sun was beginning to set. He knew that his brujo powers were especially strong during the transition from day to night, a time when liminality ruled the world and opened doors to alternative realities that a brujo could exploit.

Carlos undressed, put his shirt and pants in the canvas bag, and transformed himself into a large owl. He grasped the canvas bag containing his tools and clothes and lifted off, just barely. This damn bag is almost too heavy, he thought. It's a good thing I've changed into a very large bird of prey, and a magically empowered one at that.

He flew steadily until he'd reached and crossed over the entrance to the valley where Querobabi was located. As he flew along the rim of the valley to its far end, he could see the entire village at a glance. There were no signs of mining operations. With the exception of four figures, no one was visible in the fading light. These four — two men, a woman, and a young girl — were facing each other behind a house that from Manuel's descriptions Carlos felt confident was the home of Felipe's brother. The Indian man and woman were pleading, arms outstretched, with a swarthy Spanish man, doubtless Mateo Pizarro. One of his huge arms held a terrified Indian girl pinned to his chest.

Silently, on invisible air currents, Don Carlos glided downward and circled slowly on the side of the house away from where he'd seen the four figures. He was close enough now that his highly sensitive brujo hearing enabled him to hear what was being said. He heard a voice that he was sure was the Spanish man's say, "I'm taking your daughter to play with tonight."

On hearing this, Don Carlos landed, changed to his human form, put on his shirt and pants, and tiptoed barefoot around the house to see precisely what was going on.

The parents were weeping, imploring Pizarro to spare their child. "Please, Don Mateo, take anything you want, except her," the man begged. "Take me instead," the mother cried.

Pizarro turned back and knocked them down with a burst of invisible energy, throwing them to the ground where they lay paralyzed. "I'm taking your daughter for my pleasure," he said in a loud voice. Still clutching the daughter, he stepped over to where the child's father was lying, unbuttoned his pants, and pissed on the man. "I don't need any offers of things from you, Pepe, because I can and will take anything I want." Turning to the woman, he said with sardonic politeness. "You are very kind to offer yourself to me. Thank you. I'll be back for you some day, but tonight I fancy tender young meat." The girl struggled against him, to no effect.

Until this moment, Don Carlos had intended simply to size up the situation and then report his findings to the provincial authorities as Manuel Tapia had asked him to do. Seeing the appalling scene that was unfolding led him to change his mind. More accurately, mind had nothing to do with it; he acted without thinking, driven by emotion rather than thought.

Don Carlos had noticed Pizarro's musket leaning against the house wall. He picked it up and moved as quietly as he could toward Pizarro in order to get the best shot possible to kill or severely wound this devil in human form. Pizarro, however, sensed Carlos's presence. Without displaying any apparent concern, he turned around, looked Carlos up and down, and demanded, "Who are you?"

Don Carlos's answer was to aim the musket directly at Pizarro's chest and fire, but the sorcerer turned sideways with lightning speed and the musket ball struck him a glancing blow, falling harmlessly to the ground behind him. "You'll have to do better than that to injure me," he sneered.

Don Carlos took one of the galena crystals from his bag and hurled the lead cube at Pizarro, who leaped to one side, pushing away the child he'd held because she was impeding his freedom of movement. He was quick enough to escape a serious blow, although the crystal caused a gash on his shoulder that produced a trickle of blood.

Don Carlos's use of a crystal alerted Pizarro to the fact that his opponent was not an ordinary man, and he picked up the galena cube from where it had fallen next to him and hurled it back at Carlos, who evaded it easily. Carlos thereupon launched a more elaborate attack: three lead crystals thrown at the same time in trajectories sufficiently separate from each other that Pizarro wouldn't be able to dodge all three. Moving with astonishing quickness, Pizarro evaded two of the three, but the third struck him on the knee. He winced, but swiftly went on the counterattack.

Pizarro's attack consisted of picking up a stone the size of a man's head — this guy's pretty strong and very tough, Carlos thought — and throwing it at Carlos's chest. Carlos could have dodged the rock, but he chose instead to smash it to bits with his fist, a move that seemed, at last, to cause Pizarro to treat Carlos as a serious mortal threat.

But Pizarro posed a grave danger to Don Carlos's well-being too, and the wisdom of attacking Pizarro didn't seem all that clear to Carlos once he'd witnessed the great powers his opponent displayed. Carlos, however, was never one to linger on feelings of self-doubt. In any case, now that the battle was joined, he could not back out. Trying to leave the scene might very well be more dangerous than continuing the fight. He simply had to summon from deep within powers that had long lain unused. As he prepared to do so, he had a faint memory that in a previous life he had once fought another evil sorcerer in a battle to the death. But this was not the time for reflection, and he pushed the memory aside, sweeping it entirely away to clear his mind for the challenge at hand.

Pizarro next threw himself into the air, soaring over the house and out of sight. Don Carlos knew better than to try to follow him, even if he could manage it, by the same path, suspecting that Pizarro would be waiting on the other side of the house to deal him a blow. To evade a possible trap, Carlos, guessing that Pizarro would be looking upward in expectation that Carlos would come from above, ran around the corner of the house and was pleased that Pizarro's back was partly turned to him. He launched the last two lead crystals he had toward his enemy, one of which struck him solidly on his upper arm, the other grazing his neck. The resultant wounds didn't seem to bother him much. He turned to face Carlos, as if preparing to counterattack.

Don Carlos didn't wait to see what Pizarro might do, immediately switching weapons to try his luck with a knife. He had applied jimson weed oil to the knife's blade to poison anyone it struck and to give the victim hallucinations. Hurled with great force, the knife reached Pizarro almost before he could react. Consequently, he had to catch the knife by the blade to prevent it from striking him deeply just above the heart. His hand bled and a small stab wound showed on his chest.

Although Pizarro grunted when struck by the knife, it was going to take more than lead cubes or a knife to bring him down. The sorcerer gave Don Carlos a dark look and flung himself upward to a rock overhang fifty feet away on the steepest part of the canyon wall. No direct route of attack was apparent to Carlos, so he ran to a boulder about the size of a large watermelon, picked it up, and threw it at the canyon wall above Pizarro's head. The boulder's impact triggered a small avalanche that dislodged Pizarro from the wall to which he'd attached himself. The sorcerer fell to the ground below, landing heavily with a loud grunt, but he quickly regained his composure. He even managed a sour laugh and challenged Carlos with the words, "You are no match for me; prepare to die before the night is out."

Pizarro was right about one thing. It was now pitch dark. Both Pizarro and Carlos were using their sorcerer's night vision to continue the fight.

Pizarro took off up the canyon with strides of ten feet or more. Don Carlos followed carefully, wary of being trapped in a place where Pizarro knew the lay of the land better than he did. At the side of the canyon, against a sheer wall, it became plain what Pizarro would try next. In a single, prodigious leap, he hurled himself upward and landed on the top of the ridge. He then began rolling huge boulders down the slope and sending large chunks of the cliff wall down at Carlos, apparently hoping to stun or kill him.

It took Carlos many jumps—Pizarro was vastly superior at great leaps—to reach a spot fifty yards from his opponent's position on the ridge line. Pizarro responded by launching a lightning bolt in Carlos's direction. Carlos shielded himself with a wall of sorcerer's energy that acted as a mirror and returned the bolt toward its original source. Pizarro fought back by adopting the same technique, and so it went, the bolt of lightning going back and forth, each exchange accompanied by a loud crash of thunder, until the lightning's charge weakened and the bolt diminished to nothing.

Such was his concentration on the task at hand that it seemed to Don Carlos that the battle had lasted only a short time, but in fact hours had passed. By now Carlos knew that his powers and Pizarro's were almost equal. In battles between equals, luck rather than skill often determines the contest's outcome. Both he and Pizarro were tiring. It was only a matter of time until luck determined the victor and led to the death of the other.

Desperate situations call for desperate measures. Don Carlos dug deeply and came up with another means of attack. Transformations, he told himself, may be the only advantage I have over this devil. And so it was that he now attempted an exceedingly difficult transformation, one more extraordinary than any he had ever achieved in his previous lives.

Standing barely twenty feet from Pizarro at a high point on the ridge line, Don Carlos began to turn in place at an incredible speed until the energy of his aura created a powerful vortex of tornado-like motion that sucked stones, sticks, dust, and other debris into a broad column. Pizarro stepped back, uncertain how to attack. Next, in the most virtuosic move of all, Don Carlos divided the column into four parts connected low to the ground by tendrils of dust charged with energy. Within one of the columns, the one from which he watched the scene, he held a large rock, while surrounding Pizarro with the remaining three columns of debris. Keeping the whirlwind that contained the rock somewhat away from the main action, he blocked Pizarro's every effort to evade the other three whirlwinds as they closed in on him. Each time Pizarro attempted to crash through the columns, the whirling, debris-filled clouds buffeted him so severely that he was driven back. Finally, when Pizarro was dazed and completely confused as to where the next attack would originate, Don Carlos swept forward inside the fourth column and delivered a crushing blow to Pizarro's head with the rock he had been holding.

Pizarro crumpled and his body fell to the canyon floor below. Don Carlos followed warily until he was sure his opponent had been knocked out and was not likely to regain consciousness soon. Repulsive though the thought was to him, he knew what needed to be done next. He took Pizarro's belt, used it to tie Pizarro's feet together and to string him upside down from a tree limb. He took his one remaining knife and slit Pizarro's throat. He squatted nearby and watched as every last drop of blood drained from Pizarro's body. The sorcerer never regained consciousness, and his soul did not escape. He was dead, both his body and his soul.

According to custom among brujos of Don Carlos's type, the body of a dead sorcerer was to be treated with the utmost respect. The one exception to this rule, an exception that definitely applied to Mateo Pizarro, was when the sorcerer had used his powers for evil means. Carlos used his knife to cut Pizarro's clothes from his body, leaving him swinging naked in the wind. Several buzzards, apparently early risers, circled greedily above.

The first light of dawn was showing on the horizon. Don Carlos walked to a place not far from the home of Pepe and Rosa, but he did not knock on their door immediately. This delay was necessitated by the fact that Don Carlos's body was surrounded by an aura of bright light, a consequence of the intense practice of sorcery in which he had been engaged. He waited for his aura to fade, concerned lest an ordinary person in close proximity to such a strong aura might be harmed by it, and he had no intention of harming Pepe, Rosa, or their daughter.

Once he felt it was safe to do so, he knocked on the door, and Rosa opened it. Without entering, Don Carlos asked, "Do you have some water for me to drink? I've been up all night watching Mateo Pizarro's violent energy turn against him. Don't be afraid. He's dead."

Rosa brought Carlos a large mug filled with water. Once he'd drunk his fill, she said, "There are still those four men who live at the entrance to the canyon."

"Do you have any idea why they haven't come looking for Pizarro to ask him about last night's violent storms?"

"Pizarro ordered them never to leave their post at the mouth of the canyon unless he gave them permission."

"They may run off now that he's dead," he suggested gently. "In any case, if they stick around, they won't have any power over you without Pizarro to force you to obey them. As for myself, all I ask is that you go inside, pull the curtains, and promise never to tell anyone, even your husband and daughter when they get up, that you saw a stranger in the canyon this morning." She nodded her assent.

Don Carlos crept stealthily toward the men's cabin. Two of them were outside in an agitated state, looking anxiously up the canyon. Don Carlos assumed the other two thugs must be inside the cabin. Although close to exhaustion, he decided to put into practice the boulder-rolling exercise he'd recently done on his trip to Nombre de Dios.

The thugs' cabin was located at the base of a steep, boulder-covered slope. Carlos climbed the slope, gathered his strength, and began rolling big boulders toward the cabin. Enhancing the frightening effect of seeing boulders bearing down on them, Don Carlos repeatedly screamed an eerie wail that seemed to come from the boulders themselves. The two men who were outside shouted for their companions to get out of the cabin, and they managed to escape only an instant before the boulders crashed into it, demolishing the flimsy structure.

Don Carlos now undertook what he hoped would be his final transformation for the day. He formed himself into a ferocious-looking monster. The beast had the body of a bear, the sharp talons of a bird of prey, and the head of a wolf whose gleaming teeth dripped saliva and whose throat gave forth blood-curdling howls.

The four terrified thugs fled down the road toward town, as Don Carlos had hoped they would. He continued to pursue them until a posse led by Manuel Tapia came galloping toward them. Given the choice between being captured by a posse of humans and being devoured by a huge demonic monster, the four villains made the logical choice and offered no resistance to Manuel and his companions.

Seeing that all was well, Don Carlos hurried back into the canyon, undressed, packed his flight bag, transformed himself into a red-tailed hawk, and flew to Nombre de Dios. After returning to human form, he dressed and walked to Manuel's stable and found its owner relaxing in his office. Manuel greeted Carlos with great enthusiasm and reported excitedly that he and some friends had captured the four thugs who'd aided Pizarro in persecuting the inhabitants of Querobabi. To Manuel's questions regarding precisely what Don Carlos had seen or done while at the canyon, the only answer Carlos gave was that he had watched from the canyon rim as Pizarro's powers had somehow turned against him. "His violent nature," Carlos suggested, "apparently became so uncontrollable that it led to his death. He won't," Carlos assured Manuel, "bother the canyon's residents again." Manuel shook his head in amazement.

"One more thing," Carlos continued, "I would greatly appreciate it if you didn't in any way connect my name with the events of the past twenty-four hours. I was, after all, simply a bystander."

Manuel readily agreed, and sensing that Carlos wasn't going to tell him anything more, he contented himself with saying, "There was a terrific amount of thunder and lightning over the canyon last night. It went on and on. The very earth trembled. That's what led us to ride up the canyon road to see what had happened."

Carlos nodded his head. "Yes, I saw the lightning and heard the thunder. The storm was unusually strong and of long duration." He then asked, "Do you have any idea what Pizarro's motives were? He seemed to pursue evil deeds for the mere pleasure of doing them."

"I've been talking with his four henchmen about precisely that," Manuel replied. "They say Pizarro didn't intend to stay in the canyon much longer, that he had a teacher or mentor he was supposed to meet soon, and that this teacher had some large project in mind that he expected Pizarro's aid in completing. The whole idea behind Pizarro's actions in the canyon, according to the four thugs, was that by exercising his powers over a whole village, Pizarro would strengthen himself for an even greater battle to come."

"In a perverse way," Carlos declared, "that makes some sense. I suppose we should be thankful that he was stripped of his powers before doing any more harm. But more important to me at the moment, I want to thank you for your offer of hospitality. Although I must get going tomorrow, rest assured that I'll stop to see you on my return trip."

Manuel did his best to persuade Carlos to stay longer, but without success.

The next morning the two friends parted. The rest of Don Carlos's trip was uneventful, and seen from the outside, his experiences during the four more weeks of hard riding it took to reach Mexico City doubtless looked mundane, even boring. Not that the three men Manuel had assigned to accompany him were boring. He shared with them the kind of male camaraderie that soldiers, seamen, and vaqueros enjoy when with each other. Every night around the campfire they would tell stories, some of them true, most of them tall tales, about women they'd loved, fights they'd fought, and adventures of all sorts.

For Don Carlos the underlying mood of the trip was one of high excitement about the brujo's powers he'd recaptured. He was also aware that in his battle with Mateo Pizarro, he had used those powers to benefit others and not himself, something, to the best of his memory, he had rarely done in his previous lives, caught up as he was then by self-centered pleasures and excitements. Carlos knew it was likely that once he reached the civilized environs of Mexico City, his consciousness of his brujo self would weaken, if not for all practical purposes disappear. But he had reconnected with that self in a powerful new way during his tussles with Inéz and his battle with Pizarro, and that renewed and even strengthened connection with his true inner nature was a hugely energizing experience.

The one shadow that lingered over his reflections was his puzzlement about Pizarro's apparent relationship with a powerful mentor. Of course, this was logical enough. Indeed, it was the only explanation for the fierce attack that Pizarro had been able to mount. The sorcerer had been, without a doubt, a more powerful opponent than all but one that Don Carlos could remember encountering in the past, that sole exception being Don Malvolio. Malvolio, therefore, was most likely the master sorcerer to whom Pizarro was beholden. What, Don Carlos wondered, was the larger project that Don Malvolio had been training Pizarro to pursue? Could it be that he, Carlos, was the target of Don Malvolio's plan?

Lacking any solid basis for answering this question, Don Carlos finally decided not to indulge in further speculation about the topic. He had always been one to avoid what he referred to as "forward worrying." What was the point? His preference, a preference that fit perfectly with his temperament, was to deal with whatever arose, whether positive or negative in nature, when it became a real and present pleasure or danger.

14

Mexico

Carlos and his companions arrived in the city long after dark had fallen. Everything looked so familiar that Carlos immediately felt at home. He took his three companions to a tavern that had been one of his favorite places for socializing with friends, and lo and behold several of his old acquaintances were there drinking wine before going home for dinner. They were delighted to have him back in the city, even if it was just a short visit, and an hour passed swiftly in good conversation. They had many interesting stories to exchange, Carlos about life on the northern frontier of New Spain, and his friends' reports on who'd married whom, the names of new fencers who were challenging the old champions, and who had won the most recent horse races. All his old friends expressed regret that he was no longer in Mexico City to share adventures and to participate in the equestrian drill team that performed for the public now and then and on which Carlos had been the star rider. Don Carlos observed how quickly his awareness of his brujo self faded away, superseded by a comfortable social identity: Don Alfonso Cabeza de Vaca, the well-to-do aristocrat.

He reached his mother's residence just as she and his stepfather were sitting down to a fashionably late dinner. They had eight guests, four couples Carlos had never met before. He found that the closet in his childhood bedroom still contained many suits of clothes that he hadn't been able to take to New Mexico. He chose a stylish outfit that he liked, dressed quickly, and joined his family and their guests. His stepfather greeted him with what struck Carlos as considerable reserve, his mother with great warmth. It worried him that she was pale and drawn, having lost weight since he'd last seen her barely more than a year ago.

Dinner passed amiably enough, with the usual upper-class gossip and chit-chat. Afterward, the men withdrew to the library and the ladies to the drawing room. Only a half hour later, Carlos's mother came to the entrance of the library and announced that she was tiring and needed to go to bed. Carlos, excusing himself by saying he'd had an exhausting trip, accompanied his mother to her bedroom. To his expressions of concern about her health and the fact that she tired so easily, she replied, "Don't worry about me, Alfonso. I've had many bouts with this swamp fever, during which I alternate between chills and fevers. These episodes sap my strength but they're bearable. Let's talk more in the morning."

Carlos slept later than he'd expected, though he had a restless night. For the first time since leaving Santa Fe he had a dream in which Camila appeared. It wasn't a happy dream. She was walking across Santa Fe's main square, arm in arm with Rafael, listening attentively to whatever he had to say and laughing frequently in response. When Don Carlos got up, he felt uneasy. This was just what he'd feared. While I'm away, he thought, Rafael will win Camila's heart. He made an effort, with only modest success, to convince himself that this was a dream born of his worries, not a reflection of reality. His uneasiness, however, contributed to his subsequent decision to seek the consolation of the company of other women in Mexico City.

On arriving downstairs, he found his mother had a guest who was about to leave. This turned out to be Señora Mariana Pérez. "You remember Señora Pérez, don't you?" his mother asked. He certainly did. Señora Pérez was the first woman with whom he'd made love. He had been barely sixteen at the time. His original goal had been to seduce Señora Pérez's daughter

Daniela, who was also sixteen, but Mariana (as he called her when they were alone) was one of those vigilant mothers who managed to preserve her daughter's virginity until she was married. Mariana was a young mother, eighteen years older than Carlos, which would have made her in her late thirties now. She looked every bit as handsome today as when she had offered herself as a substitute for her daughter in Carlos's quest for a mistress.

Mariana had given him a memorable introduction to the art of love. "For a first time in particular," she had said, "one should make the experience last a very long time." She instructed him to follow her lead and relax — well, mostly relax, except at moments when fervor was appropriate. With that, she took Carlos by the hand and led him to a heavy drape which she pulled aside to reveal a narrow door hidden behind it. With a key that had been hanging around her neck, she unlocked the door and ushered Carlos into a room that was warm and pleasantly humid. She locked the door behind them. "This," she told him, "is my private sanctuary. Admission is by invitation only."

Half of the small room where they stood was taken up by a pool of water. "Let's undress each other," Mariana had proposed. "Once we're in the water, I'll tell you more about this room."

Mariana had undressed Carlos first, a process she carried out with great skill. When it was his turn, his inexperience with undoing women's clothing caused her to giggle delightedly at his clumsiness. "You'll get much better at this with a little practice," she assured him.

When they were both naked, she had him join her in "my Roman bath," as she called it. While they sat in hot water up to the middle of their torsos — with Mariana's body, glistening with wetness, commanding Carlos's rapt attention — Mariana told him that the sunken bathtub they were occupying was a wedding gift. "A dear uncle," she said, "who admired my pursuit of sensual pleasure, had it made for me. The design is modeled after Roman baths my uncle had seen while traveling in southern Europe. The turquoise-colored titles that line the bath below water level were my idea because they made me think of sun-drenched shallows I once saw in the bays of Caribbean islands. The ceramic frieze above the water line, with its images of Roman couples kissing, embracing, and cavorting, will, my uncle and I hoped, inspire the pool's occupants to do likewise."

Under ordinary circumstances, which these definitely were not, Don Carlos might have asked Mariana to tell him about the pool's drainage system, which did not resemble any he'd ever seen, but Mariana picked up a bar of soap and, with a gleam in her eye, began to lather his chest. His interest in Roman plumbing vanished immediately. After a pleasant interval of luxurious caresses, she rinsed Carlos off and they climbed out of the tub, whereupon Mariana tenderly dried him with a soft towel and led him to her bedroom. Only then did they make love.

These memories flashed through Carlos's mind upon seeing his first mistress standing next to his mother, and he stepped forward to greet Mariana with a kiss on her proffered hand.

Mariana received the kiss with her usual cheery manner and told him, "I must run now, Alfonso, but I'd love it if you would drop by my mansion this afternoon and tell me about your adventures in the wild Northern provinces." They agreed on an hour.

His mother seemed delighted that Mariana had been so friendly with her son. "Mariana is one of my dearest friends," she said, "and I'm so glad you're going to visit her while you're here. I hope you'll do so often." From her statement he assumed that his mother had never heard the rumors that he and Mariana had been lovers. He beamed at her appreciatively, gave her a kiss on the cheek that brought color to her face, and headed off to the pantry to see if the maids had saved any pastries for him to eat. They had.

After this late breakfast, Carlos called on Agustina Vazquez and delivered Lucila Arculeta's letter to her. She was dressed in an expensive gown that Carlos believed must have been imported from Spain. Gazing around the room, he could see in its rich furnishings further evidence that Señor Vazquez was exceedingly successful in his business as a lawyer defending members of the elite involved in property disputes. "May I stay while you read the letter?" he asked.

"Of course," she replied, "I'm so happy to hear from my dearest friend" — not, he was sure, having the slightest idea of the letter's contents. However, it didn't take long for her to grasp the import of what Doña Arculeta had written. She grew very pale; her eyes filled with tears, and her hands shook almost uncontrollably. "Do you know this girl Camila Lobo?" she asked in a barely audible voice.

"Yes, she's a good friend."

"Do you know about the contents of this letter?"

"Yes, Doña Arculeta took me into her confidence and asked me, as a friend of Camila's, to deliver the letter to you and to answer any questions of yours that I can."

Distraught, Señora Vazquez said, "I'll certainly have questions eventually, but at this moment my mind is overwhelmed by a rush of emotions. Even if this information about Señorita Lobo's identity is true, and I don't deny that it might be, I can scarcely comprehend all the ramifications of this news. I'll need some time to decide what, if anything, to do. Can you return another day, possibly after I've sent a note to your residence?" It was so decided.

Carlos knew that by all rights he should go next to the orphanage where Camila had grown up and ask the mother superior and the older nuns whether they could provide Camila with information about her mother's identity. But his encounter with Mariana led him to head directly to her residence.

After a maid had shown Carlos to Mariana's drawing room, Mariana greeted him with the warmest of smiles. "My!" she exclaimed. "You're more handsome than ever."

They chatted amiably for a while, and then she said, "I assume you'd like to know how Daniela is. I'm well aware that she was your first choice for a lover, but I believe you weren't disappointed in me," to which he assented with genuine enthusiasm, though he remembered that Daniela, the daughter who'd escaped him, was nubile and physically mature for her age.

"Daniela is now married and more ravishing than ever. Knowing how desirable she is, her husband, an unattractive but very rich man, keeps her under close surveillance. She's never unwatched, except, and this should interest you, when she visits me. The old fool she's married to believes that I'll keep lovers away. But I've arranged several assignations. Let me get in touch with her and invite her to meet you here tomorrow to renew your friendship" — an offer she delivered with a merry wink.

"On another topic," she continued, "it may surprise you to know that not long after you left the city, I bought a fine harpsichord." She gestured to the instrument at one end of the room. "If you will excuse me for a moment, I will come back and give you a brief concert."

Mariana rose and started to leave the room. "Make yourself comfortable on the couch," she told him over her shoulder.

When Mariana returned, she was barefooted and wearing a silk dressing gown. The concert, as she'd called it, turned out to consist of a three-note song of seduction. With only a glance at him, she sat down at the harpsichord and played a single note, after which she let her dressing gown slip to the floor. She was naked.

She turned to face his direction and played a second note. She picked up a bottle from on top the harpsichord, poured oil into the palms of her hands, and rubbed the oil on her torso.

Mariana looked over at Carlos, smiled, played a third note, and stood up. She crossed from the harpsichord to the couch where Carlos was lying. As she did so, the sun came from behind a cloud and sunlight streamed through a roof window, bathing both Carlos and Mariana in a sensual golden glow. She broke the silence, saying, "You probably don't realize it, few men do, but when women get together, they sometimes share intimate details of their love lives. Only last week a young friend of mine told me that her husband, who is twice her age, likes to see her naked, but nothing ever comes of it because he can't...." Mariana beamed at Carlos with a sweet expression on her face. "I see," she said, "that your condition is quite the opposite of that old man's. Shall we commence?"

Later the thought came to Don Carlos that "sweet," the word that best described the way Mariana had smiled at him, also described her lovemaking: tender, languid, soft, gently sensual. Afterward, they lay in silence in each other's arms until she finally said, "Very nice," adding with a beatific smile, "as always."

"My pleasure too," he replied.

Upon leaving Mariana's, Carlos felt a pang of guilt for indulging his desires when he had serious tasks to pursue. He therefore headed without further delay for the orphanage where Camila had grown up. It was located on Via de Córdoba, a broad street in a nice district. The orphanage itself was a large building with a drab exterior. Inside the front hall, the overwhelming impression was of a pervasive grayness. Stations of the Cross were the only decorations that lined the corridor leading to the mother superior's office. A young nun went ahead and entered the office, returning soon with the news that Mother Veronica was at afternoon prayers and could not be disturbed. He should come back tomorrow at a later hour. Carlos asked whether the young sister could show him around. She agreed to do so. They went through many rooms. All he remembered later was face after face of little children who turned to him with sad eyes. Outside, he felt a wave of sympathy for Camila, who had once been one of those children who watched visitors with a mixture of hope and despair.

All his close relatives, at least the ones who weren't in convents, were at his mother's for dinner that night. This included his stepfather and his mother, who, from where he sat, looked very unwell. The general's two sons, both now married to daughters of rich aristocrats, had arrived just before him. Also present were his sister Fortunata and her husband, Emiliano Alaniz, back from Lima, Peru, to visit friends and family in Mexico City. Carlos's mother welcomed him with great warmth, and both Emil and Fortunata were clearly delighted to see him. By contrast, his stepfather and stepbrothers received him in a decidedly chilly way. It's going to be a long night, he thought to himself. Had it not been for Fortunata's cheery chatter about her son, Vicente — "My father's middle name," she explained — now six months old, the early part of the evening would have been quite dreary.

As dessert was served, his stepfather turned to him and said severely. "What is this I am hearing about you proposing marriage to a maid? What on earth were you thinking? Don't tell me that she's beautiful. I know that from when we saw Joaquin and Francesca off. But a maid! That's embarrassing. You may not realize it, but the expenses of setting your brothers (stepbrothers, Carlos thought to himself) up in appropriate houses, with servants and funds for entertainment, has greatly depleted your father's legacy to the family. If you want to have anything remotely resembling a life proper for persons of our class when you come of age and marry, you had better switch your affections to an upper-class woman whose father will provide her with a very large dowry."

Carlos didn't feel like arguing. In any case, one didn't argue with the general when he was on his high horse. Neither did he feel like conceding anything; instead, he said blandly, "Let's wait to see how things work out. The young woman in question has other suitors whom she may prefer to me."

He was not intimidated by his stepfather's angry "Bah! You are unworthy of your mother," but he was distressed to see how alarmed his mother was by his stepfather's anger.

Walking his mother to her room at bedtime, he tried to reassure her. "Please don't let your husband's outburst worry you, Mother. I have resources of my own that he doesn't know about. I'm not going to end up in the poorhouse. What does worry me is the state of your health, and please don't brush my concerns aside. It's not as though you didn't warn me about your declining health in the letter you sent me. That news is what prompted me to make the long journey here from Santa Fe now, rather than waiting until after my twenty-first birthday when I planned to return to Mexico City and claim my title and inheritance. After you've had a good night's sleep, we simply must have a frank talk. I love you too much to do otherwise."

As he left his mother's room, Carlos met Fortunata, who had come to the door and was about to enter. "I've come to see Mother before Emil and I leave. Alfonso, I heard and saw some things tonight that bothered me. Emil and I are staying with his parents. I hope you'll join us for dinner sometime soon. We can talk things over then."

Unfortunately, Carlos's proposed visit with his mother the following morning never happened. Before breakfast, Rosita, her personal maid of many years, informed Carlos that his mother had had a bad night and had only now, with the aid of sedatives, fallen asleep. Rosita added that his mother begged him to be patient and to come to her that afternoon after she had gotten some rest.

Not wanting to stick around the house, Don Carlos grabbed a quick breakfast and went to see to his old fencing master, Don Ignacio de Tortuga. Don Ignacio clapped his hands with glee and embraced Carlos. "It's wonderful that you've come to visit your old teacher. I've a few young fencers who think they're the best there is; perhaps you could show them otherwise."

Two of the aforementioned young men were there practicing. Don Carlos borrowed equipment and immediately engaged the two in bouts. He easily defeated both in round after round. Neither achieved even a single hit. Don Ignacio was delighted. "You're better than ever. How have you managed to stay so sharp?"

Part of the answer, Don Carlos realized, was that his time in the high desert had awakened his brujo's powers and enhanced skills that were useful to success in fencing, especially his capacity to anticipate an opponent's next move. Although he couldn't tell Don Ignacio that sorcery gave him an edge over competitors, he saw no reason not to give a frank answer to the part of the question that could be safely addressed. "A Basque woman, Inéz de Recalde, arrived in Santa Fe recently," he replied. "She's a formidable opponent who's forced me to reach a new level of skill."

Don Ignacio's face darkened. "Watch out for her. True, she's an excellent fencer. She turned up here before leaving for the north and defeated everyone in the place. Rumor had it that her first husband died suddenly under suspicious circumstances, and that the man she calls her father is a lover who's no blood relation whatsoever. She is, I'll admit, strikingly beautiful and not a bit shy. My suspicion is that once she sets out to seduce a man, the fellow doesn't stand a chance. As I said, watch out."

Don Carlos asked whether anyone else in the city was likely to know anything more about Inéz. "Now that I have a relationship of sorts with her," Carlos said, "I'm curious to learn whatever I can about her past." Don Ignacio couldn't provide more information offhand, but he promised to ask around.

Don Carlos avoided his family's residence for both lunch and dinner, leaving a note with the family's most faithful and venerable servant, a handsome, gray-haired Spaniard named Leon, that he would be taking today's meals with friends. However, he did manage to slip in to see his mother in the middle of the afternoon. She'd rested and claimed she was feeling better. He left her room feeling a little less anxious about her health than he had been earlier. Still, he sensed that her illness was more serious than she was willing to admit.

He had a pleasant day calling on old friends and late in the afternoon stopped to see if Fortunata and Emil were home. Luckily, they'd just returned from a round of visits. Once they'd settled in the drawing room, Fortunata handed Carlos little Vicente. "Time to become acquainted with your only nephew," she said with a smile that soon became a laugh when she saw that Carlos wasn't used to holding a baby. Fortunately, Vicente didn't fuss at Carlos's ineptitude and, in any case, a nursemaid soon came and took the baby away, rescuing Carlos from his duties as an uncle.

Fortunata immediately expressed her concerns. "I'm very worried about Mother," she said. "We made this trip home after receiving a letter from her, I suppose you got one too, saying that she wasn't feeling well, and I'm shocked to see how her health has declined. Emil has recommended that she seek help from another doctor, but that's all we can think to do.

"Then there's the way General Alvarez spoke to you last night. That was rude and offensive. I was speechless, and you know that's not my natural condition. From what he said about your inheritance, I received the impression that he's used a significant portion of it to set his two younger sons up in society. I'm wondering whether you have any legal recourse, since I know he had himself appointed as your guardian and it doesn't seem appropriate, legally or morally, for him to draw on your inheritance to the benefit of your stepbrothers."

Carlos, Fortunata, and Emil talked further about the inheritance problem without reaching any definite conclusions. Carlos told Emil and Fortunata that he certainly didn't want to initiate any legal action while their mother was alive, since having him engaged in a legal battle with her husband would be exceedingly upsetting to her. Also, and he asked them to keep this information to themselves, he assured them that he had other financial resources besides income from his father's estate. "I've kept them secret from him," he added, "out of concern that he would try to gain control over them. When I'm in his presence, I make no effort to show that I have some common sense about financial matters. To be sure, New Mexico is materially poor compared with this city, so much so that coins of any kind, whether reales or pesos, are very scarce. Most exchange is done by barter. Despite that fact, I've been able to squirrel away enough pesos and reales to fill a small chest."

Eventually the conversation drifted onto other topics, particularly how Emil and Fortunata liked their life in Peru. "Very well," Fortunata replied. "I've made many friends, and Emil's business is flourishing. He's also developed an obsession of sorts with the history and medical practices of the Native people of Peru, the Incas."

Emil disagreed with the description of himself as obsessed, although he acknowledged that Fortunata had used the word in an amiable way. "And it is true," he continued, "that I have taken a great interest in the history and medical practices of the Peruvians. In the course of those inquiries, I've made at least one discovery of which I'm particularly proud.

"When we first arrived in Peru," Emil continued, "I was shocked to learn that mine owners distribute a stimulant called coca to their workers to enable the laborers, who are close to being enslaved, to work longer hours and to endure the pain associated with their jobs. Leaves from the coca plant are given out to Peruvian workers three or four times a day. The Natives have an ancient practice of chewing coca leaves, so that's nothing new, and the fact that chewing coca leaves is a traditional custom is what finally reconciled me to the practice.

"I nevertheless became interested in the history of coca use among the Incas and learned that it was both a religious practice — inducing visions among priests who used coca — and a general social custom. All that's well known. Where I uncovered a little-known fact was through contact with descendants of an unusual man, Luis Valera, a Spaniard who took part in the conquest of the Incas, and Valera's wife, a Native woman named Francisca Pérez. One of their sons, Blas Valera, became a Jesuit priest, but the thing that fascinated me was that Father Valera used his knowledge of both Spanish and Native languages to investigate Incan history and culture. He uncovered many important facts and wrote about them, but the one that intrigued me in relation to my investigation of coca was that a powdered form of coca had been used medically. The ingestion of coca by chewing coca leaves to induce contentment and to enable workers to labor long hours at arduous jobs is well known. The medical use of coca in a powdered form is, as far as I can tell, unheard of among our Spanish compatriots."

"Then how did you learn about powdered coca and its medical uses?" Carlos asked.

"That's in some ways the best part of my story. I spent quite a bit of money trying to win the confidence of Native informants. I finally received information on a descendant of Luis Valera, a mestizo man who lives in a mountain village some sixty miles from Lima. This man told me about his distant relative's discovery of powdered coca and told me that it could be applied to wounds to stop bleeding, ease pain, and speed healing. I've tried it, and it works."

Although Carlos's mind was more focused on his own problems than Emil's account, he nevertheless managed to display enough interest to ask, "I assume you've brought some of this powder along to Mexico City to show to a few physicians here."

"Yes!" Emil replied, grinning broadly. "Let me show it to you." He left the room, returning shortly with a small box that contained a grayish-green powder. "Here it is!" Emil exclaimed. "Wet the tip of your finger, dip it into the powder, and put a tiny bit on your tongue." Carlos tried it and made a sour face. "Yes," Emil said, "it has a bitter taste, but I hope to interest colleagues in the city in its potential benefits when used on open sores and wounds."

His curiosity aroused by this odd substance and what Emil had told him about it, Carlos asked, "Is powdered coca obtained by drying the leaves and grinding them up? That seems so simple that I would think powdered coca would be well known."

"Apparently it's not so simple, though my informant was not very forthcoming about how it's made. All he would tell me was that he soaks coca leaves in a special solution—he wouldn't say what it was—repeating the process several times until the effect of the dried leaves is greatly enhanced."

Emil clearly wanted to say more, but the family's butler came to the door and announced that dinner was served. Other topics dominated the dinner-table conversation.

After dinner with Emil and Fortunata, Carlos returned to his mother's home late in the evening. Leon met him in the entryway and handed him four envelopes.

All the letters were from people who hoped to see him the next day. Don Ignacio wrote that to his surprise he'd found someone who could provide additional information about Dr. Loreto Tiburcio and his daughter Inéz de Recalde. Another note, this from Mother Veronica, expressed regret at not having been available when he'd come by; could he, she asked, possibly return at an earlier hour tomorrow? Señora Vazquez wrote that she was emotionally overwrought and hoped that meeting him would help calm her down. Finally, a note from Mariana reported that her daughter Daniela was going to be at her house at half past ten the following morning and was eager to see him. All four messages contained rich possibilities, but it was in his nature to look forward with the greatest anticipation to the proposed rendezvous with Daniela.

15

Proof

Don Carlos spent a restless night. He tossed and turned when his previous night's dream returned with a vengeance. Once again he saw Camila and Rafael walking past his house arm in arm. They seemed to be taunting him by displaying their mutual affection. Worse yet, he could hear the endearments they were whispering to each other: "Darling Camila!" "Dearest Rafael!" And worst of all, he couldn't move or speak. He tried shouting at them to stop tormenting him, but no sound came, and he couldn't move to intervene because he was tightly bound hand and foot to one of the pillars of his house's veranda.

Later, during a period when he was awake, he realized that he was mystified why he couldn't jump into this dream as he had with Inéz. What was the difference? Perhaps it was simply that in the city his brujo's powers were so diminished that he couldn't successfully apply the technique of "entering the dream." The whole business of his dream states, especially their content, left him confused and upset. Once again, he wasn't sure whether what he'd seen was a true dream, an accurate representation of reality, or only a fantasy, a nightmare that his dream consciousness had concocted out of his anxieties about his relationship with Camila. He was glad when dawn came and he could start the day. The very first thing he did was to look for Rosita. She told him his mother was resting, which he took as a good sign.

Don Ignacio was an early riser, so Carlos headed directly to the old fencing master's residence. A servant, one of Don Ignacio's students, let Carlos in and showed him to a small parlor where Don Ignacio was drinking coffee. He rose to greet Carlos and declared, "Purely by coincidence, very soon after you left yesterday my barber dropped by, and when I asked him if Dr. Tiburcio had been a customer of his, he said yes. He remembered that Tiburcio and a daughter named Inéz had lived at a small hotel on a narrow lane named Calle de las Pulgas. "It's a shabby place," Don Ignacio said, "with a blue banner hanging above the door. Just walk along Avenida de Salinas, turn right at Calle de las Pulgas, and the hotel is on your left in the middle of the block."

"That's very helpful information," Don Carlos replied. "Did he report any other details?"

"I asked him for more," Don Ignacio replied, "but he didn't know much. He said the doctor never shared any personal information and was, on the whole, close-mouthed about everything except news of the latest bullfight."

Don Carlos stayed to have breakfast with his old teacher. They chatted amicably about Don Ignacio's current students. "Unfortunately," the master reported, "none of them has either the skill or the potential that you displayed. That makes my life a little less interesting. You, at least, often surprised me with the innovative moves you achieved, especially when you had a worthy opponent challenging you."

When the two men parted, Don Ignacio urged Carlos to stop by his fencing rooms at least once more before leaving town.

Carlos knew he didn't have time to get to Calle de las Pulgas before his rendezvous with Daniela. Much as he was curious to learn more about Dr. Tiburcio and his daughter, that project would have to wait until tomorrow.

He felt a spring come into his step in happy anticipation of his visit with Daniela and the pleasurable time they might have together.

Mariana's house was just off a main avenue but sufficiently far from the crowded thoroughfare to be quiet. Daniela answered his knock at the door and ushered him inside, where she planted a kiss firmly on his mouth. (He observed to himself that the shy sixteen-year-old of four years ago had definitely shed her reserved manner.)

Daniela spoke with a lilting voice that made him think of small birds singing happily. "It's wonderful to see you again, Alfonso. I'm so glad you've come. Mother is off on a shopping trip with both of the maids, so we have the place to ourselves." Taking him by the hand, she said, "Let's wait to exchange news later and get started on our main purpose right away."

Daniela led him to the small room with the large Roman bath that he remembered vividly. Someone, perhaps Mariana and Daniela together, had made very thorough preparations. Steam rising from the hot water had dampened the walls. "Let's undress each other," she proposed cheerfully. (Like mother, like daughter, he thought.)

The undressing process went rapidly. Carlos couldn't resist saying, "I've gotten better at this, just as your mother predicted when she and I first used this room."

"Yes, I heard about that," she replied with a laugh. "Mother and I have no secrets from each other, at least not when it comes to our love lives."

Carlos and Daniela slipped into the water. She leaned back and closed her eyes with enjoyment. He kept his open. He was entranced and didn't make any effort to stop staring at her.

Daniela opened her deep brown eyes. "Everything look okay?" she asked, laughing again.

"Perfect in every respect," he replied.

She smiled. "I would like to try something a bit different. I would like you to make love to me in a standing position."

Carlos was surprised but more than willing to try, and said so. After luxuriating in silence in the bath until the water began to cool, they climbed out. When Carlos reached for a towel, Daniela stopped him. "Not yet," she said.

She stepped to the wall and stood with her back against it. He took her in his arms and she wrapped hers around him. Eventually, Daniela sighed deeply and they separated.

After they'd dried off, she said, "Gather up your clothes and bring them to my bedroom, an inner sanctum that I know you've long aspired to enter. It's right next door. We can lie on the bed and talk."

Once they'd settled down, Daniela asked Carlos, "Tell me about any women friends you have in Santa Fe, Alfonso. I enjoy hearing about other people's love affairs."

Carlos gave her a concise description of his relationships with Inéz, his seductive fencing partner, and Camila, the ladies' maid to whom he'd proposed. Daniela asked him to fill in a few more details and then spoke. "I don't understand you, Alfonso. This Inéz is inviting you to be her lover and yet you haven't taken advantage. What's the problem? If she's gorgeous and willing, why hold back? This doesn't sound like the eager lover of all willing women that you were reputed to be when you lived here."

Hoping not to go too deeply into the topic of Inéz, he gave a terse response. "Let's just say that Inéz is a possessive woman, extremely possessive. I feel she hopes to dominate me, in a way to own me, and I don't want that sort of mistress."

"That's a good reason to hold back," Daniela said in a reflective way. "My husband is exceedingly possessive and jealous. He has me closely watched all the time. I can't develop a liaison with anyone from the city because talk might get back to him. Mother has helped sometimes by recruiting a temporary partner from among visitors to the city. But that's about it."

"Does your husband make love to you?"

"Oh yes," she replied. "Antonio is a creature of habit who follows a rigid schedule, day and night, every day. On Thursday evenings he tells me to wait for him in my bedroom. He comes to me precisely at eight o'clock. I'm expected to lie on my back and not move or make a sound. I'm glad to say that these episodes do not take long. After I've done my 'duty,' as he calls it, he has his dinner and goes off to his separate bedroom."

"How wasteful he is of a splendid lover!" Don Carlos exclaimed. "What would happen if he ever caught you cheating on him?

"I know precisely what he'd do, because that happened once. He made me lie face down and naked on my bed while he gave me a severe whipping."

Carlos was scandalized. "The brute! Whipped you with what?"

"One of those rawhide whips with many strands that the penitents use. Believe me, it hurt like hell and left me bleeding from the marks it made. Mother treated me with healing ointments; I didn't dare let anyone else know. One scar still hasn't healed completely," and she rolled on her side to show him a red line eight inches long just under her shoulder blade.

"That's horrible. He should be prosecuted and jailed."

"I don't think the law will touch the master of the house, and the priests would sympathize with him. After all, I had committed adultery."

At this point, Daniela was lying on her side with her hand on Carlos's belly. Feeling an intense desire to embrace her again, he pulled Daniela on top of him.

When they were lying back again, Carlos spoke. "I don't know why her name came to mind yesterday, but I wonder whether you know what's become of Virginia Espejo."

"You mean Nicaela Espejo. She started using Nicaela, her middle name, after cruel remarks about her first name stung too deeply. You probably thought of her because she belongs to that period when you were trying to bed all of us, especially me, and she was the only girl who would accommodate you."

"Didn't she leave town to marry not long after she, as you put it, accommodated me?"

"Yes, and Nica's story is a sad one. She'd gotten pregnant, and her parents forced her to marry a man from Puebla whose status was well below hers. The parents died soon thereafter, and her husband—her married name's Azebes—moved her back to Mexico City and used her dowry and inheritance to buy a small hotel. It's in a run-down neighborhood on a narrow lane named Calle de las Pulgas." (From this description Carlos realized that Azebes's hotel and the hotel where Inéz had lived were doubtless one and the same.) "The stupid man gambled all their estate away, including the hotel, died an early death, and left her a widow with a small child. It's strange you should ask because I learned all this when I chanced to meet her downtown a few Sundays ago. She and her little girl were begging on the street. After I gave her all the money I had in my purse, she told me they have some income beyond what they get from begging because she works part-time as a maid at the hotel that used to belong to her husband. Imagine: from upper-class girl to a maid! What a terrible loss of status!"

The somber mood of the moment didn't last long. The lovers soon cheered up and got dressed to go their respective ways, parting with a warm kiss in the knowledge that Daniela probably couldn't arrange another rendezvous during the brief time that Carlos was in town.

Important tasks remained, and highest on Carlos's list was visiting

Mother Veronica at the orphanage. She met him in her office and greeted him with welcome news. "After receiving Camila's letter, I initially doubted that I could provide any information about her mother's identity. We don't refuse to give such information out, but because most foundlings are left anonymously, we rarely know who the mother is. Happily, Camila may be in luck. An older nun, Sister Caridad, who has lived here for more than thirty years, has for most of that time been our baker, a job that requires her to rise daily before dawn. The kitchen overlooks the street and the orphanage's front door. I asked her, and she said she remembers the morning that the basket holding Camila was placed on our doorstep. It was just getting light, and she happened to glance out the window, saw a woman approach the door, knock on it, and hurry away. Curious, Sister Caridad went to the door, where she found the basket, and in it a swaddled Camila. She looked down the street and saw the woman cross to the other side and enter the Hotel Monterrey, the big place on the corner. She also remembered that for the preceding week she'd seen an obviously pregnant woman, dressed in black and wearing a veil, coming and going from that hotel. The veiled woman was always accompanied by a second woman in a brown dress. Sister Caridad says it was the second woman who left Camila to us. Perhaps if you ask at the hotel, their guest register will give you some clue as to these women's identities."

Carlos thanked Mother Veronica profusely. To be sure, he already knew Camila's mother's name, but being able to tell Camila a story about locating a hotel register would explain how he tracked her mother down without bringing Lucila Arculeta's name into his account.

His inquiries at the hotel were successful. The hotel's manager, Angel Carpineta, turned out to be a pack rat. He had saved the guest registry books back to the dates Carlos wanted. There on the pages for December 1 to 16, 1686, was the name he was seeking: Agustina Terradas. Although she had not used her true family name, which had been Sotomayor, she had used her correct first name. The dates and her use of "Agustina" were adequate proof, and if he'd needed more, there was the matter of her handwriting.

On the chance that he might learn even more, Carlos asked Señor Carpineta whether he remembered an obviously pregnant woman, veiled and probably dressed in black, who had stayed at the hotel on those dates and who left after giving birth.

"Yes," the manager replied. "One doesn't forget such an incident." The veiled woman was accompanied by another woman—a midwife, he now surmised. The birth, he said, had taken place upstairs; other occupants of the hotel had complained the next day of moans in the night, and the sheets, of course, were ruined. By the time the maid discovered the state of the sheets the women were gone, but they had paid for two week's lodging and had only stayed for one, so the sheets and even the mattress could be replaced. He was certain that these women had registered as Agustina Terradas and companion.

As Carlos knocked on the door to Agustina Vazquez's residence, he was encouraged by the thought that everything was falling into place nicely. Señora Vazquez met him at the door and showed him to a small parlor. She checked to see that no one was about, and though no one else seemed to be at home, she closed the door quietly and spoke in a voice that was hardly more than a whisper. She immediately addressed the business at hand. "I've written a letter," she told Carlos, "for you to deliver to my daughter. I regret that it probably won't be entirely satisfactory to her, but it's the best I can do at this time. Let me read it to you for your opinion.

Dearest Camila, your very clever friend has somehow managed to track me down. I'm glad to hear that you're all right, but please accept my deepest regrets for abandoning you to an orphanage. That was, far beyond any other, the saddest day of my life. As I gave the basket with you in it to the midwife to take to the orphanage, you gazed up at me with the most endearing look. It was heart-breaking.

I hope you will forgive me for what I did once you hear about my circumstances. I was an unmarried girl from a very conservative Catholic family and engaged to a man who was, if anything, more rigidly conservative than my parents. In the year I was to be married, I foolishly, yes, stupidly, gave in to an infatuation with a blue-eyed Basque (yes, your blue eyes come from him) and became pregnant. I was terrified. If even the slightest rumor of my affair and my pregnancy came to my family's attention, my father — who'd made his views plain on the topic of girls who got 'into trouble,' as the phrase goes — would have disowned me and thrown me out of his house without anything more than the clothes on my back. Needless to add, my fiancé would have done likewise. Under those circumstances, as a girl only eighteen years old, I saw no option except to give you up.

I can tell you with all the pain that comes to a mother's heart that not a day has passed since your birth without my experiencing deep regret for losing you. Even now, I've asked your friend Don Alfonso not to reveal my name to you. I wish things could be otherwise, but my husband has become even more fixed in his conservative ways than he was when we married, and if the fact of your existence were to come to his attention, I have no doubt that he would denounce me publicly and cut me off totally. I hope you wouldn't want that to happen, even if, as would be quite reasonable, you hate me for what I did.

With tears, your mother.

Señora Vazquez gave Carlos the letter, saying, "Please leave. I need to cry alone."

Carlos did not leave until he told her his sense of the situation. "I believe Camila will understand your predicament, then and now. I'm also sure she does not hate you. She has an eminently practical approach to life and will be grateful to you for writing as you have."

Señora Vazquez tried to smile but didn't succeed, breaking instead into sobs. She waved him out the door. Carlos observed that although he had now accomplished one of his goals in coming to Mexico City, finding Camila's mother, his second purpose, visiting his mother, couldn't be considered complete as long as her health remained so uncertain. He would have to stay in town for a while longer.

Carlos dined at a hotel with old friends, lingering over dessert and wine as he'd typically done in former days. He felt a few pangs of nostalgia for days past when the topic of the year's horse race around Plaza Mayor came up. How he wished he and Eagle could have been there to compete with the other young men and their mounts! One of his companions reported that Concepción Marcaida, a beautiful young woman in their circle he had tried unsuccessfully to seduce, had recently married an elderly widower chosen by her parents to be her husband. The friend who related this news added, in disgust, "What a waste! She has a fantastic figure and a lively personality and now she's consigned to a living death with an old man who's probably too decrepit to enjoy fully the fruits of his rare acquisition—all because her parents coveted the man's titled status."

Carlos thought immediately of Daniela and wondered whether Concepción's elderly spouse would be as vigilant as Daniela's husband in seeking to prevent his wife from having extra-marital liaisons. Without naming names, he gave a general account of Daniela's situation and mentioned to his friend that Concepción might appreciate visits, the precise purpose to remain open-ended and dependent on the signals she conveyed about her attitude toward consolation outside of marriage. "Move ahead slowly, exercising patience," Carlos counseled. "You know the old saying: 'All things come to him who waits.' What she might say now and what she'll say after a year or more of total boredom could be two quite different things." This advice elicited a round of ribald remarks from his friends on the subject of Carlos's expertise in such matters.

After he and his friends parted he walked home, arriving there quite late. The house was quiet. Everyone except Rosita had gone to bed. He found her napping on a chair in the hallway outside his mother's bedroom and asked after his mother. Rosita told him that his mother's condition had not improved, though she'd slept through most of the day and was now asleep again. Rosita also reported that his mother hoped he would look in on her the following morning. Carlos had every intention of doing so, and remained very concerned about his mother's health. Nevertheless, as he lay down to sleep, the images that entered his mind were memories of Daniela's glorious body and a fantasy of a rendezvous with Concepción, who was holding her arms out to him in anticipation of a passionate embrace.

16

Endings

Some days are just plain bad days, out-and-out bad.

Don Carlos's bad day started before he'd even gotten up. His recurrent nightmare about Camila and Rafael returned in a variation that was the worst yet. In this version Camila and Rafael were seated on the couch in Joaquin and Francie's Santa Fe house. They were embracing and kissing passionately. Unable to make himself heard or to get their attention by any other means, a very frustrated Carlos heaved himself into the air and off his bed, landed on the floor with a bone-crushing thud, and woke up. He was sweating profusely and shaking all over as though he had a deep chill. Dawn was breaking, so he changed to his daytime clothes.

Carlos left his room soon thereafter and walked down the hall. As he passed his mother's bedroom, Rosita came out looking very worried. "Your mother's not at all well this morning, worse than ever before."

Alarmed, Carlos knocked softly and, receiving no response, went in. His mother did look bad. She was flushed, apparently in the grip of a high fever. Nevertheless, she gave him a wan smile and said, "Good morning, dear son."

"Mother!" he exclaimed. "I'm very worried about you."

"That's sweet of you," she replied in a very soft voice, speaking slowly, "You were always a dear child, especially when you were little. I remember the Kissy Bird game you invented for us to play together. The part where I caught and hugged the precious little bird was so sweet. Please don't worry. This fever comes and goes, and when it goes, it turns into chills, which are worse than the fever. Rosita just gave me something to help me sleep, and the doctor is supposed to come by later this morning."

Almost immediately his mother fell asleep. He supposed this was the best one could hope for, although her color was bad, a touch of jaundice, he feared. He couldn't shake the feeling that she was worse off than anyone admitted. Had his sorcerer's vision been active, which it wasn't in the city environment, he would have seen a shadowy black figure hovering over his mother's left shoulder, death waiting to claim her. As it was, he consoled himself with the thought that Rosita was, as always, doing her best. Rest would certainly be more beneficial than a doctor's visit. After sitting by his mother's bedside, holding her hand, he slipped out to begin his business for the day.

Carlos's stepfather was waiting for him at the bottom of the stairs. I wonder how long he's been lurking there, Carlos thought to himself with considerable malice.

"I want to see you in my office," the general said, making no effort to soften the demand—it was a demand rather than a request—with a perfunctory "please." The general came to his point immediately. "I'm very disappointed in you. I found you an excellent post, and you spent your time romancing a house servant." (Camila had been demoted, Carlos noted, from ladies' maid to house servant.) "You waste your money buying a house, when you ought to be saving it by living at the Presidio barracks where you'd receive free room and board, something I could easily have arranged.

Earlier you gave your most expensive possession, a fine stallion, away. While here the past week, you've frittered away your time, visiting lady friends as though you didn't have a care in the world.

"Your mother has always protected you, and that's probably the root of the problem. You're soft. A mother's boy. And sad though it is, it ought to be obvious that she's too sick to protect you any longer. I've therefore come to a decision." (The hammer falls, Carlos said to himself.) "It's less than a half year until you come of age and have the title of marquis that's yours by inheritance. You'll also inherit some money, although very little due to the bills I've had to pay on the family's behalf. I believe that if you don't become more financially responsible immediately, you will impoverish yourself and sink drastically in status. For that reason, I've decided to cut off your allowance in hopes of forcing you to mature." (That, Carlos thought cynically, will also leave you more money to spend on your two younger sons.)

With an air of finality that indicated their interview was over, the general handed Carlos an envelope and said, "This contains a three-month installment of your allowance, which should be more than enough, assuming you have any wisdom about money, to tide you over until you are back on the job in Santa Fe. Good day now. I have more important things to do."

Carlos didn't say a word in response. He felt a momentary surge of anger at his stepfather, but pushed that aside as unfruitful. Instead, he concentrated on the secret pleasure he took in knowing that his stepfather was unaware of the large sum in silver bullion he had been promised by Manuel Tapia. He was also glad that he'd already decided to leave the city as soon as possible. His only hesitation now was occasioned by his mother's bad health. He didn't want to leave until her health improved.

The first and only business on his schedule was to visit the hotel where Dr. Tiburcio and his daughter Inéz, if she was truly his daughter, had lived while in the city. He had no trouble finding the place, and he was confident that he would find Nicaela Azebes there too. The ambiance of the dingy street and the still more dingy face of the building did nothing to lift his depression.

He asked at the front desk for Nicaela Azebes, having to remind himself not to refer to her as Virginia Espejo, as she had been when he knew her.

He didn't have to wait long for her to appear, followed by a little girl in a dirty dress. The desk clerk immediately made himself scarce. Nica didn't recognize him until he introduced himself as an old acquaintance, Alfonso Cabeza de Vaca. The crudity of her response embarrassed and shamed him. "Oh yes," she said, curling her lip. "I always wondered. Did you manage to stick it into other girls, or just me?"

"I have other business in mind today," Carlos replied with dignity.

Ignoring the various meanings his statement could have had, Nica focused on a single word in his answer. "Yes, I'm sure you're here on business." Turning to her daughter she said, "Run off to the kitchen, Suzanne, until this man leaves." The girl gave him a knowing look, displaying a disturbing degree of worldly knowledge for a child her age, and ran off. Turning back to him, Nica said, with a hard face—everything about her was hard now, and she looked ten years older than Carlos rather than only two—"it's not free any more. If you want to get laid, I get paid."

To Carlos's mind, this was a thoroughly unappetizing prospect, but he decided to play along to see what she charged. She mentioned a figure which he suspected was higher than usual for the type of clients she probably attracted. He handed her the sum she'd requested and said, "That's out of regret for any harm I did you in the past. But I'm not here to 'get laid,' as you assume. I'm looking for information about two former residents of this hotel, and if you can provide information that's useful to me, I'll show my gratitude by giving you yet more money."

Her eyes narrowed with suspicion. "Who are these former residents?"

"Do you happen to remember Dr. Loreto Tiburcio and his daughter Inéz de Recalde?"

"Sure, they stayed here the better part of a year, very high and mighty they were, the doctor, in particular."

"Was Dr. Tiburcio engaged in any sort of medical practice?"

"Not obviously," she replied, "although he was often out and told us that if anyone asked, he was at his office. He never shared his office's address with us, so a lot of good it did to tell us he was at his office unless the person asking knew the address already."

"Any impressions about what sort of doctor he was?" Carlos asked.

"Some sort of herbalist, I think. He had a lot of jars full of herbs—I can't tell you what they were—on his dresser. I saw them when I made his bed," she added hastily, as though to fend off any suspicion that she'd entered the room without the doctor's permission.

"Any other details about the doctor and Inéz come to your attention?

"I think they're some sort of religious fanatics."

"Religious fanatics? How so?" Carlos was genuinely surprised.

"My room's in the very back of the building. The doctor's was next to mine and Inéz's one door down the corridor from his. I could hear anything noisy that happened in his room and hers too."

"And?"

"I'm getting to that, Alfonso. Don't be so pushy. What made me think they were religious fanatics was that sometimes I could hear, clear as I can hear you, Inéz beating the doctor with a whip."

This was most interesting, though what it meant Carlos wasn't sure. "How do you know it was Inéz beating the doctor rather than him whipping her?" he asked.

"I know it for sure. Every time I heard such noises, the next day I found that the sheets on the doctor's bed were bloody."

"But perhaps he beat Inéz while she was lying on his bed," Carlos suggested, pressing the point.

"No, I'm sure that wasn't the case. One day after I'd changed the bloody sheets in the doctor's room, I went into Inéz's room to change hers. Apparently, she didn't hear my knock because when I entered, she was standing there stark naked toweling herself off after a bath. There were no marks on her back. And if you don't know, she has a beautiful body. Seeing her like that, it was the only time I've felt a sexual attraction for another woman, I mean, understood why some women take other women as lovers. And she's a smart one; she picked up on what I was thinking. Right away she said, 'Do you want to make my bed while I'm here?' It came out sounding as though she'd said, 'Do you want to make me in my bed?' I was so embarrassed that I gave myself a black eye by running into the door jamb in my rush to get out of there. She thought it was pretty funny. I could hear a fit of laughter coming from her room as I hurried off."

Don Carlos asked Nica a few more questions, without learning anything more of a substantial sort. He was grateful for the information she'd given him, and he also felt sorry for her, with the result that he gave her a significant sum of money. She received it eagerly. "Are you sure you don't want to get laid?" she asked. That only made him feel more depressed. The whole scene at the hotel was depressing: Nica herself, the knowing look on her little daughter's face, the front-desk clerk scurrying off to get out of the way of an illegal business transaction, and the run-down quality of the establishment.

In hopes of cheering himself up, Don Carlos stopped by Mariana's house. Her maid came to the door with a message that she couldn't see him today.

He went over to Don Ignacio de Tortuga's fencing salon. The fencing master was out, and the servant who answered the door claimed he had no idea precisely when Don Ignacio would return, though it would likely be late in the evening because Don Ignacio had gone out to dinner with an old friend from Madrid.

For want of anything else to do, Don Carlos went to his favorite tavern and found a couple of old friends with whom to drink wine. Somehow the topic of their education came up. One of them, like many young men of their class, had had Jesuit tutors. "I particularly liked Father Stefano," the fellow volunteered. "I was totally thick-headed about my studies, unlike you, his star pupil, but he was always patient and kind—a generous man. When I asked him why he bothered to tutor rich boys like us, he explained that although his first love was a life of prayer, he felt it was his Christian obligation to do something more than seek personal spiritual fulfillment."

"Do you know if Father Stefano is still alive?" Carlos asked. "Even two years ago he seemed in frail health." As far as Carlos's friend knew Father Stefano was still alive, although he'd heard that their former tutor no longer came to the city to meet with students. His few remaining pupils all rode out to study with him at his residence, the Jesuit Seminary at Tepotzotlán.

Carlos's worries about his mother's health led him to return to her residence later that afternoon. He was puzzled when he saw a number of carriages drawn up in front of the house. He decided to go in the back door. Leon was there trying to comfort Rosita. Leon turned to Carlos and said, "Your mother took a turn for the worse today; you'd better hurry upstairs if you want to see her before she dies."

Carlos knew where to go—he'd grown up in this house—but his legs were unsteady and seemingly unable to get him there. When he finally reached her bedroom door, he saw his stepfather, a doctor, a priest, and Fortunata hovering around his mother. He went to the bed and took her hand in his. She opened her eyes, brightened, and spoke in a faint voice. "Dear Alfonso, I'm sorry I'm leaving you. I want you to know that the day you did a somersault in my womb was nearly the happiest day of my life. I adored you. Of all the things I'll miss from earth when, God willing, I get to heaven, I'll miss you most. And don't," she said with a feeble smile, "be in a hurry to join me there." With this, she closed her eyes.

"Can't you see that you're exhausting her?" his stepfather barked. His mother was scarcely breathing.

The priest stepped forward and looked at the bedside group. "I fear it's time for the rite of Extreme Unction. Please join me in prayer." With that, he began anointing Carlos's mother and saying the solemn words. By the time he finished, she had passed on.

Carlos's stepfather went to the bedroom door and motioned to Carlos to follow him. In no mood to yield to the tyrant in his stepfather, Carlos stayed where he was, holding his mother's still-warm hand in his. He remembered so many happy moments with her; now she'd no longer be lying in wait to catch the Kissy Bird.

Fortunata stayed also, holding their mother's other hand. After they'd sat in silence for a while, Carlos spoke to his sister. "I'm sorry Mother's final words made so much of how she loved me. I know it used to make you and Valentina jealous when she showed such an excess of affection for me."

"Thank you for saying so," Fortunata replied. "Yes, we were the perfect little spiteful sisters, though even then I understood things well enough to see that she was desperate to have a boy child to satisfy our father's anxieties about who would inherit his title. I've come to terms with that in recent years, especially since I married Emil and had a baby of my own. Also, not long before you came in today, Mother said the most tender and loving things to me, and I'll treasure those words forever. Don't worry about our relationship. She loved me; she loved you; we loved her, and I love you too." Shortly after this exchange, which Carlos found very comforting, he slipped out of his mother's room and headed downstairs. His stepfather was waiting for him in the first-floor hallway.

Predictably, his stepfather was furious at Carlos for defying his demand that Carlos leave his mother's side immediately. "That's it," he spat. "You are no longer welcome in my house. Collect your things from your room and leave. Stay away from the wake and funeral."

"I can't guarantee that I'll do that. Having thrown me out of my mother's house" — Carlos put special emphasis on 'my mother's house' to make the point that it had been hers before it was the general's — "you have no control whatsoever over what I do next."

"Get out!" the general shouted, his face red.

Burning his bridges without regret, Carlos lashed out, "To hell with you. I'll see you at the lawyer's offices when I'm twenty-one," and he turned on his heel and stomped off.

In the end, his old fencing master came to his rescue and invited him to stay at his place until he left town. Don Ignacio urged him to fence. "Activity is the best antidote to depression," he advised, "and you have every right to be depressed." Carlos didn't feel much like fencing, but he agreed that it was better to do something than to slump in a chair and think dark thoughts. Several of Don Ignacio's better students were delighted to fence with a man who was so highly regarded as a swordsman. Unfortunately for them, he took out his anger at his stepfather on his opponents, fencing aggressively and giving no quarter. Although he could see that they were capable fencers, they barely managed to score a hit on him in twenty exchanges apiece.

The day of the Requiem Mass for his mother Carlos waited until everyone was in the cathedral and the Mass had started before slipping into a pew at the very back of the church. All the women he loved were there—notably Mariana Pérez and her daughter Daniela—accompanied by their husbands, of course. He made no effort to speak with them or Fortunata either, although Emil managed to turn around and catch his eye before he hurried out as the Mass was ending. Assuming that Emil would protect his wish for anonymity by not mentioning to anyone except Fortunata that he'd seen Carlos, there would surely be gossip about his apparent absence, which his stepfather would try to put in the worst possible light. But Carlos was in no mood for explanations. Those could be made later, if ever. Right now he simply wanted to get back to Don Ignacio's to pack and leave town. This city isn't my home any more, he said to himself. That phase of my life is ending.

17

Zoila

Upon returning to Don Ignacio's fencing parlors after his mother's funeral, Don Carlos packed his few belongings, thanked the fencing master for having given him a place to sleep (not to speak of many other favors over the years), and stepped outdoors onto the street. His plan was to head directly to the stable to collect the horse he intended to use for the first part of his trip northward. But he was stopped by someone calling his name, and when Carlos turned to see who it was, he was immediately enveloped in a bear hug. "Alfonso, what great good fortune to run into you!" the giant who'd embraced him said. "Where are you going?"

"Out of town," Carlos replied. The giant was Sebastian Reyes, perhaps his dearest friend from two years earlier. Sebastian was six years older than Carlos, and as best friends they had engaged in an informal competition to see which of them could seduce at least one of the most desirable unmarried upper-class girls in their circle. Neither succeeded.

"You were looking rather glum just now," Sebastian said. "What's the matter?"

"I've just come from my mother's funeral and am in a rush to leave Mexico City."

"That's terrible news, Alfonso. I'm so sorry to hear about your mother. She was such a nice person. Please accept my sincere condolences, but since you're leaving town anyway, I hope you'll come with me and two lovely ladies who are waiting in the carriage across the street."

Carlos mistook this for an invitation to join Sebastian in seducing the young women in question, as they so often had attempted to do in the past. He was in no mood for amorous adventures on the day of his mother's funeral. "Thank you, but it's time for me to start on my trip home."

"And where's home now?" Sebastian asked.

"Santa Fe in New Mexico province."

"That's at least a two-month-long trip, and if you leave now, I may never see you again. I insist that you come with me to Puebla, where I'm going to be married three days from now. The three of us have come all the way from Lima, Peru, where we live, so that my fiancée and her sister can meet my parents." Sebastian grabbed Carlos firmly by the arm and steered him toward a waiting carriage. "Surely you won't refuse to come to my wedding? Sebastian married at last! When you meet the girl, you'll understand why."

Sebastian's enthusiasm was irresistible. Having crossed the street, Carlos and Sebastian climbed into the carriage. Seated across from him were two lovely young women — young, though perhaps closer to Sebastian's age than Carlos's. Sebastian launched into introductions: "The beautiful woman on the right is my almond-eyed fiancée, Belén. The other beauty is Belén's cinnamon-skinned sister, Zoila. And this, my lovely ladies, is one of my dearest friends, Alfonso Cabeza de Vaca."

"The masterful seducer of young women?" Belén said with a wicked grin.

"Sebastian!" Carlos protested. "What exaggerated tales have you been telling about me?"

"Sebastian always made you sound very nice," Zoila offered appeasingly. "Besides, we wouldn't criticize you for loving pretty girls. In any case, surely you can see that the three of us are exuding happiness from every pore. That's because in three days Sebastian and Belén will marry and Belén and I will celebrate our twenty-sixth birthdays."

"You're sisters?" Don Carlos's doubts were clear from his tone of voice. They couldn't be twins, not even fraternal twins. Belén was slender with brown hair and ivory skin and, as Sebastian had said, almond-colored eyes. Zoila was taller and more voluptuous and had naturally curly black hair, dark brown eyes, and, as described, cinnamon skin. "Oh! I understand," Carlos exclaimed, the light dawning. "You have the same father but different mothers."

"He's smart as well as handsome," Belén said. "We're so glad you're coming with us to Puebla. That'll add greatly to our pleasure. To pass the time on the road we can tell you how we two sisters by different mothers came to be born on the same day. We won't force the story on you, if you're not interested. But if you are, which of us would you like to hear from first?"

"I'm most interested," Carlos said truthfully. "As to the sequence of the story-telling, you're both so pretty, I can't choose. Why not go in alphabetical order, Belén first?"

"Your suggested order indicates a naturally diplomatic nature, and in any case, for reasons that you'll soon understand, it's probably the best starting point."

Zoila chimed in. "Warning: the story's long and complicated."

"I'm not worried," Belén stated. "We'll dazzle Alfonso with many fascinating details. Our father's name was Enrique Orrente. From early boyhood onward, he was, as you'll see, a remarkable man. He was born in Santiago de Compostela, the famous pilgrimage site in Galicia, the northwesternmost province in Spain. Enrique—let's call him that most of the time—worked for his father, who ran an inn that catered to pilgrims. In the course of assisting pilgrims, Enrique, who from his youth onward sought to learn everything he could, became familiar with many languages and diverse ideas. His first love was art, and he spent at least a few hours every day sketching scenes in the town's main square, depicting people as well as buildings. He sold these sketches to pilgrims who wanted mementos of their journey. One such customer turned out to be a young physician from Madrid. This doctor was so impressed with Enrique's drawings that he urged him to come to Madrid, promising to introduce Enrique, who was only eighteen, to the great artists who resided in the capital city.

"Now Enrique, our father, always grasped the main chance, so off he went. His doctor-patron did very well by him. He found a position for Enrique in the household of Juan Bautista del Mazo, one of the greatest Spanish artists of that century, who happened to be the son-in-law of a greater artist yet: Diego Velázquez. Since Mazo did much of his own work in Velázquez's studio, our father, Enrique, had a chance to learn from two great masters. Velázquez died in 1660, slightly less than two years after Enrique came into his circle. But the son-in-law's mentoring of our father lasted another seven years, until Mazo died in 1667.

"As of 1667, Enrique was twenty-seven. By then he was a respected assistant to better-known artists, but his income from his own art remained meager. Enrique was, by nature, a practical idealist. Even during the ten years he worked in the studios of these great masters, he found time to study medicine. By 1667, he was well trained as both an artist and a physician, though he rarely practiced medicine. He was also feeling restless. He spent the next five years traveling in Europe—to France and to the great artistic locales of Italy. He returned from these travels in 1672 and went to see his father and mother in Santiago de Compostela."

Zoila interrupted her sister: "You are taking too long, Belén, monopolizing the conversation. We're about to stop for lunch. When do I get to tell my half of the story?"

"Your turn's about to come, dear sister," Belén replied, "right after I introduce Alfonso to the heart of the story, the moment when our father, Enrique, met my mother, Teresa Cabete."

The stop for lunch interrupted Belén's story. During lunch, and for several hours thereafter, Don Carlos's three friends from Peru fell into a lively discussion of practical matters about Belén and Sebastian's wedding and their future life together. Should Belén wear the jewels her mother had given her, or would that be flaunting her family's wealth too ostentatiously? How would Sebastian's parents, Bartolome and Florencia Reyes, react to the fact that she, Belén, loved wine and could consume a great deal without appearing drunk? Was her wedding gown too low cut in front—a question she'd apparently been fussing about all the way from Lima, at least to judge from the groans and helpless gestures Sebastian and Zoila made in response. Finally, Zoila intervened. "This has gone on long enough. Get back to your story, so I can tell mine."

Belén laughed and began again. "This is the story of Enrique and Teresa's courtship and marriage. In the spring of 1673, our father was still visiting his parents when a party of four pilgrims—my mother and three of her brothers—completed their pilgrimage on the Camino de Santiago and took rooms at the inn run by Enrique's father. I should add that Teresa and her brothers were natives of Goa, descendents of Portuguese merchants who had settled there more than a century earlier. Teresa's father, Joaquim Cabete, had amassed a huge fortune through his ownership of ships that carried goods from Goa to Portugal and many points between.

"If our parents are to be believed, and it's also possible that this is a fable they concocted to amuse their daughters, when Enrique laid eyes on Teresa, it was love at first sight for him. The same wasn't true for her. When Enrique, totally infatuated, proposed to her after knowing her for only two weeks, she brushed his proposal aside, asserting that it was nothing more than a device to seduce her. After he protested vehemently, Teresa told him that she wouldn't take him seriously unless he came to Goa to court her in that distant outpost of Portuguese commercial expansion. She didn't think there was a ghost of a chance that he'd accept her challenge, but a little more than a year later he knocked on her door in Goa."

Zoila stamped her foot in mock anger. "You've had your turn," she complained. "Now it's time for me to take over." She did so without waiting for Belén to agree. "Our parents, Enrique and Teresa, did not marry until Enrique had lived in Goa and traveled throughout neighboring cities and kingdoms for two full years. During his travels, he became fascinated by the erotic element in temple art, art in which lovers were entwined in a wide variety of postures. He became obsessed with learning precisely how many varieties were depicted. He sketched each of the types he found, and by 1677, he had drawings of twenty-seven different postures."

It was Carlos's turn to interrupt. "Twenty-seven! That's a very large number, and you're saying these representations are viewable in public places?"

"Absolutely," Zoila replied with a laugh. "Actually, the most important classical sources on the subject describe many more traditional postures, and our father could have saved himself a lot of trouble had he had the nerve to show his sketches to knowledgeable locals. But he refrained from doing so out of fear that his prospective in-laws, the Cabetes, and their good Catholic friends would be scandalized by a man who had what would have seemed to them such prurient interests. Worse yet, her parents might reject him as a suitor of their daughter.

"Finally, Enrique met a young Vedic scholar named Avadhuth Shama, who introduced him to the most senior Vedic scholar in Goa, Krishnades Bhatia. Bhatia laughed in a kindly way at Enrique's apparent embarrassment about his project. Bhatia told our father about ancient Hindu writings, such as the *Kama Sutra*, that teach how the sexual union of a man and a woman can be a means toward union with—well, with the creative force you Catholics call God."

Carlos was somewhat embarrassed by the direction their female companions were taking the discussion, a direction that would have been rare among Spanish Catholics of their class in social settings where both men and women were present, but he couldn't think of what to say.

"I like to call the book in question the *Cama Sutra*," interjected Sebastian, "the sutra of lovemaking in bed. Belén and I have..."

Belén gave her fiancé a withering look and cut him off before he could say more. "That play on words wasn't very funny the first time you used it. By now, it's just annoying, and I'll thank you to maintain some discretion where our love life is concerned."

Sebastian looked suitably contrite, but protested, "You never chided me for talking freely about the two of us with Zoila."

"She's my sister, and I don't have secrets from her. Alfonso might safely hear your revelations, but I worry that you'll burst out with something along those lines when we're with your parents and family. That could be embarrassing. Please show some discretion."

Carlos plunged in, quite clumsily, he later realized. "Sexual relations as a spiritual path is a new concept to me. Frankly, I'm finding the idea hard to accept."

Zoila took up the gauntlet. "I suppose you believe the principal reasons for sexual union are procreation and sensual pleasure."

"Yes, I suppose I do," Carlos replied. Sensing from the look on Zoila's face that this answer didn't come up to her standards, he added, "Of course, sexual union between two people who are deeply in love would not be simply about sensual pleasure. It might also strengthen their love for each other."

"You have the beginnings of a good answer," Zoila replied. "You also have a lot to learn. A moment ago I heard the driver call out that he's turning into the driveway of the inn where we're staying tonight. Perhaps we can pursue your education in spiritual matters tonight after dinner. I'll finish the rest of my story tomorrow after we're on the road again."

By the time dinner ended, it was nearly eleven o'clock. Belén and Sebastian claimed a need to get some sleep in anticipation of the day to come. Zoila and Carlos lingered only a little longer before heading down the corridor to their rooms. At her door Zoila put her hand lightly on Carlos's arm and said, "Tonight I'll talk you through a bare-bones version of the first step in this practice about which you've expressed great skepticism. Once everything's completely quiet, I'll come to your room. By way of preparation, you'll want to be barefoot and in loose clothing. No tight collars or belts."

Zoila slipped inside her bedroom and closed the door. Carlos made his way to his room, his imagination fired by the prospect of making love with this intriguing woman. A taste in his mouth, a unique combination of sweet and sour in his saliva, something he'd experienced before in similar situations, was a welcome sign. Inside his room he followed Zoila's instructions and took off his belt and removed his shoes.

An hour passed before Zoila entered his room. She was wearing an exquisite blouse. It was, she told him later, made of fine Chinese silk, and had been given her by Belén's grandparents as a farewell gift when she and her sister left Goa. Like him, she was barefoot. Instead of a skirt, she was wearing loose pants that matched her top. She was carrying a pillow that appeared to be very firm.

"Let the lessons begin," she said with a beguiling smile. "I hope you'll realize that our discussion of what its practitioners call Tantric meditation will be very sketchy. Our time together is short, and there's no way I can be remotely fair to a tradition that stretches back perhaps two thousand years and about which tens of thousands of pages of scripture have been written. Also, you need to be aware that what I'll teach you is only one of many existing approaches to Tantric practice. I follow the one taught me by my grandfather. The key to everything he taught is an emphasis on simplicity.

"In accordance with his school of thought, my instructions will be as simple as possible. First, sit on this cushion. It will lift your pelvis off the floor and make it easier for you to proceed to the second step, assuming the classic yogic meditative pose. Watch me, and follow me step by step as I assume the correct posture. Straighten your back without tensing. Cross your legs, placing your left foot on your right thigh and your right foot on your other thigh. Many beginners find it difficult to tuck themselves into this pose, which is called the Full Lotus, but I see that you're quite limber; just don't stay in it until you get stuck and need help to extract yourself." (Carlos wasn't worried. From as far back as he could remember, he had been blessed with a flexible body, and he didn't expect to experience any difficulty holding the Full Lotus.) "Finally, put your hands thusly" — she put the tips of her thumbs and ring fingers together — "and rest them on the upper part of your thighs."

Zoila continued. "Now to the purpose of tonight's meditation. According to Tantric theory, shared by many other schools of Hindu and Buddhist practice, all humans have centers of energy in their spines. These are called chakras. In some schools one is taught to visualize the chakras as light-filled medallions or as lotus blossoms. Like my grandfather, I prefer something simpler. Focus your attention on the base of your spine, where the first chakra is located. Your assignment tonight is to attune yourself to the energy of the first chakra, and once you've found it, proceed upward to find the other chakras. I'll come by shortly after dawn to hear what you've found: how many chakras there are and where they're located. Good luck, and don't hesitate to take a nap, if you become fatigued." With that, Zoila exited quietly.

For an hour or more Carlos could not escape the deep disappointment he'd felt when it was clear that Zoila had no intention of spending the night making love with him. But, it being his nature to find something positive in even the most negative situations, he eventually settled down to his assigned task. Having had long experience and great success with the brujo's technique of Watching, he soon worked his way into an intensely quiet state. What had often accompanied this state in his practice was a pulsing sensation that he felt throughout his body. On such occasions, it seemed to him that he could feel his blood coursing out to his farthest extremities and then returning back toward his heart. The experience, though exhilarating, also brought a deep sense of calm.

Once he'd reached a state of deep calm, he focused his attention on the first chakra. Immediately, he felt the pulse as though it originated from the base of his spine and soon perceived this pulsing energy rise to his sacrum. Over the next two hours, he identified five more energy centers: just below his diaphragm, in the heart area, in the vertebrae of his neck, at a point in the very center of his forehead, and at the crown of his skull. Reaching this final chakra, if that's what it was, he experienced a profound interior and exterior silence. It was as though he had stepped from a very quiet room into another room where the silence was deeper yet.

Zoila came back shortly before dawn. As she had suggested he might wish to do, he was taking a nap. She woke him with a gentle shake. She spoke to him in a kind, sympathetic voice. "I know you weren't happy with me for leaving without being intimate with you. Simply bear in mind that the unique thing I can share with you is not sensual pleasure, which any willing woman could do, but the Tantric approach to sexual union as a spiritual path."

Having gotten over his initial disappointment, Carlos saw no point in discussing his earlier state of mind, so he told her that he'd found seven chakras and described where he believed they were located. Zoila seemed extremely pleased. "The first step of Tantric practice is attuning to physical sensations. You've done splendidly in correctly identifying the seven classical chakras. A powerful creative energy, which the yogis call kundalini, Sanskrit for snake, resides at the base of the spine. What you experienced as you moved upward from chakra to chakra was, metaphorically, the snake uncoiling and rising. Since you did well at this exercise, we can move on to a second level tomorrow night. Right now, we need to show up for breakfast and get on the road again."

Once on the road, Zoila resumed her narrative of what happened after her father was introduced to the eminent Vedic scholar Krishnades Bhatia.

"Enrique found Krishnades Bhatia wise and generous. Bhatia described the many Vedic scriptures that dealt with love-making. Since my father was half-convinced already, it wasn't difficult for Krishnades to persuade Enrique that European understandings of relations between men and women were much inferior to those conveyed through the ancient Vedic scriptures. With this, Enrique had found his life's work, a project that combined his deep commitment to art with the sort of search for spiritual fulfillment that he'd observed among many pilgrims to Santiago de Compostela. He set out to draw, in color, pictures of all the postures described in the *Kama Sutra*. He also became interested in the meditative path that some Hindu yogis follow called the Tantric way."

"It would be a huge sidetrack if you tell us everything you know about that topic," Belén objected.

"I agree. The story of how Zoila and I came into the world in 1679 can be completed quite concisely. Enrique spent so much time at the residence of Krishnades Bhatia that he was accepted as a friend. The Bhatias had ten children, eight daughters and two sons, and because Krishnades Bhatia's small estate was insufficient to provide dowries for eight daughters, he despaired of finding suitable husbands for all of them.

"Particularly large obstacles existed in the case of his youngest daughter, Sushmita, whose left arm had been crushed in a childhood accident and who was left with a badly deformed limb. Who would want to marry a crippled girl? Believing Sushmita had no chance of marrying, her father chose a radical course of action and made her his student of Vedic scripture, with particular emphasis on what was known of ancient practices of Tantric meditation. She, seeing that Enrique was eager to learn more about Tantric theory, suggested that she help Enrique with his studies. Although this was highly unconventional, Krishnades Bhatia was not governed by conventional ideas and agreed to his daughter's proposal. One thing led to another, and Sushmita and Enrique became lovers. Under the circumstances it wouldn't be correct to call the erotic element of their relationship forbidden love, because spiritual seeking rather than simple sensual desire was always their primary goal. Nevertheless, as can happen, Sushmita became pregnant. She died giving birth to me." This statement brought tears to Zoila's eyes, and it took her a few minutes to recover her composure before she resumed her narrative.

"At the time that Enrique began his Tantric studies with Sushmita, he was already engaged to Teresa Cabete and had begun a sexual relationship with her. Teresa was, in her own way, a rebel because she believed the bonds of love between a man and a woman were more important than the rules of Catholic doctrine. She also became pregnant, and her baby, Belén, was born the same day as me. Shortly after that, Enrique and Teresa married, and because my grandparents, the Bhatias, were getting old and lacked the resources to raise another child, Enrique and Teresa took me into their family as Belén's sister.

"When our father died two years ago, Belén and I moved to Lima, Peru, to live next door to one of Belén's brothers who had a wife and a family there. Belén's mother chose to stay in Goa to take care of her aging parents, Joaquim and Carmen Cabete. You know the rest, or at least the key parts of it. Sebastian, who had recently begun a diplomatic assignment in Lima, met Belén, fell in love, and now they're to be married."

Carlos had a question for Zoila, having noticed that she wore a wedding ring. "It appears as though somewhere in this story you married."

"Yes," Zoila replied, "my husband, Claudio Herrera, is the captain of a merchant ship and is often gone from Lima for a year or more at a time. Claudio was born in Barcelona, Spain's largest port on the Mediterranean. His father was a sea captain, and on his father's last voyage, Claudio, then barely twenty years old, went along as second mate on a Portuguese merchant vessel that stopped in Goa to pick up cargo. I was twenty also, and when we met, romantic sparks flew. However, his father's ship left only a week later, and I thought that Claudio and I would never see each other again. The next year he showed up at Lima, the captain of his own ship. Still infatuated with each other, we married then and there. I've seen him only four times since, but I assure you that the fire's not gone out."

As this seemed a natural place to change the topic, Sebastian did so by saying, "Let's go over our plans one more time. Tonight we'll reach the summer home my parents own eight miles outside of Puebla. My parents and brothers and their wives and children will be there to meet us and spend the rest of the afternoon and the evening eating, drinking, and getting to know each other. The next morning we'll all take carriages into Puebla, where my beloved and I will be married. After the Mass we'll celebrate well into the night with dancing and more eating and drinking. I'm sure it will be a memorable day and a half for all concerned, especially for Belén and me."

Belén interrupted Sebastian to complain that it was all very well and good for him to believe everything was going to be fine, but if his family didn't like her, the whole occasion would be a disaster. Having heard these laments before, Sebastian and Zoila rolled their eyes and insisted that she had nothing to worry about.

Events proved their soothing assurances true. All of the Reyes family received Belén with warmth and a spirit of delight in Sebastian's good fortune to be marrying such a lovely, intelligent, and vivacious woman. The Reyes parents and sons, who'd known Carlos in Mexico City, made it plain that they were pleased to see him also, and they expressed their deepest sympathy for his recent loss of his mother. Animated conversations, unhurried consumption of several types of wine, and a six-course meal kept everyone up far into the evening. It was midnight before Carlos and Zoila headed to their rooms.

Don Carlos didn't have to wait long for Zoila to come to him. She wasted no time on chit-chat, settling down immediately to give him his instructions. "Sit as you did last night," she said, "when you successfully explored the physical aspect of the chakras, their number and their location. Tonight your task is to explore the mental and emotional energies associated with each chakra. Simply return to a meditative state and examine them one at a time. I'll come by for your report shortly before sunrise."

Using his brujo's technique of Watching, Don Carlos quickly achieved a meditative state. To his surprise, much of what followed was unpleasant. He spent little time on the first chakra, considering it mainly a starting point, not too significant in its own right. When he turned his attention to the second chakra, the one he associated with his sacrum, he met with image after image of women with whom he'd made love. There was Mariana, seated unclothed at her harpsichord, and when that image faded, it was immediately replaced by Daniela's gorgeous body across from him in her Roman bath. Instead of prompting pleasant memories, these sights produced a state of dissatisfaction. He now considered Mariana and Daniela to be lost loves because he was cutting his ties with Mexico City and might never see them again. An overwhelming sense of sadness at what he was losing left him feeling profoundly depressed.

He was glad to shift his attention to his third chakra just below his diaphragm, but that also produced unhappy thoughts. The images that came most strongly to mind were those of family members with whom he'd had conflicts: his sisters tormenting him as a little boy, family dinners at which his stepfather spoke scathingly of his views and behavior, and other episodes of his stepfather's hostility to him.

The fourth or heart chakra brought no relief. He had hoped that it would bring memories of his loving relationship with his mother. Instead, he was overwhelmed by feelings of grief. No more hugs for the Kissy Bird. No more soft murmurings of approval for his past, present, and future achievements.

The dominant feeling that arose as he explored the throat chakra was frustration at not being able to voice his feelings in the dreams he'd had about Camila and Rafael. Regardless of whether those dreams were true or mere imaginings, his inability to reaffirm his love to Camila only added to his anxieties about his relationship with her.

Finally, in reaching the sixth chakra, he achieved some calm after an inner voice spoke the words, "All phenomena are as they are. There is no 'ought' in the world of truth."

The mental and emotional aspects of the crown chakra were, he decided, beyond words. Even though he found it difficult to stay fully aware of the pulsing sensation that arose in the top of his head, he felt a deep calm. He was sure he had much more to learn about this state.

Zoila listened intently to his report, especially to his complaint that he'd thought chakra meditation would produce altogether positive mind states, whereas from the second through the fifth chakras his primary emotion had been misery.

"You aren't spiritually pure enough to attain an exalted state of equanimity, at least not for very long," Zoila told him. "When wine ferments it throws off all sorts of gas and internal debris in the process of becoming clear and delicious. During your life, right to the present, you have accumulated a large number of hungry ghosts who've come to plague you. Take heart. You have begun the process of expelling them, although you and everyone else who's human can never get entirely rid of those emotions and memories. If we had time, you and I could begin to work on techniques for dealing with such unwelcome visitations. I'm confident you'll find the way yourself if you persist in this practice.

"As for the thoughts and emotions you attributed to each chakra, what you described resembles how they are portrayed in classical Vedic literature — an excellent accomplishment for an initial exploration. A purist would say that your descriptions are off the target on many details and rudimentary when compared with traditional literature on the topic. Bear in mind, however, that I'm a follower of my grandfather's bare-bones style of chakra study, and I share his belief that a deeply felt personal understanding of the chakras is often vastly superior, and certainly not inferior, to classical formulations on the topic."

She looked at Carlos questioningly. "What training have you had that's enabled you to make such swift progress in chakra study? Obviously, you have some appropriate background."

Don Carlos wondered how much to reveal. He decided the best place to start was by telling her about his practice of Watching. "I discovered what I call Watching when I was a little boy, and I've done it ever since. Whenever my family visited a rural place, I would find a pond to sit by at night and wait for wild animals to come to drink. I discovered that they wouldn't come unless I sat absolutely still. Once a deer walked right up to me and sniffed my ear.

"In the course of doing my Watching game, I first experienced the body pulsing phenomenon that I told you about. Paying close attention to the pulsations in my extremities was a great aid to concentration.

"The only instructions I ever received that might be considered philosophical in nature came from an old man named Don Serafino. He told me that most people spend their lives in states of disappointment and suffering because they have no self-discipline and simply react to events out of fear or greed. When they finally acquire something they desire or manage to avoid something of which they were afraid, the relief is always temporary because another object of desire or fear arises immediately. According to Don Serafino, the only escape from perpetual dissatisfaction is freeing oneself from reactivity."

Zoila was unusually alert during Don Carlos's description of Don Serafino's teachings. "Had this man Don Serafino ever visited the East and studied with masters there?"

"I doubt it," Don Carlos replied, genuinely not sure. "But I have no basis for knowing because he seldom spoke about his life before we met."

"His advice was very good," Zoila observed. "I could add to what he told you, but we have to stop talking because we need to get dressed for the wedding."

Belén and Sebastian's wedding day was glorious. Family members left the Reyes summer home early in the morning, the men departing twenty minutes before the ladies, whose arrival at the cathedral would mark the ceremony's beginning. The bride was beautiful; her gown splendid; the groom handsome; the Nuptial Mass properly solemn, with the prominence of the Reyes family in Puebla life abundantly evident from the fact that the bishop of Puebla celebrated the Mass and the church was packed with stylishly outfitted members of the city's elite. A reception, a lavish luncheon, and a dance followed to everyone's great satisfaction. Don Carlos danced with many attractive women, none of them, to his eye, as beautiful as Zoila. The only dark cloud over the affair from Carlos's viewpoint was that he'd overheard Belén and Sebastian urging Zoila to stay longer and her replying that she had to leave first thing the next day. Carlos very much did not want his lessons with her to end. Finally, the festivities wound down and the newlyweds headed off to some secret location where they would spend their wedding night.

Zoila and Carlos returned to their rooms at the Reyes residence. The hallway to their rooms was deserted. The day had been very warm, and when Zoila opened the door to her bedroom, she found that the maids, swamped with other things to do, had neglected to close the bedroom blinds to keep the midday sun out. "Check your room," she whispered to Carlos. "Is it as hot as mine?" He found that it was and went to open the windows. Zoila told him not to do so. "Let's use this to our advantage. As the old adage goes, a crisis can be an opportunity." She went into her room and returned with a long towel of light linen. "For your final lesson I suggest you emulate the way a Hindu mystic would dress. Take off all your clothes and wrap this cloth around your waist and legs, knotting it just below your belly button. Don't look so alarmed; Hindu men, especially spiritual seekers like my grandfather, all wear skirts. Once you're dressed properly, sit as I've taught you, and settle into a state of concentration. Don't start on the chakra meditation until I come to be with you."

Don Carlos followed Zoila's instructions, feeling strange about putting on a skirt, though he had to admit that the combination of the skirt with a bare chest seemed suitable for the hot room. He waited quietly for Zoila to return.

18

Parting

Don Carlos's mood was buoyant as he waited for Zoila to arrive to give him his third lesson in Tantric practice. The only shadow on his happiness was his awareness that Zoila planned to leave the next morning. He dissipated that shadow by advising himself to stay with the moment, and nothing in the moment was other than positive. He was, he realized, happier than he'd been for a long time.

Using his technique of Watching, he took only a few minutes to locate the pulsing sensation throughout his body and to reach a highly concentrated state. He heard the sound of Zoila entering his room, but he did not allow the sound to trigger a reaction of any sort, either expectations or images. The result was like watching the surface of an absolutely calm pond. The sound of Zoila's entrance produced a tiny bubble on the pond's surface, but his attention to watching and not reacting kept the bubble from growing and bursting into a thought or picture in his mind.

Zoila came around in front of him wearing the same outfit she'd always worn to these sessions: a silk blouse and loose trousers of the same material. Standing in front of him and looking him up and down, she said, "I see you're ready." He took her meaning to be simply that he had dressed as she suggested and had assumed a proper yogic posture. Later she told him that she meant energetically ready, a reference to the faint halo of golden light around his whole body that signified to her that he was prepared to take the next step in Tantric study.

Zoila slipped her blouse off and dropped her trousers softly to the floor. Carlos's eyes dilated and warmth flooded his body.

Sensing his reaction, Zoila put the tips of her fingers on his forehead and said, "Don't be greedy. Remember what your teacher Don Serafino told you. Today we're after spiritual fulfillment, not erotic pleasure. Stick with our chakra practice." After a bit of a struggle, Carlos regained a quiet mental state despite the fact that he remained physically aroused.

Zoila next bent forward and unknotted the makeshift skirt around his waist, dropping it aside. In a single lithe movement she settled down on him and they were joined. The erotic impact brought Carlos's concentration close to collapse. She murmured in his ear, "Stick with our chakra practice. You may put your arms around me at my waist. Once we're both in a state of deep awareness, I will guide you through the chakras by pressing the fingers of my left hand on your back, stopping at the location of each chakra. We won't pause long at the second chakra because yours is already energetically overactive."

With these words, the session commenced. Already in a quiet space, he soon dropped into the even quieter abode of deep silence. True to her word, Zoila did not leave her fingers on his second chakra for long. Still, it was long enough for him to revisit some of the scenes with Mariana and Daniela that had seemed stressful the previous day. However, tonight both of these women who had accepted his sexual attentions smiled at him in an uncomplicated, friendly way that he experienced as completely benign.

Upon revisiting the third chakra, the family events—his sisters' jealousy, his stepfather's hostility—that had presented themselves as disturbing the previous day now surfaced in a totally different light. These memories were still not pleasant, but he was aware that all his relatives' negative behavior was rooted in their being dominated by fear and greed. He ceased to feel anger toward them and, instead, grieved for them in their suffering.

Zoila moved her fingers to touch his fourth chakra. Feelings of love for his mother swept through his consciousness. He recalled that he had chosen to be born to her to give her the male baby she desperately needed, and felt again the great joy that had led him to turn a somersault in her womb.

As Zoila touched his neck at the throat chakra, he once again saw the scene of Camila and Rafael arm in arm that had caused him so much distress in his dreams. Today, however, he knew he could speak to them and knew also that if they were present to hear his words, he would tell them that if they'd come to love each other, then theirs was a sacred bond with which he would in no way interfere. Perhaps, he thought, it was the great tenderness with which Zoila had been touching him that softened his heart to his relatives and to Camila and Rafael. He opened his eyes ever so slightly and noticed that an aura of golden light surrounded Zoila's whole body. He closed his eyes.

Little happened when his kundalini energy rose to what he'd come to think of as the wisdom chakra in the middle of his forehead. Little, that is, except a release of the last few bits of images and thoughts from his past after an internal voice had said, "Everything is as it is."

The full meaning of the last and greatest chakra, the crown chakra, still eluded him, although he was aware, as his consciousness focused on the top of his head, that he seemed to be breathing, ever so lightly and slowly, through the crown chakra area. His inhalations seemed to draw energy from a vast space above his head, and his exhalations seemed to push into the same vast space. For the second time, he opened his eyes. Zoila's golden aura and his had merged into a single golden sphere of light. The two had become one.

When Don Carlos's heightened state of awareness eventually began to fade, he heard himself saying in a barely audible voice, "Zoila, I'm losing it."

"Perhaps it's time to end the lesson," she said, and in the sweetest, most gentle way, she lifted herself off him and sat back.

Don Carlos pulled the pillow out from under himself and leaned back on his elbows. "I'm sorry," he said to Zoila.

Zoila laughed a light, lovely laugh and said, "There's nothing to feel sorry for. You were magnificent. According to Tantric adepts, many men can't achieve such a degree of composure and concentration, even after ten years of practice." She reached for her clothes.

"Please, not yet," he said. "I want to look at you a little longer. It will help me remember you as you are now, a memory I know I'll treasure." She relented from dressing.

He had been forming something in his mind and now expressed it. "The golden aura that surrounded you as we embraced made me think of the way saints are portrayed in art. And if a Jesuit teacher of mine who'd studied Hindu religion in hopes of being a missionary in the East is to be believed, the Hindus have many gods, not one. The way I saw you when our session reached the crown chakra leads me to believe I've held a goddess in my arms."

Zoila laughed, but his statement didn't seem to displease her. "If that's so, Don Alfonso Cabeza de Vaca, what does that make you? Your body aura was every bit as bright as mine, and indeed, ours joined completely, precisely the spiritual state Tantric adepts seek."

"I suppose," Carlos replied, "I'm reluctant to claim either sainthood or divinity for myself, knowing that I still have, as you pointed out, a great many impurities to purge."

"All right, if that's how you want it, but what we've seen today is clear evidence that the Divine resides in you. Alfonso, listen to me with your sixth chakra!" This was said with great seriousness. "I believe in my grandfather Bhatia's teaching that all of us are gods. You and I today embodied Shiva and Shakti, divine lovers whose transcendent love sustains the universe. Please believe in this truth, which you've just seen demonstrated, indeed, participated in fully. The difference between us and most people is that you and I are aware of our divine nature. As my grandfather always said, 'Everyone has divine nature; few realize it.'

"Now we really must end this session, Alfonso. I hear sounds that the household is getting up, and if I don't leave your room immediately — after I put my clothes on, of course — the Reyes family will be scandalized at the apparent fact that their new daughter-in-law's sister, a married woman, is sleeping around."

"Do you really have to leave today?" Carlos managed to ask as she reached the door.

"Yes, and I'm leaving right after breakfast. I'm in a great hurry to get to Veracruz."

"I might as well leave too," Carlos replied. "Perhaps we can share the road for a while, at least until the fork where the right branch goes to Veracruz and left takes me to Mexico City."

"Oh, what a good idea!" Zoila exclaimed. "Let's settle the details at breakfast."

The morning was sunny and, at least for the moment, less humid and hot. All the Reyes family and their guests were in high spirits. Zoila and Carlos shared a table with a pleasant couple, the Souzas, who were former neighbors in Goa of Belén's grandparents. A few years ago they had moved to Lisbon, Portugal. An amazing coincidence during their voyage from Portugal to Mexico was that their ship stopped in Havana, Cuba for provisions at the same time that a ship whose captain happened to be Zoila's husband, Claudio Herrera, was also in port. During a conversation on the docks, Claudio asked the Souzas why they were traveling to Mexico. Claudio was exited to learn from them that Zoila was in Mexico, and in a city not far from Veracruz, where he expected to arrive in a few weeks. He asked the Souzas to carry a message from him urging Zoila to meet him at Veracruz.

With a little assistance from Sebastian's father, Carlos and Zoila were able to travel together upon leaving Puebla a few hours later. Señor Reyes provided a carriage and driver to take Zoila to Veracruz, where he owned a warehouse. Carlos would ride in the carriage with her to the turnoff for Veracruz. Bernardo, a stable hand in Señor Reyes's employ, would ride behind the carriage leading an extra horse intended for Carlos to ride. When Zoila and Carlos parted, Carlos would continue to Mexico City to pick up his own mount there. The stable hand would accompany him and then bring the Reyes horse back to Puebla.

Every member of the Reyes family stood on the front veranda of the house to see Don Carlos and Zoila off. Zoila embraced Belén and Sebastian tenderly, her eyes bright but without tears, knowing that once she finished her travels with her husband and the newlyweds made it back to Peru, they would live next door to each other in Lima.

The carriage had scarcely left the Reyes residence behind when Zoila launched a series of questions at Don Carlos. "Tell me about the women who have the strongest claims on your inner life. I am not asking about the two women, Mariana and Daniela, you told me about yesterday, whom you seek out for casual erotic pleasure. Surely, you're more serious about one or two other women."

"Yes," Don Carlos replied. "There are two. One, whose name is Camila, is my age, a foundling, an illegitimate child raised in an orphanage. I met her because she is my sister-in-law's personal maid. Camila is beautiful physically, an attribute to which I'm not indifferent, but it was her high-spirited manner that drew me to her. We started out fencing verbally; gradually we spoke more openly from our hearts. She declared that she believed she would never marry. I, too, had vague feelings that I would never marry. That freed us to become friends and confidantes, and to develop an affectionate relationship not unlike that between a brother and sister. But when the son of the province's governor proposed to Camila, I was alarmed that I would lose her as my best friend. In a panic, I also proposed to her. She told Rafael and me that she couldn't answer either of us while she still had some hope of finding out who her mother was. The three of us agreed to a waiting period of nine months, now nearly down to five, before she would give us her answer. Part of the reason for my trip to Mexico City was to try to locate her mother.

"The other woman, Inéz, is another story altogether. Six months ago she moved to Santa Fe with her father, a physician. We were told that she's a young widow, and although I don't know her precise age, she's probably three or four years older than I am. From our very first meeting she's been aggressively provocative. She challenged me to try to match her skills as a fencer. I am an excellent swordsman—Sebastian probably told you that— and I bested her, but not easily. I was impressed with her skills and yes, I was not immune to her erotic appeal, so I agreed to meet her weekly at her house for fencing matches. It seemed clear to me that she wished to seduce me, and only my wariness enabled me to resist, although we did share one highly charged erotic embrace that left me weak in the knees. You may wonder why I am resisting a beautiful woman who's offering to be my mistress. The clues are rather subtle, but I believe she wants to possess me, to dominate me. She has a darker side. I admit she fascinates me, even so."

Zoila had been listening intently. "I asked about your love interests because those who pursue the Tantric path benefit greatly from having a partner who's a soul mate. From what you say, neither of these women is ideal. Camila might be a suitable partner in most respects, but you don't know enough about her to say whether she'd find this an appealing spiritual path. In any case, I sense that you don't really want to marry her and only proposed, as you readily admit, out of fear of losing her friendship.

"Inéz sounds like a better choice as your partner in pursuing the Tantric way of knowing. But what bothers me in your description of her is that she's too urgent about her sexual needs. The most skillful Tantric yogis have a large measure of self-restraint. An individual without self-restraint might be tempted to pursue what we call the impure path, or Vamachara, whose adherents indulge in sexual debauchery. The path that my grandfather taught, and to which I adhere, emphasizes self-discipline in the pursuit of union with the Divine."

"I confess," Carlos said, "until now, I never thought of devoting my life to a spiritual journey. I'm not even sure what I mean when I use the word spiritual, although last night's experience with you opened me to some significant possibilities. At the very least, I see that I'm going to have to reconsider everything about my life if I choose that way, and I hasten to add that as of now, I definitely want to learn more. But how? What about you, Zoila? Does Claudio share your commitment to the Tantric way?"

"No, far from it," she replied. "Although he understands that I need to follow the practices I learned from my grandfather, he's too much of a worldly adventurer and practical man to have any interest in mysticism. I love him nonetheless, and I know he treasures his relationship with me. What's important to me is that Claudio has never tried to obstruct my path, and I have shown him the same respect. That's not so common in this world, Alfonso, a man and a woman who support each other's growth, even if that takes them in quite different directions."

"What about your meditative practice?" Don Carlos asked, thinking about the intimacy of their time together the previous night.

"I know what you're asking, Alfonso," Zoila replied without hesitation. "A spiritual quest, an authentic one at any rate, can be a lonely path to undertake. I haven't meditated with anyone as I did with you last night since my marriage to Claudio, and not because of our marriage. I've simply not found anyone in the Americas, except now you, who can work with me the way you did last night. Hearing what you've told me about Camila and Inéz, I'm not confident that you're any better off. However, it's perfectly possible for you to continue doing chakra practice, even if you don't have a meditation partner. I hope you'll persevere."

"Somehow we'll have to keep in touch," Don Carlos ventured.

"That's a nice thought; however, the practical fact is that Lima, Peru is a very long way from Santa Fe, New Mexico. Are you planning any very long trips?" Zoila asked with a smile.

"Perhaps there's another way," Don Carlos ventured to say. "Perhaps we can come together in dreams."

Zoila was amused. "After last night I'll probably have dreams about you, although Claudio is going to monopolize my nights for the next two or three months. And I'll be very disappointed in you, if you don't dream about me after all the time we spent together these past few days."

"I have something else in mind. Let me explain. Inéz pursued me in my dreams on the way south from Santa Fe to Mexico City. At first, I thought the dream was coming entirely from me and was the result of that intense erotic embrace we once shared. However, when the dream repeated night after night, I decided that she was somehow projecting herself into my dreams. I did something that I'd heard about but never attempted, which was to enter the dream. It was as though there was a thin membrane between Inéz and me, and I forced my way through it, and grappled with her physically, could smell her perfume, and could hear her voice."

"You have a very active imagination," Zoila observed, her skepticism plain.

"Maybe that's all there is to it, but I don't think so, and after last night you can't deny that I can draw on some strong energetic forces. I think we should try it."

"Wait a minute," Zoila exclaimed, "what you're talking about is s...."

Don Carlos put his finger on her lips. "Let's avoid that word."

A mischievous look came over Zoila's face, and she leaned forward suddenly as though to pick up something on the floor. Covering her mouth with her hand and whispering as if to share a secret with someone, she said, "The word is sorcery." She then sat up and added, "I'm not offended by that, and I'm not frightened by it either. If it's true that you're a sorcerer, it would explain a lot—especially how quickly you learned to raise kundalini energy. Is Don Serafino, that old teacher of yours, a sorcerer?"

"Yes, Don Serafino is a sorcerer. We prefer the word brujo; yet it's undeniable that we use sorcery in our practice and treat the words sorcerer and brujo as interchangeable. I hesitated about calling what I'd done sorcery because for so many people sorcery is associated with black magic that's pursued in order to do harm to others or to have power over them. Associating sorcery with the black arts is not inaccurate; the vast majority of men and women who practice sorcery belong to a loose alliance Don Serafino always referred to as the Moon Moiety. Brujos of Don Serafino's type, which are very few in number, are aligned with the Sun Moiety of sorcerers, men and women pledged to honor the motto 'Do no harm.'"

"Have you successfully lived up to this motto?" Zoila asked. "Please don't be offended. I'm simply curious. You seem from what Sebastian told us very much given over to the pleasures of life. I hadn't detected any serious intentions in you until we began to study the chakras together."

"I regret to say," Carlos admitted, "that I've never consciously sought to do good deeds. You're quite accurate when you suggest that I've been a highly self-centered man, enjoying the pleasures of life, which I suppose you could summarize in the usual way as wine, women, and song. If I've managed to honor the Sun Moiety's goals, it's only in not intending to harm anyone."

"Surely a handsome man and ardent lover such as you," Zoila suggested in a teasing way, "has broken more than a few young women's hearts."

Even though Zoila made her point with a smile, its import struck home and left him feeling embarrassed. "I can't offer a good defense of my conduct on that subject," he replied. "I have yet to find a way of breaking off with a woman when romance fades."

"Perhaps that's why you're drawn to your friend Inéz, or Mariana and Daniela for that matter. They don't demand anything of you except erotic play. But we've wandered off on a sidetrack. We must use the brief time we have together wisely. This technique of entering the dream: is that something you learned from your teacher, Don Serafino?"

"He mentioned it once, but I've pretty much developed my own understanding of what it might be and only applied that understanding once — the dream of Inéz that I described to you."

"Tell me how it's done, this 'entering the dream' technique."

"I'm not entirely sure," Carlos acknowledged, "but I believe that since I've done it, there's no reason why I can't figure out how to do it again. I suggest that we set a certain date, perhaps a week of nights, and see whether I can enter your dreams. If I'm right and we can see, talk, and touch each other, it ought to be possible to practice Tantric meditation together."

"I'm willing to try, if you can put off our experiment for two or three months. According to the Souzas, Claudio has several shipping jobs that will take him to a variety of Caribbean ports for the next two months. He wants me to come on board and play captain's wife while he makes those rounds. When he's finished that business, he'll drop me off at Panama City. I'll find transport to the Pacific side of the Isthmus and catch a boat home to Peru. While I'm with Claudio, my nights will be fully devoted to him. No interruptions, please."

"Fair enough. By the way, do you dream a lot?"

"Yes," Zoila answered. "All the time; vivid dreams in bright colors."

"That's promising," Carlos observed. "How about first week of May? That should give you plenty of time to get home and me some time to practice entering into dreams, though I have no idea who's going to be the recipient of my visits."

"Hmmm," she mused. "Probably Inéz, as you've already met in dreams. I have no objections, nor any right to object. But I hope you'll be careful."

"An idea just came to me," Don Carlos said. "If we can think of something appropriate, we should exchange objects that have personal value to us and wear or hold them each night that I'm trying to come to you in your dreams."

"I agree. That makes sense — something that's impregnated with your energy and mine. I have just the thing." She took a ring off her right little finger. "This was given by my grandfather to my mother and then, after her death, to me. It's too small for you to wear on your hand; put it on a chain around your neck and hold it in your palm when you go to sleep."

For a moment Don Carlos couldn't think of anything comparable that he could give Zoila. Then he remembered a locket his mother had given him; it contained a lock of her hair. He rummaged around in his saddlebag and found it. "Here," he said. "This was a love gift to me from my mother. The lock of hair inside is hers. I've carried it with me for many years."

The carriage drew to a halt and the driver broke into their conversation by announcing that they'd reached the junction where Carlos had to go his way and Zoila hers. Carlos was loath to say goodbye; he held both her hands for a moment, looked into her eyes, gave her a kiss on the cheek, and then stepped out of the carriage.

As the carriage turned toward the coast, Zoila leaned out of it with a big smile on her face and called to Carlos, "See you in my dreams."

19

Seeker

After the carriage with Zoila turned onto the road to Veracruz, Don Carlos and Bernardo, the stable hand Señor Reyes had loaned Carlos for his trip to Mexico City, continued on their two-day journey, arriving at the city's outskirts as night was falling on the second day. Carlos, not wanting to be seen by friends or relatives, found a small inn on the edge of the city where the two men stayed until dawn. The city was barely awake when they entered it and reached the stable where Carlos had left his horse and the accoutrements—musket, bedroll, oil-cloth slicker, and other items—he had brought from Santa Fe. While his horse was being readied, he bid Bernardo adios, giving the young man a generous tip for his help.

Don Carlos was out of the city before most of its residents were sitting down to breakfast. His destination, the Jesuit Seminary at Tepotzotlán, was almost thirty miles north of Mexico City. As he rode along, alone for the first time since he'd met Zoila, Carlos engaged in serious self-examination. He saw clearly that he no longer felt part of the city, of any city, but particularly of Mexico City. The glitter of upper-class society, its comforts and pleasures that had completely dominated his youth, now seemed to him as cold as ashes. Thinking back to his previous lives as a brujo, he had to admit that in those lives he had not been much different. For the most part he had been a womanizer and daredevil who used his brujo powers more to amuse himself and assert his mastery over the physical world than to benefit anyone else. Reflecting on these facts in the light of the door to spiritual growth Zoila had opened for him, he swore that he would try to change his ways.

By pushing the pace, he reached Tepotzotlán in mid-afternoon and paused for a moment to view the sprawling grounds of the seminary, the residences of the Jesuit priests and students, and the magnificent ultra-baroque Church of San Francisco Javier, which was still under construction. He asked a gatekeeper where he might find Father Stefano, his favorite among his Jesuit tutors. He was told that he could find Father Stefano in the main library.

A stoop-shouldered and gray-haired man with sad eyes, Father Stefano looked up and instantly recognized Carlos. "Don Alfonso," he said, "I'm glad you've come by, and I want you to know that I'm sorry about your mother. I attended her funeral and looked for you. When I failed to see you, I asked where you were and was told that you had quarreled with your stepfather and had broken with your family."

"That's only his version of the story," Carlos replied, anger welling in him as he spoke. "What he conveniently leaves out is how outrageous his behavior was toward me on the day my mother died. I did go to the funeral, though I didn't spot you. I arrived after the Mass began and left as it ended in order to avoid having any contact whatsoever with my stepfather."

Father Stefano, hearing the anger in Carlos's voice, received it for a moment in silence. "Ah," he said at last. "Can you make an effort to reconcile with your stepfather?"

Carlos let out an exasperated snort. "That would be the wise thing to do, if I had any evidence that he wanted to have good relations with me. But he's given every indication that he never wants to talk with me again, and his hostility to me was quite obvious before our recent run-in." Carlos's mouth pulled down in a grimace. "As I see things now, he's unintentionally done me a great favor. After he verbally chased me out of the house that's rightfully my inheritance—and that was the incident that occasioned my angry words to him—I realized, not immediately, but over the week after it happened, that I don't wish to be a resident of Mexico City, nor do I want anything to do with my stepfather's family, except for my stepbrother Joaquin who lives in Santa Fe, where I now make my home."

"Those are drastic changes," Father Stefano replied with a look of concern.

"Yes," Carlos agreed, "and I'm leaving for Santa Fe as soon as possible. I came to say goodbye." (Carlos's sudden angry mood had made him completely forget his original intention in seeking out Father Stefano, which was to tell him about his experiences with Zoila.)

"Ah," said Father Stefano again. "Perhaps we should have a walk in the garden while we talk some more."

Gently shepherded by Father Stefano into the monastery's garden, Carlos felt his mood lighten and was aware again of the tranquil beauty of the place itself and the majestic mountains looming in the distance. "There were other things I wanted to speak with you about," he said at last. "It concerns my meeting with a lovely woman—don't frown, this isn't a casual love affair, or a love affair at all—named Zoila Herrera. She introduced me to a view of the world that shook the foundations of my old attitudes toward life. In the barely three days that we were together, she taught me as much as she could about following a spiritual path based on ancient Hindu scriptures. Her mentor on this path is her grandfather, a Vedic scholar, Krishnades Bhatia, who lives in Goa."

"I've heard of him," Father Stefano said. "Jesuit missionaries who've visited me here say that he's a highly respected scholar of classical Vedic scriptures."

Carlos continued. "The event that shook me to my roots happened while Zoila and I were meditating together. Toward the end of hours of concentration, I saw, and she did too, that both of us were surrounded by a luminous aura of golden light. I apologize if I'm claiming too much, given my general ignorance on the subject of spirituality, but this aura or halo—words fail me here—reminded me of the golden light that surrounds the heads of saints in religious art. And this phenomenon was accompanied by feelings of reverence for and connectedness with the whole universe. Zoila said it was an experience of union with the One, or whatever word—God, Great Spirit, Universal Truth, the Divine—is used to describe it."

"This was," Father Stefano asked, "I suppose, from what I know of Bhatia's teachings, an experience of Tantric meditation?"

"Yes," Carlos admitted, a little embarrassed that Father Stefano might disapprove.

"I thought so," Father Stefano replied, seeming to reflect on the significance of what he was hearing. "From what I know, Tantric practice can be a spiritual path full of dangers, not the least of which is that its practitioners lose themselves in the pursuit of sensual pleasures. If, however, the practitioners are properly schooled in self-restraint, then it can produce—as your first experience seems to illustrate—a powerful opening to the Divine. Tantric study might be appropriate for you, if you can pursue it in a disciplined way."

"Thank you," Carlos said. "The difficulty I'm facing, and the reason I've come to you, is that my friend Zoila, a married woman, lives in Lima, Peru, and is returning there. It seems unlikely that we'll meet again. That being the case, short of going to Lima to visit her or traveling to Goa to speak with her grandfather, I don't have any way to learn more about the spiritual path Zoila's set me on. She encouraged me to continue doing chakra meditation on my own, and I intend to do so, but I'm very much in need of further guidance. I came to visit you in part because I knew that you've read some Vedic scriptures, and now you've told me that you've heard of Krishnades Bhatia. Can you advise me regarding what steps I can take next in reorienting my life?"

"Before we start on the topic of your next steps," Father Stefano said, "Let me say that the changes you are drawn to make are ones I welcome. To be frank, you were a source of great frustration to me as your tutor. You seemed so much more mature than your actual age, and you had many talents. You absorbed literary classics and languages with amazing speed. Moreover, you seemed to enjoy learning. But when you left the classroom, you immediately immersed yourself in worldly pleasures. You showed no interest in undertaking, as I suggested you might, advanced studies here at Tepotzotlán."

"My mistake, no doubt, Father," Carlos replied. "Although it may be that I had to waste time when I was younger in order to recognize the value of not wasting it now. Were you going to go on and suggest readings I might do to further my understanding of the path to which my friend introduced me? The teachings I heard as a Catholic boy seemed more directed at controlling Catholics' social behavior than anything specifically spiritual."

"Don't," Father Stefan warned him, "denigrate the Church's role in preserving doctrine, or the fact that an emphasis on moral conduct and loyalty to the Church is necessary for social order. But what you're describing is the path of mystical surrender that's found in all great traditions — Catholic, Jewish, Hindu — although only a tiny minority of adherents to those faiths discover afresh the need to directly experience union with God.

"Please bear in mind," Father Stefano continued, "that by portraying the mystics of other faiths as legitimate in their pursuit of union with the One, I'm expressing a heretical point of view. Despite Church dogma that there is but one God and one true faith, I've always found much to admire in other traditions. Indeed, I suspect that my interest in Eastern wisdom was the principal obstacle to my receiving a missionary assignment to the Indies. My spiritual advisor probably felt that the attraction of the East for me was so strong that had I reached the Indies, I might have left the Church and become a wandering monk-mystic." This thought seemed to please Father Stefano, whose face broke into a broad smile.

"So where do I begin?" Carlos asked.

"I'm going to give you information on three different approaches," Father Stefano replied. "The first is from Jesuit teaching. Saint Ignatius Loyola, the founder of our order, the Society of Jesus, had a deep spirituality and a powerful intellect. He was also a warrior, a fact that might impress you because you may not associate deep spirituality with militant practicality. St. Ignatius wrote a devotional book, *The Spiritual Exercises*, which takes you through many rigorously described steps to spiritual knowledge. You could do worse than to follow his direction.

"Given that it was Vedic, or more specifically Tantric, meditation that has awakened you to a new perspective on your life, we should spend as much time as possible in the next two days reviewing what I know on the topic. After that I will begin a two-week solitary retreat. I feel a special urgency about this retreat because I'm not well and may not have more than a few months to live."

"That's terrible news!" Carlos exclaimed. "Perhaps you shouldn't waste your time on my concerns, given your need to focus on your own soul."

"I can give you two days, Alfonso," Father Stefano replied, "and I very much want to do so. As for what I believe is my impending death, surely you realize that all of us are born, and all of us die. That's the rule of our existence.

"The third tradition I want to tell you about is that of the Desert Fathers. Even as the early Church became more institutionalized and its teachings were formulated in creeds, a few mystics sought direct inspiration from God. These men retreated into the desert, living in small communities or as hermits. Many of them believed, as I do, that God resides in us.

"Don't look so surprised," Father Stefano said with good humor. "You and I read the Gospels together as part of your study of Latin, and doesn't the Gospel of John report our Savior's words to the effect, 'I am in you and you are in me'? After reaching Santa Fe, you wrote me that you felt your inner spirit most strongly in the desert. So, perhaps, the words of the Desert Fathers will speak to you with particular force. But for now, we should arrange stabling for your horse and also get you a room where you can wash up and sleep tonight. Then we can begin."

Father Stefano and Don Carlos devoted the next two days, with no breaks except to eat and sleep, to studying the three traditions Father Stefano had described. By the end of forty-eight hours, Carlos's head was spinning, full of all the information he'd been given, so much information, in fact, that he wondered how much he would remember.

Don Carlos prepared to leave on the morning that Father Stefano was to begin his two-week solitary retreat. Once Carlos had mounted his horse, Father Stefano handed him a small package. "This is a gift from me of three books. The first is a copy of St. Ignatius's *Spiritual Exercises*. The second is a selection of Vedic writings, in particular a few that refer to Tantric theory, which I've translated into Spanish. The third is a journal of notes I made of sayings and insights I came across over many years of reading the early Desert Fathers."

"Surely this is the only copy that exists," Don Carlos said.

"True," Father Stefano replied, "but who better to have it than an aspiring mystic headed to the deserts of New Spain? Having said that, I need to add a cautionary note. You've had a profound experience of spiritual bliss, and had it at a very young age. I wish you many more such experiences, but you need to be aware that grace in that degree and kind may not fall on you again. The more you strive to repeat that deep experience, the more you may get in the way of having it. Desire, one of the great obstacles to mystical union with the Divine, can undermine your efforts.

"Perhaps the best antidote to excessive desire, even for something as desirable as Divine Union, is to keep your life simple and devoted to loving all creation — humans, animals, and all nature.

"Let me leave you with an example from one of Christ's parables, the parable of the Good Samaritan. It's found in several Gospels. Do you remember it?"

"Yes, a traveler is set upon by robbers who beat him nearly to death and take all his money. A priest comes along, but hurries past the man without offering any help. A businessman, or some such person, also hurries by. Finally, a Samaritan, a person despised by the Jews as inferior, sees the injured man, binds his wounds, and takes him to an inn to recover. This Samaritan promises the innkeeper that he will pay all the injured man's bills."

"Very good," Father Stefano replied. "The reason I mention it is that you may often find yourself in the position of the Samaritan. To the degree that you give up the conventional way of life in the city, the life of your class and family, you will be choosing to be an outsider — a man, as it were, from Samaria — not an easy path to follow. However, the Samaritan showed what should be done, regardless of one's status. Even if you forget all the deep words we've studied the past few days, you can always go back to a simple rule: 'Where help is needed, give help.'"

With these words, the two men parted.

20

Uncertainty

*F*ollowing directions Father Stefano had given him, Don Carlos left the seminary by way of a road that headed generally northeast. Three miles later he came to the junction with the Camino Real, the main north-south route on which he had arrived from Santa Fe two weeks earlier. His impulse to leave Mexico City still prodded him onward, but he was no longer hurrying back to Santa Fe to get to Camila as soon as possible for fear that Rafael would win her; he had become convinced that his dreams of Camila and Rafael having fallen in love during his absence were true dreams. Why rush back to Santa Fe to confirm the inevitable?

Once he turned north on the Camino Real, the reality of the 1,500-mile journey ahead struck him with full force. Because of his anger at his stepfather, he had left Mexico City impulsively, without making careful preparations, and without trying to find others he could travel with. In his previous trips between Mexico City and Santa Fe he had always been part of a group or small party — a wagon train escorted by soldiers to Santa Fe and, on his return trip to Mexico City, first by three soldiers, then with two silver-mine owners, and finally by the three vaqueros Manuel Tapia assigned to accompany him. Now he was heading north by himself, having made no plans, with only one horse, his saddlebags containing some pesos and a change of clothes, his musket in a scabbard, and a bedroll for nights when he had to camp out.

As a brujo he was accustomed to thinking of himself as alone and acting without any direction except his instincts, and much of what Zoila had said suggested that if he pursued the path to which she had introduced him he would in all likelihood again be alone. But suddenly he felt his aloneness in a new way. It was as if the way forward required a leap into the unknown, into a terra incognita. The sensation was not altogether unpleasant, rather like the feeling of taking a risk, standing at the edge of an abyss, a totally dark space into which he could not see. If he stayed within the boundaries of his past lives as a brujo, he could in large degree control events, as he always had. Yet these new sensations interested him, and Don Carlos the risk-taker was drawn not to simply stay in safe territory.

He breathed more deeply and his apprehensions diminished. Although he didn't understand exactly what was happening, he sensed that it had something to do with his experience with Zoila. His breathing slowed even more. He became aware of the motion of his horse walking under his seat and felt connected with the horse's calm energy. He looked at the deep cut made by the river on one side of the road and at the steep bluffs rising on the other side and the silhouette of tall mountains on the horizon. After a while he felt a pulsing sensation in his forehead, followed by a great calm. The sixth chakra, he said to himself. My sixth chakra opened.

As he rounded a bend in the road he looked ahead and saw a small party of horsemen no more than a half mile away, potential companions for this section of the road. And in the distance he saw a little grouping of houses on the right-hand side of the road. A place to stay for the night, he said to himself, though it was too early to stop yet. But he felt that the presence of the horsemen and the little settlement conveyed a message. There would be companions on the way and places to stay. He would trust himself to the unfolding of the journey.

That night, a little before sunset, he came to a small town and found an inn where he was able to get food for himself and his horse and places for each of them to rest. Without his planning it, a pattern emerged over the days that followed. He often found other travelers riding in his direction and joined them on the road. Every night he found a place to stay – an inn or a ranch that welcomed travelers.

The only plan he imposed on himself was to make an effort to meditate every morning before breakfast. Since he never needed more than four hours sleep a night, it was a simple matter for him to rise before dawn and meditate. As his method of meditation, he combined techniques with which he'd had success in the past, starting with his Watching practice, following the pulsing sensations that arose in his body, and finally directing his attention to the chakras.

In the time he'd allowed himself for meditation practice each day – he did three hours, when one or two didn't produce the results he sought – he moved readily enough from Watching to body-pulsing sensations, and having reached that stage, he usually achieved a state of strong mental concentration. However, his chakra practice did not progress so well. On most mornings his kundalini energies did not rise beyond his throat chakra, and even when, on another day, he did achieve some contact with his crown chakra, it was faint and came and went. After two weeks of practice, he became disillusioned and began to feel that he was wasting his time. Only the memory of Father Stefano's cautionary advice that he might never again experience spiritual bliss with the intensity he had with Zoila kept him going through this period when his practice seemed so dry and unrewarding.

His initial effort to do some spiritual reading in St. Ignatius's *Spiritual Exercises* didn't help much. The exercises St. Ignatius prescribed struck Carlos as too formulaic, and the emphasis St. Ignatius placed on sin and penance didn't appeal to him in the least. Only a two-page passage entitled "Contemplation to Attain Divine Love" touched Carlos's heart. "Love," St. Ignatius had written, "ought to be manifested in deeds rather than words." How this injunction might apply to his travels he wasn't sure. That uncertainty seemed at the core of his situation.

Late one afternoon after he'd been on the road for three weeks he entered a hilly area with no homes in sight, and he began to believe that he was going to end up sleeping in a field. He had an eye out for a good camping spot when he saw a ranch ahead with a big house, a handsome barn, and an empty pasture with enough grass for fifteen or more cattle.

A knock on the front door did not produce an answer. He tethered his horse at a hitching post and walked around the side of the house. A little girl, perhaps twelve years old, came tearing into view from the back of the house. She had a look of eager anticipation on her face until she saw him, at which point she looked extremely disappointed and a little frightened. "Hey!" Don Carlos said. "Don't worry. I'm looking for a place to sleep and hope your parents will let me stay in your barn."

The child hesitated before speaking, probably, Carlos thought, having been warned not to talk to strangers. "No one's home except me," the girl burst out, "and Clara is in a terrible state. Please help me!"

"Slow down," Don Carlos said in as calming a way as he could muster. "Where is everyone, who is Clara, and what's her problem?"

"Daddy and my two brothers went off yesterday afternoon chasing some rustlers who stole our cattle. My mother was home last night, but she left early this morning after getting word that an old woman who lives in the hills west of here had fallen ill and urgently needed Momma's help. Not ten minutes after Momma went off, Clara" — mentioning the name again brought tears to her eyes — "began to have trouble. She's daddy's favorite milk cow, and no one expected her to begin calving for a week or more, but she's having a calf, except the calf is stuck and has been stuck for nearly all day; Clara and her calf are going to die if you don't help."

Don Carlos, who knew nothing about calving or the birth of any animal except the kittens the maids had raised in the kitchen at his mother's house, was more than a little alarmed by the prospect that Clara and her calf's lives depended on help from him. Nevertheless, he said, "Okay, little girl, take me to Clara; what's your name, by the way?"

"I'm Micaela," she replied, taking him by the hand and dragging him toward the barn.

He was startled to hear himself say, "I'm Carlos."

Micaela led Don Carlos inside the barn to a stall. Clara was leaning against the wall, and Carlos could see that one of the calf's hooves was visible just outside the birth canal. Micaela explained that it had been lodged there for hours, which probably meant that the calf's other foreleg was bent back and caught at the start of the birth canal. After hearing Micaela's succinct description of the problem Carlos said, "You seem to know what's wrong; what has stopped you from helping Clara out?"

"You'll see," Micaela declared. "You have to start by pushing the calf back into the womb. I've seen my father do it, but I don't have near enough strength to manage it. Then you have to reach one arm in the womb and reposition the leg that's caught so that it's in front of the calf's head like the other leg is. My arm isn't long enough to reach that far."

"Will I need to put lard or something on my arm to slip it into the birth canal?" Carlos asked.

"You won't need it; she's already soaking wet inside."

Don Carlos rolled up his sleeves and told Micaela, "I'm going to see if I can help Clara. Tell me again what part of the calf should emerge first?" he asked.

"The forelegs should come out with the head between them, but first you need to push the calf back and free the other foreleg or the calf won't come out."

Don Carlos set about to push the calf back into its mother, grasping its leg and inserting his right arm as far as it would go. Clara's contractions created a significant difficulty in this process. Her instincts not only worked against Carlos's goals by pushing in the opposite direction, but each contraction powerfully squeezed his arm. "You're right," he told Micaela in a masterful understatement. "This isn't easy." Micaela was also right about another thing, he decided. You needed long arms to do this job. By the time he succeeded in getting the calf back into Clara's womb, his right arm was inside Clara almost up to his shoulder.

Getting the calf back inside had not solved the problem of the foreleg that was bent and somehow caught at the entrance to the birth canal. Don Carlos found the whole geography of his rescue mission perplexing because it was difficult to feel, with only one hand to do so, which leg was which leg. The crowded interior of Clara's womb was a major obstacle to his sorting things out. Only after considerable awkward groping did he locate what he hoped was a second foreleg. He tugged it forward until he could feel two of the calf's legs—he hoped they were the correct ones—with the calf's head between them.

Micaela added another detail to Carlos's education in birthing a calf. "The calf," she said, "has to emerge on its belly—the same position you'd take if you were diving into a swimming hole. Is that the way it feels to you?"

"I think so," he replied, though what he meant was "I hope so but am not sure."

At that very moment he was aware of the sound of hoofbeats approaching and stopping outside the barn. He glanced over his shoulder and saw a mature man with a deeply tanned face scowling at him. "What the hell are you doing, stranger?" the man asked.

"Daddy!" Micaela exclaimed. "Carlos is trying to help Clara's calf. She's been stuck for hours and there was no one else to help."

Ignoring his daughter, the man demanded, "Do you know what you're doing?"

"No," Carlos admitted, feeling it would probably be obvious soon, if it wasn't already.

"Damn it, then," the man growled. "Get your arm out of Clara and let me take over. You've probably made a total mess of things."

Carlos was glad to let Micaela's father take over and grateful when Micaela spoke up in his defense. "He was just trying to help. I asked him to."

"Where's your mother?" the man shot back. "And haven't you been told never to talk to strangers?" Before Micaela could reply, her father gruffly told her, "Go to the house and don't come out until I tell you it's okay." Micaela ran off with tears in her eyes.

"Your daughter told me," Carlos said, "that your wife was called away to help a neighbor woman who was suddenly taken very ill."

"Did I ask you?" Micaela's father snapped as he started to put his arm into Clara's vagina. "You better get going yourself. If this birth doesn't work out, I'll take out my anger at you for having botched it. Now! Git!"

Carlos was willing enough to leave, even though he was very worried about Clara and her calf. Riding north on the Camino Real, he passed two craggy-faced young men, Micaela's brothers, he was sure, driving ten cattle toward their ranch. He was glad he wouldn't be at the ranch if Clara's calf arrived stillborn, since, given the father's belligerence, the three of them would probably have tried to beat him up. He knew he could have used his brujo powers to prevent them from hurting him, although that seemed small consolation. What good had his brujo powers been when faced with the practical problem of helping Clara's calf be born alive and well?

There were black clouds gathering on the horizon, and as far as the eye could see there was not another ranch or a town or inn. He hurried on until the first raindrops began to fall. He turned off the road, found a pine tree that offered a little shelter, tethered his horse in a patch of grass, and spread out his bedroll and the rain tarp that was packed with it. He didn't have much to eat, only a piece of bread and some beef jerky that he'd saved from lunch at a ranch many hours ago—not that it mattered once the rain began falling in sheets. He crouched under the tarp, trying to keep himself, his saddlebags, and his saddle dry. It was a losing cause. Soon he was dripping wet. Trying to keep his spirits up, he reminded himself that a fictional hero of his—Don Quixote—had nearly always failed in his quest to do good deeds, often being beaten up or chased off. At least he, Carlos, had escaped being assaulted by angry ranchers.

Over the next week, Carlos had better luck, whether alone or with companions, finding accommodations. He nearly always came to a small town with an inn or a ranch that would provide a bed and breakfast. After his daily meditation, he tried reading in the materials Father Stefano had given him, turning his attention to the book of sayings by Christian monks who'd gone into the desert to pray more than a thousand years earlier. Carlos particularly liked a story about a Desert Father whose hermitage was robbed of nearly all his possessions and who, when he discovered that the thief had overlooked one item, ran after the thief to give it to him.

Several days later Carlos passed through a stretch of road on which he met no fellow travelers and didn't come across any towns or ranches. It was growing dark, and he decided he again needed to spend the night camped out. He had just passed the mouth of an arroyo on his right. When he spotted a clump of trees up a gentle slope ahead to his left, he assumed, correctly as it turned out, that the trees might be clustered around a spring.

He camped beside it and spent his remaining waking hours thinking about the Desert Fathers.

After a Spartan breakfast the next morning, he rode downhill, returning to the road he'd been following northward. He had just turned north when he was startled by the sound of hooves crashing through brush on his right. He rode toward the edge of the steep embankment and saw a lanky steer bolting toward the entrance of the arroyo, followed by a paint horse, which, though wearing a saddle, had no rider.

Don Carlos rode slowly north along the edge of the embankment, scanning the arroyo below. Several dozen yards farther along, he saw a cowboy lying among the sand and rocks below. Carlos called to him, but the man didn't move or answer.

The situation didn't look good to Don Carlos, and he wished he could reach the fallen vaquero immediately, but he had to double back southward on the road to reach the mouth of the arroyo and then pick his way back northward among the rocks and brush in the dry creek bed. By the time he reached the place where the vaquero was lying, the man had regained consciousness and was half sitting up, propped on his elbows. "Damn!" he said. "I'm glad you came along. If you hadn't I might have died here, and all you'd find next year would be bones."

The man's statement struck Carlos as more dire than the situation warranted, but it turned out the cowboy had a point. "That damn Loco — that's the horse's name, for obvious reasons," the man declared. "When the steer I was trying to drive back to the ranch bolted out of the underbrush, Loco pivoted so fast that he fell on me. From the way my leg hurts, I'm sure it's broken. Then the damn horse runs off and leaves me here to fry in the sun."

"When Loco shows up, won't your friends at the ranch know something's wrong and start looking for you?"

"Unlikely. I had to borrow Loco from a neighbor's ranch, and those hired hands know what a lunatic Loco is. They'll probably have a good laugh at my expense when he turns up. 'Sure serves old Alberto Iglesias right for borrowing that crazy horse' — that's what they'll be saying. They'll figure I'll walk back to my home ranch. No one will be looking for me until tomorrow. Even then, they'll have no idea that steer led me a merry chase up this arroyo."

"Is your ranch far from here?" Don Carlos asked.

"Close to five miles."

"Then let's see if you can stand up," Carlos suggested.

With Don Carlos lifting, and Alberto pushing with his good leg, the cowboy managed to stand on one leg. Alberto then tried to put weight on his other leg. Carlos could see from the look that came on his face that he was in a lot of pain. "The bad news," Carlos said, "seems to be that your leg's broken; the only good news is that it's broken down in the boot, and the boot is acting like a splint."

Don Carlos called his horse over. "We need to get you mounted. You can't walk anywhere the way you are. I'll give you a leg up with your good leg, and you can pitch your broken leg over the saddle. It'll probably hurt like hell, but I don't see what else to do except leave you and go for help. Even if I succeed in bringing some men back, you're still going to need to get on a horse; a wagon won't fit in here or anywhere nearby."

Fortunately Alberto made it into the saddle with Carlos's help about as smoothly as could be expected under difficult conditions. Carlos dug around in his saddlebags and brought out a bottle of brandy. "Drink as much of this as you can," he told Alberto. "Alcohol will dull the pain a little during the ride ahead."

Alberto swallowed half of the bottle before he stopped drinking. "That's all I can handle," he said. "It's pretty strong stuff, but" — and here he displayed a little good humor — "I could get used to it. Very tasty."

Don Carlos and Alberto started off, Carlos leading the horse, Alberto riding. A half hour later Alberto announced that his head was fuzzy and his leg wasn't hurting nearly as much as it had when they started off. It took nearly three hours to reach Alberto's home ranch. "No sign of Loco," Alberto said. "I'm sure he went to his own barn."

As they came through the gate of Alberto's home ranch, five vaqueros spotted their approach and burst out of their bunkhouse to greet the two new arrivals. Carlos and Alberto filled Alberto's co-workers in on what had happened. Alberto's friends helped him down and carried him into the bunkhouse. His leg had swollen up, making it impossible to remove his boot without cutting it off him. Necessity required that it be done, but Alberto looked on sadly. "Best pair of boots I've ever had," he declared. One of the five vaqueros was an experienced bonesetter, and he skillfully returned the two broken pieces of leg bone to their correct position, splinted the leg, and bound it up. The whole affair, the bonesetter told Carlos, would have a happy ending, although Alberto wouldn't be fully healed for at least six weeks.

Alberto and his friends made much of how crucial Don Carlos's help had been. Carlos was pleased that everything was working out. By this time it was mid-afternoon, and he asked if he could spend the night in the ranch's barn. No one would hear of it. The vaqueros gave him the best bed in the bunkhouse and put together a splendid meal of steak, potatoes, squash, beans, and mince pie—all he could eat and more.

The next morning Don Carlos went to see how Alberto was doing. "Pretty well," the vaquero told him, "though I wouldn't mind another slug of that tasty stuff you gave me yesterday—just to dull the pain, of course," he said with a wry smile. "Is there anything I can do by way of return?"

"Yes," Don Carlos replied, "though you may have trouble believing it's what I want."

Carlos was right about that. What he proposed was that he would trade his riding clothes for Alberto's work outfit, which would fit him because the two men were about the same size.

Alberto expressed astonishment at Don Carlos's request. "Your clothes are much finer than mine. It's not a fair trade at all. It doesn't make any sense."

"I hope you'll make the swap anyway," Don Carlos replied. Not wanting to discuss his real motives, Carlos offered a practical explanation for his proposal. "Bandits," he observed, "are active along this part of the Camino Real. They're less likely to bother me if I'm not wearing a rich man's clothes." (Carlos had also noticed that poorer people, both Native and mestizo, looked uncomfortable when he, a Spaniard dressed in an upper-class person's outfit, asked for a place to stay, and that made him uncomfortable in return.)

Don Carlos's point about not wanting to attract bandits seemed to make sense to Alberto, and he agreed to the exchange. Carlos then continued his journey northward looking a bit less like an upper-class gentleman.

During the weeks it took him to complete the remaining distance to Nombre de Dios mission, where Eagle was boarding at Manuel Tapia's stable, Don Carlos began to investigate the selections from Vedic wisdom literature that Father Stefano had spent years translating into Spanish. What struck him forcefully was the prominence given to female deities throughout these Hindu scriptures. Shakti, as best as he could tell, was a supreme being, a deity venerated as the personification of primal energies, the creative forces that underlie all life.

Prior to meeting Zoila, Don Carlos's only religious education was in Roman Catholic teachings. While he had never given the matter much thought, even though the Virgin Mary, the mother of Christ, was venerated, it was obvious that the status of men was privileged in Christianity. Christianity had no goddesses, and all the Christian apostles and Catholic popes, bishops, and priests were men. Only men could consecrate the bread and wine during the Eucharist. Women, even saints and mother superiors who were monastic leaders, were not allowed such central roles in the faith. Yet it was a woman, Zoila, whose example had opened him to the possibility of personal spiritual transformation.

He realized that he was mixing many categories — the gender of gods, the relative power of men and women within the Church, and the influence of gender on spiritual inspiration. As he was trying to sort out these varied topics, he noticed a rough road that went off to his left. A small shrine to Our Lady of Guadalupe marked the turnoff.

Don Carlos was curious. What sort of place did the road lead to? He was familiar with the story of the Our Lady of Guadalupe, having been to the church built in her honor on the outskirts of Mexico City, and he knew it was a popular pilgrimage site. In 1531 a young Native woman in her mid-teens, her body illuminated by a halo of golden light, had appeared to a Native peasant named Juan Diego and had spoken to him in the local Indian language, Nahuatl. Carlos felt that learning more about Juan Diego's vision might shed light, albeit indirectly, on the questions that were presently on his mind.

Less than a half mile down the road he saw a cluster of buildings that either had been or still were part of a small ranch. Two women who were sitting on the front porch of what appeared to be the main building ran inside it the moment they saw him. He got off his horse and walked toward the building. Perhaps, he thought, my appearance is so shabby I've frightened those women into thinking I'm a bandit or a drifter.

He was about to step to the front door when it was opened by a middle-aged mestizo woman with a frown on her face. "What do you want?" the woman asked, though her tone of voice was less unfriendly than her facial expression.

"Permit me to introduce myself, Señorita," he said. (One always used señorita, the term for unmarried virgins, rather than señora, the word for a married woman, until the woman made her status clear.) "My name is Alfonso Cabeza de Vaca. I work for the military governor in Santa Fe and am returning home from a business trip that took me to Mexico City. I have an interest in all things spiritual and wondered what connection this place has with the church dedicated to Our Lady of Guadalupe on the outskirts of Mexico City."

The woman looked him up and down, obviously wondering why an employee of the military governor of New Mexico would be so poorly dressed. "I am Señora Vargas. This is a refuge I've founded for women who have been abused, widowed, abandoned, or scorned by society. We honor the Virgin of Guadalupe as a female figure of great spiritual power who appeared among us. Quite a few of our residents are Native women, for whom Our Lady has special significance. She appeared at the site of a temple the Spanish had destroyed that had been dedicated to a female Aztec deity, Tonantzin, and she delivered her message in Nahuatl. That's at least a partial answer to your question."

"Yes, it is," Don Carlos replied, "and what you've just said leads me to another question."

Señora Vargas waited without speaking for Carlos to ask his question.

"I hope that what I say won't scandalize you. I've been reading about Hindu religion and have come across references to Hindu goddesses who share equal status with Hindu male gods. Indeed, female Hindu deities, especially one named Shakti, are said to be the source of the creative energy that is essential to all living things. My question is this: would your Native women regard Aztec goddesses as deities comparable to Christ?"

After a long pause, Señora Vargas replied. "What you're asking is well beyond my ability to judge for certain. But if you were a good friend of a Native woman who prays at the Church of Our Lady of Guadalupe, I believe she might tell you that she prays to Tonantzin, and that she considers Tonantzin the equal of any male deity, Christian or Aztec. Our Catholic bishop would, of course, vehemently disagree. I am simply giving you the impression I've formed from working with Native women."

"I'm grateful for your frankness," Don Carlos said. "Before I go, may I also ask how you support your mission financially? All I see are a few small gardens and a dozen chickens scratching in the dust. That can't possibly be sufficient to support your efforts adequately."

"We depend entirely on the charity of our neighbors, most of whom are poor. I don't mind that, except that there is such a great need for the work we do. Right now we could easily fill that ramshackle outbuilding you see to your left, but I can't pay what the carpenters require to renovate it."

"How much would it cost?" Carlos asked. Señora Vargas named a sum, significant but not huge. Carlos went to his saddlebags, took out the purse in which he kept his money, and counted how many pesos he had on hand. It was almost exactly what Señora Vargas needed. "Here," he said, handing the money to her. "Take this as a gift from a wandering seeker."

A look of astonishment, disbelief, and joy came over Señora Vargas's face, but she expressed concern that he would be stranded, peso-less, on the road ahead. "You give me too much credit," he said, with heartfelt candor. "I'm embarrassed to say that I've given you money I can afford to give. I'm not a poor person sacrificing my last peso to do the right thing."

He was about to mount his horse to leave when a young woman in ragged clothes came into sight walking down the road to the mission. Even at a distance it was obvious that she was in a bad way, and as she approached Don Carlos and Señora Vargas, they could see that the woman had a large bruise on her left cheek and was crying.

Filled with sympathy, Señora Vargas stepped forward and took the woman, whose name turned out to be Josephina, in her arms and asked, "What happened?"

Amid many sobs and wails of grief, Josephina's story gradually came out. "My husband, Miguel, was deeply in debt. First, he sold our small farm; then he sold my little baby to Gypsies."

Don Carlos was incredulous. "Sold your baby to Gypsies?"

"I tried to stop him and we fought. That's how I came to have these bruises."

"How long ago was this?" Don Carlos asked, thinking that he could pursue the Gypsies in order to recover the child.

"Three days ago. I've been walking day and night on the road to this place, which I heard was a safe haven for women like me. I would have gotten here sooner, but I was frightened and hid off the road whenever I heard anyone approaching. I was afraid that men who found a woman alone would rape her."

"Which way did these Gypsies go—north or south?" Don Carlos asked.

"I have no idea. Miguel knocked me unconscious when he took my baby, and by the time I awakened, they were nowhere to be seen."

"Were these people mounted?" When Josephina said yes, Carlos despaired of catching up with the Gypsies who'd taken her baby. Even if he used his brujo powers and transformed himself into a hawk, they had too big a lead. The area he'd need to survey was much too large. He felt powerless to do anything useful.

"Sadly," Señora Vargas declared, "this type of situation is all too common. We're terribly crowded right now, but when I hear a story like this, I can't turn the Josephinas of the world away. With the money you just gave me, I'll contact carpenters and soon we'll have more space."

"I wish I could do more," Don Carlos said, feeling great sadness that stories like Josephina's were apparently so commonplace. He left the refuge of Our Lady of Guadalupe in a somber mood, chastened by the great gulf between his spiritual aspirations and his lack of ability to fulfill them. As a brujo, he had been able to overcome every obstacle he faced. Now he'd become painfully aware of the limits of his power to control human events.

In this somber mood he made his farewells to Señora Vargas and Josephina. He mounted his horse and headed back to the Camino Real. Nombre de Dios mission was less than a day's ride ahead, and he told his horse, "Well, old girl, I think it's time we pushed the pace a little so that I can sleep in a soft bed and you can have all the grass you want in that pasture in back of Manuel Tapia's stable."

It was dusk when they reached Nombre de Dios. Carlos rode directly to Manuel Tapia's house, which was located next to his stable. He turned his horse over to a stableboy and enjoyed a quick reunion with Manuel, after which excused himself by saying, "We can talk more later tonight; right now I want to say hello to Eagle."

From the fence around the field where a dozen or so horses were pastured, Carlos could see Eagle grazing. "Eagle!" Carlos shouted, whereupon his equine friend lifted his head, pricked up his ears, and sniffed the air; then he trotted across the field right up to Don Carlos and pressed his face gently against Carlos's chest. Carlos gave Eagle the carrot he'd brought him and said, "I'm very glad to see you too."

21

Xochiquetzal

The morning after arriving at the mission town of Nombre de Dios, Don Carlos rose to find his host waiting to have breakfast with him. They were midway through their meal when Carlos asked Manuel whether he had heard of any more instances of sorcery in the area since Carlos's epic battle with Mateo Pizarro.

"Two incidents come to mind," Manuel replied. "About three weeks after you'd left for Mexico City, an old man with a mean face came by accompanied by a young man who seemed to be his servant or apprentice. I say the mean-faced man was old, but he seemed to have the energy of a much younger man. He was dressed in black and had a way of asking questions that suggested he would just as soon kill you as wait for an answer. The younger man was tall and extraordinarily handsome; women probably swoon at his attentions. But I sensed that there was something dark and sinister about him too.

"The man in black asked whether I knew what had become of Mateo Pizarro. 'I visited the valley,' he said, 'where Don Mateo used to live and found that his house had been wrecked. The Natives, ignorant peasants all of them, claimed they didn't know how it had happened. They said all they knew was that one morning they'd found Pizarro hanging, dead and naked, from a tree. Even though by the time I got there nothing was left of him but a pile of bones below the tree, the peasants were still too terrified to go near the place.'

"This man in black was obviously angry about what he'd found. He called Pizarro 'my best student ever' and muttered to himself, 'I had great plans for him.' Immediately, he demanded to know whether I'd heard anything about how that evil sorcerer died. I suspected that this fellow would be out to get you if I admitted any knowledge of your part in Pizarro's disappearance, and I said, as was true and therefore something I could say with great conviction, that I'd never been in the valley and knew only that there had been a huge thunderstorm in the mountains about three weeks earlier. He nodded his head, as though that confirmed his suspicions, turned on his heel, and left."

"Did he give you his name?" Carlos wanted to know.

"No, but as he was leaving, the tall young man who seemed to be his assistant said to him, 'Don Malvolio, doesn't this sound like the work of your old enemy, Don Carlos?'" The mean-faced man in black hit the young man hard on the head with his riding whip and snapped, 'Shut up! That's for me to decide.'"

Don Carlos regarded it as bad news that Don Malvolio was still alive and searching for him, but he wasn't about to let his concern show to Manuel, who had no reason to connect the Don Carlos of Don Malvolio's statement with the Don Alfonso who was seated in front of him.

"This Malvolio," Carlos told Manuel, "sounds like a nasty fellow. Thank you for not mentioning me. It's a good thing that the peasants he spoke with apparently didn't mention either of us in connection with whatever happened to Pizarro. Had they done so, this Malvolio fellow might have made an ugly scene with you. But, to change the topic, didn't you speak of two incidents? What was the second one?"

Manuel replied, "A month after the first incident, I heard about a woman who seems to be a powerful bruja. She calls herself 'Xochi,' possibly after an ancient Aztec goddess, and lives in a small valley between the two lines of hills west of here." Pointing toward the nearest of the hills, Manuel added, "You can see that there's a steep trail that follows a zigzag route over the ridge."

"That looks like a difficult climb," Carlos observed, "especially if it's a rock-strewn trail." Manuel indicated that it was narrow and rough.

Curious about Xochi's contact with the outside world, Carlos asked, "Does anyone visit her?"

"None of the locals will go near the place," Manuel said. "They believe it's haunted by the ghost of a man who had built a one-room house there and was murdered, or so the locals believe, by dark entities who left his headless corpse behind. But a month ago two Indian men came to town and asked me whether there were any brujos in the area. I told them that the woman who calls herself Xochi might be a bruja and warned them that the locals regarded her as dangerous. They insisted on learning where she lived, so I gave them the best directions I could to her place, and off they went.

"What happened next was terrible. Within less than a week both returned, though separately, in bad shape. From what they told me they had drawn straws to see which of them would approach Xochi first, thinking it would be to the winner's advantage. The man who called himself Jorge drew the long straw. He walked over the ridge toward Xochi's place until he saw a woman on the path ahead. She shouted, 'Go away!' He told her he wanted to study sorcery with her; she replied that she didn't take students unless they brought her a dozen dark green crystals. The crystals had to be perfect: transparent, eight-sided, and unchipped. If he didn't have crystals of that sort, he should go away before she cut his private parts off. He promised to search for dark green crystals and then, when he didn't leave immediately, she turned an angry shade of purple, leapt at him, threw him to the ground, and bit off his ear.

"His companion, a man who went by his last name only, Olmos, was much larger and tougher than Jorge. Olmos had killed several rivals in fights and was a powerful wrestler. He asked Jorge how big the woman was, and Jorge replied that she couldn't have been more than five feet three inches, almost nine inches shorter than Olmos and half his weight. 'You stupid coward,' Olmos said, 'a woman like that needs to be shown who's boss. You should have grabbed her, thrown her on the ground, and taken your pleasure. I'll bring her some violet-colored crystals, and she'll either settle for them or I'll do as I wish with her.'

"Olmos went off. He was gone a long time, at least three days. When he returned, he was a broken man. He couldn't even give us a coherent account of what had happened to him. Now he spends his days sitting on a bench in the plaza, staring into space and mumbling to himself about a witch who took his soul and his manhood from him."

Xochi sounded like a very dangerous woman; she also seemed to have powers that might indicate knowledge Don Carlos could use to his benefit. He asked Manuel where dark green crystals were found in the region. "Nowhere that I know of," Manuel replied. "In my extensive searches for crystals, the only colors I've found are clear, violet, and black. I can't help you." The two of them dropped the subject of Xochi.

Don Carlos decided to visit Xochi. He could see that the steep trail up the hill would be hard going for Eagle, and since the base of the trail appeared to be in walking distance, he set off on foot across dry fields with little vegetation. It was still early enough in the morning that dewdrops clung to clumps of stubble in low spots that had until a few minutes earlier been in the shade. The first rays of sun to strike the dewdrops created a phenomenon that Carlos had always found magical. Each dewdrop sparkled with rainbow colors, a tiny universe in a single drop of water.

When he reached the base of the trail, he sat down to rest next to a small, spring-fed pool. He was beginning to have some doubts. Here he was again possibly risking his neck by courting a potentially dangerous encounter, which was precisely the type of act he'd told Camila he had no intention of undertaking. But after a brief mental struggle, his love of adventure won out over any desire to be prudent.

Just at that moment he became aware that a cougar was standing silently about twenty feet away from him. Don Carlos remained motionless. As the cougar approached in a leisurely fashion, he recognized her as the same cougar he'd met about a day's ride north of Nombre de Dios on his way to Mexico City. She was eyeing him with interest, apparently aware that she'd met him before. "You're a long way," he said to her, "from the watering hole where we met last winter."

She walked to the edge of the pool, took a leisurely drink, and finally spoke. "You seem to underestimate four-leggeds of my type. Each of us has a large range. What brings you here? If you came in hopes of mounting me, you're too late. I would have welcomed it when we first met, but I subsequently found a big strong male who mounted me, and now I'm pregnant."

"I'm glad to see you nevertheless," Don Carlos said with genuine politeness. "Although I couldn't help you get pregnant" — that had never been part of his plan — "I hope you'll still be willing to help me, if you can. What I'm looking for are dark green crystals that are eight-sided and transparent. Have you seen any such crystals around here?"

"Only in one place," she replied, "a narrow crevice that's hidden in some bushes just beyond that boulder over to your right. I'll show you the place, if you'll just wait while I have another drink. If that's smoked beef I smell in your knapsack, I'd love to have it all." Don Carlos handed the beef over without hesitation.

The cougar, whose named turned out to be Ramona, made good on her promise. She showed him the crevice and without another word waved a paw at him and went off into the brush. Using the knife that he had in his belt, he carefully pried out nineteen crystals. Twelve of them could be used to bargain with Xochi. The other seven he would give to his friend Manuel.

He started up the steep, winding trail to the top of the hills and soon came across a cactus laden with blossoms. The thought came to him to take some blossoms to Xochi as a peace offering.

He cut off several dozen blossoms, apologizing to the plant, and began to develop a plan. He was wearing the worn work clothes that he'd obtained from Alberto Iglesias, the cowboy with the broken leg. Apparently Alberto had planned to repair a hole in his shirt, because there was a needle and thread in the shirt's breast pocket. Don Carlos had kept the items in the pocket, intending to do the repair work himself sometime. Now he thought to use them to thread the cactus blossoms he'd just collected into a flower chain. Very pleased with the way that small sewing job turned out, he carefully stored the flower chain in his knapsack.

After a strenuous climb, he reached the top of the hill and started down its other side. A half hour later he came to the edge of a meadow, rounded a bend in the trail, and saw a pool of steaming water, apparently a hot spring, ahead. On the side of the pool toward Carlos a young Indian woman was climbing out of the water. She was naked and wet from head to toe. Her body was firm and well-muscled. She had a stocky figure, with thick thighs and broad shoulders, not a female body type that particularly appealed to Don Carlos, though he conceded that she was nevertheless physically attractive. Clearly startled by Carlos's sudden appearance, she snatched a light-brown one-piece dress from the ground and hastily put it on. In an effort to cover her surprise, she went on the attack. "Go away! You're not welcome here." Carlos was sure he'd found Xochi.

In a calm, reasonable tone of voice, Don Carlos replied, "In the valley they say that you're a powerful bruja; if that's so, I have some questions to ask you."

"If you want answers, you should have brought me twelve dark green crystals, perfect eight-sided transparent crystals."

"Your answer," Don Carlos replied, testing her, "suggests that you aren't much of a bruja, since a powerful bruja would know whether I've brought the dark green crystals you want."

Don Carlos's statement stopped Xochi for only a moment. "I wasn't looking at your energy," she said curtly. "If you've brought me dark green crystals, show them to me."

Don Carlos put down his knapsack, took out three of the largest crystals from his horde, and held them in his palm where they were plainly visible. "Xochi, these are excellent quality, perfectly transparent and eight-sided, and from a place I found not far from here." He worded his statement to suggest that his powers had enabled him to find crystals that her lesser powers had failed to locate.

"Do you have twelve?" she asked, her eyes narrowing.

"Yes, quite a few more, in fact."

"Are you so stupid that you don't realize that I can easily kill you and take all of them without answering any questions?" she said.

"That might be more difficult than you believe," he replied. Putting the three crystals in his shirt pocket, he added, "Look. Can't we stop barking at each other like dogs? The simplest course is for me to ask you my questions. Regardless of what you say or don't say, I'll give you the three crystals I showed you, and the more information you give me, the more crystals I'll give you."

"Simple isn't my way," she said.

"So I gather," Don Carlos replied, and broke out into peals of laughter.

Xochi smiled, an insincere smile that Don Carlos could tell was a ruse to disarm him while she gathered power in her right arm to hurl a deadly blast of energy at him. When she sent the blast at his chest a moment later, he had already chosen his favorite response among the three available to him: dodge the blast, deflect it with a blast of his own, or turn it around and send it back at Xochi. With lightning speed he chose the third option, and the returning blast caught Xochi on the arm (he had aimed it there so as to not give her a mortal wound) and caused her to cry out in pain.

Her cry of pain immediately changed to a cry of rage, and her anger seemed to inflate her body. She swelled up until she looked like a hairy beast the same light-brown color as her dress. Though she appeared taller than before, Don Carlos's sorcerer's vision enabled him to see that this was an illusion. Although she projected an image of greater size, she remained small compared to him. Nevertheless, when the beast-Xochi opened her mouth and snarled, the vicious, sharp teeth she bared would have been sufficient to frighten a lesser man out of his wits.

The beast-Xochi leaped at Don Carlos, intent on either killing him or doing him grave harm. He swiftly transformed himself into a gigantic cougar, an animal form that was clearest in his mind from his recent encounter with Ramona. Meeting aggression with aggression, the cougar-Carlos stepped forward and with one swipe of his huge paw struck the beast-Xochi a blow that sent her sprawling in a heap fifteen feet to one side.

Stunned, the beast-Xochi lay motionless on the ground, gradually losing any semblance of a non-human form. That process was completed when Xochi regained full consciousness. She was bleeding, though not seriously, from the side of her head, where Don Carlos had struck her beast form.

Xochi changed tactics. She straightened her hair and dress and smiled in a beguiling way. "You're right," she said. "There's no need to fight. I've been foolish to attack such a powerful brujo. Give me those three crystals"—at this point she began walking toward him—"and I'll answer your questions."

The thought crossed Don Carlos's mind that this pleasant version of Xochi projected a strong feminine erotic appeal, stocky or not. Noticing the drift of his thinking, he warned himself to be careful. With his guard up, he became aware of subtle signs, invisible to the ordinary man's eyes, that Xochi was not sincere in her offer to cooperate with him.

Once more, he was a step ahead of Xochi when she again attacked him, leaping at him from four feet away with bared teeth and an intention to kill him by biting his jugular vein. Don Carlos caught her in mid-air, grabbing her by the waist and spinning her forcefully around. He maneuvered both of them to a nearby rock and sat on it. He was now holding her face down over his knees. With one hand he held her head up by the hair, preventing her from biting him on the leg, and with his other hand he pressed down hard on the middle of her back, pinning her to his lap. Xochi kicked violently and screamed angrily, "Let me go! Take your hands off of me!" She twisted and turned in an unsuccessful effort to break loose.

Her protests did not diminish. "Let go of me, you ##<*#>&," she screamed—he couldn't tell what name she'd called him because it was in a language he didn't know, but he was sure it wasn't complimentary.

Out of a clear blue sky a lightning bolt struck the ground not twenty feet from the spot where Carlos and Xochi were grappling. "Stop that, you idiot!" Don Carlos exclaimed. "You'll kill both of us if you keep that up. I'm not letting you go until you promise to deal with me honestly."

A long silence followed. Don Carlos listened to bees buzzing in the brush and heard a hawk's cry in the distance. At last, with obvious reluctance, Xochi spoke. "All right. If you let me go, I won't attack you again."

Don Carlos tossed Xochi as gently as possible to his right, and she landed on her feet about a man's height away from him. She was still seething, and she glared at him with her mouth set in a straight line and her eyes afire with hatred.

Don Carlos reached in his pocket and brought out the three large dark green crystals that he had collected. "I mean you no harm," he said. "Here. Take these three crystals as a peace offering; no conditions. No answers to my questions required."

Xochi's expression altered ever so slightly. "I never expected anyone to show up with the rare type of crystal I demanded. The whole idea was to require an impossible task of visitors so they'd leave me alone. Put them on that rock and step back so I can pick them up and examine them without coming too close to you."

Don Carlos did as she asked and used the act of backing away to go over to his knapsack and take out the chain of cactus flowers he'd made. "I brought these flowers for you," he said, stepping forward to put the flower garland on the rock and again backing off.

She observed his careful effort to keep his distance. "What do you want of Xochiquetzal?" she asked, pronouncing her full name.

"Xochiquetzal" — he repeated the name to prove he'd noticed — "it's as I said earlier. I have some questions I'd like to ask you."

Xochi's attention seemed focused on a distant place. "In the Old Times, Xochiquetzal's followers frequently brought her flowers, and every eighth year they held a huge ceremonial procession in her honor — carrying her, bedecked in flowers, to her temple on a platform, while birds and butterflies fluttered all around her. Those happy days ended long ago."

"When was all this?" Don Carlos asked.

The angry look returned to Xochi's face. "That was two centuries ago, before you Spaniards conquered my people — killing, raping, and enslaving them. Before you came Xochiquetzal was beloved as the guardian of mothers and their children, revered as the embodiment of female sexual prowess, and worshipped as the source of fertility among our people. Then you Spanish came, killed our priests, burned our sacred books, and imposed your language, religion, clothing, and morals on us. Everything of living value was taken from us."

"Is Xochiquetzal still venerated by anyone, anywhere?" Don Carlos asked.

"A few continue to worship her under difficult circumstances," Xochi replied. She had put the garland of cactus flowers around her neck and stroked one of the flowers. But with words that showed she was still wary of Don Carlos, she said. "I'll tell you more of the story, if you follow all my requests precisely. Come with me to my dwelling, walking ahead of me and keeping at least your height in distance between us."

Don Carlos and Xochi walked in this fashion a short distance up a path to her tiny house. She had furnished it with a few Native weavings and wall-mounted wooden carvings painted in vivid colors. The carvings seemed to be stylized images of Aztec deities. Turning to him, she asked,

"Would you like some anise tea?" She was still staying a safe distance away from him.

Don Carlos hesitated a moment too long. "I see that you still don't trust me any more than I trust you," she said. It was a statement of fact, made nonjudgmentally.

"Is that any wonder," he replied, "given that the way you greeted me was something less than friendly? Anise tea will be fine," he added.

Neither spoke while Xochi made the tea. As she set the tea in front of him, Don Carlos broke the silence. "How do you feed yourself in this remote place?"

"I do very well," she replied. "My needs are minimal, and this place supplies them adequately. I harvest fruit from cactus plants and gather nuts and roots. The meadow collects sufficient moisture from rain and snow to enable me to have a small garden for squash, beans, and corn. I keep two female goats and milk them when they are not nursing newborn kids.

"When I need something I can't get here, I take my burro, Luz (she smiled at the name), and go disguised as a man into the valley and trade with an old woman herbal healer. She's too crippled to gather many herbs herself, so I bring her herbs that I've harvested and dried. I also bring honey that she sells for me in a nearby town. I never enter the town and I visit her on its outskirts at night so as to not be seen. I lack for nothing in the way of material goods.

"Before we get to your questions, it might help you understand me if I tell you about my own history. You asked whether anyone still honors Xochiquetzal. Yes, a few do, although they are so scattered and demoralized by the conquest of two hundred years ago that the force of their veneration is much weaker than it was in the Old Times. All my women forebears, both before and after the Conquest, honored Xochiquetzal and prayed to her for help in love, childbirth, and sickness. No women were excluded from their prayers, not even prostitutes.

"When the Spanish conquerors tried to eradicate Aztec culture, my distant grandmothers had to disguise their adherence to the Old Ways. Each grandmother in my line passed on to her eldest daughter stories of Xochiquetzal's loving nature. The first girl child in each generation was named Xochi, and my ancestors' devotion to Xochiquetzal was expressed by their becoming, in every generation, midwives and healers. They lived in relative isolation in rugged mountain valleys to the north and west of Mexico City.

"I could tell you much more, as it was passed on to me. For example, some people say that the cult of Xochiquetzal survives in Tlaxcala. Each May the people of Tlaxcala hold a Festival of the Virgin of Ocotlán, during which a procession moves through the town in a manner that's said to resemble the older festivals that were held every eighth year in honor of Xochiquetzal. That may well be; however, my grandmothers never participated in that festival because they remembered that the Tlaxcalans aided the Spanish in the Conquest and that their chiefs were baptized Catholics. My grandmothers were purists who prayed to Xochiquetzal in secret. If anyone asked about their special devotions, they would describe them as a shamanic practice related to their work as healers."

Don Carlos interrupted Xochi. "Pardon me," he said. "What about the veneration of the Virgin of Guadalupe, a Native woman who appeared in a vision to a Native man? I heard that the spot where the church in her honor was built had previously been a temple to an Aztec goddess and that even today Native people, women in particular, go to the church to pray to this goddess, Tonantzin, rather than to the Virgin Mary, the mother of Jesus. Surely you could have found friendship among such women rather than living here alone."

"I'm surprised that a Spaniard knows about the women who pray to Tonantzin, which is a general name that applies to many female Aztec deities, but your story illustrates my point all too well: that Natives must hide their devotion to the Old Ways from the Catholic priests. As for the reason why I haven't stayed among those Native women who honor the Old Ways, even though they have to disguise their beliefs—well, you'll understand better once I've told you the most painful part of my story."

Xochi continued without pausing. "My mother died several years ago, when I was only nineteen years old. My father and every other close relative having died earlier, I was left with sole responsibility for my younger sister. My mother had taught me some skills as a midwife and healer, and I thought my sister and I could manage all right with a small garden, a few goats and chickens, and herbs we would gather to sell or trade.

"The great misfortune we soon suffered came at the hands of a large mestizo family that had established a cattle ranch near our town. This family had eleven boys in it, brothers and cousins, who were rowdy and violent. One night, completely drunk, they came to the small house at the edge of town that I shared with my sister. They threatened us with knives and took turns raping us time and again. A few who dragged my sister off to a separate room were so drunk that they eventually passed out, and she was able to escape. The next day, after these horrible men finally tired of me and went away, I found her hanging from a tree behind our house, dead by her own hand. Is it any wonder, I ask you, that I want nothing to do with men?

"Fearful that these monsters would return, I buried my sister — the priests would not help because she'd committed suicide — and loaded my few possessions on Luz and slipped out of town in the night two days later. I fled for several months. Along the way I met an old woman, a sorceress, who taught me the two ways to protect myself that I tried on you: the throwing of a bolt of sorcerer's energy, and the trick of projecting the appearance of a ferocious beast."

"Did you use a bolt of sorcerer's energy to drive off those two men, Jorge and Olmos, who came here months ago?" Don Carlos asked.

"Yes," she replied. "Olmos was especially threatening. He tried to make me take violet-colored crystals rather than the dark green crystals I'd demanded, and when I rejected his pitiful substitutes, he jumped at me. It was clear that he intended to rape me, so I knocked him down with a burst of sorcerer's energy and while he was too paralyzed to prevent it, I emasculated him. I don't feel guilty at all for having injured him so terribly. He was the type of brute who raped me and my sister. He didn't deserve any mercy."

Don Carlos made no effort to argue with her, in large part because he believed that she was entirely correct in her interpretation of Olmos's intentions. "I notice," he said, "that you described your ability to seem to be a terrible beast as a trick of projecting the appearance of a beast rather than an actual transformation into the animal."

"That's correct," she agreed. "I can't truly change myself into a beast or animal as you did. The old sorceress explained to me that true transformations are very difficult and that the brujos who can achieve them are few in number. Obviously, you're one of those rare brujos who's learned transformations."

"Still," he observed, "you managed to project the appearance of a beast, which seems to me not far removed from actually becoming the beast."

"If you've ever seen a dove confront an enemy," she replied, "you've seen how the bird puffs up her feathers and spreads her wings to appear larger than she is. The defense succeeds if the dove's opponent is fooled, and my imitation of ferocity and strength, which is born of fear and anger and therefore has powerful emotions underlying it, works well enough with ordinary men."

"What about the bolt of lightning that nearly struck us?" Don Carlos asked.

A sober look came to Xochi's face. "I'm not skilled enough to always be able to control these energies once I've raised them."

"Thank you for telling me your story, even though it's a sad and terrible one. Would it be all right if we move on to my questions now?"

"Yes," Xochi replied. "I'll do my best to provide answers."

Don Carlos described his experience of "entering a dream" with Inéz and his Tantric practice with Zoila. "Do you have any idea," he asked, "how I can contact Zoila in dreams?"

"I don't have any direct knowledge from either my grandmothers or my mother," Xochi replied. "I don't even know if what you want to do is possible. Nevertheless, a few ideas for things you could try come to mind. If you'll pardon me for saying so, I sense that had you lived in the Old Times, your pursuit of love with women would have led you to honor Xochiquetzal. Even so, this Zoila's teaching that one can attain union with the gods through love-making is new to me, although, who knows, it may have been taught among Xochiquetzal's followers before the Conquest. Much has been lost.

"As for mastering the art of entering a dream, your experience with Inéz suggests that the two parties to such an encounter would need to have an exceedingly powerful emotional connection, even if the connection mixes positive and negative energies. Also, it sounds as though at least one party must have a strong intention to contact the other. I doubt that the technique would work if the practitioner simply went to sleep without first holding the intention to dream in mind. My best practical suggestion, however, would be based on shamanic methods my grandmothers and my mother used. All of them ingested vision-inducing plants like the buds found on the peyote cactus in order to attain special states in which they could visit the spirit world and receive wisdom that might benefit people who'd sought the shaman's help. My mother taught that chewing peyote cactus buds can enable a healer to speak with plants and ask them to reveal what healing properties they have. I've done that with some success."

"The use of vision-inducing plants sounds promising," Don Carlos exclaimed. "Thank you for the suggestion."

"You're welcome," Xochi said, though a worried look had come on her face. "I have a concern that I must share. If you return unharmed from here, and people hear about it, the fear that's kept most of them away will end, and I will be harassed and possibly injured."

"Perhaps it's time for you to consider returning to the world," Don Carlos suggested. He could tell that this statement alarmed her all the more. "No, don't worry," he continued. "For one thing, I promise that I will resume my journey northward as anonymously as possible without telling anyone I've met you. My apparent disappearance ought to keep people wary of coming here. For a bolder suggestion, hear me out.

"During my recent visit to Mexico City," he told her, "I spoke with a man who has a close acquaintance with the ancient wisdom of Eastern cultures. When I asked what the pursuit of this wisdom path would require of me, he said that a meditative practice leading to liberation from greed, fear, and ignorance would lead me to develop compassion for the suffering most humans endure all the time and motivate me to seek to alleviate their suffering."

"That's a lovely ideal," Xochi said. "As a midwife and healer, my mother used every bit of knowledge she had, including shamanic practice, to bring happiness and well-being to people who sought her help. But I don't see what your Eastern wisdom path has to do with me. I lack knowledge, I'm vulnerable, and I live in fear."

"This has everything to do with you," Don Carlos replied. "Yours is a giving heart that's been injured by violent men, and your fear of experiencing more pain has trapped you into isolating yourself from life. I believe you can return to the world, perhaps disguising your connection to the goddess Xochiquetzal, but applying what you have learned from your mother and grandmothers to help Native people, especially women. I have what I believe is a perfect place for you to begin. Outside Hatawatl, about a half day's travel from here, I came across a refuge run by a mestizo woman, Raquel Vargas, who takes in women who have been abandoned and abused by their husbands, families, and lovers. Some of these women were prostitutes; many have children. These are precisely the women for whom Xochiquetzal was a guardian goddess. It's perhaps also of interest that Señora Vargas is the person who told me about Tonantzin and that she has dedicated her refuge to the Virgin of Guadalupe.

"Señora Vargas does the best she can with limited resources, and I did what I could to help her by giving her a gift of money. An even better contribution I could make to her work would be to convince you to assist her."

Don Carlos and Xochi argued through the night, not even taking a brief break to rest, until finally Carlos convinced Xochi that his proposal would serve to protect her against the danger she might face if she remained alone in her mountain hideaway and also give her a meaningful way to reenter the world and help others. Once the decision was made, it took them most of the day to organize Xochi's belongings for the move. They divided her belongings into three piles—a large one for him to carry, a slightly smaller one for her, and a substantial one for Luz. That night they rested and early the next morning they hiked out with the goods they'd packed, leading Xochi's goats. As they descended the steep trail from the top of the ridge to the valley in which Nombre de Dios was located, they moved slowly to prevent any mishap from occurring. When they reached flat terrain, they went directly to the edge of town to the home of the old woman healer in whom Xochi had complete trust. Carlos left Xochi, Luz, and the goats there while he went into Nombre de Dios to collect Eagle. He also asked Manuel for the loan of two horses, one for Xochi to ride and the other as a packhorse for the goods he and Xochi had carried away with them.

Soon they were on their way, a small caravan consisting of two people, three horses, a burro, and Xochi's goats. They made good time, arriving at Señora Vargas' hospice in the afternoon. Upon hearing Xochi's story and being told of her devotion to the healing arts, Señora Vargas welcomed Xochi with open arms.

Don Carlos returned to Nombre de Dios and left Eagle at Manuel Tapia's stable without speaking with anyone except a new groom who didn't know his name. He spent the night with Manuel Tapia and made his friend a present of the rare green crystals he'd found. In the course of their conversations that evening and at breakfast the next day, Carlos asked Manuel swear to tell anyone who asked that he had no idea what had become of the upper-class man known as Don Alfonso, either in association with Pizarro's death or in connection with Xochi. And to maintain the reputation of the site of Xochi's former home as haunted, Manuel agreed to tell anyone who asked that as far as he knew it remained too dangerous to visit safely.

As Carlos made preparations to leave, Manuel urged him to join three of his men who were driving a dozen horses to El Paso del Norte. "You have," Manuel observed, "saddlebags loaded with pesos I've given you, and there are many thieves between here and El Paso del Norte who'd like to get their hands on that small fortune."

After initially resisting Manuel's proposal, Carlos finally accepted it. He also adopted Manuel's suggestion that he should rendezvous with the three vaqueros north of Nombre de Dios and introduce himself as an ex-soldier named Ricardo de Silva. The ruse ought to work, Manuel maintained; the shabby clothes Carlos had acquired on his trip were suitable for a former soldier, and the three vaqueros came from Durango and would not recognize Eagle as belonging to the gentleman Don Alfonso.

Before joining Manuel's three men to resume his journey north, Don Carlos made a side trip to Señora Vargas's refuge to see how she and Xochi were getting along. Xochi already looked relaxed and happy in her new home. "Thank you for everything," she said. "You're a kind, gentle man."

Embarrassed, he protested, "Gentle? I was a pretty rough with you initially, and"—thinking of his rage at his stepfather—"my inner feelings aren't always kind."

"I wouldn't know about that," she replied. "All I know is that you could have used your powers to squash me like a bug. Instead, you patiently waited for me to stop being so hostile and then went out of your way to help me."

When, in parting, Don Carlos reached for Xochi to give her a farewell hug, she held him away by putting her hand on his chest. With a shake of her head, she said, "I'm sorry, Don Alfonso. I'm not ready to embrace any man, even you who have befriended me and to whom I am exceedingly grateful."

Don Carlos was not at all surprised, once he thought about it. "Would you object," he asked, "if I kissed your hand, Xochiquetzal?"

Xochi laughed heartily. "I suppose I can accept that—after all, you're a titled aristocrat, and out of courtesy I should learn to observe some of the niceties appropriate to your class." She extended her hand, and he kissed it lightly.

"That kiss," Carlos told Eagle later as they made their way north, "was in its own way as precious as any of the kisses I have given women in the past."

22
Memories

Don Carlos had had every intention of returning to Santa Fe before his twenty-first birthday, which was on June 21, 1705. He failed to achieve this goal because his return trip from Mexico City was taking six weeks longer than he'd originally planned, and he was so absorbed in his adventures along the way that he didn't think of his birthday until several days after it had passed. He finally remembered it as he rolled up in his blanket to sleep on the first night after leaving Nombre de Dios. He reflected that had he remained permanently in Mexico City and reached his majority there, his life would have been drastically different. He would have inherited an aristocratic title and whatever was left of his father's estate—his mother's house, if nothing else, assuming his stepfather hadn't borrowed against the property and been unable to repay the mortgage. And he would have continued in the role of a young upper-class man. Far from regretting these matters, Carlos felt nothing but positive emotions about his being free of titles and riches. He liked his life as it was without the social, political, legal, and financial entanglements of the world he had once inhabited.

That night, and for each of the next three nights that he was on the road from Nombre de Dios to El Paso del Norte, he dreamed colorful, elaborate dreams. These were true dreams based on memories of his life five lives earlier, the first in which he had been a brujo, an apprentice to Don Serafino Romero, the greatest of all Sun Moiety brujos.

The first night he dreamed along these lines he and Don Serafino were living on the outskirts of a port city. He didn't know (or remember when he woke up) the city's name, and the sea wasn't visible from their house, but when the wind blew from a certain direction, he could smell salt water.

He found himself as an eighteen-year-old Chibcha Indian in service to Don Serafino, whose public identity was as a physician. But in their times alone together, Don Serafino made it plain to Carlos that he was a brujo intent on training Carlos to follow the Brujo's Way. "Your first lesson," Don

Serafino told his young apprentice one night, "is to learn alertness. You must be eternally vigilant, alert every moment of your life to every threat that presents itself. Failure to succeed at alertness and, equally important, to react appropriately to whatever arises, can mean certain death." He concluded his introductory statement about alertness in a voice that barely rose above a whisper, though he projected his words with such great force from a place deep within himself that Carlos's whole body vibrated as if he was standing in the center of a huge bell tolling a call to worship. "Alertness," he insisted, "is a life-and-death matter."

As Carlos's tutor in alertness, Don Serafino introduced a tough-looking Spanish ex-sailor into the household. "Sanchez will cook for us," Don Serafino remarked, "and keep you alert. He is an excellent cook and has killed dozens of men by various means while fighting for Spain." Carlos wished Don Serafino had not mentioned Sanchez's military exploits. The knowledge that the man was adept at killing made Carlos very nervous.

Nervous, but not, as it turned out, alert, or at least not alert enough. The very night that Sanchez joined the household, Don Serafino and Carlos were seated at the kitchen table eating a tasty stew Sanchez had made when suddenly Sanchez threw a small block of wood across the room that struck Carlos in the chest. (Thinking about the incident later, Carlos realized that he had seen Sanchez's hand move out of the corner of his eye without recognizing the significance of the movement or being quick enough to dodge the block of wood.) "If that had been a knife," Don Serafino observed without looking up from his bowl of stew, "you'd be dead."

Thus began Carlos's training in alertness. Sanchez assaulted him with objects time and time again and under any and all conditions: when Carlos was eating dinner, when he was pulling on his boots, when he was taking a pee, when he was studying a book on sorcery Don Serafino had given him to read. The inventiveness of Sanchez's attacks made them totally unpredictable, and the variety of objects he employed was equally varied: wood blocks, rocks, a fragment of pottery, a piece of fruit, a spoon, and a knife. As Carlos grew more skillful in his responses, he was able to snatch most of these objects out of the air; however, he dodged the knife. Don Serafino scolded him roundly. "That knife was a dangerous weapon. By not catching it, you're giving your assailant an opportunity to pick it up and use it against you."

All of Sanchez's initial assaults had been with objects thrown at Carlos from directly in front of him. After Carlos reached the point at which he either caught or dodged missiles launched directly at him, Sanchez began to try to catch him off guard from the side—not just in the house, but in the yard, on the street, and in the local farmers' market. To reduce the chances of Carlos simply fixing his attention on Sanchez, the wily fellow adopted disguises—an old man, a fat woman, a priest, a laborer, a soldier, and an astonishing range of other false roles. "Your enemy may be anyone, anywhere," Don Serafino warned his apprentice.

On one occasion Sanchez hid behind vines on a second-floor balcony and managed to hit Carlos on the side of the head with a rock that drew blood. "Ouch!" Carlos cried.

Don Serafino, who had been walking beside Carlos, sternly rebuked him. "No! You should never let your enemy know that he's hurt you. Doing so will only give your opponent confidence, and confidence is a great aid to success."

The final phase of training in alertness involved attacks from behind. Initially, Carlos had great difficulty with this exercise and was hit repeatedly by objects that Sanchez hurled at him. By himself one night in the house, he took off his shirt and examined his back in a mirror. His pale olive skin was covered with cuts and bruises.

"How," he complained to Don Serafino, "can I be expected to prevent blows from behind when I can't even see the attacker?"

"It's about time you asked," Don Serafino replied. "After a reasonable period of time trying to figure it out on your own, you shouldn't be too proud to ask. I am your teacher, not your enemy. Attacks from behind are very challenging. Since your eyes can't provide a warning, you must use your ears."

"If I don't hear the rustle of a sleeve or the sound of steps made by the attacker, it's too late, isn't it?" Carlos protested.

"Not at all," Don Serafino told him. "A brujo hears the object approaching in the air."

Astonished, Carlos lodged another protest. "A rock once thrown is silent, isn't it?"

"The prospective victim certainly won't hear it if his senses are dull," Don Serafino agreed. "However, every object makes a sound—granted, it's hard to detect—while it's approaching in the air. Close your eyes; you've been depending too much on sight alone. Sanchez and I will throw objects around the room. Tell us what they are before they hit the wall or the floor. We can start the process with you blindfolded to wean you from trying to use your eyes." He picked up a bandanna and wrapped it around Carlos's head, covering his eyes.

Carlos's immediate response was that Don Serafino was asking him to do something impossible. It took arduous practice to sensitize his hearing. After hours and hours that stretched into days and days Carlos's awareness finally became sufficiently acute not only to hear objects in the air but identify what they were. Eventually, he made no mistakes, shouting out the object's identity before it reached its destination: "Rock!" "Lemon!" "Piece of leather!" "Tea cup!" "Spoon!"

Finally, Don Serafino declared him proficient. "Good," he said by way of congratulations. "You are ready for your final test in alertness."

"What's that?" Carlos asked, disappointed because he'd thought he'd mastered the skill and wouldn't be tested any further.

Don Serafino clapped him on the back and laughed. "If I told you in advance," he said, "it wouldn't be much of a test."

Two days passed without anything extraordinary happening. Don Serafino spent most of the time with Carlos, inculcating him with the importance of the Sun Moiety's motto, "Do no harm."

Early one afternoon, Don Serafino declared, "We've studied enough for now. Let's go out for a walk." He stood up, went to the front door, and opened it, motioning to Carlos to come along. Carlos also rose and walked toward the open door, in the process turning his back to Sanchez, who was cooking dinner on the stove. But Carlos heard something, spun around incredibly fast, and caught a knife by its handle that would have otherwise struck him on the shoulder.

Don Carlos woke up with a start from his dream. A feeling of exhilaration swept over him, even though he was trembling slightly from the intensity of what he'd dreamed. When he returned to camp from answering a call of nature, he found his three companions beginning to prepare breakfast.

During breakfast that first morning on the trail, Manuel Tapia's three employees—two Native men (Andreo and Paz) and one mestizo (Blas)—subjected Carlos to some good-natured teasing. "You were tossing around in your bedroll," Blas ventured, "as though you were dodging knives."

"Maybe he was trying to catch flies in his sleep," Andreo, the older of the two Native men, suggested. "You have to move really fast to catch flies."

Carlos laughed along with them and answered in an ambiguous way, "Maybe so."

As for his companions' observation that he'd tossed and turned in his sleep, he had to acknowledge that they were right. Fending off objects and attacks all night, even dream objects, took a lot of energy, and he had gotten up wondering whether he would be tired all day. He was pleased to find that the contrary was true. He felt refreshed by his dream experience and was in high spirits all day.

That night, the second on the road with Manuel's three men, Carlos's dream memories were on another subject altogether from alertness. This second night's dream began with Don Serafino walking next to him on the street one block from the house where they lived. Without any preliminaries, Don Serafino launched into a new lesson. "Today," he began, "you're going to study auras. Every person, in fact, everything in the world whether animal, plant, or inanimate, has an aura of light around him, her, or it. The most commonplace representations of auras are in portraits of saints and the Virgin Mary, whose heads are often shown to be surrounded by golden light."

"I thought those were halos," Carlos observed.

"Possibly that's what the artist thought he was depicting," Don Serafino replied, "but even if they didn't recognize it as such, they were at some level aware of the exceptionally strong auras that spiritually advanced men and women have. The strength of the aura is a byproduct of the life energy of whatever you're looking at, and because the life energy of people and things varies greatly, a given aura will be bright, dull, or virtually undetectable. Also, all auras have distinctive colors that are determined by the nature or temperament of whatever you're observing. Today I want you to watch people we meet and after we've passed them tell me the color of the person's aura. Don't think too much. Let your intuition and instincts take charge; say whatever comes to mind."

For several blocks Carlos didn't see anything that remotely resembled what he expected to see from Don Serafino's description. No halos of light; no colors of any sort, except the color of people's clothing. "I don't get it," he complained.

"You are thinking too much," Don Serafino asserted. "You're trying to use your mind to analyze the situation, weighing everything rather than simply letting your instincts provide the answer. You're seeing without seeing."

Don Serafino grabbed Carlos by the arm and spun him halfway around so suddenly that Carlos felt momentarily dizzy. "Quick!" he said in an urgent way. "Across the street; the short man. Say the first color that comes to mind."

"Red," Carlos replied, having no idea why he'd said so.

"Exactly!" Don Serafino agreed. "He's a soldier who's wearing civilian attire today. He's as belligerent as they come. Let's keep out of his way."

"Shall I quit trying to figure things out," Carlos asked, "and simply guess?"

"Good idea, Carlosito," Don Serafino told him, using the pet name he'd given Carlos.

Carlos and Don Serafino continued the stroll and walked for hours. Carlos guessed, and guessed, and guessed—sometimes gaining Don Serafino's approval, often missing the mark. Strangely, or it seemed strange to him, as he grew more tired, he grew better at the exercise. He said as much to Don Serafino, who nodded knowingly and replied, "You're seeing better because you're seeing with your belly button rather than your eyes and brain. Focus your awareness on your belly button and use your eyes as little as you can."

Walking on, a dialogue of terse exchanges developed as they passed each new person, Carlos guessing, Don Serafino either confirming or rejecting his guesses.

C: "Green?"

S: "No."

C: "Red?"

S: "Definitely."

C: "Blue."

S: "Light or dark?"

C: "Light blue."

S: "Correct."

C (astonished): "That young woman radiated golden light in large amounts."

S: "Yes, to an unusual degree, though your interest in young women, natural enough for a man your age, may have led you to exaggerate a little."

C: "Dull brown; very weak."

S: "Good!"

C: "Red."

S: "Yes."

C: "Another red, even brighter and deeper. So many reds."

S: "Not surprising, since we're surrounded by a population of

Spanish conquerors who have used violence to establish their dominance over others."

After seemingly endless guesses over a week's time, Carlos began to feel that he knew rather than simply guessed the correct answers—that he had actually begun to see auras. Nearly every guess he made won Don Serafino's endorsement. "I think," Carlos ventured, "I'm seeing auras much better now."

"Yes," Don Serafino replied. "You're learning very fast. In fact, let's quit for the day and go to the inn for wine to celebrate. You can, and should, keep watching; only there's no longer a need to tell me what you're seeing."

One block later, as the two men were only three doors down from the inn, Carlos saw something entirely new in the way of an aura. They passed a middle-aged man, most of whose body aura was gray except for a large black cloud that was clinging to the left side of his upper torso. The black cloud seemed to have tendrils that reached into the man's body.

After they'd passed the man, Carlos whispered to Don Serafino, "That man looked sick!"

"Very sick," Don Serafino agreed.

They heard a commotion behind them and turned to look. The man had collapsed.

A woman kneeling beside him cried out, "He was walking along and suddenly, without warning, he dropped dead!"

"There was ample warning," Don Serafino told Carlos. "I saw it, as did you. The black cloud was death clinging to him."

Carlos awoke from this dream, feeling sad for the man who had lived with no awareness of his condition. "Lack of awareness," Don Serafino asserted while they drank their wine after the incident of the man collapsing on the sidewalk, "is one of the three deadly enemies of wisdom. The others are greed and aversion. Although no one can completely eliminate ignorance, desire, and aversion from his mind, as brujos we train ourselves to recognize these obstacles to truth and to avoid being drawn into giving them power by believing in them."

Don Carlos got up wondering what sort of breakfast-time commentary his three companions would make about his behavior through the night.

"You didn't thrash around so much last night," Andreo, the older Native man, reported, "but you sure talked up a storm. You sounded as though you were shouting colors: 'Red!' 'Yellow!'"

"Were you dreaming in color?" Blas asked.

"Yes, vivid color," Carlos replied.

"That's amazing," Andreo declared. "I dream a lot, but I can't remember any dreams that were in color."

"I don't dream much at all," Paz, the younger of the two Native men, said a bit glumly.

Carlos's companions began to discuss dreams they remembered and to argue—the three of them seemed to enjoy arguing about almost any topic—whether or not it mattered if one dreamed in color, without colors, or not at all. By the time they'd saddled up and gotten their herd of horses organized, they seemed to have forgotten about Carlos shouting colors throughout the night.

Don Carlos, his companions, and the horses they were driving north covered more territory that day than on previous days. All our auras, Carlos observed with an inward chuckle, look bright today. Perhaps that accounts for our extra stamina, the additional energy that led us to make one less rest stop than usual and to eat lunch quickly rather than dawdling. For his part, he knew he was eager for darkness to fall and permit him to bed down and sleep. Two nights of fascinating dreams in which he'd remembered many long-forgotten events made him curious to see what memories he'd have tonight.

He'd always been one to fall asleep immediately upon lying down, and tonight was no different. The third in this series of dreams began right away. He and Don Serafino were seated at their dinner table, having just finished lunch. Sanchez came in the door with a small black dog. Carlos wondered what that was about. They'd never had any pets. "This is Perrocito," Don Serafino said. "He's to be your teacher."

Carlos was perplexed, and his confusion must have showed on his face. Don Serafino laughed and explained. "Every brujo benefits from having at least one sorcerer's skill at which he's unusually adept. Mine is astral projection, leaping across distances in a moment's time. I don't know of any other brujo, whether from the Moon or the Sun Moiety, who can do that. A few brujos of the Sun Moiety are remarkable for their capacity to heal sick people, even people who are nearly dead. And that doesn't exhaust the list of special skills that are found among brujos—superhuman physical strength, a capacity for foreknowledge, or a talent for entering into dreams other people are having.

"I've been asking myself," Don Serafino explained, "what brujo's technique might be particularly useful for you to develop as your specialty.

I've decided, without knowing for sure whether this will work out, to try to train you in transformations."

"What do you mean by transformations?" Carlos asked.

"Let me show you," Don Serafino replied, and he stood up and walked over next to Perrocito. Instantly, he disappeared and in his place was a black dog that could have been Perrocito's twin. Carlos's jaw dropped in amazement.

Sanchez declared, "That's an astounding example of a transformation. Now all you have to do is to learn how to do it." At that moment, the second black dog changed back into Don Serafino. The original Perrocito, who'd been eyeing his twin nervously, immediately relaxed.

"What you need to do," Don Serafino asserted, "is to study Perrocito — the way he walks, how he eats and breathes, what interests him and what doesn't, even how he sleeps. If you can familiarize yourself sufficiently with every detail of his existence, then it's possible that you'll be able to enter into a dog form simply by repressing your human energy patterns and taking on a dog's."

"When you're a dog, don't forget what it's like to be human," Sanchez added with a chuckle. "You'll need to remember that, if you want to get back to your human form."

"Don't worry," Don Serafino assured Carlos. "If you're having trouble, I can help you return to being our beloved Carlosito. Begin studying Perrocito."

Thus began Carlos's intensive study of dog life, at least Perrocito's version of a dog's life. Carlos ate when Perrocito ate, scratched at fleas when he did, went out in the yard and peed whenever Perrocito did, rambled around the city's streets investigating alleys and sniffing trees, barked, stretched, lay down, slept, and even tried to breathe at the same pace as Perrocito. He reported these activities and many others in great detail to Don Serafino, but whenever his master told him, "Close your eyes, Carlosito, and become a dog," nothing at all happened.

Carlos lamented his lack of success at learning to do transformations, but Don Serafino urged him not to be discouraged. "Transformations are very difficult; even powerful brujos often lack the ability to change their forms. Your problem may be that you have no affinity for dogs. Let's introduce you to a cat; you may be more cat-like than canine in your temperament."

The next day Sanchez showed up after breakfast with a handsome gray female cat. The cat proved to be very friendly, sauntering over to

Carlos and jumping up on his lap. "I think she likes you," Don Serafino commented. "That's a promising beginning."

Once again, Carlos began to study an animal. The cat, soon named Lucy, seemed to enjoy his attention. Carlos watched closely as she lapped up milk and soon could describe in detail how she managed to get the milk into her mouth. He enjoyed observing her lick her paws and then wash her face and behind her ears, and he watched the way she prowled around hunting squirrels. She also slept a lot—most of the day, and most of the night too. The only trouble was that Carlos found it impossible to sleep as much as she did.

After a week, Don Serafino suggested, "It's about time for you to try to transform yourself into a cat. Close your eyes and feel the fur that covers your body, the smells that you're picking up from breakfast, the sounds of birds outside, and the regular in-and-out of your cat-like breathing."

Carlos tried to follow these instructions, and for a moment he could almost picture himself as a big cat, but imagining himself as a cat and actually becoming one were apparently two very different things.

This failure was followed by more failures. Carlos became despondent. "I'm not making any progress," he complained. "Perhaps I don't have any talent for transformations. Isn't there some other sorcerer's specialty, maybe something easier to do, that I could learn to master?"

"I thought you reported that you almost felt cat-like yesterday," Don Serafino replied. "Don't give up so easily. A brujo must be stubborn to the point of seeming insane in his pursuit of mastery of the Brujo's Way."

Carlos tried again and again to change himself into a cat's form, all without success, even though he felt more kinship with Lucy than he had had with Perrocito, who lacked the qualities of stealth and calm-mindedness that Carlos observed and admired in Lucy. Still, he felt he wasn't getting anywhere. "It's time for you to try another animal," Don Serafino declared. "I'm thinking maybe birds would suit you, although usually flying beings are more of a challenge than grounded beings like dogs and cats. But there's no firm rule; what works for one brujo may not for another, even a more powerful brujo.

"In addition to shifting your study to birds," Don Serafino added, "I think you should study birds in the wild. Perrocito and Lucy, as domestic animals, may lack some quality of being that wild creatures have. For all that you're a well-behaved young man with lots of self-control, you may have a wild streak hiding in yourself. If you get in touch with that deeper level of your character, a certain wildness, it may unleash the power you need to achieve transformations."

In search of wild birds to study, Don Serafino and Carlos traveled for several days away from the city into the countryside. They watched birds every chance they got while on the trip. Finally they found a hermit living on a mountainside who said he would be willing to let them occupy his house for three days while he took some carvings he'd made to sell in the city.

Toward the evening of the second day that Carlos and Don Serafino stayed at the hermit's hut, Carlos was able to report that he had been studying a pair of small nesting birds that lived in a tree behind the hut. He described in great detail the way the birds flew, what they ate, how they moved their bodies when sitting on a tree branch, and much more. He was even able to give such a good imitation of the male bird's call that the male flew over to a place above him, apparently alarmed that a rival might be moving into the area.

"That's it!" Don Serafino exclaimed, hitting him on the shoulder so forcefully that Carlos's brains were momentarily scrambled. "Listen to the bird. What do you hear?"

"A lovely, melodic sound," Carlos replied.

"That's only half the answer," Don Serafino insisted, and then with great power he delivered a command that gave Carlos's body a jolt: "Give yourself to the sound!"

Immediately, the bird's call came again. Carlos felt a strange sensation, as though he wasn't sitting on a bench next to Don Serafino but perched on a branch looking down at two men. He reported this feeling. Although it didn't strike Carlos as having much to do with transformations — he was obviously still in human form — Don Serafino seemed exceedingly pleased. "You're ready to take the next step."

No amount of pleading by Carlos could get Don Serafino to describe the next step. When the hermit returned the following day, Don Serafino paid him a handsome sum for the use of his house, and when the old man invited them to stay longer, Don Serafino replied, "Thank you, but we must move on."

Don Serafino led Carlos up a mountain path to a ridge above the tree line. In spite of feeling confused about their destination and specific purpose, Carlos found himself enjoying their surroundings. A hawk circling above caught his eye, and he watched as it made leisurely circles, seldom needing to use its wings to maintain altitude and repeatedly voicing a cry that seemed calculated to cause its prospective prey to make a panicky dash for cover. The overall effect was mesmerizing, and Carlos lost all sense of time. He imagined what it must be like to be lifted by the air currents alone and to feel the exhilarating rush of air past his body.

Suddenly the hawk went into a steep dive and landed not twenty feet from where Carlos and Don Serafino were standing. A snake writhed, caught in the hawk's talons.

A curious feeling, or rather several curious feelings, came over Carlos. When the hawk hit the ground, a jolt of energy had run through Carlos's lower legs and he clutched his toes as though they were talons. His arms felt larger than usual, especially his shoulders, and his neck swiveled three-quarters of the way around as he checked out his surroundings. He could see five times better than his normal sight permitted. "You make a very fine hawk," Don Serafino said, looming over Carlos from his position beside him. Sure enough, when Carlos looked down at his body, he was a perfectly formed hawk, and his clothes lay in a pile around him. Only some time afterward did it occur to him to wonder how Don Serafino had transformed himself into a dog without his clothes interfering. "That's a much more complicated process," Don Serafino told him. "For now the simpler method, which is to get undressed before you change your form, is best."

After this initial success in the art of transformations Carlos, with help from Don Serafino, practiced changing himself into all manner of animals, though from the first his favorite transformations were into hawks during the day and owls at night. "I can see," Don Serafino commented, "that you're drawn to adopt the forms of birds of prey. I admit that I'm surprised. I had thought of you as a quiet young man, and I certainly didn't expect that you'd have the aggressive spirit of a bird that depends on hunting and killing."

"Do you now believe I'm a violent person?" Carlos asked, dismayed by the thought.

"No," Don Serafino replied, "although that's a possibility, if you choose to turn in that direction. You have a warrior's mentality—ready to fight if necessary and to defend yourself resourcefully. But that combination of qualities doesn't necessarily mean that you're drawn to violence."

"Hawks and owls kill to survive," Carlos observed, a question disguised as a statement.

"True enough," Don Serafino told him, "but they don't kill, as a violent man does, out of rage or for the thrill of it. You might even say that they are matter-of-fact or businesslike in their hunts. They don't indulge in greedy behavior, as is characteristic of violent men."

It was still dark, at least two hours before dawn, when Don Carlos awakened from his dream. He didn't feel the least bit sleepy, so he walked out of camp and changed himself into an owl. The thought came to him that he achieved such transformations easily now, but the dream he'd had the previous night reminded him that the technique of transformations had originally been very difficult. He was warmed by the memory of Don Serafino telling him at the end of his training, "Transformations aren't easy. Despite your doubts, you learned to change yourself into other forms quite quickly, and you've now achieved an extraordinary mastery of this aspect of the brujo's art."

Soaring over the Camino Real to the north of his camp, Don Carlos saw no indication of the presence of the highway robbers that often roamed the area. He relaxed and let himself experience the great delight of being an owl. He made it back to camp to join his companions for breakfast.

"We began to worry," the mestizo said, "that you'd wandered off for good or had been carried away by brigands."

"Not a chance," Don Carlos replied with a laugh. "You'd have heard me screaming bloody murder. No, I like to pray alone for an hour or two before dawn; I was never far away."

With only one more night on the road until he reached El Paso del Norte, Carlos felt intense curiosity about what he might dream that evening.

23

Celeste

Anticipation can make time seem to go slowly. In his eagerness for night to come and the chance it would provide to dream, Carlos spent the whole day in an impatient mood. As if his impatience were infecting the others, he noticed that he and his companions were making very good time. He wasn't the only one, he decided, who was eager to get somewhere, though Manuel's three men probably were pushing the pace to reach El Paso del Norte sooner rather than later, while he was mentally hurrying forward to nightfall.

As luck would have it, his three companions were in no rush to eat dinner and get to sleep once they'd set up camp for the night. Today, the two young Native men announced, was their mestizo captain's birthday, and they'd planned a party to celebrate. Carlos had not been aware that Paz, the younger Native cowboy, had spent every spare moment during rest periods that day hunting through the brush for rattlesnakes. He'd managed to find and kill four and reported his success with great pride.

Andreo, the older of the two Natives, barely more than a boy himself, was cooking a special dish — rattlesnake with onions in gravy flavored with chili peppers and other spices — that his mother had taught him. "It's a great treat!" he announced. Served rolled up in corn tortillas, the rattlesnake recipe, Carlos agreed, was very tasty. A side dish of pan-fried potatoes added the bulk to the meal that four hungry men needed after working all day.

Carlos was amused by the stealth with which Andreo and Paz had gone about their preparations. Andreo had brought onions and potatoes in a string bag from Nombre de Dios, and Paz and had managed to conduct his rattlesnake hunts without either Carlos or Blas, the birthday person, catching on to their ultimate purpose.

The most astonishing aspect of Andreo and Paz's preparations was that they had managed to hide three bottles of wine in a pack of blankets that one of the extra horses was carrying. "I apologize that there aren't four bottles," Andreo said, "one for each of us; we'll just have to make do with two bottles for Blas, and the three of us will share the third." This statement prompted a burst of raucous laughter from Carlos's companions. Apparently, Blas loved to drink and often kept drinking until he was blind drunk.

"You scoundrels!" Blas declared, pretending to be outraged. "You've had this wine along for days without telling me!"

"We didn't dare tell you," Andreo replied with a laugh. "If you'd known about the wine, none of it would be left for your party."

Don Carlos took only one cup of wine, nursing it along while Andreo and Paz downed the rest of the bottle they'd designated for themselves. Blas, meanwhile, consumed cup after cup and finally, when he'd reached the second half of the second bottle, dispensed with the formality of pouring the wine into a cup and began to drink directly from the bottle.

Quite drunk now, Blas began to brag about fights he'd won and the women, a great many of them, according to him, that he'd seduced. He challenged Andreo, saying, "You can't hold a candle to me as a fighter or seducer of women."

Andreo, himself a little drunk, though considerably less so than Blas, asserted that he'd always avoided brawling, but that he had seduced every woman in his village before leaving for Nombre de Dios.

Blas scoffed at this boast. "How many women was that, two? I once heard you say you came from a small village."

Paz spoke up at last. "Maybe seducing his neighbors' wives, daughters, and grandmothers was why he had to leave his old village."

Blas was amazed. "Did everyone notice?" he asked. "Paz actually made a joke; I never thought I'd see the day."

Andreo refused to let Paz's jibe go unanswered. "Ha!" he replied. "Coming from a boy who's never been with a woman, that doesn't mean anything."

Paz looked thoroughly deflated and miserable. Blas came to his rescue. "Don't worry, Paz. We'll find you a pretty señorita in El Paso del Norte who will enjoy showing you how it's done."

Paz turned pink in the face, but he didn't look displeased at this prospect.

The banter among Manuel's three hired hands continued in this fashion long after dark, with Don Carlos an amused observer, even though he was impatient to get to sleep.

That was not to be. For the past hour the companions had heard thunder and seen frequent flashes of lightning in the mountains to the west. These signs of a major thunderstorm had grown closer and closer as the evening progressed, and the horses, both those in the herd and the men's mounts—all except for Eagle, who was as steady as they come—were moving about restlessly. Drops of rain had begun to fall.

"Maybe we should see what we can do to keep the horses calm," Don Carlos suggested.

Too late. A huge lightning bolt, followed by a tremendous clap of thunder, struck close to the camp. Three of the horses in the herd made a run for it, breaking their picket lines and charging away from camp. "I'll go after them," Carlos shouted, running to Eagle and jumping on his bare back.

Paz called out, "I'll get a saddle on my horse and try to keep the herd here." Andreo leaped up to do likewise; Blas toppled over in an alcohol-induced stupor, no use at all.

With just a halter and a lead rope to work with, Carlos would have had a tough time keeping Eagle on task, except that their longstanding friendship produced complete cooperation between them. Eagle responded alertly to every signal from Carlos, and for much of the time that he and his master were pursuing the runaways, Eagle didn't need guidance. He was a very smart horse who understood precisely what the situation required.

After a chase of at least ten minutes, Carlos and Eagle finally cornered the three runaways in a dry arroyo that dead-ended only a short distance from the road. The rain was diminishing, and the slackening of the downpour perhaps contributed to the runaways' decision to stop when they did. Although the three milled around in a confused way, they couldn't muster the motivation to try to bolt past Carlos and Eagle, who were partly blocking the escape route.

Now came the tough part. It was one thing to have caught up with the runaways, but how, Carlos asked himself, am I going to get them back to camp? Fortunately, despite the downpour, the lightning strikes and thunder had abated somewhat; even so, the runaways were still in a state of alarm, ready to charge off again at the slightest provocation.

Carlos finally remembered that he'd stored some lumps of sugar in his pocket as future rewards for Eagle. He dismounted and walked toward the calmest of the runaways, which happened to be the one he knew best, a sturdy bay horse unimaginatively named Big Boy. Holding some of the sugar out invitingly and speaking quietly to him — "Easy there, Big Boy" — Carlos succeeded in feeding the sugar to the nervous creature. While Big Boy was eating a lump of sugar, Carlos gently picked up the lead rope that was attached to the horse's halter.

By making a sugar offering to the other two runaways, he was able to grasp their lead ropes also and to walk all three horses over to where Eagle was standing. Remounting Eagle, the lead ropes firmly in hand, he started out of the arroyo at a very slow walk. To his great relief, the runaways followed dutifully along.

Back at the camp, where Blas was only now beginning to come to, Don Carlos learned that Andreo and Paz, both experienced horsemen despite their youth, had succeeded in checking the best efforts of several horses in the herd to run off. With the Carlos's return with the three runaways, all twelve horses were accounted for.

No sooner were the four men congratulating themselves on having gotten the situation under control than torrents of rain began to fall again. Combined with the darkness, the downpour made it impossible to see more than ten feet in any direction. A few minutes later, Don Carlos's acute hearing alerted him to another danger. They had camped on the edge of a tiny trickle of water that, though it scarcely qualified to be called a creek, was a watercourse, and Don Carlos could hear that a flash flood was rushing in their direction from the mountain slopes to the west.

"Quick!" he shouted. "In a few minutes a flash flood is going to sweep through here. I can hear the wall of water up the canyon."

None of his companions could hear the oncoming flood waters, but they weren't about to question Don Carlos's perception. They scrambled to gather up what they could—a few cooking utensils, blankets, and their gear—threw everything on their mounts, and started to herd the other horses north to higher ground. Blas, though still very drunk, and therefore not much help, managed to clamber on his horse (which Carlos had quickly saddled) and follow everyone else to safety.

They barely made it. Only minutes after they'd left their camp, a ten-foot-high wall of water swept through, carrying pieces of wood and even small boulders along with it. In the darkness, the four men couldn't see the site of their former camp, but they knew that anything they'd had to leave behind was gone for good.

"We're lucky we were still up and dressed or we'd have lost our boots and clothes," Don Carlos observed.

"I think there may have been some wine left in that second bottle," Blas said sorrowfully.

"And how would you know?" Andreo asked. "You were too drunk to see straight, much less think straight."

Everyone had a good laugh at Blas's expense, and he joined in. Don Carlos liked these men and men of their type. Life knocked them around, but they didn't dwell on their losses. They'd escaped danger to live another day. That was good enough.

A steady rain was still falling. Everyone and everything was wet and getting wetter by the minute. "We're soaked to the skin," Don Carlos declared. "Why don't we keep riding, which at least will help us keep warm? This thunderstorm may have been local enough that we'll find dry ground a few miles from here. If and when we do, we can stop and try to get some rest."

An hour later the small caravan came to drier ground and a flat spot with a little grass for the horses and room for the four men to spread out their blankets and use their saddles for pillows, admittedly pillows of an uncomfortable sort. The blankets were still damp, with the result that conditions were barely tolerable.

Despite these impediments to rest, Don Carlos had no trouble falling asleep almost as soon as he lay down. The last words he heard were from Andreo. "There he goes again. The way the man can go to sleep at the drop of a hat is nothing short of amazing." From the laughter that greeted this statement, it seemed that everyone found Carlos's capacity for sleep both astonishing and amusing. At least, Carlos observed to himself, I'm a source of innocent merriment.

Not long after falling asleep Carlos began to dream again about his life with Don Serafino. Although they were sitting together in a house that hadn't appeared in any of the three previous dreams, Carlos assumed the place was in the same city because the air smelled salty.

The principal feature of the room was a fencing strip. Three young men were packing swords into bags. The oldest of the three had a very sour look on his face. "Leon," Don Serafino commented quietly to Carlos, "doesn't like to lose, and you defeated him soundly again and again."

Even though Leon couldn't possibly have heard what Don Serafino said from across the room, he glanced angrily at Carlos and stomped off.

"The problem," Don Serafino remarked, "is that you've become too good for the local competition. No one can win even one exchange with you, much less a best of seven bout. That's fine, except that you're still nowhere as good as you could be or ought to be if you're going to go into the world, as I hope you will, as a fencer of unparalleled skill."

"I'd like to improve," Carlos replied. "What can be done?"

"Luckily for you," Don Serafino told him, "I have a solution. Two weeks ago an old friend of mine arrived in the city from Cuba. My friend is an excellent fencer, much better than you at present, though perhaps not better than you can become. Do you remember that narrow lane we sometimes pass, the one with red impatiens blooming lushly on each side?"

"Yes, I know it well," Carlos answered, "though I've never gone down it."

Don Serafino replied, "My friend lives at the end of the lane in a pink adobe house. Go over there right away. Knock three times on the door. I'm confident my friend will teach you a great deal."

Carlos packed up his equipment, eager to test himself against a fine fencer. He knew that the best way to improve was to fence with someone who had skills superior to his own.

The lane in question was only four blocks from Don Serafino's residence and Carlos turned into it with a spring in his step. The pink house was small, with fragrant flowers of many types hanging from pots on the veranda or planted in rows around the base of the house's walls. The effect of the varied fragrances wafting through the air was delightful.

As instructed, Carlos knocked three times. He heard soft footsteps within. The door opened and a woman who appeared to be twice his age, perhaps forty years old, looked at him and asked, "Are you Don Serafino's student?"

She laughed at the expression on his face. He had expected to be greeted by a man, only to be confronted by a handsome Spanish woman in the tight shirt and pants that fencers wore for their bouts. Obviously, she was Don Serafino's friend and his, Carlos's, prospective tutor. Her laugh had a lovely quality to it, not unlike the joyful sound of a lark. "That old scoundrel!" she exclaimed. "I can see from the look on your face that he didn't tell you that your fencing master is a woman."

"No, he didn't," Carlos managed to stammer.

"And you've never heard of such a thing," she guessed.

Hesitating a bare second, he confessed, "No, I never knew that women fence, much less that they could be masters of fencing."

"Well," she observed cheerfully, "at the moment you have only Don Serafino's word for it. Come in, and we'll fence, and you can judge for yourself. The fencing strip is in the interior patio garden. By the way, my name is Celeste."

Indicating that he was to follow her, she turned and led him to the patio. When they reached it, she turned to him again and looked at him in a friendly manner. Her eyes were deep brown, not just deep in color but somehow deep in an emotional way. He made this observation without any prior experience in reading eyes for their emotional qualities. Eyes had always been just eyes to him until now.

"Why don't we get right to it?" she suggested, as she picked up her sword. He unpacked his and they took up their positions and immediately began to fence.

They agreed to score their bouts on the basis that the first competitor to achieve seven hits would be the winner, after which they would immediately begin another bout.

In their initial bout Celeste scored the required seven hits, while he achieved only two. She was a magnificent fencer — lightning fast and creative. His best thrusts, variations on attacks that almost always succeeded against the men with whom he had been fencing, were nearly always parried, and often Celeste's ripostes produced a hit for her.

During the next three bouts, Carlos attempted a variety of strategies — going all out on the offense, fencing in a defensive mode, and trying a mix of both that he hoped would be sufficiently unpredictable to break through and score touché. Time and time again, Celeste responded with great flexibility to everything he offered. It seemed as though she was always one step ahead of him, even to the point that she appeared to know what he was trying to do before he knew.

Over the course of eight bouts, all of them completed without a break to rest, Carlos managed to improve somewhat. In the seventh bout he made three touches, and in the eighth four, still well short of Celeste's total. Upon scoring the final hit of the eighth bout, she dropped her guard and declared, "Perhaps that's enough for today. I hope you'll return tomorrow so that we can resume our practice." He nodded and told her that he would look forward to it.

The following day it seemed as though Celeste raised the level of her fencing. Carlos had hoped that he would start where he had left off, achieving three or four touches and gradually increasing his successes. He was dismayed when he lost the first three bouts two touches to her seven. Gathering himself, he bore down, fencing with a passion born of not liking to be bested. His renewed vigor produced results, and by the eighth bout of the day he'd once again achieved four hits to her seven.

"Good," she told him. "You have a lot of natural talent. We will meet again tomorrow at the same time, I hope." He agreed.

The next day he was dismayed to find that he was once again at the point he'd been when he'd begun the sessions with Celeste. During the first four bouts, his successes were minimal: one hit, two, two again, and back to one, even though he believed he was fencing well above the level that he'd displayed only three days earlier. The trouble was that Celeste matched every advance in his skill with a higher level of fencing on her part.

This pattern was repeated for the next five days. Every improvement that he made was matched and exceeded by Celeste. After a particularly brilliant exchange that he ultimately lost, he asked, "Do you have any suggestions for me? I seem unable to break through."

"Break through to another level?" she replied. "The fact is that you're fencing at a much higher level than the rather amateurish one you brought to our first day's bouts. As for what you could do to improve even more, my suggestion is that you slow down the exchanges, seeing my actions as though they were happening in slow motion. Think about that strategy, and see if you can apply it tomorrow."

Carlos had no idea what Celeste had meant. How did one slow down an opponent who, as in Celeste's case, thrust and parried with incredible speed? He even asked Don Serafino that evening if he could explain what Celeste meant. "How should I know?" his mentor replied. "I'm no fencer."

Before he could consider how rude his answer might seem, Carlos burst out, "Why do I think you know more than you're telling me?"

"Perhaps so," Don Serafino told him. "Just remember that words are concepts, and actions are realities."

Armed with this advice, though not truly understanding how to apply it, Carlos knocked on Celeste's door the next morning. She greeted him as always. The only difference was that today she'd chosen to wear a deep-red fencing outfit with a low neckline. Carlos had come to admire her body greatly, to the point that he dreamed about her shapely figure. They fenced in his dreams, and he didn't do any better in his dreams than in reality.

The first three bouts of the day went badly for him. He scored fewer touches than ever, only one in two of the bouts and none at all in the other. She stopped and dropped her guard. "I told you to slow down the exchanges. I didn't tell you to fence slowly, but you're being incredibly slow today considering what you can do. Let me repeat the instruction: You must see your opponent's every move as though it's happening slowly, slowly enough for you to anticipate and preempt your opponent's every initiative."

"I haven't figured out how to do that," he said.

"You passed Don Serafino's course in alertness, didn't you? No, he didn't tell me; he didn't need to. I can see it. Surely, he advised you to stop thinking with your head and to be guided by instincts arising from your belly button. That's what he always said to me."

This was the first hint that Celeste had once been, and possibly remained, a student of Don Serefino's.

"Focus on your belly button," she instructed him. "Or, more accurately, focus deep inside your abdomen a few inches below your navel."

"Let me gather my wits," he said, amused at the idea that according to Celeste his wits were located just below his belly button.

For the rest of that day and during the next two days, Carlos achieved greater success as he began to understand what Celeste meant by seeing one's opponent in slow motion. The number of hits he achieved in each bout gradually increased from two to three, from three to four, and then, in almost every bout, from four to five.

During the seventh bout of the day, and after he'd twice achieved five touches in earlier bouts, he and Celeste were tied at five to five. His attention had reached a level of concentration that heretofore would have seemed inconceivable. On the next exchange Celeste suddenly lunged forward, stretching out toward him farther than she'd ever reached before. It could have been a major error, as it left her less well-balanced, her weight far forward. But as she'd made this move, her breasts had pressed visibly into the V-shaped neckline of her snug fencing outfit, and Carlos's attention shifted completely. He felt that he was being drawn to her bosom as if by a powerful magnet. Triumphantly, she cried, "Touché!"

"I was momentarily distracted," he admitted, somehow finding it amusing.

"Yes," she said drily. "I noticed. But having sexual energy is one thing, and letting it cause you to lose your concentration in a bout is quite another."

He couldn't believe what she had said. "A point lost because I glimpsed Paradise? I'm not sure that's such a bad exchange."

Celeste hooted. "Paradise? You are very young. I hope to teach you better. For instance, are you aware of my aura? Surely, Don Serafino has taught you about auras."

"Yes," Carlos replied. "You have a golden aura, tinged with a yellow luminosity. It's also amazingly strong, extending well beyond your body to nearly fill the room."

"A slight exaggeration, perhaps," she declared, "that phrase about nearly filling the room. However, my question is whether you see what happens to my aura when I make a thrust or riposte that's intended to produce a hit."

"I haven't noticed any change," he admitted.

Tapping him solemnly on the shoulder with the blade of her sword, she said, "Pay attention! Your assignment for tomorrow is to notice what happens and describe it to me."

Carlos wasn't sure what it was about this most recent session with Celeste that left him vaguely dissatisfied. Was it that she'd used a trick to disrupt his concentration, and he'd fallen for it? Or was it that he'd been doing so well until she pulled the rug out from under him? Or that she'd given him another focus for his attention—her aura—when he already had almost too much to handle, including the incredible speed of their exchanges, the constant innovations with which she confronted him, and the practice of slowing things down?

He arrived on her doorstep to find that she was seated on the house's veranda. She was wearing a black outfit that covered her front halfway up her neck. "I promise not to be bad," she teased him, "and distract you—now that I know you're distractible"

They fenced intensely, and he consistently won four or five exchanges to every seven she won. Then, after the fourth such bout, he noticed that every time she launched one of her successful attacks there was a tiny shift in her aura. He began to watch for it, and soon confirmed that the shift resembled a small bubble that appeared near the hand in which she held her sword. Having confirmed this impression during the fifth bout of the day, he tried to use what he was seeing, reacting to these small shifts in her aura before they developed fully. To his astonishment he achieved seven touches to her four during the bout.

"Ah!" she declared approvingly. "You've seen how my aura changes at those decisive moments. Do you know what you're seeing?"

"It's rather like a bubble rises...," he began.

"Yes, that's what it looks like, but what is it?" she insisted.

After only a moment's pause, he simply said, "Intention."

"Exactly!" she agreed. "Now that I know for certain that you can see my intentions, as I've seen yours all along, let's continue and see how things go."

They resumed their bouts and found that they were now almost equally matched. He won some seven touches to her five or six, and during the next bout the results would be reversed. They became so absorbed in their exchanges that they didn't stop, as had been their custom, when they'd completed eight bouts. Only once they'd completed the tenth bout did Celeste say, "Perhaps we should call it a day."

The day had been extremely hot and humid, and their exertions had left both of them drenched with sweat. "I could wring my clothes out," Carlos observed, "and fill a bucket with the water."

"Me too," she agreed. "What I need now is a shower. Will you help me do so?"

"How?" he asked, perplexed.

"The shower in this house consists of a bucket with holes in it. When water is poured in, you get a shower. Pails with water in them are up on a shelf above the alcove where you stand while taking a shower. If I dump the water in the bucket and climb down the ladder next to the shelf, half the water is out before I get under the bucket. If you'll pour the water into the bucket for me, I'll get my first full shower in this place."

"I guess I can do that," Carlos said.

"It's simpler than fencing with me," Celeste told him with a laugh. Then she showed him where the shower alcove was located. "Climb the ladder," she said, "and stand on the shelf; don't worry. It's plenty strong. I'll be back in a moment."

Carlos noticed that there were four pails full of water on the shelf. He positioned himself and waited. He didn't have long to wait. Celeste came back, her shoulders and feet bare, a large towel wrapped around her body. She smiled up at him. "I'm going to drop the towel, and I want you to pour the water with your eyes closed."

"What?" he protested. "How can I manage that?"

"Use your inner body awareness of where you are in space and let the pouring of the water be directed by that."

He was already holding the pail full of water, and he found he was able to dump water from the pail into the bucket with holes. He believed he could hear the water begin to run down Celeste's body.

She called up to him. "That's good, but you must remember to dump the second pail into the bucket before the first has completely run out." He managed to follow her instructions with his eyes closed.

He was raising the third pail preparatory to pouring it in the bucket when Celeste told him, "That's enough for now. You can open your eyes and climb down."

She had stepped out of the shower alcove and wrapped the towel around herself. When he climbed down, being so close to her made him feel a little dizzy. She fixed him with a look that penetrated deeply into his eyes. "Your turn," she said.

"My turn?"

"Yes, you're just as sweaty as I was. Take your clothes off and get in the alcove. I'll climb up on the shelf and pour water on you. One good turn deserves another."

He hesitated. "What's the matter?" she asked.

He hesitated again. "It's just that it's going to be embarrassing to be naked at this moment."

"So I'll close my eyes," she said.

Carlos undressed quickly and moved into the alcove below the shower bucket. Celeste, still wrapped in her towel but eyes averted, climbed up the ladder and, eyes closed, began to pour water.

Two buckets of water later he felt a lot cleaner. Celeste climbed down the ladder without looking in his direction. She took two robes off a hook and handed one to him. "Put this on," she said. "What's the point of getting fresh and clean and then putting on our sweaty clothes?" She turned her back, undid her towel, slipped into the robe, and knotted its belt around her waist.

"Come have a glass of wine," she said. "Perhaps your clothes will dry in the sun if we give them a little time." She picked up their outfits and carried them down the corridor to the patio, where she spread them over chairs along the path to a dining room. Inside the dining room was a table on which stood a bottle of wine and two glasses.

Celeste poured two glasses of wine, indicated that he should sit down, and, once he'd done so, sat down also. She raised her glass in a toast. "You've reached a whole new level of fencing today. At the moment we're evenly matched, but I can tell that soon, with practice, you'll be far more skillful than I am. That's good. They say that when the student exceeds the teacher, he or she is ready to be on his own. Although you're not quite there, you're well on the way to mastering three skills crucial to excelling: tactical creativity, slowing down your opponent's actions, and taking advantage of your ability to read your opponent's intentions."

"I'm very grateful to you," Carlos replied.

"Let me propose," she suggested, "that you keep coming for daily practice until you are much my superior at fencing. At the pace you're progressing that won't take long, and it's just as well because I will be leaving soon to return to Cuba."

Carlos's heart sank. He realized that he'd fallen in love with Celeste, the difference in their ages be damned. Even though they scarcely knew each other, except as fencing partners, he didn't want to lose her. He said so: "I don't want you to leave."

"That's very sweet of you, Carlos. But Don Serafino, my mentor as he is yours, has goals for me; and given those goals we shouldn't be living in the same place — not the same country, much less the same city."

Carlos mulled over what she'd just said and had many questions. "Have you been Don Serafino's apprentice for long, and if so, why does that require you to go back to Cuba?"

She looked at him intently. "Every twenty years Don Serafino recruits more apprentices, usually four in all. Don Serafino gives each of us tasks to do. I'm sure he'll explain those to you eventually. Since there are so few of us — I seem to be the sole survivor of the generation of apprentices before yours — he sends us to different places."

"The sole survivor?" Carlos felt alarm at this news. "What happened to the others?"

"We are brujos aligned with the Sun Moiety. Our purpose is to live in such a way that at worst we do no harm to anyone or anything, and at best help all beings be happy. There were five of us in my generation of initiates twenty years ago. We've lost contact with all of them except me. Some may have died forgetting that they were brujos and thus were reborn as ordinary men and women, unaware of their past lives as brujos. Others may have been killed by members of the Moon Moiety of sorcerers, ghastly individuals who take joy in causing misery in the world. They despise us because our goals are totally opposite to theirs, a fact that they find deeply threatening."

"What do you do in Cuba?" Carlos asked.

"Dear Carlos. I've probably said too much already. Don Serafino is the one you should hear most of this from. I'll simply say that you'd never recognize me in any of the disguises I use in Cuba. Most commonly I'm an old crone who's a curandera."

"An old crone!" Carlos exclaimed. "I can't believe it. You're much too beautiful."

"What a nice thing to say," Celeste replied. "But you would be amazed how little it takes to fool people, most of whom see only the surface of things. A little powder in my hair to gray it, a stooped posture like that of a worn-out old woman, a cackle for a voice, and a shuffling, weak gait, and most people accept my story that I'm an aged seller of herbal cures. No more questions for now. Come tomorrow and fence with me. I'm enjoying the challenge."

Over the next two weeks, Carlos's superiority at fencing grew undeniable. The point was soon reached at which he achieved three or four touches to each of Celeste's. On very hot days they helped each other take showers, and on rainy days they fenced in the open corridor under the roof of the veranda that faced the patio. Always they sat in Celeste's dining room and drank wine after their sessions were over. A small innovation on Carlos's part was that he began to bring his teacher presents: most often flowers, but once a tiger's-eye bracelet that caught his eye in the market, and another day a necklace made of black obsidian beads that made him think of Celeste's hair. She always gave him a light kiss on the cheek, a tender response that kept him plotting what present to bring her next.

Finally, the day came when Carlos, inspired by Celeste's challenge that he show her the very best he could do, won seven straight exchanges in two successive bouts. This seemed to delight her. "Let's not waste time on something you do so much better than me, although I enjoy losing to you more than I enjoy defeating most opponents. Let's go straight to the shower."

At first they followed their usual routine. Two pails of water for Celeste; two for Carlos. But when she climbed down, she said softly, "Don't put your robe on. Let's go to my bedroom and let the breeze dry us." He was surprised by how comfortable being naked with her felt.

For a while they lay on their backs on her bed without speaking.

Since lying down, Celeste had had her eyes closed, but now she opened them and looked at him with great seriousness. "Do you," she asked, "have a girlfriend or mistress, Carlos?"

He was embarrassed to say "No," which was the truth; he was twenty years old, an age at which he supposed he should have been able to answer affirmatively.

"Permit me to say that I'm surprised," she replied. "You are such a handsome man, so attractive, and from what I've seen, you have very strong erotic inclinations. I guess you simply don't act on them. I've been wondering, for example, why you never touch me. Even our kisses are always initiated by me. And, though we are lying on the bed together, you haven't reached out to touch me."

"It's not that I haven't wanted to," Carlos said.

"Well, then...," she said, opening to him a way that was not just physical.

Ever so tentatively Carlos did what he'd hungered to do for many weeks. He reached over and stroked her arm. He ran his hand over her belly and touched her hip and bent to kiss her lips. She opened her mouth and kissed him deeply. Soon they were entwined.

When their embrace ended, they lay back and she put her hand on his chest. "You understand the principle involved here, don't you?" she asked.

"I have no idea what principle you're talking about," he replied, genuinely puzzled.

"It's all very simple, really," she told him. "Men and women are like two halves of one being. Separately, they are incomplete. Joined together in love their union fulfills them; they are whole."

Carlos came back as usual every day for the next week, only now they spent less time fencing and more time making love. He experienced bliss, both physical and emotional. Then one day she insisted that he continue to hold her in his arms long after they'd finished. She broke the silence by saying, "I'm sad to say that I must return to Cuba. I've greatly overstayed my vacation from my duties there, and you're the reason, which I hope will please you. I would like you to meet me at the docks tomorrow morning. I'm sailing on the ebb tide."

Carlos had known this would happen; still, he was shocked and sad. He admitted as much to Celeste. He also told her that their time together had been an unforgettable pleasure, and he wasn't going to spoil the moment or her memory by moping around. Her response was to pull him into her arms and make love to him.

Don Serafino accompanied him to the docks the next morning. Celeste was there, her luggage already on board. She embraced her friends warmly, kissing each of them on the mouth. Then she addressed them. "Although I normally abhor farewell platitudes, please allow me to voice one from my heart. I hope to see you both again, in this life or a future life." With that, she hurried up the gangplank and stood on deck, waving and smiling until she was out of sight.

Don Serafino had recently explained to Carlos that brujos of the Sun Moiety learned to retain their consciousness as they died and consequently were reborn knowing that they were brujos—so Carlos didn't need to ask what Celeste had meant about possibly seeing him in another life. He turned to Don Serafino and said, "Thank you for finding me such an incomparable instructor in the art of fencing."

"Fencing?" Don Serafino replied with a shake of his head. "Is the art of fencing the only thing you thought this was about? I could have found any number of top-notch men to teach you the art of fencing. I chose Celeste specifically to tutor you in the art of love."

Don Carlos woke from his dream to find himself, still damp from last night's storm, banked up against a saddle he'd used as a pillow. His three companions were also stirring, and they had a good laugh at his expense when he admitted that he'd had another dream.

"We'd never have known," Blas remarked, grinning as though he was sharing a big secret with the other hired hands, "except that you were thrashing around and moaning in your sleep, which is pretty standard for you, I'd say."

Carlos smiled, a smile occasioned less by Blas's good-natured teasing than by thoughts of another time and place. By some unusual form of mental chemistry, he felt that Celeste, his first love, a woman he'd known only briefly more than a century and a half ago, was nevertheless near at hand.

24

Alejandro

As the outskirts of El Paso del Norte came into view Carlos and the three vaqueros who'd accompanied him on his journey northward broke into smiles of relief. Their journey from Nombre de Dios was nearly complete. Carlos could rest two or three days and then start the last leg of his trek back to Santa Fe. Manuel Tapia's men — Blas, Andreo, and Paz — could deliver the horses they'd herded north and enjoy a brief holiday in El Paso del Norte before heading home. The four men had had a good time together and had avoided bandits and calamities due to storms. They had every reason to be pleased with their successes.

Don Carlos took Blas and the two young Native men to an inn and treated them to a big meal and drinks. Some friendly kidding ensued as Manuel's three hired hands tried to get Carlos to tell them details of his dreams. After fending off questions for a while, Carlos decided that half a truth might satisfy their curiosity. "The first night," he said, "I dreamed about being perpetually on the alert for possible attacks on my person. The content of the second was more fantastic, involving my encounters with a variety of people, all of whom glowed with one color or another—red, yellow, blue, and even black—from some inner source. In the third I had the experience of flying like a hawk, and the fourth night brought dreams of romance."

"You must be thinking about a girl waiting for you in Santa Fe," Blas ventured.

"A woman to whom I've proposed," Don Carlos told them, "lives in Santa Fe; whether she's waiting for me is another matter."

"You mean she might have given up on you because you were gone so long?" Andreo asked.

"That's altogether possible," Don Carlos replied. "A rival for her hand remained in Santa Fe. I have a feeling that he might have won her heart while I was away."

"Would that bother you a lot?" Blas wanted to know. "It's none of my business, of course, but you don't seem too upset."

"My answer," Don Carlos said, "is that I've suspected for so long that she might fall in love with my rival that I've armored myself against that possibility."

"Women are so fickle!" Andreo declared out of nowhere.

"And how would you know?" Blas demanded, and the three men began to argue about whether or not women could be trusted, with Blas and Andreo contending that woman were treacherous beings and only Paz, the youngest and the one with no experience of love, holding a more charitable view. The last thing Carlos heard from the three after he excused himself and went about his business was Blas scoffing at Paz's idealism. "Once a woman has broken your heart," he said, "you'll have a different opinion."

El Paso del Norte's army garrison was barely three blocks from the inn where Carlos and his friends had enjoyed their meal. He walked directly to the commandant's offices and asked for Colonel Gabriel Encarnación. The colonel was in his office and very glad to see Carlos. "Don Alfonso," he exclaimed. "We began to wonder whether you were coming back; you've taken much longer than you expected."

"Quite true, colonel," Carlos replied. "Many events pulled me away from my original timetable. My mother died; a friend insisted that I attend his wedding in Puebla, and the necessity of helping a variety of people I encountered on the trip north from Mexico repeatedly delayed me."

"You were exceedingly generous," the colonel observed.

"I simply did what was necessary," Carlos said. "But tell me; are the three soldiers who accompanied me here from Santa Fe all right? They must have worried that I'd abandoned them."

"On the whole," Colonel Encarnación replied, "I dare say that they've enjoyed their time here—enjoyed it, that is, with two possible exceptions. In the first case, because of an increased number of attacks by Native raiders on travelers north of here on the Camino Real, I had to include them in a punitive expedition against the raiders. We got into a nasty fight with a large Apache war party, and one of your friends, Gonzalo Navarro, was badly wounded. I'm glad to say that he's fully recovered.

"In the second case, Alejandro Guzman got into trouble because of a young woman he was romancing. The details are obscure. As I understand it, he and a mestizo girl met at the Saturday markets and became enamored of each other, or at least he began to view her as his sweetheart. Apparently, someone—despite our best efforts we haven't been able to find out who—attacked him one night, dragged him into a dark alley, and beat him nearly to death. He, too, has recovered, though he strikes me as anxious for his own safety. His assailants are still at large. The sergeant in charge of his unit reports that he jumps at shadows and prefers to stay in his quarters rather than go onto the town streets, even in the company of other soldiers."

"Do you feel he'll be unable to make the trip back to Santa Fe?" Carlos wondered.

"My impression," the colonel replied, "is that he's eager to get out of town. I suspect he can't wait for you to be on your way, but I hope you'll tarry a bit and join me and my family for dinner tonight and any other night you're here."

Carlos accepted the colonel's invitation and took advantage of his hospitality three nights in a row. The fare at Colonel Encarnación's, though not elegant, was far superior to the very limited diet that was available on the road. So Carlos justified his decision to stay three days by reasoning that both he and Eagle, especially Eagle, needed to rest and eat more heartily than had been possible on the trail.

Only on the third day of his stay in El Paso del Norte did Don Carlos seek out the three young soldiers who were going to accompany him on the trek north to Santa Fe. The two younger men, Luis and Gonzalo, said they were happy to see him. Gonzalo showed no visible signs of the injuries he'd sustained in battle.

Alejandro Guzman was another matter altogether. Although he was fully recovered from the beating he'd received, his nerves were shot. When Don Carlos invited him to walk to the inn for a meal and drinks, Alejandro initially refused. Carlos had to coax him to come along, using assurances that no one would attack him in broad daylight and that if anyone tried to do so he, Carlos, would deal harshly with the attackers. Alejandro eventually, though with obvious reluctance, agreed to the outing.

After they'd been served lunch, Don Carlos said, "I gather you had a bad experience involving a girl and someone, probably several someones, who attacked you. Are you sure the two things — the girl and the attackers — were directly connected? Isn't it possible that the attackers had nothing to do with the girl?"

Alejandro replied with a shudder. "No! As they were beating me, one of them — there were at least three — hissed, 'Leave Rosa alone, and if you don't, you won't get off so easily the next time.'"

"Did they rob you?" Don Carlos asked.

"They stole my money — I'd just gotten my pay — stripped me naked, and went off with my clothes. I was in such bad shape it was all I could do to drag myself back to the barracks."

"Nasty, very nasty," Don Carlos observed. "You have no idea who they were?"

"No. I never met any brothers, cousins, or men of any sort connected with Rosa. When Colonel Encarnación questioned an aunt of hers, the woman claimed that Rosa didn't have any male relatives who could have been my attackers."

"And the girl, Rosa," Don Carlos inquired, "never hinted that anyone would mind that you were courting her?"

"Not at all," Alejandro said with a grimace. "In fact, she pretty much took the initiative. She flirted with me the first time we met and always encouraged me. Granted, she may have done so because she wanted the gifts I brought her. She was open enough about that. She would point to something—a bracelet or a shawl, for example—and say, 'If you love me, you'll buy that for me.' And she was sexually bold too—she wasn't innocent...." His voice trailed off, and he looked miserable.

"Have you seen her or tried to since being beaten?"

Alejandro flinched at the thought. "I haven't dared, and I don't think it would do any good to try. Colonel Encarnación and the local police attempted to locate her and couldn't. The other women in the market, even her aunt, claim they have no idea where she's gone. It's all very mysterious. Everyone's given up on trying to figure out what's become of her and my attackers." Carlos privately suspected that Rosa and the men who attacked Alejandro had been in cahoots from the very beginning, but he had no intention of saying so.

"I guess you'll be glad to leave El Paso del Norte," Don Carlos suggested gently.

Alejandro looked doubtful. "I'd like to get out of here, even though I don't think I'll be of much use to you as a bodyguard. I've found out that I'm not much of a warrior."

"You mean because three men jumped out of the dark and beat you up?" Don Carlos replied. "That's no disgrace. Please answer a question for me. How long ago did this attack take place?"

"Nearly a month ago now."

"I'd like you to show me the alley where you were beaten."

"I don't want to go near that place ever again!" Alejandro said.

"The best way to deal with fear is to meet it head on," Don Carlos told him. "I can't help you unless you're willing to cooperate. Come, take me to the alley." Alejandro balked at first, but eventually complied.

The alley proved to be a narrow lane off a dark side street. It was a perfect place for thugs to set upon a lone pedestrian at night. "I gather you were headed back to the barracks after a rendezvous with this Rosa?" Don Carlos suggested.

Alejandro looked downcast. "I can't believe I was so stupid. I was walking along thinking of Rosa and not paying any attention to my surroundings. I wasn't aware of the thugs until they jumped on me, knocked me down, and dragged me into the alley."

Although Alejandro wouldn't enter the alley, Carlos did so and found signs of a scuffle. Poor Alejandro wouldn't have had much of a chance under these conditions, he decided. Faint remnants of red auras still lingered from the mugging. Carlos believed that, given enough time, there was a good chance he could track down the attackers from their energy imprints, but he didn't really have the time. He was determined to start north to Santa Fe the next morning.

Don Carlos and his three-soldier escort—Alejandro, Luis, and Gonzalo—left El Paso del Norte at the crack of dawn the next day. In addition to their own mounts, they brought two extra horses and loaded them with supplies: blankets, food, and cooking utensils. Carlos invited Alejandro to ride next to him and instructed Luis and Gonzalo to form a second pair with the pack horses on lead lines.

Carlos studied Alejandro. The young mestizo—he'd turned eighteen while Carlos was on his trip to Mexico City and back—was good looking. It wasn't difficult to see that a young woman might have enjoyed being courted by him, even though in Carlos's opinion this Rosa woman had probably been up to no good from the start. On their first trip together Alejandro had struck Carlos as shy and rather soft-mannered for a man who'd chosen to enlist in the military. But his present fearfulness was new. Carlos began to mull over what he could do to help Alejandro, and he soon had a few ideas. If nothing else, he thought, doing something for Alejandro would be an interesting project to pursue during the eight or nine days it would take to get back to Santa Fe.

Having dealt with that topic, he turned his attention to his own feelings. He examined the reasons for his lack of urgency in returning to Camila. Was it simply a matter, he wondered, of a reluctance to marry because marrying might end his life as a brujo? There seemed to be unknowns beneath the surface of his feelings. Had he secretly hoped that Camila would fall in love with Rafael and thus solve his problem for him? Well, he decided, there's nothing to be done now; whatever will be, will be.

By noon the July sun was beating down on the four travelers and Carlos began to look for a place with water where they could stop, water their horses, and take a break. A small hacienda that he'd not noticed on the southward phase of his journey turned up at just the right moment. When Carlos made it plain to the owner that he could pay in pesos for the man's hospitality, the old fellow was delighted. Silver coins were very hard to come by on the New Mexican frontier.

A small stand of poplar trees gave Don Carlos and his companions a shady place to rest during the hottest part of the afternoon. An inspiration came to Carlos and he asked the young soldiers, "You have daggers, but do you ever practice their use? I've seen your comrades in arms training with their muskets and swords but never with their daggers, even though daggers are standard equipment."

Gonzalo shook his head. "I've had almost no training in the use of a dagger," he said. Alejandro and Luis agreed that the same was true for them.

Don Carlos jumped up energetically. "Then let's not pass the time idly. Let's use our break to learn something. You may not realize it, but many people regard me as the finest fencer in New Spain and New Mexico. It's been many years since I've been bested in a bout. I'll grant you that the dagger is a very different weapon from a sword; nevertheless, I suspect certain features of a dagger's use resemble fencing. If Luis will loan me his dagger, Gonzalo and I can test our skill against each other. We'll wrap a piece of leather around the points of our weapons to be certain no one gets hurt."

Carlos had, as he'd acknowledged, no experience in using a dagger, at least not in his present lifetime. Still, he had many advantages. The footwork of a knife fight came easily to him, and many of the maneuvers—feinting, lunging, and parrying—resembled moves used in fencing. His other advantages included quickness, the ability to anticipate his opponent's next move, and creativity in responding moment-by-moment to the contest's imperatives. He easily bested Gonzalo, repeatedly penetrating his defenses without even once permitting Gonzalo to break through his.

He next worked with Luis and with the same result. Alejandro was an even weaker opponent. His fear defeated him almost before each new exchange began. In a bout with Gonzalo, Alejandro had no better success.

At the end of the fifth exchange between Gonzalo and Alejandro, Don Carlos held up his hand. "Would you agree, Alejandro," he asked, "that you're having the least success with the dagger, and for that reason your life would be at great risk in an actual knife fight?"

Alejandro's cast down his eyes. "I'm ashamed to admit," he replied, "that you're right."

"Shame isn't relevant to a practice session," Don Carlos told him. Turning to Luis and Gonzalo, Carlos added, "I'm going to take Alejandro off behind the barn over there and give him some instruction. We'll see what difference that makes in his skill."

Once out of sight behind the barn, Carlos spent nearly an hour practicing different techniques with Alejandro. First, he showed him how to avoid an opponent's attack, either by stepping back or to the side or by deflecting an attempt to stab him; next, he demonstrated the art of feinting, of confusing one's opponent with false attacks that one had no intention of completing; and finally, he gave him hints on two different ways to strike an opponent after a successful feint or evasive maneuver. Carlos constantly encouraged Alejandro's every success, no matter how small.

By the time Don Carlos and Alejandro returned to their companions' resting place, Carlos was confident that Alejandro would at the very least be able to hold his own in a bout with Gonzalo. As it happened, he did much better than hold his own, and as he succeeded two times out of every three, his confidence increased. He became bolder and more decisive.

Not wanting his companions to exhaust themselves in the heat, Don Carlos soon called a halt to the practice session and told the three soldiers, "You can see how much improvement can be achieved with a little coaching. Don't worry, Gonzalo and Luis, now that I've tutored Alejandro, I promise to do the same for you before we get back to Santa Fe. You ought to be able to win some bets with comrades by besting them in the use of your daggers."

The four travelers pushed ahead at a fast pace after the sun was low in the west and the temperature began to drop. They didn't need to stop again until after dark because a half moon provided enough light for them to set up camp, cook, and walk the horses to a nearby spring for water.

The second day passed much the same as the first. The four men made good time before noon, took their midday break at one of the well-established rest stops on the Camino Real, and practiced with their daggers. Tutored by Don Carlos, all three men made good progress.

The small caravan pressed on as the day cooled down. By nightfall they'd reached the southern end of the most dangerous part of the trail, the Jornada del Muerto. Carlos had been planning another activity to build his companions' confidence in themselves and was delighted when he spotted an ideal location to put his plan into effect, a flat area large enough for four men and six horses to use as a campsite. It was surrounded on three sides by low-lying, boulder-strewn hills. He motioned to his companions and told them, "We'll spend the night here."

This announcement was greeted with disbelief. Finally, Gonzalo spoke up. "Don Alfonso," he protested. "The ground is covered with rocks."

"You have a point," Don Carlos agreed. "But none of the rocks are very big; the largest aren't as big as a child's head, and the smallest is about the size of an apple. We are strong men; surely rubble like this isn't going to prevent us from making camp here."

All three soldiers gave Don Carlos looks that clearly said, Are you crazy? "You shouldn't give in to doubt so easily," Carlos declared. "Let me show you how we can fix this place up; future travelers will benefit from our efforts."

With this, he dismounted and told them to do likewise. "You will observe," he said, "that these nearby rocks are very soft, crumbly sandstone. Up the slope a bit is a vein of much harder rock. We'll collect a few of the hard rocks, bring them down here, and pound on these small rocks, pulverizing them into sand that will make soft beds for us. To be sure that no one injures his hands, I'll loan you some leather gloves I acquired in El Paso del Norte."

Passive resistance came next. None of his three companions made a move. "All right," Don Carlos announced cheerfully, "I'll show you how it's done. First, retrieve a hard stone from the slope." He bounded up the slope and rolled a half dozen of the hard stones down to his young companions. Returning to the base of the hill, he put on a leather glove, picked up one of the hard stones, and gave one of the apple-sized sandstone rocks a hard whack. It broke into small pieces, and with a few more strikes — whack, whack, whack — Carlos produced a pile of sand.

"Now," he told his companions, "this can be a lot of fun, if you simply use the right approach. For every sandstone boulder, imagine the face or head of someone you still bear anger toward, no matter how long ago the incident that made you angry took place. Surely, you can think of someone to fit this description. Gonzalo?" he asked.

Gonzalo got the point right away. "The drill sergeant I had when I first enlisted," he said, "used to pick on me until I hated him and wished I could punch him in the face."

"How about you, Luis?" Don Carlos asked.

After only a moment's hesitation, Luis replied, "When I was a boy a cousin of mine used to take the greatest pleasure in beating me up. He was older and much bigger than me at the time. If I tried to run off, he'd chase me down, throw me to the ground, and pummel me."

"And you, Alejandro?" Don Carlos inquired.

Alejandro's answer was no surprise. "I get furious every time I think of those thugs who dragged me into the alley and practically killed me."

"All right then," Don Carlos summed up what he'd heard. "We all have people who harmed us in ways for which we'd like to exact revenge. Let me show you how it's done." He knelt next to a boulder that was almost the size of his head. "Very well, Mr. Malicious," he growled, cautiously refraining from using Malvolio's name, "you've given many people pain; see how you like it when the tables are turned on you. Take that, you bastard!" he yelled, and struck the boulder so hard that it broke into fist-sized pieces. "And that, and that, and that, and that!" he shouted as he smashed the smaller pieces into piles of sand.

His three companions got the point and joined him in attacking defenseless sandstone boulders.

Gonzalo picked up a hard stone and banged it down on the largest sandstone rock in his vicinity. "Here's payback for your meanness, you pathetic excuse for a sergeant!" he shouted.

Luis picked up a similar theme: "Hey! Tough-guy cousin!" he snarled. "Here are a dozen whacks for every time you kicked or hit me!"

Alejandro wasn't far behind. He lined up three medium-sized sandstone boulders and carried a hard rock over to them. He exploded in a frenzy of anger. "You yellow-bellied sons-of-bitches!" he cried as he bashed away at the sandstone boulders, reducing them to tiny fragments in no time.

Angry red auras so bright that they practically lit up the area surrounded each of the three soldiers as they vented their feelings. Gonzalo was the most creative in the epithets he used, among others: "You're stupider than a buffalo's afterbirth!" "Your mother's face is uglier than a turkey vulture's!" "Take that, cesspool breath, you pile of cow dung!"

Alejandro won the intensity-of-outrage prize. "You chicken-shit assholes" was one of the milder forms of address he used for the men who'd jumped him.

Don Carlos pummeled sandstone boulders at a great rate too, although initially he didn't feel a strong personal need to express anger. He began his assault on sandstone boulders by placing Don Malvolio's face on them and attacked with an outburst of fury he found he couldn't sustain for long. Don Malvolio had done harm to many people over many lifetimes, actions that were reprehensible in the extreme; yet Carlos's anger with Malvolio had a curiously impersonal quality. For all that Malvolio had sought to harm Carlos, his success had been limited. Even in the instance of Malvolio's use of Violeta to entrap him, Carlos had escaped.

As the intensity of Carlos's ire at Don Malvolio faded, he found he was seeing his stepfather's face on the rock he was smashing. He began beating rocks into sand with renewed vigor, and he fell into a blind rage, the strength of which startled him. Alarmed at the depth of his rage, he stopped pummeling boulders and stood up, breathing deeply.

It seemed a good time to stop anyway. Forty-five minutes had passed, and he sensed that his three companions had gotten about as much out of the exercise as was possible for the time being. "All right, guys," he shouted over the din of boulder-bashing, "we've definitely improved this place." And he was right about that. Having worked at a frenzied pace, he and the three soldiers had cleared a circle of ground more than adequate for accommodating their bedrolls.

"That turned out to be fun," Luis declared, and with a nod of his head and a big grin, Gonzalo indicated that he agreed. Alejandro looked brighter too, though less so than his two mates. Venting his anger today wouldn't, Carlos supposed, heal him completely or immediately.

"I thought everyone looked exceedingly happy smashing things," Don Carlos observed, and he broke out in a belly laugh that the soldiers found contagious. Although the hilarity had a somewhat hysterical quality to it, Carlos was pleased.

That night Carlos dreamed for the first time since dreaming about Celeste four nights earlier. His new dream was a strange one. He had entered the drawing room of a house he didn't recognize. Camila was seated across from him, holding a baby on her lap. The baby's blue eyes seemed to indicate that the baby was hers.

Carlos was shocked by Camila's appearance. She had put on weight, and she looked matronly. What troubled him more than her changed figure was something in her manner that conveyed a deeply ingrained conventionality. Was this, he wondered even as he dreamed, a vision of the future? He'd heard that some brujos had the capacity for precognition, though he'd never supposed that he was among their number. Yet if this was a vision of the future, he found the scene thoroughly troubling. Given the aspect of Camila's character that this dream seemed to reveal, he felt certain that she would not be able to accept his brujo identity and that if they married, he would have to keep that identity secret and give up being a practicing brujo.

These thoughts filled him with dread as he pondered what might happen when he reached Santa Fe. He considered himself a man of honor, and if on his return Camila accepted his proposal of marriage, he would be honor-bound to go through with it. He certainly couldn't back out based on a dream.

25

Hostilities

*B*y dawn, two hours after he'd awakened, Don Carlos was in good spirits again. He had done his daily meditation and had shrugged aside the anxiety that had beset him after his dream of the matronly Camila. Allowing worries to drag him down went counter to his nature. He encouraged himself with the thought that his capacity for love and his inner strength would help his relationship with Camila remain a warm one if they married.

Two other topics were on his mind: How to get through the Jornada del Muerto section of the Camino Real without harm, and whether he could do anything more for Alejandro Guzman. Thanks to the dagger-fight training and the boulder-bashing exercise the young soldier was in better emotional shape than he'd been when they'd left El Paso del Norte, but he had a long way to go. Carlos determined to remain on the lookout for anything else he could do for Alejandro.

The more pressing challenge was to make a safe passage in two full days or less through the Jornada del Muerto, the most dangerous section of the Camino Real between El Paso del Norte and Santa Fe. Colonel Encarnación had warned them that Apache raiders were very active in the area, despite the Spanish military's best efforts to discourage war parties from attacking travelers.

After Don Carlos and his three companions were mounted, he addressed them briefly. "As you know," he said, "the most dangerous part of the trail is ahead. Even with long July days, it's doubtful that we can make the whole transit of the Jornada del Muerto in a single day. My hope is that we can push forward and reach Laguna del Muerto by nightfall today. It's an excellent place to water our horses; the only problem is that Native raiders are aware of that fact, and it's one of the sites they favor for ambushes and surprise attacks. As a small party, we might appear to them to be ideal victims for their mischief. But let's not look for trouble. Simply keep alert, and if we see anything suspicious, we'll take necessary precautions."

Don Carlos was impressed that none of his three young companions either complained about the dangers ahead or asked what sort of "necessary precautions" he had in mind. In their own fashion they were tough-minded realists who took whatever came their way.

The party pushed forward at a good pace. The only difference from previous days was that despite the scorching July heat they didn't pause for a long break at midday, though they did make one short stop around noon at a small spring near one of the *paraje* or camps customarily used by overland travelers. Carlos excused himself for a moment, telling his companions that he wanted to check the countryside for signs of any recent activity by Native raiders. He did so, except not in the way his friends assumed he'd meant, which was to walk around the immediate vicinity. What he actually did once he was out of sight was to transform himself into a red-tailed hawk and make a reconnaissance of a much larger area than he could have done on foot. He was pleased to see no signs that raiders were hiding in the ten miles of road immediately ahead.

Back on their mounts, the four men picked up the pace a little and arrived at their destination, Laguna del Muerto, as night was falling. They quickly made camp and cooked dinner, but Carlos didn't waste much time eating. He gulped down his beans and tortillas and once again excused himself. "This is the most dangerous spot of all," he declared. "I'm going to make another reconnaissance. If I'm not back in an hour, saddle up and keep going on the trail with your muskets at the ready."

Night surveillance required that he take a bird form other than a hawk. He transformed himself into a screech owl and flew concentric circles around the camp, spiraling outward farther and farther in search of any signs of Native raiders. He located a war party of twelve raiders camped next to the road a little more than two miles ahead. They were in a position to ambush Don Carlos's party if it continued northward after dark or to make a surprise attack on the Spaniards if Don Carlos and his friends settled down for the night.

Don Carlos flew back to his take-off point near the camp, returned to his human form, and walked into camp to brief his companions on what he'd seen. "I've spotted a war party of twelve raiders less than three miles north of here," he said. "I believe they'll wait a few hours and then creep up on us, hoping to catch us asleep."

"Twelve to four isn't great odds," Gonzalo, ever the practical one, observed.

"You're right," Don Carlos agreed, "but only if we stay here like sitting ducks waiting to be attacked. As a swordsman I've learned that taking the offensive against a strong opponent is sometimes the best strategy. My suggestion is that we ambush them before they can ambush us. Let's use a surprise attack strategy to our advantage.

"Here's what I have in mind," he continued. "Gonzalo, Alejandro, and I will sneak up on the raiders on foot. Luis will follow us on the road with our horses. The three of us will attack; if we succeed in driving the raiders off, then we'll return here for a good night's sleep."

"Even a relatively good night's sleep," Gonzalo said, "may not be possible with raiders so close at hand."

"True," Don Carlos acknowledged. "And we also have to consider that things may go badly, in which case we'll retreat to the horses Luis will be holding for us and take off to the south as fast as we can."

"By leaving Luis back with the horses," Alejandro objected, "you made the odds even worse, changing them from four to twelve to only three to twelve. That's extremely risky."

"Tonight you will see that you are a great soldier," Don Carlos told him with a firm voice that conveyed confidence, "no matter what the odds. Don't worry; I'm certain we can pull this off."

In complete darkness, the Spaniards loaded their goods on their horses, checked to see that their muskets were ready for use, and began to move up the road together on horseback. After a mile, the three designated attackers—Don Carlos, Gonzalo, and Alejandro—dismounted, grabbed their muskets, ammunition, swords, and daggers, and began to walk toward the Native camp at a brisk pace. "We ought to be in position for our ambush in about fifteen minutes," Don Carlos whispered.

"The raiders' war ponies," he reported, "are on the east side of the road in a small grassy area; the warriors themselves are to the west. We're going to divide our attack between the horses and the warriors."

"Divide our already-small forces!" Gonzalo protested. "That goes against every rule for battlefield tactics that I've ever learned."

"Divide may not be precisely the correct word," Don Carlos replied. "I will move down the east side of the road, drive the herd of war ponies into the brush, and start launching arrows at the warriors' camp to the west."

"Slow down!" Alejandro objected nervously. "Where are you going to get arrows?"

"Patience, my young friend," Don Carlos told him. "I'll get them from the two warriors who are guarding the horses. Here's our plan of attack: Our first move will be to creep a little farther forward. When we can see the warriors' camp, I'll break off and ambush the horses' guards. You'll hear a huge ruckus from me shouting bloody murder as though I represent at least ten attackers. At the same time I'll shoot some arrows in the direction of the warriors' camp. That's the signal for you to fire your muskets. Since both of you have two muskets—Gonzalo can have mine as well as his own, and Alejandro, you already have yours and Luis's—I want you to fire once from your first position and save your second shot for use in case the raiders attack you. But don't stay in the place from which you initially fire at them. Move closer to the road so that, if necessary, we can meet on the road and retreat to where Luis is holding our mounts. Any arrows shot toward your former location will land where you were rather than where you are."

"This feels very risky to me," Gonzalo declared.

"That's true," Don Carlos agreed. "But remember that there are only twelve warriors. I'll do in the two guards; I believe one or two of my arrows will find their marks; if you shoot straight, as I'm sure you can, you'll kill or wound two more warriors. After our initial attack their numbers will be cut in half. I believe they'll panic and try to flee.

"Let's get going," Don Carlos added. "If we don't hurry, they'll launch their attack on us before we can ambush them."

Don Carlos had no intention of leaving much to chance. Once he was alone, he could use his full powers as a brujo, and he did precisely that. He transformed himself into a screech owl to get within less than ten feet of the guards. He could hear them speaking, and though he didn't know many words in their language, he knew enough to confirm the fact that they were Apaches. Positioning himself behind them, he returned to his human form, attacked them with the butt end of his dagger and knocked both of them unconscious.

He was pleased that both warriors had quivers full of arrows, ten apiece—obviously in anticipation of a full-scale attack on the Spaniards. This was the moment of truth. He put the bows and arrows in position for immediate use, cut the tethers that were restraining the horses, let out a series of screams, howls, and moans that panicked the horses, and drove them away from the grazing site.

Immediately, the raiders across the road leaped up and grabbed their weapons. Using his sorcerer's vision, he could see that two had muskets, so he fired at them first and followed quickly with three more arrows. Most of his arrows hit their marks, killing one warrior and wounding three others. Adding these casualties to the two guards he had incapacitated, he figured that meant that the score was six down and only six to go.

The Apache warriors were completely confused by the sounds of their war ponies stampeding and by an attack coming from the direction where their comrades had been posted. Nevertheless, they did their best to organize a counterattack. At precisely that moment, Gonzalo and Alejandro, in a position that was now to the right flank of the Apache camp, opened fire. At least one musket ball struck down a warrior.

Five to our three, Don Carlos observed. The odds were getting better. He shot off two more arrows, wounding yet another warrior, and moved back toward Gonzalo and Alejandro.

At this juncture the unpredictability of battle led to a development with potentially dangerous implications for Don Carlos and his companions. Although two of the uninjured raiders fled northward, away from the attacking Spaniards, aiding their wounded comrades to escape the battlefield, the remaining two uninjured Apaches ran in the direction of Gonzalo and Alejandro, hugging the ground so closely that Carlos lost sight of them.

Don Carlos crashed through the brush as fast as he could toward his companions. Before he could reach them, he heard two more musket shots — obviously, or so he hoped, Gonzalo and Alejandro discharging their second muskets. Moments later he burst onto the scene of a skirmish between the two soldiers and the two Apache raiders.

As best Don Carlos could tell Alejandro's second musket shot had killed one of the raiders. Gonzalo's shot was a misfire and did no damage, and the remaining Apache ran forward, knocked him down, and attacked him with a flint knife. Alejandro saved the day by drawing his dagger and stabbing the warrior in the back. The raider twisted around and was trying to stab Alejandro, when Alejandro, putting his recent lessons in knife fighting to good use, parried the warrior's attempted blow and dispatched him with his dagger.

Seeing that the immediate danger was past, Don Carlos called to Alejandro and Gonzalo to return to where Luis was holding their mounts. "I'll meet you there shortly," he said. He slipped off into the darkness to the place where he'd left his clothes when he made his screech-owl transformation. He dressed and rejoined his three friends at the appointed spot.

"Let's keep going for an hour or two," Don Carlos suggested. "I don't believe the Apaches who survived our ambush are any great threat to us. Even the two horse guards that I knocked out but didn't kill aren't much of a menace, since I broke their bows before joining Alejandro and Gonzalo in their attack. Nevertheless, I'd like to get well away from here on the off chance that they're still determined to ambush us."

An hour later the Spaniards agreed to keep going for another hour, and an hour after that they voted to keep going a little longer. Although they were bone weary by now, they didn't feel safe stopping. Finally Don Carlos announced, "Enough! The three of you and our horses need rest. I have exceptional night vision. Let me keep watch. I'll give the alarm if there's any danger."

The night passed without any further trouble. After a leisurely breakfast, the four Spaniards continued to their next destination, the Chavez hacienda east of the Rio Grande from the former town of Socorro. Nothing was said of the previous night's battle and the killings it involved, yet Carlos was sure that even a killing done of necessity wounded a soldier's inner spirit. At the very least it was sobering to consider that things might have gone differently, and that they could have been fatalities rather than the agents of other men's deaths. Unless one's a hard man, Carlos reflected, someone who thrives on inflicting harm on others, war was a trauma for the victor as well as the vanquished.

Don Carlos and his companions reached their destination in the middle of the afternoon. A Saturday market day was still going strong in the open space adjacent to the Chavez hacienda, which served as the only inn in the area. A few spots where vendors had laid out their goods on blankets earlier in the day were vacant now, but Carlos was relieved to see that a few dozen traders were still doing business and that a variety of goods — blankets, clothes, jewelry, knives, and pottery — were still available. Only this morning had it dawned on him that he ought to bring presents to his friends in Santa Fe. This market offered almost his last chance to shop for gifts.

Although his list of potential recipients wasn't long, he wanted to give gifts that were both appropriate and special. He mentally checked off friends as he found suitable gifts for them.

Pedro and María: an especially fine wool blanket, not useful at present on hot July nights, but definitely good for next winter, and it was a handsome piece of weaving besides.

Diego: a saddle pad of high quality—this one would be for special occasions—and a pair of beautifully made spurs.

He considered and then rejected the idea of bringing Inéz a gift because he wasn't sure he wanted to encourage that relationship overtly.

Choosing something for his stepbrother Joaquin and sister-in-law Francie was a problem. They seemed to have everything they needed in the way of household goods. A luxury item then. He finally found something he liked and thought they could use too: a finely crafted silver tray.

Shopping for a gift for Camila proved to be most difficult, and stirred up larger uncertainties within him. So much depended on what their relationship would be once they were reunited. If they were to marry, a ring would be the perfect choice. But if they were not to marry, what then? It was impossible, he decided, to buy her a ring. Far down in his mind a thought stirred: it was impossible to marry her. Quickly, he covered it over; he had proposed; he was honor-bound.

He made two complete tours of the booths around the market without finding a gift for Camila. My brujo powers, he noted to himself, so valuable in fighting off an Apache raiding party on the Jornada del Muerto, are useless in other areas of human affairs, such as what present to buy for a woman.

At that moment he was for the second time looking over jewelry being offered for sale by a handsome Spanish woman. She was interesting in her own right, and he'd moved quickly past the items on her blanket the first time around because he found himself strongly attracted to her. With her was a young woman she introduced to another customer as her daughter Yolanda. Yolanda was pretty and a mestizo, which indicated to Carlos that the Spanish woman was married to a Pueblo Indian man who might not take kindly to Carlos flirting with his wife.

The second time around he cast caution to the wind and initiated negotiations with the Spanish woman for an unusual silver necklace with small blue stones that reminded him of Camila's blue eyes.

"I am traveling from Mexico City to Santa Fe," he told the woman, whose name turned out to be Esperanza, "and I can pay for this necklace with pesos. What are you asking for it?"

"It is extremely fine craftsmanship and the stones are rare too," she replied. "I am asking ten pesos." It was a price both Carlos and the Spanish woman knew was too high.

Don Carlos wasn't pretending when he told her, "That is too much. Three pesos and six reales will enable you to buy many necessities, or luxuries if you're so inclined, because people in these parts don't have silver coins and value them greatly."

"Your offer is insultingly low," she scoffed, "and you know it. Look at the fine craftsmanship involved in the way the stones are set into the silver." She held the necklace out to him and indicated the features of it to which she'd referred.

"Is this necklace more valuable to you," he asked, "because your husband made it?"

"Don't be rude," she said sharply. "You don't need to know about my private life in order to see how beautifully made this necklace is."

Esperanza's marital status apparently was a touchy topic between the two women, because Yolanda remarked irritably. "Oh, Mother! Why not admit that you don't have a husband?"

Yolanda's interruption set off a heated exchange between mother and daughter in a Pueblo language that Carlos didn't know well, but he gathered that Esperanza was angry out of fear that her daughter's remarks would drive Carlos off without buying the necklace.

"Ladies, please!" Don Carlos protested. "I didn't mean to start an argument. My interest is in the necklace. To show my good faith, I'm willing to pay five pesos for it, still a high price, I trust you'd agree."

"No, I don't," Esperanza declared. "But to show that I believe you are a gentleman and thus well intentioned, I'll let you have the necklace for eight pesos."

Carlos had not noticed until now that there was an infant sleeping in a basket next to Yolanda. The baby woke up and began to cry. Esperanza spoke sharply to her daughter. "Yolanda, he's hungry. Feed him."

"I know he's hungry," Yolanda murmured. Turning away, she unbuttoned her blouse and picked up the baby so he could suckle. Carlos politely averted his eyes.

Alejandro, standing next to Carlos, was not so quick to look away.

Yolanda's mother, taking note of the direction of Alejandro's gaze, cleared her throat disapprovingly. Alejandro reddened and turned to look elsewhere.

Esperanza resumed bargaining by repeating, "The price is seven pesos."

Carlos objected, saying, "six pesos is as much as I'm willing to pay. If that's unacceptable, I'll wait until I reach Santa Fe to see what local jewelry-makers have to offer."

"Very well," she agreed and held out her hand for the coins.

Before the transaction could be completed, a boy of about twelve ran up and announced breathlessly, "Jorge is gambling again and losing. He's already lost all the bundles of salt he earned last week and it sounded as though he was about to bet his belt."

Alarm mixed with anger flashed across Esperanza's face. "Jorge is my eldest son," she announced bitterly, "and he gambles away everything he owns and tries to get me to stake him to more. 'I'll win this time,' he promises, 'if you'll just loan me something to bet. I'll return it two times over.' This is a delusion, of course."

"Every time my brother loses at cards," Yolanda announced, "he comes home begging for us to feed and clothe him. He pretty much ends up stealing our earnings from us."

"If you can get my son away from the card table today," Esperanza told Don Carlos, "you can have this bracelet for the price you originally offered."

"Please help us," Yolanda said, tears beginning to fill her eyes.

That did it. Carlos laughed at himself. All a woman has to do, he observed, is cry and I'll rush to her aid. He grabbed Alejandro, who was standing beside him, and said, "Come along. We'll need to see if we can do anything to get Jorge away from the card table."

"What do you have in mind?" Alejandro asked.

"Nothing immediately," Don Carlos replied. "First, we have to see precisely what's going on." They walked to the hacienda's main public room where Esperanza said they'd find her son.

The situation turned out to be worse than Carlos had anticipated. Four men were hunched over a table playing cards. Jorge, much the youngest, was easy to spot by his age, the frustrated look on his face, and the lack of chips in front of him. Two middle-aged mestizo men, one of whom turned out to be a rancher and the other a farmer, each had a smallish pile of chips. The fourth man, clearly the one who'd been winning most consistently, was a hard-looking fellow dressed in black from his hat to his boots. Carlos, with

Alejandro behind him, joined the group of onlookers around the table. One of the older men told the man in black, "One more hand, Apolinar, and then I quit."

"But Señor Alvaros," Apolinar said in a persuasive tone, "you don't want to quit now. You won the last hand. Your luck has turned."

"I doubt it," Alvaros replied with a shake of his head. "It's never worked that way before. I win one and lose the next, that's the pattern."

"Very well," Apolinar agreed. "Play one more hand. But if you win a second hand in a row, you'll owe me the chance to win my money back."

Apolinar looked across the table at Jorge. "Jorge, I've already given you a loan against your bags of salt. Do you have anything else to use for credit?"

"I have a good saddle to offer," Jorge replied.

Don Carlos hadn't intended to jump in immediately, but this was too much. "A man shouldn't put his saddle at risk," he told the gambler and the many onlookers. "I will take Jorge's place at the table and test my luck."

Jorge started to protest, but Don Carlos pulled him bodily up from his chair, handed him a peso, and told him, "Here's a peso; whether I win or lose, you'll have some money to gamble with when I tire of the game."

Taking some silver coins from his pocket, Carlos inquired, "I assume no one will mind me joining the game and giving you a chance to win something other than salt and wool cloth."

Watching Apolinar's aura closely, Carlos could tell that the man, as greedy and dishonest as they come, assumed Carlos was a sucker, and a sucker and his money are soon parted.

"What are the rules of the game?" Don Carlos asked.

Apolinar described them. "Everyone gets five cards on the first deal. A round of betting follows. You discard anywhere from one to five cards and on the second hand there's another round of betting. What you're hoping for is standard: a hand composed of high cards, or cards of the same suit, or two, three, or four cards of the same face value, and so forth. You must bet at least one chip on each deal or drop out."

"That's all I need to know," Don Carlos commented, "except please tell me whether aces are high or low cards."

"Aces high," Apolinar replied.

Placing four pesos on the table, Don Carlos asked, "How many chips do I get for each peso?"

"Eight," Apolinar told him, which Carlos noted was quite a high price per chip, making the game's stakes much too rich for a man of Jorge's limited means.

Although the first five cards Carlos received were not promising, that didn't matter. He was going to bet only a few chips this time, fold early to limit his losses, and watch the game closely.

Alvaros won the game, his second success in a row. Carlos lost only two chips, shaking his head in disgust at both his first and second hand.

Alvaros was definitely hooked, just as Apolinar (in Carlos's opinion) had wanted. Carlos noted that Apolinar folded early too, losing only three chips in the process. This barely made a dent in the large pile he'd accumulated over many games.

Apolinar reminded Alvaros, "You owe me at least one chance to get my money back, or part of it anyway." Alvaros, obviously encouraged by his recent successes, agreed.

What Carlos suspected during the first game and confirmed during the second was that the game was fixed. In extremely subtle ways the cards were marked to insure that Apolinar would know when he had a stronger hand than the other participants. The backs of the cards had a pretty paisley design on them that had tiny flecks of color so close in hue that the differences were difficult to spot. For someone able to interpret the clues, however, these flecks indicated the suit—diamonds, clubs, hearts, and spades—of each card. In addition, the face cards and the ace all had very low bumps in one corner to indicate which card—jack, queen, king, or ace—it was. With this information available to him, Apolinar could bail out early if he had a losing hand or stay in the game if he was sure of winning after the second draw.

Apolinar, Carlos knew, was a name said to mean "destroyer," an appropriate name for a gambler who fixes the game and deprives others of their material wealth.

"This is a most unusual deck," Don Carlos said casually as the cards were being dealt for the second game. "Where did you get it?" he asked Apolinar.

Apolinar looked annoyed. "I bought it from an old Gypsy woman in Veracruz who had used it for telling fortunes."

"From the looks of the big pile of chips in front of you," Don Carlos declared, "it's also brought you good luck."

"Do you want to play or talk?" Apolinar replied, baring his teeth in a hostile manner.

"Oh," Don Carlos told him. "I was just passing the time until I have my cards in hand."

His hand this time was definitely better. He had three face cards: two queens and a king. He discarded the other two cards and received another king and a five of clubs. Two pair, he observed to himself, wasn't bad. He bet four chips on the second round, which Apolinar matched.

"Too rich for me," both the farmer and the rancher declared, and folded.

"Me too," Don Carlos said, but he had no intention of letting the charade go on any longer. Instead of tossing his cards onto the pile with the farmer's and rancher's cards to be collected by Apolinar, Carlos reached out and swept the farmer's and rancher's cards over to him.

"What the hell!" Apolinar exclaimed. "I'm the dealer."

"Just a moment," Don Carlos replied. "Let me show everyone here, both the players and onlookers, that I can do a card trick in which I tell you precisely which card is which. For example, this card Alvaros drew is a king of spades, and this card in the pile my friend the farmer returned is a jack of clubs." He turned the cards over to prove his point.

"It's too bad," Don Carlos continued, "that the two of you didn't draw more face cards, but I can also tell you the suit to which the remaining cards belong." Quickly sorting the farmer's discards and Alvaros's into four piles, Carlos announced, "These four cards are diamonds; these two spades, this one a heart, and the remaining cards are clubs."

Alvaros understood immediately. "You mean Apolinar has been dealing marked cards?"

"That's a damn lie," Apolinar snarled.

"The way you can identify the cards isn't easy," Don Carlos replied, ignoring Apolinar's outburst, "but the face cards are easiest to spot. Feel the corner of this card. The three little bumps tell you that it's a queen. Our quick-witted dealer over there feels the card's bumps as he deals them, memorizes who gets which face cards, and bets accordingly."

"That's it!" Apolinar growled, putting on a good show of being exceedingly aggrieved. "I don't have to put up with insults. Game's over. Give me the cards!"

"That's not the way this is going to work," Don Carlos informed him calmly. "You're going to return all the chips you've gotten through your little scheme, and I'm going to rip up these cards so that you can't use them again."

"You bastard!" Apolinar shouted. "I won these chips fair and square, and if you rip up those cards, you'll bleed for it!" He pulled a knife from his belt and demanded, "Hand those cards over!" Simultaneously, he was sweeping the chips into his hat.

Don Carlos coolly pocketed the cards that had been played in the most recent game. "Too late, Apolinar. The evidence that you've been cheating these men is there for all to see. Put the knife away. You're not going to collect your ill-gotten gains now that I've exposed you as a cheat."

Apolinar was a tough customer. He rose to his feet quickly, turning the table upside down. As the table crashed to the floor, Apolinar began to swing his knife in wide arcs from side to side. Everyone backed away, except for Carlos. He held his ground and noticed that Alejandro had maneuvered his way around the room until he was standing eight feet directly behind Apolinar. The young soldier had his hand on the hilt of his dagger, ready to draw it.

Apolinar moved towards Don Carlos, continuing to sweep his knife back and forth in a menacing way. "Give me my cards," he demanded.

The crook doesn't see when he's beaten, Carlos thought. Pulling about half the cards he'd collected from his pocket, Carlos threw them on the floor between himself and Apolinar. Seeing that he'd have to bend over if he wanted to pick the cards up, Apolinar snarled, "You son of a bitch," and lunged forward in an attempt to stab Carlos with his knife.

In a blur of motion, Carlos drew his dagger, parried Apolinar's thrust, and dealt Apolinar a wound on his knife arm that was, as Carlos had intended, fairly superficial, though an impressive amount of blood began to flow from the cut.

Apolinar, stunned and hurting, retreated three steps, only to come under attack from Alejandro, who'd approached Apolinar from behind and struck him a hard blow on the back of his head with the butt of his dagger, knocking him to the floor.

Don Carlos felt quite pleased with the way events had unfolded. He turned to Jorge, Alvaros, and the farmer and said, "Obviously, you don't owe this scoundrel anything, not so much as a grain of salt." Addressing the onlookers, he continued, "I assume that you'll see that this swindler is turned over to the local authorities or at least run out of town without his cleverly marked deck of cards." Several big men stepped forward to grab Apolinar as he groggily began to come to and struggled to rise. Several other members of the crowd went over to pick up and examine the cards

Carlos had thrown on the floor. A lot of head shaking accompanied this examination.

A chorus of admiring calls of "Thank you" was heard in the room, to which Don Carlos responded with a simple "You're welcome; it was truly my pleasure."

Jorge was doing his best to slip away but Don Carlos moved quickly to intercept him, grabbing him by his arm and asserting, "You and I are going to have a talk, Jorge. I have a bone to pick with you for the dumb way you got into this fix and tried to give away your saddle."

"I wasn't trying to give away my saddle," Jorge protested vehemently.

"Nonsense!" Don Carlos declared. "Gambling with a hardened crook like Apolinar is a sure way to loose your shirt and your saddle. You can't afford to play cards with a coyote like Apolinar. It's stupid to try."

Jorge wasn't about to give in totally, although it was obvious that he was shaken by what had happened and a bit intimidated by the force of Don Carlos's voice and words. "I didn't know Apolinar was cheating," he said.

"How long were you gambling with him?" Don Carlos asked.

"Maybe an hour and a half," he replied, which Carlos suspected was an understatement.

"An hour and a half playing cards with that cardsharp," Don Carlos said, "and you had no hint that the fix was in? From what little I saw, Apolinar never bet much on games he was about to lose, which cost him almost nothing, and then bet heavily and made a big haul when he did win — correct?"

"Maybe he was just having a run of good luck," Jorge suggested.

"I don't believe you're stupid," Don Carlos told him, "and unless you are, on reflection you'll see that instead of sensing that something was fishy about the game, you were totally fooled by Apolinar. He supplied the deck and never let anyone else deal, correct?"

"Yes," Jorge mumbled.

"Well, usually the person who wins the previous game deals the cards for the next," Don Carlos reminded him. "The fact that he supplied the deck and wouldn't let anyone else deal was a sure sign that he was up to something."

"At the start of our games," Jorge replied, "Apolinar announced that we'd let the player who won three games in a row be the dealer."

"Of course," Don Carlos observed, belaboring the obvious a bit more than he liked, "no one except Apolinar ever won three games in a row."

"He didn't always win three times in a row," Jorge objected.

Tired of Jorge refusing to admit his mistakes, Don Carlos took him by the arm, shook him vigorously, and, leaning over to put his mouth next to Jorge's ear, shouted at him, "Stop defending your stupidity. Everyone makes mistakes; the greater error, the sign of deep-seated stupidity, is not learning from your mistakes. The way you're talking, you're setting yourself up to become a perennial loser."

Jorge was trembling slightly, afraid of Don Carlos and the overwhelming power with which he delivered his message. "The chief message you should take away from today's events," Carlos continued, "is that you should never play cards or any other game of chance for money. You lack the killer instinct it takes to be a successful gambler. That's no disgrace; be glad you don't have a ruthless temperament."

"I knew I had crossed some line," Jorge admitted, "when I found myself betting my saddle. I heard myself voicing those words, and I knew my saddle was something I couldn't afford to lose, but I couldn't stop myself."

"So what should you do in the future?" Don Carlos asked.

"I guess I should stop before I start," Jorge replied.

"That's the right answer," Don Carlos told him. "You have a habit; you have to break it; that's not easy to do because the potential thrill of winning will always beckon like a beautiful woman who wants to seduce you."

Speaking of beautiful women, the direction Don Carlos and Jorge had been walking had by now brought them to the part of the market where Jorge's mother and sister were beginning to pack up their goods. Jorge's little brother was there too and Luis and Gonzalo were nearby, putting their heads together with Alejandro, who was filling them in on what had happened during the card games.

Esperanza looked at her son with great sadness in her eyes. "I heard what happened," she said. "Being prepared to bet your saddle is a new low."

Before Jorge could say anything his mother held her hand up to stop him. "I've tried scolding and nagging, and neither did any good. I can only hope that you'll take to heart what this gentleman, whose name I don't know, told you about the ways of the world. That's a mother's wish for you."

"I'll try, Mother," Jorge contritely replied.

"I have an idea that might help," Don Carlos declared. He reached in his pocket and brought out the cards he'd taken from Apolinar. Sorting quickly through them, he found one card from each suit, two of which were face cards — an ace of spades and a jack of hearts — and handed the four cards to Jorge. "Carry these with you at all times," he urged Jorge, "at least until you're sure you've successfully repressed your desire to gamble. If you catch yourself about to join a game of chance, take two of these cards out as a reminder of this day and your resolve to give up gambling. If nothing else, the feel of the markings on the face cards ought to give you fair warning."

Jorge took the cards and asked, "Do you want the peso you gave me back?"

"If you'll promise me to give that peso to your mother or to buy her a present in return for all the sorrow you've brought her," Don Carlos replied, "then you may keep it."

Esperanza held out the necklace, the price of which she and Don Carlos had been negotiating before the need to help Jorge intervened. "Here," she said, "gentleman whose name I don't know. The least I can do for the great kindness you performed for my son, my family, and me today is to make a gift of this necklace to you."

"I couldn't take it without paying," Don Carlos protested. "The two transactions — our negotiations regarding the purchase of this necklace and my intervention on behalf of your son — were separate. No, I should pay you the price we agreed upon, six pesos."

"I can't accept that full sum," Esperanza told him. "You'd end up paying more to my family's coffers as a result of a favor you've done all of us. Let's agree to deduct the peso you gave my son and make the price to me five pesos."

"Fair enough," Don Carlos agreed, handing her five pesos and taking the necklace she passed to him. After a pause he added, "Now if you'll excuse me, my young soldiers and I need to find a place to stay tonight, the inn being full. But I see Alvaros, the gambling rancher, on the other side of the market, and I'll bet he'll find room for us and our horses. I wish you well."

Don Carlos joined his three soldier companions and started across the market toward where Alvaros was standing. "That was a timely intervention on your part, Alejandro," he told his young friend.

"I feel good about clobbering that cheat," Alejandro replied. "But

I feel badly that the jewelry vendor, Esperanza, caught me staring at her daughter nursing her baby. It was only a glimpse, and I should have averted my eyes sooner."

Don Carlos agreed. "You're right, and I'm sure that in the future you'll be more discrete."

Gonzalo and Luis, overhearing what had happened, took the exchange in a more ribald direction. Gonzalo crowed, "This Alejandro fellow has all the luck!"

Don Carlos wasn't comfortable with this particular bit of banter and he was about to reprove them when he felt someone tug at his sleeve. It was Esperanza's younger son. "Please, sir," the boy asked, "my mother wishes to know the name of our benefactor."

Don Carlos looked across the plaza to where Esperanza was standing and gave her a friendly wave. Returning his attention to the boy, he said, "Please tell your mother that I apologize for not introducing myself sooner. The necklace she sold me will be carried north to Santa Fe by Don Alfonso Cabeza de Vaca, personal secretary to General Juan Villela, military governor of Santa Fe Province."

26

Homecoming

*T*he morning of the fourth day after their overnight stay with Alvaros (who had been delighted to put them up at his ranch), Don Carlos and his three companions rose early in anticipation of reaching Santa Fe later that day. The four-day trip to their present camp had gone well, unmarked by either unexpected problems or notable adventures. They'd had an easy time of it, taking long breaks through the heat of the day and resuming their journey on the Camino Real late in the afternoon as the shadows lengthened and the temperature dropped.

Don Carlos was amused by his companions' ongoing discussions of seemingly any topic that occurred to them. The three soldiers had become more voluble as the trip progressed, or perhaps they'd always been talkative but had kept their thoughts to themselves until they knew him better.

A typical debate topic was what should have been done to punish Apolinar. Luis got things started by asserting, "They should have strung him up then and there."

"That's too harsh," Alejandro objected. "He was a cheat, not a murderer. On the principle of an eye for an eye, he didn't kill anyone, so taking his life would have been excessive."

"They hang horse thieves," Gonzalo observed, "not that I'm in favor of that. I believe a horse thief can be reformed, and hanging him cuts off any chance he'd have to change his ways."

"I think," Alejandro mused, "that on the eye-for-an-eye principle the right thing to do to a scoundrel like Apolinar who cheated his victims out of material goods would be to take everything he owned from him except the clothes on his back, and his boots, of course."

"What about his horse?" Luis asked. "Taking a man's horse is pretty cruel."

"Now look who's being softhearted," Gonzalo snorted. "A moment ago you were ready to hang this Apolinar fellow on the spot."

"If we're going to let him live," Luis replied, "he ought to be allowed to keep his horse, if for no other reason than that he'll need some way of getting out of town."

A half hour later the three soldiers were still debating whether to leave Apolinar his horse. At least they now seemed to agree that hanging him was too harsh.

Yolanda's breast also became a topic of conversation. Gonzalo got things started by teasingly asking Alejandro, "What were you thinking of when you were staring so intently at her breast?"

"I wasn't staring at her," Alejandro protested. "It was just a momentary glimpse of a mother nursing her baby."

Gonzalo didn't give up. "But even that glimpse aroused you, didn't it?"

Alejandro denied that he'd become aroused or even had improper thoughts. "You're way off target there, Gonzalo," he insisted. But under persistent criticism that he wasn't being honest with his comrades, he finally conceded that there was some truth to Gonzalo's accusation. Having made this admission, Alejandro retorted, "So what?"

"So what?" Gonzalo repeated. "So nothing! So why won't you let us in on those thoughts? Come on, give! Tell us what you saw and what you thought!"

Alejandro shot back, "You're just jealous because I saw what I saw and you didn't."

"I'll grant you that," Gonzalo replied.

Don Carlos thought that Alejandro's confession and Gonzalo's admission would bring an end to discussions of Yolanda's breast, but nothing of the sort happened. The two soldiers, joined now and then by Luis, came back to the topic again and again, going over the same ground repeatedly, sometimes using exactly the same words as they had on the first go-around.

The repetitiveness of these conversations eventually triggered in Carlos an important understanding of his companions. All three — Alejandro, Gonzalo, and Luis — were from rural backgrounds. In small towns and rural settings, most of life progresses in highly routine ways. When something occurs that deviates from these day-to-day routines, no matter how small the deviation, the event becomes a topic for conversation. Until something new comes along, and that might not happen for days or even weeks, the natural thing to do is to continue to chew over the novel events of the past. That the novelty is slow to wear off, Carlos observed, is a testimony to the human spirit, to people's curiosity and aliveness even in constricted social circumstances.

The next time Don Carlos eavesdropped on his companions' discussions they were arguing about whether Jorge would be able to give up gambling. "I doubt it," Gonzalo contended. "Once a gambler, always a gambler; it's like the lust for wealth. Once you get in the grip of greed, it's too late to develop more modest desires."

"I thought you were arguing earlier," Luis said, "for the possibility that a crook like Apolinar might turn over a new leaf and be reformed."

Gonzalo came right back, asserting, "Apolinar was a crook, but he wasn't a slave to gambling; he gambled as a way of making a living. Jorge was a slave to his gambling habit the way some men are slaves to the bottle, drinking too much no matter what it does to their bodies and fortunes."

"Perhaps Jorge should join the army," Alejandro suggested. "That would give him a purpose in life, a discipline to organize his days."

Alejandro's suggestion turned the debate in a totally different direction. Would Jorge benefit from the soldier's life? Wouldn't he continue to gamble? And what was so great about military discipline anyway? Like all their arguments, at least as far as Don Carlos could tell, this topic remained unresolved, in spite of the many times they came back to it during the trek to Santa Fe.

The last day of the journey home they set out at dawn, having a ride of only a few hours left. A mile outside of Santa Fe, Carlos's travel-weary horse began to recognize landmarks he'd seen in the past. Eagle's walk, which until then had been perfunctory, suddenly showed much more energy. As Carlos and his three companions reached the outskirts of Santa Fe, Eagle went, unasked, into a higher gear, trotting down the street with his ears tilted forward. Carlos didn't have to guide him to turn into the street where the front porch of Carlos's house could be seen from the plaza. Down the street he went to the back of the house and his old home, a four-stall stable.

Diego was mucking out Pepper's stall. He looked up and a huge smile broke out on his face. "You're home! You're home!" he cried, and then, shouting in the direction of the house, "He's home! Don Alfonso is home!"

Carlos dismounted, and Diego ran to Carlos and gave him a bear hug. The kid has grown a foot, Carlos observed to himself, exaggerating a little.

Gordo came dashing out of the house, wagging his tail enthusiastically, leaping in full circles, and barking joyfully.

María and Pedro emerged next. They had been cooking breakfast and urged Carlos to join them. They were plainly pleased to see him. María surprised him with the fervor of her welcome-home hug. Pedro pounded him on the back and said, "You've been gone a long time."

Eagle too got a big welcome from Pepper, who neighed loudly and repeatedly.

After Eagle was safely in his stall eating hay, the four humans sat down to breakfast and began to exchange news. Before too long, Carlos excused himself. "I have a letter for Camila. My search for her mother was successful."

"She'll be ecstatic!" María exclaimed.

"I hope so," Carlos replied.

Carlos walked the short distance to Joaquin and Francie's house at the Presidio and knocked. It was a typical July morning in Santa Fe, with the temperature already close to seventy and headed into the mid-eighties or even higher.

Camila answered the door and said, "News travels fast. I heard you were back." She brushed her cheek to his; not overwhelmingly warm, as welcome-home kisses go, but nice nevertheless. She showed him into the parlor.

"Let's leave small talk for later," Carlos said. "I located your mother and have a letter from her. I imagine you'll want to read it immediately. We can go over any details you need explained after you're done reading."

Camila opened the letter and read slowly through it. Carlos got the impression that she read and then reread some passages before continuing onward. "This letter explains a great deal," she finally said. "I'm sorry she doesn't want to give me her name and has doubtless asked you to swear not to reveal it. Still, it's a very loving letter; I'm immensely moved. It lifts a dark cloud of unknowing that's hovered over my life until now. How on earth did you track her down?"

"The short story," Carlos replied (one with some significant omissions), "is that your letter to Mother Veronica had already produced results. An elderly sister remembered seeing a woman deposit you on the orphanage's steps, and she had noticed that the woman returned to a hotel down the street. I spoke with the hotel's manager, and he had a guest register that had been signed by your mother. Although she didn't use her full name, there were enough clues that I was able to track her down."

"Can you tell me anything about her as a person?" Camila asked.

Choosing his words with care, Carlos replied. "She's a very nice person and has a husband who has prospered in his business; they have a handsome home. She and her husband have children of their own, but I got the impression that you have never been far from her thoughts all these years, despite her not having any idea of what had become of you. Unfortunately, as her letter indicates, her husband is a narrow-minded man who would react very badly if he knew about your existence."

"Oh, Alfonso!" she said, standing up and giving him another kiss on the cheek, this one much warmer than the first. "I'm sure you're aware how much this means to me. It changes so much in my life. Thank you from the bottom of my heart. I don't know how I'll ever repay you."

"Your joy is payment enough," Carlos replied.

"You were gone a very long time," Camila said. "I'd begun to think you weren't coming back. Most of the nine-month waiting period we'd agreed upon has passed, and, if I may say so, you look different. What is it? Something about you has changed — something more than being older."

Carlos's response was evasive. "You're probably seeing signs of the desert Alfonso."

"No, that's not it. I'm sensing something else."

Trying to make light of the subject, Carlos replied, "Perhaps I've joined the human race."

She studied him a moment before saying, "I know you meant that as one of your typical jests, but I think it's more revealing than you intended. Except for one moment when Rafael's proposal seemed to unsettle you, you've always been the master of every situation, never becoming emotionally involved."

He acknowledged part of her point by saying, "I encountered some setbacks as well as triumphs on this trip." Then he suggested, "Perhaps it's a chastened Alfonso who's returned to Santa Fe."

"Chastened? I wouldn't have put it that way," she said, "but that wouldn't be totally at odds with your statement that you've joined the human race."

She looked down at the letter he'd brought from her mother. "Although I'd like to explore the topic of how you've changed further, that could be a long conversation and I feel we should put that off until I've had a chance to show this letter to Doña Francesca and Rafael."

"Speaking of Rafael, how is he?"

"He's fine," Camila said, "though he's still waiting for my answer regarding his proposal, as you are too, I'm aware."

Camila's answer struck Carlos as ambiguous, so he decided to speak openly. "I want you to know that I often dreamed about the two of you and got the sense that your friendship grew much stronger in my absence. It was a torment to see my best friend in another man's arms, but if that's how the land lies, you can be assured that I wish both of you the very best."

"Thank you for saying that, Alfonso," Camila said. "When I got up this morning, I still wasn't ready to make my decision about marriage, but this letter opens the way to doing so sooner rather than later. Now I really must excuse myself to share my mother's letter with Doña Francesca and Rafael. I expect Rafael any minute."

"I understand," Carlos replied. "In any case I ought to be going because I have several more calls to make today."

Carlos's next stop was Joaquin's officer quarters in the opposite corner of the Presidio. Joaquin's welcome struck Carlos as quite cool. It was easy to guess why. Going right to the point, Carlos asked, "I suppose you've heard about my mother's death and my subsequent quarrel with your father?"

"Yes, he wrote me," Joaquin said with great reserve. "I was sorry to hear about your mother's death. That was sad news."

"Yes, very sad news. As for my quarrel with your father, don't believe everything he wrote, or at least don't suppose that what he wrote was all that could be said. I think you're well aware that your father tends to see everything in black and white. If I may risk being very frank, and I do so in hopes of retaining your friendship, some of his actions upset me a great deal. The very day my mother died, he told me I was no longer welcome in his house. 'His house?' By inheritance it should be my house, and in reacting to his claim of ownership, I let my emotions get the better of me and I told him to go to hell. I regret my words. If I could, I would take them back. They only made a bad situation worse.

"I was also angry because earlier he had told me that much of the money in my father's estate had been spent to buy fine mansions and household items for your two brothers. My impression is that he sent you and me off into semi-exile in order to be free to use my inheritance to the benefit of your younger brothers."

Although Joaquin started to comment, Carlos interrupted him and said, "You may think I'm wrong about your father's motives. If so, time will tell. For now let me finish telling you what I intend to do. I've concluded that the life I led in Mexico City is not the way I want to live the rest of my life. Your father's treatment of me and of my inheritance, oddly enough, reinforced my intention to forgo my inheritance, whatever little of it remains, and to abdicate any claim to my father's title of marquis."

Joaquin looked genuinely shocked. "That's drastic, Alfonso. I hope you'll reconsider."

"I appreciate your concern, Joaquin, though I've made up my mind. This isn't a hasty decision. I've had months, much of the time in solitude, to think this over. Next week I'm going to speak with the government's attorney—I'm assuming it's still Señor Nicholas Arculeta—and ask him to draw up and notarize documents indicating that I withdraw any claims to my inheritance or title. I'll have these sent to my father's lawyer in Mexico City and to my sister Fortunata, whose son will become the heir to the title and can claim it when he reaches twenty-one. I will ask that Emil, my brother-in-law and Vicente's father, be named guardian of the title until Vicente comes of age.

"I also," Carlos concluded, "want you to have copies of these documents. Keeping you informed is my way of showing that I don't want my break with your father to lead to a break with you. I very much want to remain friends with you and Francie."

"Rest assured," Joaquin replied, "that our fondness for you will in no way be diminished by this unfortunate situation, for which, as I can see from what you've told me, my father must bear much of the blame." After the briefest of pauses, Joaquin asked, "What does this radical course you've chosen mean for your material comfort? Your salary as the governor's secretary can't cover much more than your basic expenses."

"Don't worry, Joaquin," Carlos assured him, "I'm not destined for the poorhouse. When your father told me he was going to teach me a lesson in frugality by cutting off my allowance from estate funds, what he didn't realize was that I've saved a substantial amount of money from various activities I've undertaken unbeknownst to him. As a result, I'm surprisingly well off. Now if you'll excuse me, I really must keep going on my homecoming rounds."

Carlos's next stop was Governor Villela's office. The governor was in and pleased to welcome Carlos back to Santa Fe. "You've been gone a long time," he said, echoing a common theme for the day. Gesturing to the pile of papers on Carlos's desk, he said, "In your absence we fell far behind on paperwork, even with some help from Señor Arculeta. I fear it may take you the better part of a month to clear your desk."

"I assure you I'll work as quickly as I can," Carlos replied. "It's good to be back and to see you."

Next stop: Doña Arculeta's home to give her a copy of Agustina Vazquez's letter to Camila and to tell her many of the details about how he'd located Camila's mother. This conversation took quite a while and prompted Doña Arculeta to make repeated expressions of gratitude.

By the time Carlos reached his house and began an extended report to Pedro, María, and Diego it was well past lunchtime. María saw to it that Carlos had something to eat, and the four friends had spent an hour in pleasant conversation on the veranda in front of the house when they saw Camila and Rafael coming down the street holding hands. Don Carlos had no doubt what they were going to say. It didn't take a sorcerer's vision to see that Camila had made up her mind to marry Rafael.

Camila took the lead, addressing Carlos directly. "Alfonso, as you guessed, Rafael and I have grown closer during your long absence. It bothered me that you weren't here to plead your own cause, although I always believed—and you said as much—that your offer of marriage arose from a fear that you would lose my friendship if I married Rafael, rather than any enthusiasm for the institution of marriage. Believe me when I say I was deeply touched by your proposal. I hope to remain your friend, and I know Rafael sees how important you are to me because he has assured me that he will make every effort to help us maintain our friendship. That settled, and with the letter from my mother in hand, I've accepted Rafael's proposal of marriage. We'll ask to have the banns announced this Sunday and we'll marry as soon as possible thereafter, because Rafael's orders to take command of the garrison at El Paso del Norte have come through."

An outpouring of congratulations followed. Carlos joined in, his feelings a mix of regret that the man first in Camila's heart would be Rafael and relief that she'd chosen as she had. Whatever else had been at stake, his commitment to his secret identity as a brujo was no longer at risk, and he didn't have to deal with the troubling issue of whether he could marry Camila and remain a practicing brujo. But even as he sighed inwardly, the thought crossed his mind that Camila's observation that he'd changed was true, and that he couldn't simply go back to his habitual ways, playing at the masquerade of being an ordinary man while turning to his brujo powers when he faced tough situations. Also, more than in any previous life, he had formed emotional attachments to people—Fortunata, Pedro, Diego, and María, among others—and to places (his little house in Santa Fe) and four-legged friends, Eagle and Gordo.

After Camila and Rafael left, Pedro and María went inside to start cooking dinner, and Diego excused himself to care for the household's horses. It was late afternoon, and Carlos was wondering whether he ought to visit Inéz right away or wait until tomorrow morning.

Inéz settled the matter by coming to see him. The black dress she was wearing reminded him of the image of a black widow spider he associated with Violeta, who had trapped him in her web.

Inéz didn't waste any breath on welcome-back niceties. Instead, she said, "You've certainly taken your time coming to see me. Apparently, I'm low on your list of people to call on."

"I'm sorry to have given you that impression," he replied. "Shall we get together tomorrow?"

"What's wrong with right now?" she said in what sounded more like a demand than a question.

He couldn't think of a good reason why not. "I'll need to get dressed in my fencing suit and collect my equipment," he told her. "Do you want to wait here while I change or meet me at your place?"

"You know I'd rather come in and watch you change," she declared, though it seemed to him that she did so in a less aggressively flirtatious way than he'd come to expect from her. "But I'll go ahead to my place and get dressed. Come as soon as you can," she added, and turned and walked away.

Although it took him only a little time to change, she was even quicker and met him at the door to her house in an all-black fencing suit. Black seemed to fit her mood.

They went to the patio where her fencing strip was located. "Do you want to fence first, or talk?" he asked.

"Let's fence now," she replied.

They took up their swords and began to fence. Carlos won exchange after exchange. Inéz's heart didn't seem to be in it. After an exchange that Carlos won with a single parry and riposte, Inéz, in a defeated voice, said, "I'm worthless; it's not just that I'm out of practice or that you've gotten better, which you seem to be; I'm just worthless."

"Perhaps we'd better stop and talk," Carlos replied gently. "Do you want to tell me what's wrong?"

"No, I'd rather not talk about myself. I'd whine and become an object of pity in your eyes." Apparently reconsidering, she continued, "I've had some big loses in the past six months: You were the only person who interested me in Santa Fe, and you went away. My dear stallion Diablo broke a leg and had to be put down, so I'm not riding, and, obviously, I haven't been fencing either. To top it all off, my lover has been in a foul mood. He came all the way to what now seems like a God-forsaken place expecting that someone would send an important package to him here, but this package hasn't come. Sometimes the gloom and anger in this house are so thick that you could cut them with a knife. No, I don't want to say more. Tell me some stories of how you romanced pretty women; that might cheer me up."

Carlos proceeded to tell Inéz at great length about his rendezvous with Mariana and Daniela. (He did not tell her about Zoila, justifying this with the thought that his relationship with her was not, strictly speaking, a love affair.) His descriptions of making love with Mariana and Daniela seemed to cheer Inéz up a little, and she questioned him closely about many details. Her eyes widened when he described Mariana's Roman bath. "That sounds delightful," she remarked.

Hoping to shift the conversation from himself to Inéz, Don Carlos asked her, "I'm wondering about one thing. While I was in the desert you came to me in my dreams and acted in a provocative way. You'd said you would haunt my dreams. How did you manage that?"

His statement amused her. "I didn't manage anything. That last time we were together I said I would visit you in your dreams to plant the idea in your head. Apparently you took it seriously and dreamed about me. I'm delighted to hear that. I thought that after you left Santa Fe you would put me altogether out of mind. Precisely what did I do in these dreams?"

Carlos was taken aback by the news that Inéz apparently had not instigated the dreams he'd had about her, and he wasn't sure it was wise to describe the dreams in great detail. What he did tell her was that she'd come to him in the wet shirt she'd worn that memorable day and that these dreams had kept him tossing and turning for several nights in a row.

A thoughtful look came over Inéz's face. "Precisely when was this in your journey?" she asked.

"During the first week or ten days," he replied.

"Now that you mention it," she said, "at least three times during that first week or ten days after you left, I dreamed that you were in my bedroom with me. Once, no, I think it was twice, I felt as though you were embracing me. The last time I had that dream I distinctly felt you kissing me — pure wishful thinking, or so I assumed at the time. I liked the feeling of being embraced and kissed, although eventually you pushed me away, which annoyed me. Hearing that I was on your mind sufficiently to appear in your dreams pleases me more than you can know."

From what Inéz was telling him, it now seemed to Carlos that he had drawn on his brujo's powers to visit Inéz in her dreams rather than she, as he had supposed, having contrived to come into his. He was getting nervous with what the drift of their conversation might reveal about him. In an effort to shift the focus back to her, he said, "You seem a little less depressed now than earlier, which reminds me of something you told me long ago. You said anger underlies sadness. Does that apply to your present condition?"

Without hesitating, Inéz replied, "Yes, definitely."

"Then," Carlos said, "I suggest that we return to fencing and that you express your underlying anger by going on the attack."

Inéz agreed, and they picked up their swords and resumed fencing. True to her word, she went on the attack with such ferocity that it was all Carlos could do to fend her off. He won nearly all the exchanges, but on two occasions she broke through his defenses. Her eyes were afire with anger, and several times she launched her attack with a cry that was an expression of pure rage. It was a warm late afternoon, and soon sweat was pouring off their bodies. At last, in unspoken agreement, they stopped fencing and went to sit at the table.

Inéz, her padded top soaking wet, declared that she was uncomfortably hot and removed it, revealing a corset-like undergarment that exposed her shoulders. The atmosphere of their bout was suffused with erotic energy, though neither of them seemed intent on seducing the other.

Inéz poured two glasses of wine. She raised her glass as in a toast. "Thank you," she said, "I feel a bit better."

"The second time around was truly inspired fencing," Carlos replied. "I hope we can repeat this without you having to be in a foul mood when we start." As he spoke, Carlos was aware that his wish to fence with Inéz didn't derive only from the thrill of contesting with a skillful opponent, but also from the delight he felt in gazing at the extremely attractive woman seated across from him. He brushed aside the thought that the erotic undercurrents in their relationship meant he was reverting to his old way of life of pleasure-seeking. Zoila was his model. No one could question the depth of her commitment to a spiritual path, but she didn't believe that spiritual seeking required her to abandon the joys of a fulfilling sexual relationship.

Inéz's voice broke into his reverie. A look of mild alarm had come over her face, and she seemed to have slipped back into a depressed mood. "It's very late. My lover will be here any moment. Please slip out the back door."

"Doesn't he know about our fencing matches?"

"Of course, but it's better that he not see us together like this."

Carlos left by the back door, walked around Inéz's house down a narrow side lane, hid behind the corner of a house, and waited. The light from the setting sun suffused the scene with a golden-red glow, and the rich fragrance of a flower he couldn't identity filled the air. The early evening temperature was still quite warm. He watched as Inéz's father — if he was her father, or perhaps he was her lover, or her father *and* her lover — walked up to the door of the house he shared with Inéz and entered without knocking.

27

Puzzles

Governor Villela's estimate that Carlos would need the better part of a month to catch up on the paperwork that had accumulated in his absence proved to be not far off the mark. On his first day back at work, Carlos spent several hours organizing the materials that were piled on his desk into three categories: most urgent, somewhat urgent, and routine. The first pile was so large that it took five twelve-hour days, much longer than normal business hours, for him to complete it. He might have taken a more casual approach, working fewer hours and placing himself under less pressure, but he was feeling guilty for having indulged his seeker self so fully on his return trip to Santa Fe.

Even the "somewhat urgent" category was slow work. A number of documents in this pile needed to be notarized by Nicolas Arculeta, the king's attorney for the province. Other items had not been completely filled out, and he had to spend a full day walking around town to find the individuals who could give him the information he needed to complete the forms.

After nine days of intense work in his office Carlos began to chew on a question of some importance to him. He was asking himself how he could maintain a good balance in his life. He'd noticed that he'd been rushing his morning meditation, cutting the time he spent in silence by more than half. Also, he hadn't been doing any reading in the materials Father Stefano had given him. He knew that once he caught up with the backlogged chores he wouldn't need to devote so much time to office work. Still, for the moment he felt estranged from a significant part of his life.

Was it possible, he wondered, for the bureaucrat and the brujo to coexist? After less than two weeks back in Santa Fe he already felt his brujo awareness diminishing in strength. The activities that fed his soul—the desert, solitude, transformations, meditation—were missing from the days he spent devoted to his work as an imperial bureaucrat.

Toward the end of a second week of constant labor at his office job, he decided he needed a break, even though he still had many items remaining to handle in the somewhat-urgent category. He went to Governor Villela and asked him if he could take a day off.

"Dear boy," the governor replied. "By all means. You've been working extremely hard. If you keep going at this pace, you'll soon be exhausted."

"I appreciate your generosity, general," Carlos said. "But I can't help thinking that things wouldn't have piled up so much had I returned more promptly to Santa Fe."

"Think nothing of it, Alfonso," the governor told him. "The past eight months have been a difficult time for you. Your mother's death was a terrible blow, and your conflict with your stepfather had to be upsetting. Then on your return trip you had to fight your way past Apache raiders in a battle in which you displayed great courage and ingenuity. I know that for a fact because I interviewed the three soldiers who accompanied you. After hearing their praise of your leadership, I feel" — he added with a hearty laugh — "that I should be offering you an officer's commission in the army. We could use more officers with your talents."

Carlos hesitated before answering. His first impulse was to blurt out something to the effect that military life, especially the killing it sometimes involved, didn't appeal to him in the least. In an effort to be more politic, he simply said, "I would probably spend a lot of time in the guardhouse as a result of my tendency to wander off on personal pursuits."

Governor Villela chuckled; then a solemn expression came on his face. "On top of everything else," he said, "you returned to Santa Fe to find that my son has stolen your sweetheart. That, too, had to be an emotional blow."

"'Stolen' is much too strong a word for what's happened. Rafael and I were always friendly rivals for Camila's hand, and I remain his friend. Rafael is an extremely good choice for Camila. I wish the two of them nothing but the best."

Governor Villela concluded the interview abruptly by saying, "Nevertheless, you need — and have earned — a day off. I'll see you tomorrow."

Less than an hour later, Carlos rode Eagle past the outer limits of Santa Fe. He took a deep breath and immediately felt refreshed and relaxed. Too much concentrated work at a desk, he observed, has produced tension in my body. From now on, he resolved, I'll stand up every twenty or thirty minutes to stretch.

Soon Carlos and Eagle were in open country. Without any particular destination in mind, Carlos had taken a road that led northward toward Taos Pueblo. He had no intention of going to Taos itself, much too far away for a one-day round trip. He simply wanted to explore the countryside north of Santa Fe.

Eventually he spotted what looked to be a seldom-used Indian trail off to his right. Carlos had always been intrigued by what was at the end of little-used roads, and he particularly liked roads that, as he hoped would prove true of this one, terminated in a dead end.

His hopes were fulfilled when the trail opened on a small meadow that contained a pool fed from two sources: hot springs and a tiny fresh-water creek. He hopped off Eagle and put his hand in the water. Near the hot springs end it was very warm; at the place where the fresh-water creek trickled into the pool, the water was chilly. On impulse, he stripped off his riding clothes, found a spot toward the warm-water end of the pool, and slipped into the water. He lay back, submerged up to his neck, and let the water's heat penetrate deeply into his muscles. He gave a sigh of satisfaction.

He heard a bird's call high above him and looked up to see a circling red-tailed hawk, one of the birds of prey that he most enjoyed becoming when he wanted to make a sorcerer's transformation. But he didn't feel particularly drawn to flying today and settled for simply watching the hawk in full flight.

He scanned the cliffs to the east of the pool. Near the top of the cliffs he could see a bare section that seemed to glitter. In his experience that phenomenon often indicated a place where crystals could be found. He promised himself that some day he would climb up the cliff to see what, if any, crystals might be there.

The possible presence of crystals in close proximity to hot springs led him to conclude that this place might have been used, perhaps still was used, by Pueblo people for a variety of purposes: cleansing hot baths, searches for crystals with sacred qualities, or perhaps even as a site where young men made vision quests. For him, it provided an answer to the question of how to keep his brujo spirit alive and well while serving as an imperial bureaucrat. He simply had to spend at least one day every week in the desert high country reenergizing his secret inner self, the brujo self.

A more perplexing puzzle, one to which he saw no immediate solution, was what to do about his now non-existent love life. His only serious love interest in Santa Fe had been Camila. Even she had not been a source of erotic love, although he'd always had an anticipatory hope of sharing a fulfilling relationship with her after marriage. Now that prospect was no longer in the picture.

Inéz was a potential love interest, but a dangerous one. She reminded him too much of the treacherous Violeta, and until their recent reunion she'd always appeared to be a combative seductress determined to claim him as a conquest. Now he sensed that a subtle shift had taken place. He had returned from his travels stronger at the heart of his being than previously, and she seemed to have lost some of her former bravado. What was going on? What did this apparent change say about the possibility of Inéz becoming something to him other than a fencing partner and an object of casual flirtation?

Inéz's relationship with Loreto Tiburcio puzzled him even more. The man claimed to be her father, but Carlos couldn't recall Inéz ever referring to Dr. Tiburcio as her father. On the contrary, the term she had used for him more than once was "lover" — "my lover." Yet she seemed bound to him in much the same way that a child is bound to a parent. These facts coexisted uneasily with what Nica Espejo had told him in Mexico City about Dr. Tiburcio and Inéz. Whether Tiburcio was Inéz's father or her lover, Carlos could not figure out why she had been beating Tiburcio with a whip.

Everything he knew about Inéz seemed to warn him away from a love affair with her. Her sexual magnetism threatened to be entangling, almost enslaving, and as much as he was drawn to her he was wary of what involvement with her might entail. At the same time, he could not free himself of his desire for beautiful, sexually attractive women, and none of the other women in Santa Fe interested him in the least. Perhaps, he thought, I should use my days off to visit nearby towns — Bernalillo, for one — to see if any other interesting women live in the area.

Cheered by that thought, he'd started back for Santa Fe.

As Carlos neared the outskirts of town he saw a lone figure, a woman clad in black, sitting on a patch of grass next to a large mound of dirt. It looked as though the woman had brought flowers and placed them on what, Carlos now assumed, must be a grave. As soon as Carlos realized that the black-clad woman was Inéz, it dawned on him that the grave, which was very large, must be where she'd buried her beloved stallion Diablo.

Carlos approached, dismounted, and started toward Inéz. She glanced at him over her shoulder and turned her back to him. "Go away!" she said.

He held his ground. "I'm very sorry about Diablo," he told her. "And I apologize for not expressing my sympathy sooner."

"You certainly weren't in a rush. It's been nearly two weeks since you returned and we fenced and you haven't been by to see me even one more time."

He took a step toward her, but she snapped at him," "I told you to go away. Leave me alone."

"I had a mountain of paperwork waiting for me," he explained. "I still haven't gotten caught up with all of it."

"Yet you're out for a ride in the country," she scoffed. "What sort of excuse is that?"

"I badly needed to get out of town," he replied. "Come on, Inéz; let me walk you back to your place." He reached for her arm, but she pulled it away.

"No!" she said, keeping her face turned away from him.

"Why won't you look at me?" he asked.

"I'm crying, that's why. And I can't stand to be an object of your pity."

Carlos backed away and sat down. "To say I'm sorry for your loss of Diablo is not the same as saying I pity you. I'll wait here until you feel composed. Then I hope you'll let me walk you home."

"Why are you suddenly being so nice after ignoring me for almost two weeks?" she demanded.

"Business kept me away, even though I could say of you, as you did of me, that you're the most interesting person I know in Santa Fe."

She pounced. "Hah! I seem to remember a certain blue-eyed blonde that you were ready to marry." She turned and let him see her tear-stained cheeks and the pained expression on her face.

"That's over," was the best he could come up with, although after a moment's silence in which she kept looking at him, he added. "I would miss it very much if we didn't resume our fencing bouts, now that I've dealt with the most urgent items on my desk."

Inéz brightened a bit at this statement, though it was her turn to pause before speaking. Finally, she said, "All right; I'll let you walk me home."

As they started off, he leading Eagle with one hand and offering her his other arm to take, it occurred to him that the ever-seductive Inéz might simply be shifting, as she sometimes did in fencing, from the offensive to defense, employing the time-honored female tactic of arousing a man's interest by seeming to turn away.

They were nearly back to her house before she spoke again. "You still haven't claimed your prize," she reminded him, and he was on the verge of replying that he had claimed it, until he remembered that she denied any knowledge of the dream in which he'd done so. But since she seemed to be feeling better now, he encouraged her. "I think," he declared, "both of us need to have some fun. I've been working too hard, and you're suffering from several sad events."

A sparkle came in her gray eyes—a flash of the Inéz he enjoyed as a worthy opponent in fencing. "What do you have in mind?" she inquired.

"Fencing," he replied, "has always been at the heart of our relationship."

"But you've become better, while I'm worse than ever," she complained. "In fact, I scored barely any hits the other day. That can't be very interesting for you."

"There you're wrong," he insisted. "Sometimes the trip is of more interest than the destination."

"The means more interesting than the ends?" she suggested.

"Exactly!" he agreed. "What I propose is that for my prize you fence with the goal of distracting me to the point that I have fewer successes."

"How?" she asked.

"Come now, Inéz," he said with a grin. "Surely you've noticed that your beauty can distract me. Use your feminine wiles. Wear that favorite perfume of yours and that corset-like garment that exposes your shoulders. Let your hair fall loose in curls."

"What if," she asked, getting in the spirit of the moment, "I come up with a few ideas of my own?"

"Whoa, there," Carlos replied in mock dismay. "We want this to be a fair fight. I am like any other man, susceptible to female enchantments."

Inéz laughed. "You protest too much," she replied. "I don't believe you for a moment when you say that you're an ordinary man."

Mildly alarmed, but curious about what she had in mind, Carlos declared, "I have no idea what you mean."

She laughed again and didn't answer the question implicit in his latest statement. They had reached the back door to the house she shared with Dr. Tiburcio. All she did was propose, "Tomorrow—during siesta?" But then, as she was entering the house, she called after him, "The sun at midday will enhance the fragrance of my perfume."

Carlos went home buoyed by this conversation. He felt he'd made progress in solving the puzzle Inéz posed for him. On the surface it might seem he was falling into a trap of being smitten by a ravishing but possibly dangerous woman. The difference this time—the difference from his fatal relationship with Violeta—was that he was treating his affair, if that's what it was, with Inéz as play; it was not blind passion. Play, he decided, had the advantage of keeping a certain distance between himself and Inéz—something he'd failed to do with Violeta.

Work the following morning went very well. He attacked the piles of documents on his desk with great energy and efficiency. Governor Villela, who dropped by to give him yet another item, noticed right away. "You are catching up," he observed, "faster than I thought possible."

"A day off can do wonders," Carlos replied, and they both laughed.

The day off had been good, but Carlos knew that the real source of his enthusiasm was his anticipation of an early afternoon fencing bout with Inéz.

Inéz met him at the door to her house before he could even knock. She pulled him abruptly inside. "No one except you should see the way I'm dressed," she said.

Her outfit was indeed provocative. Below her waist she was wearing a normal fencing costume, light shoes and tight pants. She had let her curly black hair fall loose about her shoulders and had used kohl to enhance the shape of her eyes. The scent of her favorite perfume wafted in his direction, filling the hallway. Her simple black top added the strongest erotic note to her attire. It was cut even lower than the garment of the same type she'd worn during one of their previous bouts.

Noticing his appreciation, she smiled impishly. With effort, Carlos restrained himself from making a salacious comment. They walked to the fencing strip in the patio. As had been her custom, Inéz had put a bottle of wine and two glasses on a nearby table. "In case we wish to drink some wine while taking a break from our bout," she announced.

There was also a second, smaller bottle on the table. Inéz picked it up, poured a little oil from the bottle, and rubbed it on her shoulders and chest, applying it in a languid, sensual way.

When she'd finished, Inéz handed Carlos the bottle of oil and turned her back to him. "Please," she asked, "apply oil to my back. You'll notice that it smells of night-blooming jasmine, a fragrance that's said to bewitch lovers. And you'll also notice that I washed my hair this morning with a soap that has the fragrance that makes you dizzy."

Carlos began to apply the oil to Inéz's back. The combination of fragrances from her hair and the body oil had a mesmerizing effect that he felt it best to resist. Carlos, he warned himself, you need to concentrate fully on fencing when our bout begins.

Inéz sensed his withdrawal and asked, "What's the matter? You drifted away."

He pulled himself together and replied, "I may be about to pass out. Perhaps we'd better commence fencing while I'm still conscious."

The moment of temptation passed when he reminded himself that carelessness had once led to his death. By placing memories of Violeta in the forefront of his consciousness he brought his awareness to greater clarity.

The bout itself was well contested, even elegant in form. Both Carlos and Inéz rose to the occasion by fencing creatively. Exchange after exchange inspired them to innovation after innovation. Only Carlos's sorcerer's vision, which enabled him to anticipate Inéz's intentions, allowed him to fend off some of her best moves. Although he won nearly every exchange, his successful hits were not easily achieved.

The raw power both fencers displayed had a particularly transformative effect on Inéz. She was afire with a vitality that served to enhance her beauty in Carlos's eyes.

In the heat of the July day, both combatants were soon drenched with sweat, and Inéz's shoulders and the top of her chest gleamed, now and then catching the sun's rays directly. It reminded him of what happens when a crow's body, turning in flight in bright sunlight, suddenly becomes not black but a flash of light as bright as a reflection from a mirror.

Then Inéz, after a well-designed preparatory maneuver, made an audacious lunge toward him. As she stretched forward her breasts almost spilled over the top of her corset. She returned to an en garde position and used both hands to tug her top back up — well aware of the display she'd put on — and said, "I believe that was a hit."

He had defended himself well, and the hit she had scored was so light that he could have denied that it had happened, but he didn't. "Yes," he agreed. "That was definitely a hit." A smile of great satisfaction came over her face.

Once they resumed fencing Carlos, angry with himself for having allowed Inéz's body to distract him for even a moment, attacked with a vigor that bordered on violence. He achieved hit after hit in rapid succession, ten in a row. "Remind me," she sighed, "never to make you angry with me. Perhaps it's time to quit for today; we've fenced non-stop for more than an hour."

He agreed and they sat at the table to drink wine. After a few sips, Inéz looked at him appraisingly and declared, "I did my best to keep you interested, perhaps even to cause you to lose more often, but I've failed. I hope you're not disappointed in a prize so easily won."

"There was nothing at all easy," he insisted, "about our contest."

"You're a puzzle to me," she replied. "You keep me at arm's length. For a long time I thought that was simply out of loyalty to Camila. Now that she's no longer in the picture, you still hold back. I could feel it when you were applying oil to my back; initially you were giving yourself to the experience with great enjoyment; then you suddenly shut down.

"Also," she continued, "you've definitely changed since you went away."

Carlos didn't feel comfortable telling Inéz about Zoila's impact on his life, so he responded evasively. "All those months on the Camino Real must have had some effect."

She replied with a touch of impatience in her voice. "I'm not talking about a superficial change in your appearance. The change I'm sensing in you is something internal, something it seems you feel a need to hide. You don't have to explain, if you don't want to," she assured him. "In fact, it might be better if you didn't. A little mystery in a relationship can be a good thing."

He considered observing that much about her was a mystery to him, but he didn't. Relieved that he didn't have to explain anything, he simply told her, "I hope we'll continue our bouts. Today was splendid. Many thanks. Our session did me a world of good."

He packed his equipment and said, "I have to get back to work. You don't need to walk me to the door if you'd rather stay out of sight."

"Perhaps that's wise, though nothing that happens in this small town goes unnoticed. Word will spread quickly that you've visited me. I hate to ask, but is it within the rules you have for our relationship for you to embrace me? I would like to be held."

He'd missed holding a woman; it had been many months since he'd had that pleasure. He took her in his arms, not stroking her back or attempting anything more than a simple embrace.

Suddenly, she began to tremble, and she tried to extract herself from his embrace. "What's wrong?" he asked. "What did I do to upset you?"

She pulled back and looked directly at him. Her eyes were full of tears. "I hate being needy, especially when I need to be strong. I've had such a wonderful time with you today, and I don't want to ruin it by being sad. But the truth is that I am sad and not because of anything you've done.

Please" — this was said with a wan smile — "come again next week and I'll do my best to be entertaining." She turned away and he let himself out of the house.

28

Inéz

Inéz's moodiness weighed on Don Carlos's mind. Ordinarily she embraced life with immense enthusiasm, yet he'd returned to Santa Fe to find a dark cloud hanging over her. Despite the wariness he felt toward her, he had been glad to see her and had enjoyed their fencing sessions. He felt remiss in having waited so long before setting up their second fencing bout, and he decided he needed to do something to lift her spirits. It didn't take him long to come up with some ideas. As soon as his plans were formulated, he walked to her place, knocked, and found her at home. He described the purpose of his visit. "I couldn't help noticing how much you miss having a horse to ride since Diablo's death. I hope you'll let me take you shopping for a new horse."

Inéz shot him a questioning look without saying anything.

He continued. "Two weeks ago, as my companions and I passed Esteros de Mejía, the rest stop on the Camino Real that's just south of El Bosque Grande, we met a drover with a herd of semi-wild horses he'd rounded up. His eventual destination was Bernalillo, and he told me a big horse sale will be held there at Mariana Olviedo's hacienda this coming Saturday. What I propose is that we put together a small party — you and me, Pedro and María, and Diego — and ride to Bernalillo tomorrow and check out the available horses. A wide selection of horses will be there because two other drovers are also bringing herds for sale. What do you say?"

Inéz's response was noncommittal. "I have nothing better to do this Friday or Saturday," she replied. However, Pedro and María had already told him that they'd be interested, and Diego had said he'd be thrilled to come along because he had never been to Bernalillo and was eager to see it.

With everyone in agreement, Carlos rented horses for María and Inéz, and the five friends left for the horse sale at dawn Friday morning. The early start was necessary because Bernalillo was forty miles from Santa Fe.

Don Carlos's party arrived at Bernalillo late Friday afternoon. They made a quick tour of the horse sale being organized for the next morning. Three drovers had already shown up, each bringing forty to fifty half-wild or wild horses that were pastured in a big meadow on the east side of the river. Inéz spotted a number of horses, all of them stallions, she wanted to check out at greater length the next day. Three of the best-looking prospects were in the same herd.

Lodging for the night proved more challenging. News of the coming sale had spread widely, and every extra bed at the local farms and ranches seemed to be spoken for, leaving the prospect that Carlos and his friends might have to camp out in a meadow beside the Camino Real. Not quite ready to give up on sleeping under a roof, Carlos asked Pedro and Diego to scout around for a place to sleep while he, Inéz, and María ate dinner at the ranch where the sale was to be held. The ranch's owner, Mariana Olviedo, a handsome widow in her sixties, showed up during the meal to apologize that she had no beds left in her house for overnight guests. Pedro returned to report that he'd found a widow named Bernal, whose late husband was a descendant of the town's earliest settlers, who had space in her stable for their horses. She was also willing to let Diego sleep in the hayloft and had two vacant bedrooms, each with a single bed, that she'd rented Pedro for the night.

"That's a relief," Carlos said. "I was beginning to think we'd have to sleep in a field. Pedro and I can take one bedroom, and Inéz and María can share the other."

"I don't agree," Pedro replied sharply. "I want to share a bed with my wife. You and Inéz can work out what to do about the other bedroom between yourselves." Not waiting for Carlos's response, he helped María on her horse and the two went off together.

"I guess I can sleep in the barn with Diego," Carlos said. "I've slept in many barns over the past months."

"You'll do no such thing," Inéz declared. "The two of us can use the same room."

"If so, we'll have to establish some ground rules for behavior. If I promise not to try to seduce you, will you promise not to seduce me?"

Inéz seemed to find Carlos's "rules" highly amusing. When she stopped laughing, she said, "If that's the way you want it, I promise not to try to seduce you." Carlos was pleased both because she'd agreed to his "rules" and had done so in a light, teasing manner that seemed to indicate she was in a good mood.

The bedroom proved to be a small one, probably in normal times the room of one or two of the widow's six children. Pedro and María were next door, with a thin partition between the rooms. Inéz and Carlos, without thinking about it, spoke in low voices close to a whisper. "I'm really tired," Inéz said, "and I want to be out horse shopping before most buyers are doing business. Let's go to sleep right away. If you'll turn your back to me, I'll get undressed and slip into the bed" — which was, indeed, a single bed.

Don Carlos sat down on the floor on the other side of the bed, facing away from Inéz, and pulled off his boots and removed his belt, jacket, and shirt. He had grabbed an extra blanket from the bed and was arranging it so that he could sleep on the floor when Inéz, her movement shaking the rickety bed a little, announced, "Okay. I'm under the covers."

A long pause followed until Inéz asked, "Where are you? Aren't you coming to bed?"

"I'll sleep on the floor; it's no harder than the ground I slept on during my recent trip."

"You will not (with special emphasis on "not") sleep on the floor," Inéz asserted. "The bed is big enough for two."

"But what about our agreement not to seduce each other?"

"What about it?" Inéz replied. "We can share a bed without doing anything. Now get in here. If you don't join me in bed, then I'll have to sleep on the floor too, as my spirit of fair-mindedness would require me to do. I don't fancy sleeping on the floor, so the only option is for you to quit stalling and get in bed."

Carlos eased his way into his side of the bed, being careful not to touch Inéz.

"What now?" she asked in a grumpy tone of voice. "I'm sure part of you is hanging off the edge of the bed." (She was right about that.) "You won't get much sleep in that position. Turn over and put your front against my back. That's the only efficient way for two people to sleep in a bed this small."

Carlos turned over, as instructed, and was startled to find that Inéz was wearing only a chemise.

"Whoa! Is this your idea of not being seductive?"

"Would you stop fussing?" she replied. "Give me your hand," and she took his hand and put it around her waist. "That's nice. It's just what I need to sleep well."

"And I'm supposed to fall asleep?" Carlos asked, nevertheless enjoying the feeling of touching Inéz's body.

"Stop complaining and do something practical," Inéz said. "Surely you can feel my breathing. Regulate your in and out breaths to match mine. That'll help take your mind off other things." Carlos did as instructed and found it soothing. Inéz dropped off to sleep after only a few breaths. It took him a little longer, though before he fell asleep he became aware of her heartbeat as well as his. Unless he was imagining things, it seemed to him that their heartbeats as well as their breathing were in unison.

The next thing Carlos remembered was Inéz gently sliding over to the edge of the bed (she didn't have far to go), where she sat up and stretched. What a beautiful sight! It suddenly dawned on him that, for all that he'd bedded many women, he'd never spent the night sleeping with one. "I could wake up every morning to sights like this," he told Inéz.

She looked over her shoulder and said, "You could, if you would simply decide to acquire a wife or a mistress or both. Now please dress quickly and head down to breakfast. I want some privacy to use the commode."

Carlos was soon on the stairs on his way to breakfast, which was available buffet style in a small dining room. Pedro was there and looked up. "Get a good night's sleep?" he asked with something annoyingly like a smirk.

"Yes," Carlos replied. "I slept very well and longer than I usually do."

"I'll bet" Pedro said, his skepticism quite obvious. "Here come the ladies." Inéz and María were chatting in an animated way and laughing heartily.

"They're getting along well," Carlos observed.

"Yes," Pedro agreed. "María likes Inéz and insists that she's very nice. I may have to reconsider my doubts about Inéz. We'll see who's right."

Inéz patted Carlos on the shoulder and kissed him lightly on the top of his head. "Poor fellow," she said to María, "he fell asleep before he could make any headway seducing me."

"Liar," Carlos replied good-naturedly. "You fell asleep first."

"That's even worse, isn't it?" was Inéz's retort. "The fellow can't even get the girl's attention. But I think my version makes a better story."

After breakfast, they located Diego and gave him large helpings of leftovers from their meal. They arrived early enough to beat most of the crowd to the area where the drovers had corralled their horses. It didn't take Inéz long—she's decisive, a quick study, Carlos thought to himself—to locate a horse she liked very much: an unusually large mustang who was bullying the other horses—definitely the boss. Unable to see for certain, Inéz asked the drover if the mustang was a stallion. "No," the drover replied, "that's a mare."

"I rather had my heart set on a stallion; I've always owned stallions," Inéz said.

"Señora, that mare is the most intelligent and strongest horse in this herd, and she's a dominant mare who bosses the younger males around— the closest thing to a stallion you'll find in a mare."

"Maybe it's time for me to change my thinking," Inéz observed, and she immediately initiated bargaining with the drover, who told her his vaqueros had nicknamed the mare Bucko. Negotiations stalled when it turned out that Bucko had accepted a halter and a saddle, but had not yet been successfully ridden. "I'm satisfied with the price we've agreed upon," Inéz told the drover, "but the deal is off if I can't get on Bucko before we leave here today."

Inéz's statement clearly worried the drover, who admitted that Bucko had bucked off both his vaquero assistants. Pedro stepped into the breach and volunteered to try to ride Bucko, saying that he might succeed because while in the military, he had been in charge of his company's horses and had saddle-broken many a wild horse. The two vaqueros held Bucko's head, and Carlos boosted Pedro into the saddle.

The vaqueros gave Pedro the two lead ropes they'd used to hold Bucko steady, whereupon Bucko began bucking, whirling, and snorting in outrage at having a rider on her back. Pedro's riding skills showed to good effect, and eventually Bucko, her sides heaving from exertion, stood still for a moment, only to start bucking again as soon as she'd caught her breath. Pedro rode out this latest tantrum. Finally, Bucko stopped and seemed to be calm. Pedro relaxed and asked Bucko to walk forward by lightly touching her with his heels. Bucko started lunging, bucking, and twisting again. Pedro, off balance, began to lose his seat, and rather than be pitched onto the ground he skillfully leapt off, but he stumbled and landed hard on his side. "I'm getting too old for this sort of nonsense," he grumbled as he got up and dusted himself off.

The vaqueros eventually cornered Bucko and, with the enticement of a bucket of grain, managed to restrain her by her lead ropes. They then led her over to where the drover and Inéz were standing. Turning to Pedro, Inéz said, "Good job! You almost had her. I'll take my turn next."

Some alarm was expressed by all present at this plan, but Inéz wasn't to be talked out of it. Held by the two vaqueros, the mare rolled her eyes, showing their whites. Inéz whispered in Bucko's ear while giving her lumps of sugar. She kept at this until Bucko seemed to be listening to her. "Alfonso," she said, "give me a leg up." With considerable misgivings, Carlos did as he was told.

The moment Inéz was in the saddle, Bucko threatened to rear. "No!" she said, in a firm, no-nonsense voice. Bucko was soon quiet again.

"Let go of your lead rope," she told the vaquero on her right. Before he could hand it to her, Bucko began to twist away. "No!" she said again, more sternly. "Whoa!" Bucko calmed down and stood still. After several minutes in this holding position, Inéz told the other vaquero to hand her both the lead ropes. Bucko seemed about to start another tantrum, but Inéz said, "Walk!" and Bucko walked slowly in the direction Inéz steered her.

"She's got a lot of guts," Pedro whispered to Carlos. "And she's a hell of a rider too."

After two times around the corral, Inéz brought Bucko back to their starting point and dismounted without further incident. "This is the one for me," she said. "I love a challenge."

By the time Inéz's purchase of Bucko was complete, Diego was nowhere to be seen. "Where could that kid have gone?" Carlos asked no one in particular.

"He got bored with the business side of things," María reported, "and went off toward the main house at the Olviedo hacienda with a pretty Indian girl." Sure enough, they found Diego sharing some overripe apricots from Señora Bernal's orchard with the girl.

As quickly as they could, Don Carlos and his friends organized their trip back to Santa Fe. The only tense moment occurred when Eagle and Bucko met. Bucko snorted and squealed. Eagle replied in kind and added something highly insulting. For a moment Carlos thought he was going to have a horse fight on his hands. But Eagle, who'd always been the dominant horse in any herd he'd been in, apparently put the younger Bucko in her place, and Bucko accepted Eagle's dominance.

On the trail back to Santa Fe, Pedro and María went in front, riding side by side; Carlos came next in line, leading Bucko under Eagle's watchful eye. Inéz and Diego came last, and whenever Carlos had a chance to look back, he saw that they seemed to be having a lively conversation.

When the party reached Carlos's house in Santa Fe, Inéz asked whether she could board Bucko at his place, where the fourth stall had been empty. "Diego will take good care of Bucko," she said, "and I'd rather have him working with Bucko than those roughnecks at Arturo Barbon's stable." Carlos agreed. "Based on my chat with Diego," she added, "I believe he's discovered girls. Nothing quite like a boy in love, is there?"

"Oh my word," Carlos replied. "I suppose it had to happen sometime; God knows I was girl crazy at his age. But I'm not old enough to play dad."

"You certainly know enough about courting girls," Inéz replied, "and, like it or not, you're going to have to play dad."

They were about to go their separate ways when Inéz turned to Carlos and asked, "Wasn't that just Part A of your make-Inéz-happy program? What's Part B?"

"I'm pleased," he replied, "that you want to know. Here's Part B: Joaquin and Francie's baby is to be baptized at Mass a week from tomorrow. I hope you'll help me organize a surprise party in honor of the baby's baptism. My idea is to invite everyone in town to a big barbeque for them in the plaza. One difficult aspect will be keeping the plan a secret from Joaquin and Francie. Also, to put on a good show we'll definitely need to enlist help from leading families. Toward that end, it would be a good idea for you to come to Mass with me tomorrow and talk with the women from the town's first families."

Inéz looked uncertain. "You know I don't attend Mass, and I barely know any women from the town's elite," she said. "Is this a plot of yours to make me a respectable woman and a good Catholic who confesses her many sins and is friendly with the town's leading ladies?"

"All of the above, I suppose," Carlos replied, with a grin that told Inéz he didn't really mean it.

The following morning Carlos called for Inéz at her home. She came to the door in an elegant pale blue dress. That was a surprise. He had never seen her in anything pastel-colored—always in black, brown, dark green, or, in one instance, in a red riding outfit with gold trim. "My!" he remarked, "Don't we look fetching today."

"I'm glad you approve," she replied. "You look pretty good too in your Sunday suit. You realize, don't you, that your showing up for Mass arm in arm with me is going to set tongues wagging?"

"I do. Let's think of it as a public service. The gossip around here has gotten stale. A fresh dose of juicy gossip will raise everyone's spirits." As they entered the chapel at the Palace of the Governors, quite a few heads turned in their direction—the men in appreciation of Inéz's beauty, the ladies to admire Inéz's dress and to speculate on her relationship with Carlos.

At the end of Mass, Carlos and Inéz joined members of the town's elite who had gathered outside the chapel to greet each other. Don Carlos steered Inéz directly to Lucila Arculeta's side, introduced them, and told Lucila about the plan for a surprise party in the plaza the following Sunday. "Will you help us out?" he asked.

"Dear Alfonso," she replied, "you have done me such a great service"—Inéz's eyebrows shot up at this statement—"that I couldn't refuse you any such assistance, even if I wanted to, and I certainly want to help you with this project. Why don't I take Señora de Recalde to meet other friends of ours, all of whom I'm confident will be glad to assist such a delightful plan?"

Carlos went off to converse with his men friends, keeping an eye on Inéz's progress through the ranks of elite ladies. It seemed to him that all of them—Cristina Beltran (the rich merchant's wife), Pilar Peralta (the vice governor's wife), and Isabel Villela (the governor's wife)—initially greeted Inéz with some reserve, only to warm up to her when, Carlos supposed, they learned what she was proposing to do.

As he walked Inéz back to her place, she said, "Everyone's enthusiastic, eager to do their part. This is going to be a lot of work, which is fine with me. I was getting bored by my routines, although your return and Bucko's purchase have improved my state of mind. I should add that I've been invited to the drawing rooms of nearly every member of the town's elite, something I never expected to happen, given that my reputation is apparently suspect."

Carlos's week was crowded with chores, most of them stemming from the backlog of documents and letters that had piled up during his time away from Santa Fe. On Wednesday morning he gave Diego a message to deliver to Inéz that they would have to postpone their weekly fencing match until early the following week. Apparently, Inéz was also overwhelmed with chores, as she told Diego that preparations for Sunday's festivities—

arranging for food, tables, two bands, and gifts for the baby — were a big job that was demanding her total attention.

In the end, all the time spent on preparations made for an entirely successful event. When Joaquin and Francie passed the northwest edge of the plaza on their way to the chapel for their baby's baptism, they expressed surprise at the amount of activity there. Carlos, who was walking with them to church preparatory to becoming little Esteban's godfather, said he didn't know for sure, but he thought an event honoring some family's patron saint was planned for later in the day.

The baptism went smoothly enough. Carlos noticed that, unlike so many babies he'd observed on similar occasions, Esteban did not break out wailing when handed to the priest.

After the ceremony, as Joaquin, Francie, and the babe in arms, Esteban, left the chapel, they immediately noticed that at least half of Santa Fe's small population had gathered on the plaza. As the baptismal party came into view a cheer went up and one of the bands started playing. Governor Villela stepped forward and spoke with Esteban's parents: "Congratulations, Captain Joaquin and Señora Alvarez. We have organized a party in honor of little Esteban's baptism and the happiness his birth has brought to all your neighbors. We hope you will enjoy the day."

The party went very well. Everyone agreed that the food was unusually good and that the bands outdid themselves in the serenades and dances they played. Despite the fact that Carlos didn't get a chance to speak with Inéz, he kept track of her movements and noticed that she spoke with everyone she met, the elite and the poor, with equal graciousness. He overheard many people say that Señora de Recalde had done a remarkable job organizing the event.

As the party was winding down, Carlos was about to go over to Joaquin and Francie when he felt a hand on his elbow. He turned to find Dr. Tiburcio, Inéz's father or lover or whatever he was, standing there. In all the time that the mysterious doctor had lived in Santa Fe Carlos and he had seldom spoken; when they had, Dr. Tiburcio's contribution had always been rather brusque. Today proved to be no exception. "It may be well for you to remember," the doctor said without preamble, "that my daughter's first husband died under highly suspicious circumstances."

Don Carlos was momentarily speechless, and before he could organize his thoughts to reply, the doctor turned on his heel and walked swiftly off.

What the hell was that about? Carlos wondered to himself.

29

Loreto

Carlos couldn't get his mind off the strange incident of Dr. Tiburcio approaching him to insinuate that Inéz had caused her first husband's death. To find out more about Dr. Tiburcio he visited Lucila Arculeta, who had become a confidante as a result of the help he had given her in locating Camila's mother. She was also a highly reliable source of gossip about Santa Fe's residents.

Don Carlos asked Lucila what she knew about Dr. Tiburcio and his patients. "Does he do them any good?" he inquired.

Lucila replied, "Most of his patients get better, and he's become quite popular as a result, despite his dour and unsocial personality. The ones with physical ailments he gives herbal concoctions that usually produce good results. He has had even more success treating individuals with emotional or mental problems, though the pattern of treatment in those cases is very different, indeed, quite curious."

"Curious? How so?" Carlos asked.

"Dr. Tiburcio gives patients suffering from melancholia or emotional instability a concoction of his own making. To a liquid, usually milk, he adds a powder. The patient's mood brightens almost right away. They stay in that happy state for a while, but in a day or two they lapse back into melancholia. He returns and gives them more milk laced with the powder. The pattern repeats: temporary improvement followed by another onslaught of melancholia. On his third visit he says that his patient needs long-term treatment and after that he comes every day to administer the powder. He has four or five such patients. Although he doesn't charge much for each visit, it gives him a steady income."

"Has anyone ever recovered to the point that he can stop this treatment?" Carlos wanted to know.

"To the best of my knowledge, none of the long-term patients has ever fully recovered."

After a bit of light conversation with Lucila, Carlos excused himself and left. The question that now loomed large in his mind was whether he could get his hands on some of the powder Dr. Tiburcio administered and identify what it was. It certainly sounded as though the patients became dependent on, possibly even addicted to, the powder. Perhaps, he thought, Inéz can get a sample of the powder for me.

He was eager to talk with Inéz in any case and went directly from the Arculetas' to Inéz's residence. Before he could knock on her door, a gust of wind blew it open. He entered and was looking into the empty parlor and kitchen to his right when he heard voices from down a corridor to the left. He supposed it was the bedroom wing. He tiptoed down the corridor, feeling like a sneak thief but convinced by his sorcerer's intuition that it was important for him to hear what was going on.

Two doors down the corridor one door stood open a crack. Peering inside, he saw Inéz, three-quarters turned away from him, standing by a bed. She was wearing the corset-like undergarment she'd sometimes revealed during their duels, a black silk chemise, and black leather boots. She was holding a penitent's whip in her right hand.

Dr. Loreto Tiburcio was sitting in front of Inéz on the bed, pleading with her, "No, please no; I'll be good."

"But that's just it, Lo-lo," she replied disdainfully. "You've been naughty. Momma can always tell."

"No, no," he protested. "I've been good."

"Don't lie to me, Lo-lo. That only makes it worse. You know I have to punish you when you're bad."

"No, no," Loreto cried. "Don't whip me."

"Lo-lo," Inéz said firmly. "It hurts Momma more than it hurts you, but you know she must punish you."

"No, please, no. It hurts so much, and I haven't done anything naughty."

More firmly now: "You've been a very bad boy. I can tell, and it's no use lying about it."

"No, no," he cried, tears streaming down his face as he tried to cover his private parts with his hands.

"Take your hands off yourself, you little pervert," Inéz snarled, grabbing him by the arm. "Momma can tell you've been naughty. Take off your shirt and lie face down on the bed."

Whimpering, Loreto did as he'd been ordered to do.

"You're disgusting," Inéz shouted. "Such a nasty little boy with such nasty thoughts and habits! Momma is going to have to whip you." With that, she shifted the whip to her left hand and hit Loreto hard across his back. Whack! Loreto cried in pain.

"Disgusting," she growled. Whack!

"Filthy pervert," she snarled. Whack!

"Horse dung is cleaner!" Whack!

The epithets continued, each one followed by a blow from the whip.

Loreto wept and screamed in pain at first, but soon his screams changed to noises that sounded like moans. He reached under himself with both hands.

"You're disgusting!" Inéz bellowed in what struck Carlos as genuine anger. "All you want to do is to play with yourself." She struck him three more times in quick succession. By now his back was covered with red welts and blood.

Finally, Inéz stopped whipping Loreto and said in a soothing voice, "That's enough for this time. Sit up and tell Momma that you're going to be a good boy from now on."

Loreto sat up and turned toward Inéz, an adoring look on his face. "Thank you for forgiving me, Momma," he said. "I'll be good now." He was looking longingly at Inéz.

"All right, Lo-lo," Inéz said in a gentle voice. "Momma will hold you." She sat down on the bed and embraced Loreto, who began to make whimpering noises. Inéz's arms, now lightly around Loreto, were smeared with blood from his wounds.

"There, there," Inéz said consolingly. "Momma loves you. You're her little boy and always will be." As she spoke these words, Inéz seemed to be staring off into space, but when Carlos followed the direction of her gaze, he was dismayed to see that she was looking into a mirror on the wall and that he, Carlos, was plainly visible in the mirror.

Looking into Carlos's eyes, a pained expression on her face, Inéz mouthed the words, "Now you know."

Carlos shrank back and hurried away, ashamed of having witnessed secret deeds.

The next morning Inéz came to Carlos's house to get Bucko, now renamed Alegría, at the very moment that Don Carlos returned from a long ride he'd taken in hopes of clearing his mind of the troubled feelings he had about Inéz and Dr. Tiburcio. A wild gallop on Eagle had helped a little, and Eagle had enjoyed it a lot.

Inéz approached Carlos without looking him directly in the eye. "I hope," she said, "you're still speaking to me after what you saw, or at least that you'll give me a chance to explain before throwing me and my horse out of your life altogether."

"I don't intend to do that," Carlos declared. "Nevertheless, I want to hear your explanation, because what I saw left me extremely confused, not knowing what to think."

"It's complicated," Inéz replied. "Basically Loreto made me do those things by threatening me if I didn't. I felt I had no choice if I wanted to stay alive."

"What sort of hold did he have over you?" Carlos asked, genuinely puzzled.

"You need a little background. I was born into a very poor Basque family. My father was a cobbler who went from village to village in the mountain towns around Pamplona repairing shoes or making new ones. He drank too much and was a compulsive gambler. Unfortunately, he was never a successful gambler, and once we had to leave a town because he'd lost so much money gambling that he couldn't pay what he owed. The men to whom he owed the money came after him and beat him up. I remember seeing him with black eyes, a cut lip, and an injured arm. When I asked my mother what had happened, she said he'd had a bad accident.

"At times my childhood was happy. When I was about twelve, my father set up a shop in Pamplona, a city large enough to support his business, and he stopped drinking. I was old enough to work, and I had a job in the kitchen of a house owned by an army officer who was a fencing master. One day he caught me playing with a sword in his fencing salon. I was terrified that he would scold me and not let me continue to work for him, but instead he gave me a lesson and decided that I had some potential as a fencer. For the next two years he gave me lessons free of charge, and my skills increased at a rate that seemed to astonish him.

"When I was fourteen, everything fell apart. The fencing master reenlisted in the army, depriving me of my job and my access to fencing. Then my mother died, and my father went back to drinking and gambling. He also began to treat me badly. I was in his way, he said, costing him money he could better use for his own needs.

"Barely a week after my fifteenth birthday he brought several men to our rented rooms for a session of drinking and gambling. One of the men was Loreto Tiburcio. As the night progressed, my father got drunker and drunker and lost game after game. Loreto won so many of the games that the other two men left, leaving only my father and Loreto. My father had lost so much that it was clear he couldn't pay Loreto. Not even giving Loreto all his cobbler's equipment—which Loreto didn't want—would suffice. Loreto proposed that he would forgive my father his entire debt if he would give him me as his servant. My father called me to come into the room. I somehow knew what was going to happen. 'Here,' my father said to Loreto, 'you can have the girl. She's no use to me.'

"Loreto had me pack a few belongings and come to the rooms where he was staying. We left Pamplona the next day. At that point Loreto was an itinerant herbal healer who went from place to place selling herbal concoctions he made.

"A week later we had reached Vitoria, a small city a long way from Pamplona. I now believe that Loreto wanted to put a considerable distance between Pamplona and ourselves to be sure that I wouldn't try to run away.

"The first day in Vitoria—he was already telling people that I was his daughter—he took me to a ramshackle house where women were selling their bodies to shabbily dressed lower-class men under the watchful eye of a pimp. That night he came to my bed and forced himself on me. He told me in a fierce voice that I had no place to go and had better obey him no matter what he did or asked, because if I didn't he would sell me to that pimp to service all comers.

"Thereafter Loreto used me every day. The only relief came from fencing lessons, which he paid for. Strangely, he was proud of my accomplishments as a fencer and set up lessons for me with the best fencing master in town. He also had a great interest in horseback riding and often let me ride fine horses that he rented.

"It was as if I lived two lives—a daytime life in which I appeared to be his almost-grown daughter, went to the market, cooked his meals, and cleaned his house, and a nighttime life of sexual degradation and fear. I hated him, I feared him, and I was desperate to please him. I was convinced that if I didn't please him—and it wasn't enough if I passively endured him sexually, he wanted me to act provocatively, like a whore—he would kill me. He was an herbalist; he knew all about poisons, and I lived in fear that he would poison me.

"So, when he came up with a plan to marry me off in order to get control of my prospective husband's money, I cooperated. I was seventeen; I was pretty, and I had attracted the attention of a young man who lived next door to us in Vitoria.

"Poor Hernando! Loreto carefully cultivated a friendship among the three of us. Hernando had inherited both property and money when his parents died, but he was young and had little experience of the world. Loreto pretended to take a fatherly interest in him and encouraged his interest in me. He suggested to Hernando that he should marry me, and we would become a family.

"Hernando, who was a guileless man, took the bait and married me. Loreto cooked up a fantastic story about the life we three would have together as a family. He persuaded Hernando to sell his inherited properties and put the money in his, Loreto's, name to manage for all three of us. Prospering from Loreto's financial acumen, we would be able to travel to all the most important cities in Spain and after that, who knows, see the world. Hernando was in love with me and Loreto's plans seemed to him like a romantic adventure. Loreto arranged for us to move to Bilbao, a port city on the Bay of Biscay. Then one morning, after Hernando and I had been married less than five months, as we were eating breakfast Hernando went into convulsions, toppled off his chair, and died.

"An inquest was held, but since Loreto, as a doctor, testified that Hernando had died from an epileptic fit, that was the end of it. We left Bilbao as soon as the inquest was over. No probate proceedings were necessary because Hernando, having signed his money over to Loreto, didn't have any remaining property. What should have been my inheritance as Hernando's widow was firmly under Loreto's control.

"After Hernando's death Loreto's sexual demands on me grew increasingly perverse. From a Portuguese sailor he acquired an African aphrodisiac that created a strong arousal in men who were impotent. He began to market it in taverns and encouraged those who bought it to test its effects, in what he called an 'introductory treatment,' with me. I played my role in these 'treatments' so successfully that the men paid Loreto very well. To make matters worse, if that's possible, Loreto derived enormous pleasure from watching these sexual encounters through a hole in the wall. It's no excuse for my later behavior, Alfonso, but all of this reinforced my belief that the only worth I have in this world stems from my sexuality."

"Your worth," Carlos said emphatically, "is definitely not limited to your physical attractiveness. However, I can understand how being forced to be intimate with so many men was a deeply unpleasant experience that might lead you to that conclusion."

"It was very unpleasant," Inéz acknowledged, "and it would have been much worse had I not developed a way of distancing myself within those sexual encounters. Basically, each time I was about to serve one of Loreto's clients, I would lie down on my bed and imagine my deep self withdrawing from my body until I became only an onlooker, an observer hovering above my body, untouched."

"Remarkable," Carlos murmured half to himself. "Still," he asked, "I don't understand what hold Loreto had over you after your marriage ended. Why didn't you leave him? You're beautiful, you would have attracted another suitor, or, in the improbable case that you didn't, you could have found work as someone's servant."

"Ah," Inéz replied, "Loreto was clever. He insisted that he knew I'd poisoned Hernando. Despite what he'd said at the inquest, he told me he'd been suspicious, and he'd searched my dresser and found poison in a bottle of my perfume. If I didn't do what he told me to do or tried to run away, he said he would turn the perfume bottle over to the authorities and tell them he'd discovered that I'd poisoned Hernando.

"I knew this story was untrue, but what could I do? Even if I tried to run away, where could I go? He had all my money, and I knew he'd follow me and find me. I was trapped; I couldn't escape. I almost came to believe his story about the poison in my perfume bottle. Sometimes I imagined pouring it into his coffee...."

After a pause she went on. "For a time we traveled from place to place along the coast between Santander and Gijon. Loreto, with my forced cooperation, had a good income from his treatments for men's sexual problems. But he finally overstepped. The son of a wealthy nobleman who had heard of Loreto's cure came to him secretly. It turned out that the young man's difficulties had more to do with his lack of desire for women than with inability. I could do nothing for him, so Loreto stepped in to provide service. Somehow the young man's father found out about it and threatened Loreto with dire financial, physical, and legal consequences. Loreto decided to run for it and concluded that the safest course of action was to get out of the country altogether by moving to New Spain. We took passage on a boat, and after a long transatlantic voyage and an overland journey we reached Mexico City. Once there, he started to make demands on me for the kind of behavior you witnessed yesterday."

"That story about your allegedly poisoning Hernando is far in the past," Carlos protested. "I don't see how such an old story would have much credibility now."

"Oh! Loreto had that all worked out too," Inéz replied. "He said he would accuse me of trying to poison *him*. He would pretend to be violently ill after having seen me pour something into his morning coffee. He would say that he was convinced, from the symptoms, that my husband had died from a larger dose of the same poison, which he now realized I had administered. I could deny everything, he said, but he was sure that the courts would believe a story told by a reputable doctor rather than one told by me."

"Diabolical, all right," Carlos said. "I can see why you saw no alternative to going along with him. But what about the lover whose jealousy you hoped to inspire by having me give you a bruise from a love bite?"

Inéz looked chagrined and flushed at his question. "Oh, Alfonso, I'm so sorry; I'm ashamed too. I made that story up to get you to embrace me passionately."

"Are you saying that there was no such lover or that Loreto wasn't the lover you wanted to make jealous?"

"I never willingly made love with Loreto, and I certainly did not experience what we did as making love. It would be more accurate to say that he was my abuser. No, there was no one else. I'm ashamed of myself for deceiving you. I just wanted to be held and loved."

"You were bad," Carlos replied with a smile, "but I would be the worst liar on earth if I didn't admit how much I enjoyed giving you that love bite. But what are you going to do now?"

"I've decided to move out and suffer whatever consequences follow. I've already asked Lucila if she'd let me stay with her, and she's agreed."

"Won't that set in motion Loreto's plan to accuse you and have you tried for murder? We've got to head that off."

"I don't see how," Inéz replied. "But I can't live this lie any longer, even if it means dying on the gallows—though I'll try to avoid that by getting out of town first."

Carlos shook his head. "I don't think that will be necessary, if we can turn the tables on the doctor. Remember, in life as in fencing, sometimes the best defense is an aggressive attack. The first order of business is to get our hands on that powder he gives his patients. Can you get some for me?"

"I think I can," Inéz replied, "although there's very little left. That's one of the things that's plunged him into such a dark mood. He bought the first batch from a Peruvian in Mexico City, and although he bought a lot of the powder, he thought it would be prudent to ask the Peruvian to get more for him. But before the powder arrived from Peru, Loreto and I had to make a run for it."

"Run for it?" Carlos asked. "What was that about?"

"Loreto," Inéz said, "had been treating several clients with the powder therapy. One of them had a very bad reaction, whether it was caused by the powder or the woman's prior condition I don't know, but she suffered an attack of convulsions that frightened and angered her husband. The next time Loreto went to treat her, she warned him that her husband, who luckily wasn't home at that moment, intended to do Loreto serious bodily harm.

"Loreto rushed back to our rooms and told me to pack to leave right away. He decided on Santa Fe because it was so remote that he believed the angry husband wouldn't be able to track him down.

"Before leaving Mexico City Loreto went to see the Peruvian from whom he had agreed to buy the additional supply of powder, and he paid him to ship it to Santa Fe by wagon train. I always doubted that this arrangement would work out, and it's obvious now that the powder isn't coming, and Loreto has almost none left. Loreto doesn't have much cash left either. His income from his practice here barely covers necessities, and every time he's late with a payment toward purchasing this house, the former owner threatens to throw us out. Come to think of it, I wouldn't be surprised if Loreto may be about to make another run for it—lacking, as he does, the powder for his most loyal patients and the money to keep us in this house."

"Here's what we'll do," Carlos said. "I'll ask Lucila to find someone willing to contact Loreto and say that one of his patients needs to see him right away. As soon as he leaves the house, you and I will slip in and hope we can quickly locate some of the powder."

Don Carlos's plot was put into motion immediately. After stationing Diego and Pedro outside Loreto's house to warn him if the doctor returned, he entered and joined Inéz in searching for the powder. With a good idea of what to look for, Carlos used his sorcerer's vision and soon found a small supply of the powder hidden under a floorboard in Loreto's bedroom.

Carlos sent Inéz to stay with Lucila while he went to the governor's office. He quickly sketched the situation for his boss. "Dr. Tiburcio is doing grave harm to his patients by giving them a powder that's a common drug in Peru. It's called coca. It's made from coca leaves that are soaked in some sort of solution, dried, and then ground up. I know about it because my brother-in-law, who's a physician, lives in Lima, Peru, and he's been researching the effects of coca on its users. He showed me coca in powdered form and gave me a tiny amount to taste. It looked and tasted the same as the powder I found when I searched the doctor's house an hour ago. According to my brother-in-law, coca use is addictive, and though it may seem to have a positive effect temporarily if ingested, it creates in the patient, as Dr. Tiburcio doubtless knows, a craving for more without ever resulting in a cure."

Governor Villela was shocked. "The scoundrel! I never liked the looks of the man, but this is appalling. We must have him arrested immediately." With these words, the governor went to the door and told an assistant to bring Mauricio Castillo, the town's police chief, to his office. Castillo arrived soon and promised to arrest Loreto immediately.

A half hour later, Castillo returned frowning. "We got to Tiburcio's house, and he answered the door. I told him he was under arrest for injuring several of his patients. He protested his innocence, but swore he would cooperate. He asked only that he be given five minutes to go to the room where he stored his records to collect some items that would aid in his defense. I foolishly failed to accompany him. Ten minutes or more passed before I decided he might have tricked us. Sure enough, he'd slipped out of the house by a back door. We've been unable to find him, and the blacksmith whose shop is on the south side of town believes he saw Tiburcio mounted on a fast horse and hurrying out of town. I've sent two deputies after him, but we don't know for sure which road he took after he was outside the town limits. He may have escaped us entirely."

30

Freedom

D̲r. Loreto Tiburcio's departure from town did not immediately end the toxic impact he had had on some of Santa Fe's residents. By all odds, the individuals who suffered most were four individuals—a boy aged fourteen, two young women in their twenties, and an older woman in her forties — whom he had been treating for melancholia with his now-infamous powder. Withdrawal from addiction to coca had horrible effects on the four patients and caused enormous grief among their relatives and friends who watched, largely helpless to do anything. For several weeks after the drug was withdrawn all four endured, in varying degrees at any given time, headaches, agitation, diarrhea, and uncontrollable tremors. For two of the doctor's former patients — the boy and a twenty-three-year-old woman — life became so miserable that they attempted suicide. The boy almost succeeded, and his attempt alerted everyone to the danger all four were in. The families of the sufferers rallied bravely, and others pitched in. Don Carlos, having dropped by the boy's home for a visit, was the one who caught him in the act of trying to slit his wrists. Carlos took immediate action, recruiting Diego and three other young Pueblo Indian men to stay with the afflicted boy on a round-the-clock suicide watch. Eventually, all four victims of Dr. Tiburcio's treatments resumed their normal lives, which, unfortunately, meant that some of their previous symptoms of melancholia returned. Kindness and understanding from their friends helped a bit.

Inéz, now staying at Lucila Arculeta's house, needed a lot of kindness and understanding too. Previously, sheer force of will had carried her through her time with Dr. Tiburcio. But her willpower, exhausted by years of enduring the doctor's threats and demands, collapsed once the source of those threats and demands was removed from her life. She became a ghost of her former self. She complained of headaches, strange bodily pains, and inexplicable fatigue that left her barely able to get out of bed. She dragged herself around looking wan and miserable. She spurned Carlos's invitations to fence with him. "How could I fence?" she snapped at him. "I feel as though my body is mired in molasses!"

After weeks of having his proposals to fence turned down, Carlos conceded that perhaps fencing was too physically demanding at present for Inéz. He shifted the focus of his invitations and set out to persuade her to take rides with him on weekdays after he finished his chores at the governor's office. Her response to his initial appeal was "No. I don't want to ride today or any day in the foreseeable future."

Don Carlos protested that Alegría needed exercise and missed her. "Have Diego or Pedro or María take Alegría out for a walk," she replied.

"Not possible," Don Carlos had said with gentle firmness. "They're all too busy. Pedro now works every day at carpentry jobs to earn extra cash for himself and his bride. María is also working extra hours for Francie because little Esteban is demanding a lot of attention; Diego is deeply involved in the twenty-four-hour suicide watch over the boy who was receiving Loreto's treatments. That leaves you as the only logical person to ride Alegría. Besides, she misses you. I can tell that she doesn't understand what's become of you."

It was this appeal to Inéz's love of her horse that finally got her to agree to take rides in the country with Don Carlos and Eagle.

By coincidence, this happened shortly after Camila and Rafael's wedding and the day after the farewell party held in their honor before they left for El Paso del Norte, where Rafael was to replace Colonel Encarnación, who had decided to retire. Despite his best intentions, Carlos had found it difficult to participate wholeheartedly in these festivities, less because of losing Camila — he had for some time accepted that as inevitable — but because of his concern about Inéz, the depth of which surprised him a little.

Over the past few weeks he had found himself increasingly drawn into her affairs. One practical task that had needed attention involved things belonging to her that remained in the house she had shared with Dr. Tiburcio. Inéz refused to go anywhere near the place. "Dark entities haunt that house," she told Carlos. "You can enter it without them hurting you, but I cannot." So Don Carlos, Pedro, María, and Diego spent the better part of a Saturday clearing Inéz's things from the house and rescuing a few of the nicer pieces of furniture for eventual sale, if Inéz refused to take possession of them. Except for some of her favorite clothing, everything went into storage. The house itself was reclaimed by the former owner because Dr. Tiburcio had failed to complete the required payments toward the agreed-upon sale price.

Since Dr. Tiburcio had used all her money for a down payment on the house, Inéz was left without a peso to her name. This wasn't a short-term problem, as Lucila Arculeta was supplying all Inéz's immediate needs, but Inéz spent a lot of time worrying about her future. "What's to become of me?" she asked Carlos. "I have no resources; I've never earned my way at anything other than being in service; and I have no marketable skills, unless I start a fencing academy for women, which is a ridiculous proposition."

After listening to this lament for what seemed like the twentieth time, Carlos finally spoke up. "You're fussing too much about your financial situation. I'm sure something will come along once you feel entirely yourself again. As a matter of fact, I've recently realized that my situation is in some respects similar to yours. I'm an excellent clerk, but government clerks aren't well paid, and my expenses have always exceeded my income from my salary. Although I can't count on supplementing my income in the ways I've done in the past, I'm moving forward in the belief that I'll be able to take advantage of new opportunities when they arise. I'm sure the same will be true for you." Expressing more exasperation than the situation may have merited, he added, "So quit feeling sorry for yourself; you're going to be okay."

At this point, about three months into the healing process, Inéz stuck her tongue out at Don Carlos and said, emphatically, "Bah! Easy for you to say." Carlos regarded her playful reaction as a sign of progress.

Inéz's response led Don Carlos to say something to her that had occurred to him in the past few weeks but he hadn't mentioned because he wasn't sure she would take it well. "All right," he said, "I won't argue with you about the similarities or differences in our financial situations. However, the better I get to know you, the more I see that we're alike in many ways, possibly more alike than different."

She was clearly interested in what he had in mind. "Tell me more," she said.

"I will, if you promise to try not to reject everything I say out of hand."

"I'll try, but I'm in no position to guarantee anything about anything." This was said with great seriousness.

"Here's what I've noticed," Carlos replied. "I've always been drawn to you because you were a fascinating person, full of surprises. When we're in good spirits, both of us are passionate about life; we pursue everything that interests us — fencing, horses, love — intensely. We're both highly adept at those activities — fencing is perhaps the best example — that we care about. Unconventionality underlies a lot of what I'm describing. Although neither of us is conventional — about religion or about the proprieties of class — we both disguise that fact, I more than you, at least until now, by putting up a facade that we hope will prevent people from seeing our secret selves. And that's another similarity I've observed; we both have secrets."

All Inéz would say in response was, "That's worth thinking about. I'm going to have to turn all those parts over in my mind. Thank you for speaking so frankly and for all your efforts of late to cheer me up."

Carlos took the way she responded as a good sign.

A few days later Inéz asked for Carlos's advice. "I've been thinking," she began, "that I would benefit from going off by myself to a secluded pool fed by hot springs and sitting in the water up to my neck. I still have impurities that I'd like to cook out of my body and mind. A long soak in hot mineral water might be just the thing. Do you know of any such place?"

"I know the perfect place," he declared, and he gave her precise directions to the pool that he and Eagle had visited on one of their treks. Impatient to try it, Inéz left that very same day.

That evening Inéz returned as the sun was setting. After the briefest possible stop to give Alegría to Diego to feed and let out into the corral in back of Carlos's house, she burst into the kitchen where Carlos, Pedro, and María were having dinner. She radiated happiness as she exclaimed, "The hot mineral water and the trees and cliffs nearby did wonders for my mood. I felt the power of the place drawing all the toxins out of me. I can't thank you enough, Alfonso. It's a very special place."

As Inéz was finally recovering from melancholy, Carlos suffered an attack of the same malady. It came on in two stages, the first occasioned by a conversation with his stepbrother Joaquin. Carlos had stopped by Joaquin and Francie's residence at the Presidio. After a bit of light banter with Carlos, Joaquin grew serious. "I've just heard some news," he announced, "that could have negative consequences for both of us. One of Rafael's men arrived here yesterday from El Paso del Norte with a message. Rafael wrote to give me advance warning that a contingent of ten soldiers had stopped for two days at the El Paso del Norte garrison. Rafael reported that the captain in charge of the unit is to replace me as commander at Santa Fe."

"Are you to be given a promotion or a new command?" Carlos asked, then adding, "I guess not, from the look on your face and the fact that you said you had bad news."

"Rafael hadn't yet learned many details, except that it seems I'm going to be recalled to Mexico City as part of an investigation of charges of dereliction of duty."

Astonished, Carlos asked, "Whatever could justify such serious charges?"

"While you were away, Alfonso, I had to deal with an incident in the Jemez Springs area. Two Spaniards, both ranchers, reported that rustlers had made off with several dozen horses. The alleged rustlers were three Pueblo men, brothers from Jemez Pueblo. I led a well-armed party of soldiers to the scene and located the accused. The three Natives claimed it was all a misunderstanding. They'd come across the horses ranging freely and unbranded and had assumed that they were wild horses. They expressed regret for the confusion and offered to return the horses along with a half dozen extra horses to prove their good faith. I was convinced of their sincerity and took no action against them."

"That seems consistent," Carlos commented, "with our government's post-Revolt policy of trying to avoid excessively punitive actions against our Pueblo neighbors."

"I thought so too," Joaquin agreed, "and the fact that there have been no more incidents of that sort since indicates that my choice was a good one. However, word of my actions apparently reached my father in Mexico City. You know what he would have done under similar circumstances."

"Yes, I do," Carlos said. "He would have hanged the three accused men and gone to Jemez Pueblo and burned their property, probably hanging a few more Natives to demonstrate that crimes against Spanish property will always receive a draconian response. Still, I don't understand what motive your father could have for dragging your good name through the mud. Surely, that's bad for him and the rest of your family."

"Since I don't know for sure, I can only speculate, and that's where your name comes into the picture. The contingent of soldiers that's headed this way is accompanying a large caravan of supplies and immigrants. One of the new immigrants is rumored to be the Crown's choice to replace Governor Villela, who is said to have asked to be relieved of his duties here so that he and his wife can return to Mexico City."

"I've heard nothing of this," Carlos declared, "as you'd think I would, given that I'm the governor's personal secretary."

"I suspect," Joaquin suggested, "that Governor Villela, as a military man, does everything by the book according to the chain of command, and he's not going to make any announcement until the papers confirming the new arrangement are in his hands."

"You may be right," Carlos said. "That's consistent with the man I know. But I don't see what that has to do with me or with your situation."

"By now," Joaquin replied, "my father has learned that you intend to abandon your claims to your title in favor of your nephew and have named your brother-in-law as guardian of your nephew's future title and inherited estate. My father also knows, I'm sure, that you and I have become friends, and given his habit of dividing everyone into two camps—loyal friends or bitter enemies—I think he's been maneuvering to strike at both of us."

Feeling confused, Carlos asked, "How do I figure in this, if I do?"

"Surely you realize," Joaquin pointed out, "that Governor Villela's departure has implications for you too. The new governor will want to appoint his own staff, and there's no guarantee that he'll retain you as his private secretary. Indeed, Rafael seemed to think that the prospective new governor, who is a friend of my father's and is accompanied by a son about your age, will want to appoint his son as his secretary."

Carlos shook his head. "I guess it's too soon to be certain, but I can certainly see the likelihood that your father's hand is behind both of these moves."

"Your situation isn't yet as clear-cut as mine," Joaquin observed.

The situation seemed clear enough to Carlos. He left his stepbrother's residence in a very bad mood, furious at his stepfather. What was worse, he couldn't shrug off his anger. I'm reacting, he observed, like an ordinary man, unable to achieve the equanimity I've been taught as the Brujo's Way and that is also part of the path Zoila introduced me to. What a depressing thought! And his anger stayed with him for the rest of the day.

That night Carlos tossed and turned, unable—which was unusual for him—to sleep. When he finally fell asleep it seemed almost as if he were having a waking dream, somewhere between a normal dream state and waking consciousness.

He found himself at sea during a violent storm, hovering above a three-masted merchant ship. A big man, evidently the ship's captain, was at the helm wrestling with the ship's wheel. The top third of the ship's mainmast had broken off, and the sails of the other two masts were in shreds, whipping around in the wind. High waves were buffeting the ship from all sides, and when a huge wave lifted the stern of the ship out of the water, Don Carlos could see that the rudder had been damaged.

As Don Carlos watched, a woman emerged from the ship's main cabin and struggled up the stairs to where the captain was fighting with the wheel. He motioned to her to go back to the cabin, but she moved forward and stood behind him with her arms around his waist. Horrified, Don Carlos recognized the woman as Zoila. Another huge wave crashed over the ship and nearly swept Zoila and the captain overboard. Moments later, the biggest wave yet—Don Carlos thought it looked to be nearly a hundred feet high—hit the ship and split it in two just behind the wheelhouse. Zoila and the captain, who Carlos was certain was her husband, disappeared from view. Don Carlos frantically tried to see where they'd gone and feverishly attempted to break through the transparent film that separated him from the scene. Nothing availed, though after the longest time the sky cleared, and he could see that the surface of the ocean, now relatively calm, was strewn with floating debris. No humans, alive or dead, were to be seen. Zoila, he was sure, had drowned at sea.

For months Don Carlos had been trying to contact Zoila in his dreams. He had had no success. Night after night he tried every trick at his disposal, all of them involving some sort of preparation before going to sleep: holding the ring Zoila had given him; spending an hour or more meditating on a mental image of her; ingesting a few peyote cactus buds he'd acquired from a Native friend in order to enter an alternative state of consciousness. Nothing had worked. Now he knew why.

That morning Inéz found Carlos seated on his house's front veranda with his head in his hands. "What's the matter?" she asked. He made no reply.

"Alfonso," she said, shaking his shoulder, "say something."

"I don't want to talk; can't talk yet," was all he managed to say.

Inéz sat down next to him and put her arm around him in an affectionate way. "It's all right if you don't want to talk about what's upsetting you, but I'll sit here with you until you feel better."

A long time passed — it's very difficult to measure time under such circumstances — without Carlos saying anything. Finally, he asked Inéz, "Do you believe dreams can be true?"

"Are there true dreams? I suppose so. Is that your view too?"

"I know there are," he replied. "I had one once about Camila and Rafael. I tried to pass it off as the product of my fears, but when I got back to Santa Fe, I learned that it was true — not just in general that the two of them had fallen in love, but in every detail: how they walked together, where they walked, how they embraced, all of it. Now I've had another dream, a dreadful one, that I'm sure is true." (More than a year later he received a letter from Belén saying that her sister hadn't returned by way of Panama because while in port at Cartagena, her husband had accepted a commission to deliver a cargo to Lima, Peru, and Zoila had agreed to accompany him around South America back to Lima. Nothing further had been heard from them, and reports of unusually violent storms and gigantic rogue waves in the South Atlantic led to the conclusion that their ship was lost at sea.)

"What happened in this dream?" Inéz asked.

"The details of the dream don't matter much," Carlos replied. "But what I saw does; that a dear friend of mine died in a violent storm at sea." (Later, when he thought back to this conversation, he was struck by the fact that Inéz accepted his dream as true and didn't try to comfort him, as a more conventional person would have, by saying, "It was only a dream.")

"Who was this friend?" she asked.

"A woman named Zoila."

Trying to lighten the mood a little, Inéz said, "You were supposed to tell me about all your love affairs."

"Ours wasn't a love affair, certainly not like the others I described to you." This statement loosened the floodgates of his grief and he poured out the story of how he'd met Zoila, and how she'd told him that relations between men and women could take on spiritual meanings that were much more profound than the purely sensual pleasure he'd always derived from sexual encounters. Then, in a halting fashion because he wasn't sure Inéz would understand, he described the chakra practice he and Zoila had shared on their third night together and its awesome result: the union of their golden auras. "Does this make any sense at all to you?" he asked. "My experience with Zoila is what's led me to reexamine the way I was wasting my time before meeting her."

Inéz stroked his shoulder and replied, "I don't begin to understand everything you've said. You'll need to tell me more. And I have no experience whatsoever of sexual relations as anything but a form of violence or aggression, a few times with Hernando excepted. That there could be a spiritual element in lovemaking is entirely new to me. However, I can see how important this woman and your experience with her are for you. If she's dead, and given your deep spiritual connection with her I'm inclined to accept your dream as true, then her death is a great loss."

The next three weeks were spent in an odd reversal of their roles. For nearly three months he had been the one helping Inéz to heal; now she took a turn trying to help him deal with his grief. Not that this required anything much different from what he'd been doing for her: horseback rides, attending Sunday Mass together, and sharing meals that Pedro and María prepared for them. Gordo, an enthusiastic, happy companion at all times, provided comic relief through his playful antics. Inéz's spirits also improved from undertaking to cheer Carlos up.

One day well into this process, after a meal at Lucila Arculeta's, Inéz and Carlos were sipping wine in the drawing room. Inéz grinned at Carlos and said, "I'm feeling so much better, thanks to you, almost like my old self, and I'm not referring to the old self of my time with Loreto; I mean my younger self—the self of the years when my mother was still alive. I hope you'll help me recapture more fully the joy and optimism I felt in those years, and toward that end I'd like you to join me in a game I used to play with my girl friends. It's called 'Princess for a Day.'"

Carlos wanted to know more. "How is the game played?" he asked.

"One person," Inéz replied, "in this case me, gets to be princess for a day. The idea comes from those old-time romances in which the beautiful princess — we always considered ourselves beautiful for the purposes of the game — languishes unhappily, either under the spell of a wicked witch or because her parents don't want her to fall in love with any man other than the stuffy old king they want her to marry for political purposes. Enter a tall, dark, and handsome young man who, though he seems not to be rich or a titled aristocrat, is nevertheless the man of her dreams. Their meetings have to be kept a secret."

"Do you have a rendezvous planned for us or some secret spot at which we can play this game?" Carlos inquired.

"Rendezvous is a good description," Inéz replied. "Since this is a romantic fantasy, the princess — that's me — gets to establish the story line. All you have to do is follow along. The starting point will be a horseback ride Saturday to a remote place. I think the pool that I visited recently at your suggestion would be perfect. The princess — that's me, remember — will supply a picnic lunch. The princess — by now you surely remember that's me — is determined to have a necklace of fine crystals, the more varieties and colors the merrier, so we'll have to spend a little time collecting crystals before lunch. Mostly all you have to do is to fulfill the princess's every wish as they occur to her through the day. Locating an appropriate picnic spot and leading her to a place where she can collect crystals ought to be first on your list of dream-fulfilling activities. How does this sound?"

"It should be fun," Carlos replied. They agreed to set out for the back country at nine Saturday morning.

Don Carlos agreed with Inéz's suggestion that the secluded hot springs she'd recently visited would make a perfect place for a picnic and a search for crystals. As planned, they started northward at nine in the morning on the road to Taos Pueblo but soon turned east onto a faintly visible trail in the direction of an imposing mountain range. Not much later they arrived at the base of the mountains and rode alongside the cliffs to their right. This brought them to their destination, a meadow with a small pool formed by water from a hot spring and a fresh-water creek. Tall trees that screened the spot off from any view except from the cliffs above made it a perfect site for a private picnic, and abundant grass on the far side of the meadow provided an ideal place for Eagle and Alegría to graze while Carlos and Inéz went hunting for crystals.

Using his sorcerer's vision, Don Carlos, as he had on his previous visit to this pool with Eagle, spotted an exposed cliff near the top of the ridge that seemed to glitter. This was a phenomenon that in his experience was often associated with the presence of crystals. Having tethered their horses in the grassy area, he and Inéz began to climb the cliff above the pool. The route straight up was too steep, so they had to pick their way across the cliff's face. At one point they came to a shale slide that made further progress unsafe, and they had to double back and try a route in the opposite direction. The sun was now high and had begun to shine directly on the slope they were climbing. Don Carlos was glad he had a goatskin of water for them to drink, but he was beginning to wonder whether the effort they were having to make was worth it, given the uncertainty of finding crystals when they reached their destination.

Inéz finally complained. "The princess for a day is feeling as though this is too much work. I hope we're almost to our destination."

Fortunately, they'd reached the area Don Carlos had seen from below. "This is it," he said, relieved that the climb was over. He plopped down in the shade of a bush and urged her to do likewise. It worried him that at first glance he didn't see anything resembling a crystal.

Inéz, however, seemed energized by having reached their destination, and she began exploring. Moments later, from a crevasse behind a big boulder, she shouted, "Crystals! Lots of them!"

Don Carlos was on his feet and over to the boulder in a flash. The crystals were a fairly common type of clear quartz, but of very good quality. They dug a dozen out of their matrix with a small pickax that Carlos had brought along. They spent the next hour exploring the area—sometimes together, at other times separately. Crystals were abundantly present, and they were of different types and colors: purple amethyst, smoky quartz, and even a small cache of yellow topaz crystals. "Everything fit for a fantasy princess," Inéz declared, as they packed the crystals they wanted and sipped some water.

"We're not the first explorers to visit this place," Don Carlos announced.

"How do you know?" Inéz asked, alarmed at the thought that they might be set upon by someone hostile.

"Don't worry," Carlos replied. "We have the place all to ourselves today. But notice the print of a hand on the wall across from us, and the small antelope figure that's pecked into that boulder to your right. Also, everywhere we found crystals there were signs that previous visitors had removed a few before we did. My guess is that Native shamans knew about this place and came to it on vision quests—encounters with their sacred spirits. You may have noticed me muttering to myself now and then; I was asking forgiveness of the gods of these crystals for taking them from their homes."

After studying Carlos a while, Inéz asked, "Do you believe those Native teachings?"

"Yes," Carlos replied without stopping to think about it. "Even if I didn't believe them, I would still try to respect the Natives' sacred places, just as I would hope they'd respect my churches and religious sites."

It was time to head down the cliffs for what by now would be a late lunch. Clambering down a steep slope has its own dangers, but at least Carlos and Inéz knew a good route to follow. Although it took them far less time to get back to the spring and their horses than it had taken them to reach the crystal quarry, the climb left them hot and tired and glad to rest.

They'd barely caught their breath when Inéz jumped up and said, "I am so sticky with dried sweat and dirt that I must get into that pool. Will you please," she asked shyly, "go over and talk with Eagle, not looking in my direction, while I take a dip? I'll let you know when I'm out and dressed again. Then you can take your turn."

Carlos talked to Eagle about some of the good times they'd had together, all of which Eagle received in the most blasé fashion, lifting his head momentarily when Carlos approached and going back to grazing as soon as he understood that they weren't going anywhere.

It wasn't long before Inéz called to him. "Your turn."

A memory of Celeste offering him his turn in the shower flashed through his mind, and he observed to himself that Inéz had made fast work of her pool time. "You didn't stay in very long," he said. "I hope you stayed as long as you wanted."

"A fantasy princess," she explained, "is careful to respect the needs of her tall, dark, and handsome companion. I'll go chat with Alegría while you take a dip. I'm glad I thought to bring towels. I forgot to bring them on my first visit here and had to sit naked in the sun until I dried off—the advantage of a secluded spot, I suppose."

Carlos, mindful of how considerate Inéz had been, took a quick plunge in the water, climbed out, dried off, dressed, and invited her to join him for lunch.

Their hunger was obvious from the enthusiastic way they consumed the food they'd brought. At one point, some sauce from an enchilada spilled all over Inéz's hand, and she licked it off as best she could. She gave him a big grin and laughed. "Even fantasy princesses have accidents while eating, and sticky hands go with being fourteen."

They finished their lunch and lay back in the sun, listening to the sounds of the place — bees buzzing about, a flock of crows making indignant noises above them, and the trickle of water from the creek as it flowed into the pool. After a while, Inéz spoke. "I have a present for you," she said. "Fantasy princesses aren't all take and no give." She retrieved six peyote cactus buds from her backpack. "You told me about your meditation practice called Watching. I'd like to try Watching after chewing these peyote buds."

Carlos looked hesitant.

"I thought," Inéz said, "that you'd tried peyote before and didn't find it harmful. I haven't tried it yet and want to. My source, in case you're wondering, is a Pueblo woman herbalist who trades to acquire peyote from where it's grown south of here. As your fantasy princess I give you permission to join me or not as you prefer. It's entirely your choice, but I'd be happiest if you'd accept my present."

"It's your party," he replied in a good humor. "My role is to honor your every wish."

They chewed the tough little peyote buds and drank a lot of water before leaning back again. After nothing had happened for a while, suddenly everything they could see — they'd both simultaneously become aware of the same phenomenon — had become magical. What Don Carlos saw was that he and Inéz were surrounded by auras of golden light. Moreover, every plant and rock in the area also had a distinctive aura — luminous yellows, greens, blues, and reds. These auras were not static. They pulsed with the subtle energy inherent in each source, brightening and dimming, and even, at times, shifting from one color to another. The whole scene was entrancing, glorious, truly magical.

Don Carlos heard a rustling in the bushes. A very fat skunk waddled out into the open and headed in their direction. "Here comes trouble," Carlos whispered to Inéz.

She looked up, saw the approaching skunk, and declared, "There's nothing to worry about."

"If we get sprayed," he whispered back, "even our horses will refuse to have anything to do with us."

"We're not going to get sprayed," Inéz asserted. "She spoke to me the previous time I was here, and apparently she has something more to tell me; that's all."

The skunk walked right up to Inéz and nuzzled her ear, making some chittering noises as it did so. Soon Inéz nodded ever so slightly, and the skunk continued to chitter. From Don Carlos's vantage point—he couldn't quite hear what the skunk was saying—it was definitely conveying an important message. The skunk had a bright aquamarine aura that pulsed strongly throughout its visit to Inéz. Having finished delivering its message, the skunk went to the pool, took a long drink of water, and waddled back into the brush. Don Carlos's hearing was so acute by now that he could hear the skunk long after it had gone out of sight.

"What did your skunk friend have to say?" he asked Inéz.

"It was girl-girl talk. Elvira, that's her name, is an old skunk and she thinks she's pregnant for the final time before she dies. She wanted to tell me about life and love based on her accumulated life wisdom."

"For instance?" he was very curious.

"Secret things. In romances the fantasy princess always has secrets she keeps to herself. Don't you have secrets? I think you have some big ones, and it's not fair to ask me to tell you my secrets, if you won't tell me yours. Tell me a big secret, and I may tell you what Elvira told me."

Without a moment's thought, Don Carlos said, "In another lifetime I was a brujo."

"Wow!" she exclaimed, lifting herself up on an elbow and leaning over him. "That definitely qualifies as a big secret."

Inéz launched into questions: "Was your name Alfonso in your previous life?"

"No, my secret name has always been Carlos."

"Did you live more than one previous life as a brujo?"

"To the best of my memory there were five."

"Does anyone know about your past lives—except, now, me?"

"Yes, Pedro figured it out—or rather I needed to explain it to him—long ago. My powers of sorcery are strongest, vastly enhanced, in desert environments, and as we traveled northward to Santa Fe, he noticed some things in my behavior that couldn't be explained any other way."

"You mean you're a brujo or sorcerer, either or both, in this life also?"

Oops! The cat's out of the bag, he realized. "Yes, although my connection with my brujo self is weak when I'm in cities or towns, and in this lifetime I've spent more time in towns and cities than in deserts."

"Did your brujo's powers contribute to your success in discovering the shamanistic site where we found crystals today?"

"Yes."

"Holy Mother!" Inéz exclaimed. "That explains a lot of things about you, and the explanations have been right under my nose all the time. What a dummy I am!"

"You're no dummy," Carlos said. "Indeed, it occurs to me that you may have been a bruja in a past life. Don't look so skeptical. The early age at which you became a superior fencer—just as was true in my case—suggests that you were drawing on some inner knowledge carried over from a past life. Then there's your awareness that I was visiting you in my dream. That awareness indicates that you have latent powers; you don't know where they come from or how to use them, but you have them. And that trick you developed when serving Loreto's clients, separating your conscious self and hovering above your body, is a very difficult bruja technique. You may not remember learning it as part of a bruja's training, but you were able to draw on it. Finally, you said that Elvira the skunk spoke to you when you were here before, and you hadn't chewed any peyote buds. Also, you seem older than you are. I thought you were perhaps twenty-five. Come to find out you're twenty-one."

"The same with you. I always found it hard to believe you weren't yet twenty-one. Carlos, may I call you Carlos when we're alone together?" He nodded his assent. "How can I have been a bruja in a past life and not know it? You seem to remember your past lives."

"According to a master brujo with whom I studied several lives ago, when humans die, their souls go to a place sorcerers call the Great Soul Vat. If for some unfortunate reason, a brujo was totally unconscious of himself at the time of death, then, as is true for most ordinary people, he won't remember his past lives when he's reborn and may never rediscover his powers as a brujo. That could have happened to you. But that's a topic for another day."

"Wait a second!" she insisted. "Before you change the topic, explain how it is that you apply the words sorcerer and brujo interchangeably to yourself. I always thought sorcerers were sinister. Don't brujos and brujas practice black magic too?"

"You're right," he agreed, "in thinking that most sorcerers are malicious, and most brujos also use sorcery to do harm. But there are important, though admittedly rare, exceptions. The path taught by my original teacher, a brujo named Don Serafino Romero, is entirely different, built on the principle summarized in our motto: 'Do no harm.'"

He could tell that Inéz had more questions, and he tried to cut her off, but she insisted that he allow another question. "I am," she declared with great dignity, "princess for a day, and I get to make up the rules. You must answer one more question before I answer yours." She paused.

"What's this question?" he asked, becoming a little impatient to get some answers to his own questions.

"I was just thinking," she began, "that it must have been a huge strain to live in two worlds, playing the role of Don Alfonso, the heir to a title, most of the time, and having to suppress any sign of your inner brujo self except when you were alone in the desert. I think that would be both difficult and confusing."

"Sometimes it is difficult," he admitted, "especially when I'm living in a town or city society. I pretty much lose my ability to do even the simplest forms of sorcery."

"What's the change I've sensed in you since you returned to Santa Fe?

"You are testing the limits of your prerogatives as a fantasy princess with yet another question."

"If you answer this one promptly," she assured him, "I'll immediately reveal the secret of Elvira's message."

"My brief time with Zoila set me on yet another path. I don't have to abandon my practical skills as an ordinary man or give up my brujo powers, but I'm now determined to explore the way of wisdom to which Zoila introduced me. I can't tell you much about it because it's so new to me. I wouldn't even believe there's something to be sought, except that I once experienced it."

Inéz laid her hand gently on his arm and looked at him with the softest expression in her eyes, and did so without saying anything.

"There," he said, "I've kept my part of the bargain by telling you big secrets about myself, especially the fact that I'm a brujo, which could cause a lot of trouble for me if generally known. You have to play fair and tell me what Elvira said to you."

Inéz giggled. "That's a first," Carlos observed. "I've never heard you giggle before."

"Have you not been paying attention?" Inéz asked, with a mixture of feigned and real impatience. "Today I am trying, with some success, to recapture my fourteen-year-old self, the self I had in my last year of innocence."

"Sorry for interrupting," Carlos said, a bit chastened. "Please go on."

"Elvira's exact words were 'you can marry him if you wish, but only if you give him freedom.'"

"Am I following the story line correctly?" he asked. "We're going to marry?"

"It's inevitable! In the old romances the fantasy princess and the tall, dark, handsome stranger always marry. Her parents aren't happy about her choice, but that's not a problem in my case, since my parents aren't around to raise objections. No matter what, the princess and the handsome stranger always marry and live happily ever after."

Alarmed by this turn in their conversation, Carlos blurted out, "But brujos don't marry."

He should have anticipated her retort. "You seemed ready enough to marry that blue-eyed blonde, Camila."

"The truth," he told her with great seriousness, "is that I feared that if I did, I would have to give up my brujo life. If so, I probably would have lost my capacity to be reborn with my brujo consciousness intact."

"That would have been a huge sacrifice," she murmured, instantly seeing the significance of what he'd said. "Did you love her that much?"

"Frankly, no. I was afraid of losing her to Rafael, and in a moment of panic I proposed and then didn't see any honorable way out of it."

"No wonder you looked so stricken when I said the fantasy princess and her beloved always marry."

He was still anxious.

"You needn't worry," she said. "Elvira may have proposed a way it could be done, but this fantasy princess is far too young to marry, and even if she were as old as she seems to be, she's not sure she could apply Elvira's advice. I don't think I should marry a man who needs to be free, because I couldn't bear to let my husband go off alone into the desert, never knowing whether he'd come back to me."

"Perhaps," Carlos ventured, "this isn't a good time to say so, but I think I'm falling in love with you."

She smiled. "The usual next step in princess stories," she told him, "is for the fantasy man to kiss the fantasy princess."

"I like that part of the story," Carlos declared, pulling her into his embrace and kissing her tenderly. Over to one side, Eagle lifted his head and whinnied, which Carlos took to mean that his four-legged friend approved.

Carlos and Inéz's kiss ended. Acting as one, without needing to discuss it, they began to pack to return to Santa Fe. As they mounted their horses, Carlos couldn't resist commenting, "I don't know precisely where the journey we're beginning will take us, but I feel great happiness to have you as my companion on the way."

Inéz's brilliant smile intensified his happiness. The unknown way opened ahead.

READERS GUIDE

1. *The Brujo's Way* can be read and enjoyed simply as a story of adventure, romance, and magic whose protagonist has two identities: a public self, the young Catholic aristocrat known to his family and friends as Alfonso Cabeza de Vaca, and a secret self, the brujo (sorcerer) Don Carlos Buenaventura. But what begins as an open-ended adventure, a light-hearted picaresque narrative whose hero has more-than-usual powers and delights in their use, eventually becomes the story of Don Carlos's odyssey of self-discovery. At what point does this deeper layer of meaning begin to become evident in the narrative of the sixth life of Don Carlos Buenaventura?

2. The tone of the novel's opening chapters is playful. What does this serve to establish about Don Carlos's character? Is he simply frivolous, or is he a free spirit who loves life? There are many other possibilities for describing his character and personality. Which ones surface most strongly, when and where?

3. Carlos Buenaventura is described as a brujo with extraordinary powers in the practice of sorcery. Even as a fetus in his mother's womb, he is aware that he has had many previous lives, his brujo training having enabled him to retain the continuity of his consciousness at the moment of death and afterward. Even if this premise were possible, enabling one to retain one's memory of previous lives upon being reborn, would that be desirable?

4. Don Carlos believes that it is dangerous for a brujo to be drawn into the emotional entanglements that are inherent in human relationships. He remembers how his passion for a woman blinded him to the mortal threat she represented and how that led to his death, ending his fifth life as a brujo and nearly preventing him from being reborn with a knowledge of his previous lives as a brujo. Does he generalize too much about love relationships from this single event, or is there, perhaps, some validity to the conclusions he draws from it?

5. Don Carlos has a number of mentors, none more important than the master brujo, Don Serafino Romero, who introduces Carlos to the basics of the Brujo's Way. Don Serafino's teaching is that humans divide into two types: the ordinary person, who suffers because of a life conditioned by fear, desire, and ignorance, and brujos and brujas who achieve personal freedom and happiness by not giving themselves over to aversions and desires, refusing to pursue those all-too-human inclinations when they surface. Does this philosophy of life seem rich with possibilities, or does it seem cold in its code of detachment?

6. Don Carlos has learned the letter of Don Serafino's teachings about detachment and equanimity, but has he fully understood their spirit? He gains equanimity by shutting down on negative emotions — it is his habit, he observes, never to dwell on negative possibilities, turning instead to the positive potential of a given situation. Is this a wise approach to life, or does it seriously limit the acquisition of self-knowledge?

7. Over the course of the book it becomes evident that Don Carlos pursues courses of action that go against aspects of the Brujo's Way as taught by Don Serafino. Even after recognizing that he has acted impulsively in his relations with Camila and Inéz, he does little to change his ways. Then, despite his promise to Camila that he will be careful on his trip to Mexico City, he chooses to engage in an exceedingly dangerous battle with an evil sorcerer, Mateo Pizarro. Would it be fair to say that even when he notices he's responding to situations in ways at odds with his brujo training, he remains more attracted to risk-taking than committed to self-control?

8. The importance of consciousness — specifically Carlos's ability to retain his brujo consciousness after death, but more generally the practice of alert awareness in which he has been trained — is a major theme in *The Brujo's Way*. Does the quality or depth of Carlos's consciousness change in the course of the book?

9. Lurking mostly offstage during this account of Don Carlos's sixth life is his mortal enemy, an evil sorcerer named Don Malvolio. Don Carlos doesn't know much about Don Malvolio, and Malvolio's goals and the motivation behind his relentless enmity for Don Carlos remain murky. Don Carlos's simple explanation is that Malvolio is the type of malicious sorcerer who

gives all sorcerers a bad name, whereas he, Carlos, is aligned with a rare subgroup of sorcerers (who prefer to call themselves brujos) whose motto is "Do no harm." But in book two of the Buenaventura Series it turns out that there is much more to Malvolio than Carlos realizes. Play author. Make Malvolio into a more complex, even sympathetic character.

10. Disguises are a necessity for Carlos both in his life as an ordinary man (Don Alfonso Cabeza de Vaca) and in his secret identity as a powerful brujo, but he also takes great enjoyment in them. Although these disguises seem to serve him well, would he gain anything (and what) if he depended on them less for his safety and happiness?

11. What sort of conflicts does his need to maintain his various disguises create in Don Carlos? It's obvious, for example, that he feels a great deal of affection for his mother, yet he is certain that she could not accept his secret brujo self. This situation is echoed in his relationship with Camila, a blue-eyed beauty who insists that he be her friend — like a brother, open to frank and probing friendship — rather than her lover. But with Camila he also knows that he cannot reveal his true brujo identity. What is revealed about him when, threatened by the possible loss of his friendship with Camila, he panics and proposes to her, despite the fact that marriage to her might require him to suppress his brujo self? Is the cost worth it?

12. Carlos's relationships with father figures are no less complicated. He has positive feelings toward his several mentors — notably Don Serafino in the Brujo's Way, Don Ignacio in fencing, and Father Stefano in academic studies — but his relationships with the father-figures within his family are problematical. Even before he's born, he realizes that his father, the Marquis Alfonso Cabeza de Vaca, is a rigid, conservative Catholic who would kill Carlos at the first hint of his brujo identity. Carlos deals with this threat by repressing his deep self, adopting a persona that's intended to please. After his father's death and his mother's remarriage, Carlos is confronted with his stepfather's hostility. To what degree is the anger he feels toward his stepfather — an emotion he finds it impossible to repress, even though his brujo training insists that he should not give into aversion — intensified by a previously repressed fear of his father?

13. Don Carlos has amazing powers, especially in the sphere of transformations, a sorcerer's technique at which he's said to have unrivaled skill. His capacity to talk with animals is equally impressive, as are the acts of prodigious strength of which he's capable. But despite these extraordinary achievements, does any sense gradually emerge that his brujo training was cut short by circumstances (the details of which don't surface in this first volume of the Buenaventura Series) before Don Serafino had the opportunity to instruct him in how to apply their commitment to the motto "Do no harm," or to describe the precise nature of the enmity that Don Malvolio and his ilk feel towards Carlos and his allies? Reading between the lines, what more does he need to learn to be a better brujo of his type and a better human being?

14. Don Carlos is described as having a great love of women, and many women seem to find him exceedingly attractive. Do Carlos's brujo powers carry over into his many liaisons with women, giving him dominance in the relationships, complete mastery of those situations? Does it come as a surprise that he is thrown thoroughly out of balance when his deep friendship with Camila is threatened by another man proposing to her? What underlies this apparent emotional vulnerability, seemingly strange in a man/brujo with such great powers?

15. What does Don Carlos learn about the limits of his brujo powers in the last third of the book?

16. At the end of the book, in fact, in the final sentence, Don Carlos declares that he is about to embark on a spiritual odyssey, the precise outlines of which he cannot yet discern. Indeed, he calls this new direction in his life — distinct from his pursuit of an ordinary man's life and his practice of the extraordinary magic of his brujo life — the "unknown way." But many clues of what this "unknown way" might be are scattered throughout the book. What are some of its main components?